copyright ©Julia Blake 2014
All rights reserved

Sele Books
www.selebooks.com

This is a work of fiction. All characters and events in this publication, other than those in the public domain, are either a product of the author's imagination or are used in a fictitious manner. Any resemblance to actual persons, living or dead, or actual events is purely coincidental.

No part of this publication may be reproduced, distributed, or transmitted in any form or by any means, without the written permission of the author, except in the case of brief quotations embodied in critical reviews and certain other non-commercial uses permitted by copyright law.

For permission requests contact the author.

www.juliablakeauthor.co.uk

ISBN: 9798676765569

The Book of Eve is written in British English
It has an estimated UK cinema rating of 18
containing explicit sexual scenes,
some bad language, and scenes some
readers may find distressing

The Book of Eve is an
Authors Alike accredited book

DEDICATION

To my Parents.
Thank you for all the years of support.

To my friends who told me to go for it.
Well, I went for it. Here it is.

To Maggie
Best wishes
Julia Blake
x

CONTENTS PAGE

Copyright
Dedication
A Note for the Readers

	Prologue	1
I	Exodus	9
II	Genesis	39
III	Kings	75
IV	Esther	107
V	Acts	133
VI	Chronicles	161
VII	Ruth	197
VIII	Lamentations	227
IX	Luke	269
X	Revelations	299
XI	Judas	331
	Epilogue	347

About the Author
A Note from Julia
Other Books by the Author

ACKNOWLEDGEMENTS

A big thank you, as ever to my wonderful editor Dani. Thanks, missy, you are a stern taskmaster, but I wouldn't have you any other way.

Thank you must also go to my eagle-eyed beta readers, Caroline Noe, and M.A. Maddock. Both talented authors in their own rights, you can find them at:

carolinenoe.org
www.instagram.com/m.a_maddock/

A massive thank you needs to go to James and Becky Wright at Platform House Publishing for all their patient help with formatting and all their advice and creative input with the fabulous cover and interior graphics. Thanks, guys, you are amazing.

For all your publishing needs, contact Becky on:

www.platformhousepublishing.co.uk

And finally, a big thank you to my girl, Franki. My own personal IT department, thank you for helping your Mum with all the tricky bits.

A NOTE FOR THE READER

The Book of Eve was first published by a small press publisher in 2014, but I was never happy with the way she had been presented to the world.

Fast forward to 2020 when I received the copyright back and was finally able to showcase my beautiful, complicated, and sensitive girl Eve in a more suitable manner.

You can contact me on Facebook Julia Blake Author and Instagram at @juliablakeauthor

And you can read all about my crazy life on my weekly blog "A Little Bit of Blake" on

https://juliablakeauthor.home.blog

You can also find out all about me and my books on my website:

www.juliablakeauthor.co.uk

And I like large parties. They're so intimate. At small parties there isn't any privacy.

The Great Gatsby
F. Scott Fitzgerald

Flushed with starlight and moonlight drowned,
All the dreamers are castle-bound.
At midnight's stroke, we will unwind,
Revealing fantasies soft or unkind.
Show me your debauched nightmares or sunniest daydreams,
Come not as you are but as you wish to be seen.

House of Salt and Sorrows
Erin A. Craig

It was late now, so late that it could once again be called early – that surreal, enchanting, twilight hour between the end of a party and the unfurling of a new day. The hour when reality grows dim and hazy at the edges, where nearly anything seems possible.

The Dazzling Heights
Katharine McGee

PROLOGUE

"It's time you went back and faced your demons."

Before dawn, the dream happened again. Once more, I wearily pulled myself up the long flight of stairs, paused outside the door and knocked gently, once, twice. I waited for the answer that didn't come; that never came. Turning the handle, I pushed the door open and looked into the room.

Knowing I was dreaming but unable to break free, I waited for what would happen, for what always happened.

The room was empty. In the sudden flash of lightning which burnt through the undrawn curtains and open window, I saw the bed, pristine and unmarked by the weight of a body.

Disappointed, I left, hesitated, then turned to pace softly down the dimly lit landing, searching, needing... What? What had I been looking for?

Thunder rumbled and lightning flickered again, staccato, otherworldly. Around me, the old house held its breath. Water oozed onto the thick carpet *from my sandals, their sodden leather chafing against the chilled damp skin of my feet.*

Cold, I was so cold, so alone; confused.

I reached the next door, saw it was ajar, saw my hand stretch out. In my head I heard my despairing cries – no, don't go in there, don't...

It was too late. It was always too late.

Silently, the door swung open. I stood and waited. The room was dark, then, in an instant of blinding illumination from a lightning crack so violent it seemed the world trembled, I saw... and I saw... and I saw...

I catapulted out of sleep and away from the dream so abruptly that my teeth snapped shut over my tongue. Crying out in shock and pain, I sat bolt upright, sweat-tangled sheets clinging to my legs tentacle-like, attempting to drag me back into the dream, heart hammering violently, a desperate tattoo in rhythm with the throbbing of my skull, my breathing hoarse and ragged in the silence of the room.

The dream. *That* dream. It had been weeks, months even since it last plagued me. I thought myself free of it, but knew what had triggered this backward step, this unwanted look over my shoulder; knew what had made it come again.

By sending the email to Ruth, I had broken through the confines of my self-imposed, year-long exile. I had reached out to the past, to my old life, my old self. Was it any wonder the past had retaliated and was now reaching out to me?

I felt marginally better after I had showered, standing so long under the rusty Heath Robinson contraption that the water, lukewarm at the best of times, ran frigid, jerking me back into a sense of time and place.

The dream, banished to the corners of my mind by the routine, rumbled discontentedly, demanding attention. I ignored it.

Taking my normal cup of caffeine overload with me, I settled on the rickety wooden veranda, propping my bare feet on the handrail, knowing from year-long practice exactly where to place them to avoid the wicked splinters which sought to catch unwary flesh.

Gazing out over the expanse of Montego Bay, I felt myself begin to relax, the beauty of the view acting like an aspirin on jangled senses.

Cautiously, I sipped at the scalding black coffee. It was a special brand, unique to the island; in truth, I think it was unique to Reg. I remembered the warning he gave me along with the first packet of shiny perfect beans.

"Don't drink too much, white girl, your system, it's not used to it."

I accepted the beans but ignored the warning, much to my cost. I grinned ruefully, thinking of the chronic migraine four cups in one day had caused. The way my body had trembled for hours, the odd muzzy sensation behind the eyes, the loss of a night's sleep, and the fact that for hours after, my pee had stunk of caffeine.

Now I play it safe and stick to one cup a day, drunk first thing, sitting here on the veranda, aware of the hardness of the ancient chair solid under my rear, the thrills skittering up my spine as I swung dangerously back on its unstable legs. The breath-taking majesty of the brand-new day, the sea, the sand, the shiny-faced sun ... Why had I sent that email?

Other than the odd email to my parents, to reassure them and prevent them from listing me as a missing person, I had had no contact with anyone since arriving here. Since that night, over a year ago, when I ran away; ran as fast and as far as I could.

I knew why. The book was finished. That great cathartic purge; the story which had long niggled inside and had been let loose during my year of self-imposed solitary confinement.

A year spent without any modern-day distractions had allowed the tale to pour forth, although darker, more complex, and possibly better than I ever imagined it could be.

I had agonised over every word, and edited it forwards, backwards, and inside out. I had gone as far with it as I possibly could.

It was time, if I was serious about it, to show it to someone else, Ruth being the obvious choice. As risks go, it was a calculated one. Sure, she had my email address now, could reply if she wanted to, but had no way of knowing where in the world I was. Also, I had asked her not to tell the others and knew, for all her faults, that Ruth would probably respect my wishes.

Becoming aware of the passage of time, I hurriedly finished my coffee and washed the cup at the tiny sink in the minuscule cupboard which served as a kitchen. Grabbing my shoes, I let myself out of the house, feeling sand shift between my toes, already warm despite the fact the sun was barely out of bed.

Five minutes' walk along the beach and I reached work, surely the best commute in the world, and sat on the restaurant steps to rub sand off my feet and put on sandals.

I always ate breakfast at the restaurant. It was part of the deal. In exchange for long hours of labour, I get board and lodgings. Board being, whatever Reg had felt like cooking that day, and lodgings, the tiny house he owned along the bay. Isolated and dilapidated, it suited my new solitary nature perfectly, and I was aware of how lucky I had been to find Reg.

Those early days on the island were difficult to think about. Stunned, in a quagmire of misery so deep it would surely drown me, I quickly realised my limited funds wouldn't last long.

Stumbling across the bar one evening, I spotted the simple handwritten sign – *staff needed* – and the rest, as they say, was history.

I found the owner of the bar, Reg, alarming at first, in that he was the blackest person I had ever met. Skin the colour of over-ripe plums, so dark that light seemed absorbed by it.

He looked me up and down, taking in the obvious quality of my clothes and the Rolex on my wrist.

"You wanna work in my bar, white girl?" The inference was obvious.

"I need the money," I stated calmly.

Again, he looked me up and down before nodding slowly, a smile splitting the infinity to reveal perfect white teeth.

He had taken me on, a trial basis, which now, some eleven months later, had settled into an easy and satisfying working relationship with a healthy side order of friendship.

Then, I had been a little afraid of him – his blackness, his physical presence, his over-the-top personality, booming voice, and even louder laugh. But during the first few weeks of working for him, I came to appreciate the hidden qualities of Reg: his gruff kindness; his professional approach to his many enterprises; and his spontaneous and eclectic sense of humour. It wasn't until much later that I'd also come to understand there was a darker element to Reg.

There were those mysterious meetings I wasn't supposed to know about, the individuals Reg kept me well away from, and the odd packages stored for a brief time in his office.

I was aware the island had a murky underbelly of crime. Knew, whatever my personal views, that it was a fact of life, so I kept my mouth shut and my opinions to myself.

After finishing breakfast, I tied an apron around my waist, smoothing its crisp, clean, whiteness over the cotton dress I had pulled on that morning, and reapplied my lip balm.

My face was otherwise bare – I had left that "other" me at Heathrow Airport – my hair now a cropped mass of tangled curls, exposure to the sun bringing out golden hints in the chestnut.

I knew Reg liked me working for him and had once confided he felt I was good for business; added a touch of class.

I didn't know about that, but I understood that tourists far away from their comfort zone, whilst loving the idea of places with local colour, found it easier if they also contained colour they were used to and an accent they found familiar.

I was especially popular with English, American, and Australian tourists, a fact reflected in my tips. Thankfully so, as it was my tips I lived on, although my needs, now so simple compared to before it was almost laughable, were amply met by them.

Reg stopped me as I left the kitchen, preparing to face the day, the usual round of holidaymakers and honeymooners desperate to cram a year's relaxation into two short weeks.

"Melissa, there's an email for you,'" he said.

I paused. Met his knowing gaze with mild concern, understanding with no words being necessary he had already read it. And why not? After all, it was his computer and email account I had used. Still, I felt a twinge of annoyance.

"What does it say?" I asked, surprised when his expression softened, and he patted me awkwardly on the shoulder.

"I think you'd better read it," was all he said and turned away towards the bar where customers waited, even though it was barely ten in the morning.

Letting myself into Reg's office, I crossed to the computer and logged into the email account, seeing that my suspicions were well-founded. The email had been opened. It was from Ruth. Laced with her usual bluntness, it was brief and to the point, much like Ruth herself.

Eve, where the hell are you? Everyone has been looking for you, especially Scott. I won't mention that I've heard from you if that's what you want, but I won't lie to him. If he asks me again if I know anything, then I will tell him.

Re opening chapters, they look very promising. Have spoken to my agent and based on my recommendation she is prepared to have a look at it, perhaps with a view to representing you. Is it finished? Can you send me the rest?

Ruth.

PS. Will you be going to Annaliese's funeral?

Annaliese's funeral? Coldness touched my heart and hairs rose on the back of my neck. Annaliese's funeral? With shaking fingers, I pulled the keyboard towards me, googled her name, and read without comprehension the headlines and stark facts.

The illness I had known nothing about, the painful bitter end, the funeral scheduled for three days' time, details, details, details... they told me nothing I needed to know.

Had the others been with her at the end? Had she thought of me? Perhaps, even asked for me?

Most of all, how could she be dead when I hadn't forgiven her for what she'd done?

I left the office five minutes later, still shaking, silently beginning my duties. Disorientated, and uncertain, I picked up a tray off the bar; then stood, lost in thought.

Reg looked at me. Sliding a frosted Pina Colada to a customer, he waited until they had moved to a table then leant over the bar, gently took the tray from my hand, and placed it on the stack with the others.

"My cousin's wife's brother-in-law works at the airport," he informed me.

I blinked in dumb bewilderment. Reg's complex family arrangements were hard to follow at the best of times, let alone now when I doubted my ability to follow the plot of even the simplest nursery rhyme.

"He'll get you a ticket, very quick, very cheap."

"Ticket?" I found my voice, husky, and low.

"To England. I think, white girl, it's time," he paused, nodding sagely. "It's time you went back and faced your demons. It's time you went home."

CHAPTER I – EXODUS

"Oh, keep your bloody secrets,"

I am late reaching the church, deliberately so, my plan being to slip unnoticed into one of the back pews. I don't want to risk being seen by any of the others, especially Scott.

Scott. My heart falters at the thought that I will soon see him again. Honestly not knowing how I feel about it, my emotions and thoughts are struggling to adjust; to reacclimate.

It's strange being back in England, in this familiar little village church. It's as if time has stood still as if I'd never been away, the year in Jamaica already slipping from my memory.

Nothing has changed, yet everything is different.

Slowly my eyes wander to the beautifully crafted coffin at the front of the church, the massed banks of perfect white roses, and the assembled congregation of sombre-faced mourners in black. Couture rubbed shoulders with Marks & Spencer, Annaliese had never made any distinction of status in her friends.

I shiver in my thick coat, telling myself it is because of the abrupt change from the heat of Montego Bay to the comparative chill of a bright and sunny British September day.

Reaching up, I ensure the veil cascading from the tight cloche hat is still securely fastened over my face, concealing my features, and hiding me from recognition.

My disguise, for if I am honest that is what it is, will serve the purpose for which it was bought in London yesterday. After this is all over, I will neatly fold the clothes in a bag and give them to some charity shop. Perhaps then, finally, I will reach closure and be able to put all thoughts of Annaliese firmly from my mind forever.

Annaliese.

My lips curve in a reluctant smile as I reflect on how much she would have loved my outfit.

"Darling!" She would have exclaimed, examining with pleasure the intricate beading on the coat sleeves, stroking the downy soft collar and trying the hat on, peering at me through the Greta Garbo thick black veil, blue eyes wide and sparkling with mischief, as she preened in pure Hollywood star fashion.

"How simply divine. And how unlike you."

Yes, it was unlike me, and that, along with its thick all-concealing bulk, was what I was relying on, to shield me from curious eyes and to protect my identity. For these people, Annaliese's friends, my friends, must never know I was here; that I had been unable to keep away from Annaliese's final bash; her last party.

My eyes are again drawn unerringly to the front of the church to where she is, riding within her golden chariot, festooned with garlands and wreaths of her trademark white flowers nestled amongst glossy green foliage.

"I love all flowers," she'd once been quoted as saying, "but only wear white ones, as at least I know they'll match everything I'm wearing."

How typical, how very Annaliese I think, eyes blurring at the memory. Furiously I slip a hand under my veil and dab painfully at my eyes. I will not cry for her, will not give her that power.

But it's no use. Tears stubbornly slide down my cheeks and I am helpless against the well and churn of emotions. Maybe it is appropriate to shed a tear in memory of the woman who had once been my best friend, although that is too tame for the feelings I had had for Annaliese.

She had been the sun and the moon to me, her moods controlling the destiny of my days. One smile could uplift spirits and make my heart soar. One frown could dash all hope, leaving me bereft and despairing.

A movement at the front catches my eye. Through a momentary gap in the congregation, I see Robert sitting in the front pew. He turns to murmur something to the woman beside him, who frowns, nodding in concentration and I see it is Caro, Annaliese's faithful assistant.

Robert turns his gaze resolutely back to the box in which Annaliese now resides. His lips move as if muttering a farewell to the woman who had been his wife for twenty-seven years.

There is a rustle amongst the congregation as the vicar steps forward, his long surplice snowy white and gleaming in the shaft of light which breaks through the stained-glass window behind, bathing him and the coffin in the glorious autumnal sunshine.

Dust motes dance, and for one wild moment, I imagine it to be Annaliese's soul, spiralling and twirling upward, dancing in death the way she had loved to dance in life, her essence beginning its epic journey to heaven.

I give myself a little shake and firmly yank myself back down to reality. I gave up all such foolish romantic notions a year ago.

With a crash of notes, the organ hurls us into a hymn, one of Annaliese's favourites – *Morning Has Broken*. I have a memory of her singing it, long golden hair a tangle of morning-after-the-night-before bed-headedness, eyes bleary with a hangover, mouth twisting into a wry grin of black humour as she surveys the fallout from a monumental party in the cold light of morning.

I remember her throwing up her hands in despair and grabbing my wrist, her lilting, surprisingly deep singing voice with that faint trace of accent which only ever emerged when she sang, or in times of extreme emotion, an accent which intrigued and baffled me as I strained to catch its origin.

Twirling me around, my feet cold on the tiled floor, robe flying around my ankles, she sang loudly, *praise for the bringing of this fresh morning,* her rich laughter wrenching reluctant humour from me.

We danced down the hallway and into the kitchen where she opened a bottle of champagne. Glasses clinking, we giggled, toasting ourselves and another phenomenally successful party, the scent of her perfume faint in my nostrils.

Oh Annaliese ... Annaliese ... why? Why?

The man next to me silently and sympathetically hands me a starched, freshly laundered handkerchief. I murmur my thanks, glancing curiously from the corner of my eye.

I vaguely recognise him as Annaliese's bank manager. A man of middle years and middle-class values, he had attended some of Annaliese's more sedate gatherings and she had had him wrapped around her little finger.

Dennis, that was his name, although his surname escaped me. He belonged in the outer circle, and as such, had not been deemed worthy of the attention of the chosen few, we, the lucky ones who had the honour of being Annaliese's disciples. Her "coterie", as she called us.

Discreetly, I touched the handkerchief to a face wet with tears of bitter memory and noticed Dennis pull another from his pocket. How many had he brought, I wondered? Had he been anticipating floods of tears from Annaliese's more emotional female compatriots?

There is a sniff beside me, and a flurry of white as he raises the square of linen to his face. Dennis had come prepared for his own emotional breakdown, and I gaze in wonder as this staid, nondescript little worm of a man, sobs like a baby, his narrow shoulders shaking with unsuppressed emotion.

All around me people are breaking down, handkerchiefs and tissues being groped for in pockets and slim black clutches.

"Oh, how delicious," I can almost hear Annaliese cry in delight. "A positive sea of grief. How very Greek."

The hymn ends and the vicar begins the service, its ornate, old-fashioned language suiting the woman we are here to bid farewell to. In life, Annaliese had enjoyed the theatrically overblown, relishing complexity and confusion, so it is apt her funeral should be this grand Victorian melodrama of black and bitter tears.

She would have loved it. I wondered if she arranged it, almost immediately realising that yes, of course, she had. Annaliese was never one to leave things to chance; her meticulous planning and obsessive attention to detail the reasons her parties had been so renowned.

There is a rustle of interest in the congregation. Robert walks forward to join the vicar, turning to face us, a piece of paper clutched in blanched white knuckles. My heart turns as I see how the past year has aged him, his previously unlined face showing obvious signs of strain, his dark, well-cut suit hanging from a body that has lost weight.

He clears his throat, and an air of almost unbearable expectation grips us. Collectively, we lean forward in our seats, willing him on, flooding our support and compassion towards him as he tries to talk; falters, coughs again, and then finally, begins to speak.

His voice, faint, and wavering, gains in strength as he warms to his theme, his words rich with passion and grief. The prepared speech slips unnoticed from his fingers, and he talks to us directly from his heart, honestly and compellingly, about his Annaliese, the woman he had loved and protected for so many years.

"Annaliese loved life," he began, looking around the sea of solemn heads, all nodding in agreement. "And she had a great capacity to wring every ounce of fun out of any situation. Looking around, I see so many dearly loved and familiar faces, and I know you will all agree with me it was one of the things that made her parties legendary. She loved and enjoyed people.

"One of her greatest thrills was having so many friends. From very early on in our marriage, I had to accept that our home would always be bulging at the seams. That it would be a very rare evening I would arrive home and not find a party in full swing," he grinned wryly.

"Whether I was invited to it was another matter." There is an obliging chuckle from the congregation. "Her work was also a source of great joy to her. Although, she did once confess she felt like a fraud and was genuinely stunned that her musings and scribblings could generate such passion and fervour amongst her readers.

"I remember when her first book was published, how small her ambitions were. To be acknowledged as a writer, to see her novel in a bookshop, and that maybe someone, somewhere, would buy it."

Again, he paused, his smile was wistful and gentle. "I don't need to remind you all what happened next."

I see the wry smiles and nodding heads that greeted Robert's words. Annaliese's success was a worldwide phenomenon, the twenty novels, ten films and two TV series bringing her recognition, plaudits, and the financial wherewithal to support a lifestyle of stupendous excess and lavish generosity.

Yes, generosity. For all her faults, and as I'd discovered to my cost, Annaliese had those, she had given magnanimously of her wealth, redistributing, and sharing it with the ease of a woman who truly did not care about money.

"The greatest sorrow in her life," Robert continued, "was that she was unable to have children. Yet, Annaliese still found the strength of character to turn disappointment into hope and founded a string of children's homes throughout the country.

"It gave her great joy to visit these homes and to interact with the children, rejoicing when a child found a new home with loving parents.

"Through Annaliese's love, and her determination that every child must be given his or her chance at a decent life, many children are today leading happy and fulfilled lives."

I shifted uneasily, my sensitivity to the subject making me feel small-minded and mean, Robert's words causing a gnawing dichotomy within my heart. My hatred for Annaliese, for what she had done to me, was boundless, yet I was an adopted child.

I had been one of the lucky ones, my parents being exactly the sort that any child, given a choice, would choose. Others, I knew, had not been so fortunate.

It was hard to reconcile a woman whose personal crusade had been to help the young and vulnerable, with the heartless monster I had built her up to be in my mind.

"I can't believe she's gone," Robert's voice shook, emotions threatening to overwhelm him. I saw Caro strain forward in her seat, shoulders tense, spine stiff, poised to leap to Robert's aid.

"She was my life, my universe. I can't believe the sun will rise now she is gone. She ..." He paused, hand to eyes, shoulders shaking.

To the mingled horror, compassion, and fascination of the congregation, he began to sob, raw choking gasps of sorrow and loss.

The vicar placed a comforting hand upon his arm, as Caro reached his side, a man close behind her. Craning my neck to see around the rather large lady sitting in front of me, I realise it's Scott and the breath catches in my chest.

Gently, Scott led Robert back to his seat and Caro whispered something to the vicar who nodded, stepping back as she turned to face the congregation. It was now so quiet within the church I could hear the faint cooing of woodpigeons in the trees outside.

"Ladies and gentlemen," Caro began, her gruff voice hoarse with emotion, the accent which betrayed her Irish roots pronounced, as if control were slipping. Her eyes were red-rimmed. Even from my place at the back, I can see lines of grief and strain etched deeply around her mouth.

A woman whom only the most generous would call handsome, now Caro's honest plainness shines out, face scrubbed and shiny from the deluge of saltwater it has suffered.

I reflected how I had hardly ever seen Caro distressed before and had never seen her cry. Rarely had she displayed any emotion at all except when her small eyes had rested upon Annaliese, her friend. Then, and only then, did the burning light of an almost fanatical obsessive love cross her homely features.

Of us all, Caro had the most to lose from Annaliese's death. Not only was Annaliese her closest, her only friend, but she was also her employer. For as long as anyone could remember

Caro had been Annaliese's assistant, organising her life with the precision of a military operation.

She took care of all the tedious day-to-day details that had so bored Annaliese and ensured that Annaliese's life could be one endless round of writing, fun, friends, and laughter.

My bulldog, Annaliese had called her. Looking at her pale drawn face, small, bloodshot eyes, and dark purple circles hanging beneath them, the name seemed cruelly apt.

"Ladies and gentlemen, I would like to take this opportunity to thank you for coming. I know Annaliese would be touched to see so many of her friends here. Her friends meant the world to her. She loved you all very much and I know it was a great source of joy that every person she met in life became a friend and remained so."

Well, not all of them I think, bitterly.

"After the service, there is to be a brief interment. Then everyone is invited back to the Hall. It was Annaliese's explicit instructions, and I quote, that the boring bit where the box goes into the ground be as short as possible. Then all my lovely friends must have the most wonderful party, get very drunk on champagne, and remember all the good times we had together."

She waited, as a fond chuckle rumbled through the congregation.

"This afternoon, in the park, there is to be a tree-planting ceremony, where a young silver birch will be planted in memory of Annaliese. When I asked Annaliese what type of tree she wanted, she laughed and told me I could choose because she'd never met a tree she didn't like."

Again, there is a rustle of humour at the purely Annaliese comment.

"So," Caro continued, with a catch in her voice. 'I chose a silver birch, as I felt of all the trees in the wood, it was the one that best reflected Annaliese. Its delicate silvery beauty, its rustling leaves that love to dance in the breeze, and its slender, pale trunk, all being attributes which reminded me so much of her it seemed an obvious choice." She paused and swallowed.

"I hope you will join us," she gestured vaguely in the direction of the front pew where the other members of the coterie sat, "in planting this living memorial to the most wonderful woman that ever lived. Thank you." She walked back to the others, her stride brisk, sitting down with a relieved thump beside Robert.

Mimi slipped a comforting arm around her shoulders. For a moment, I saw Caro relax into the French woman's embrace, before pulling away, spine stiffening into its customary sergeant-major, ramrod straight posture, dabbing furiously at her eyes with a tissue plucked almost angrily from her capacious, eminently practical, black handbag.

The service continued. We bowed our heads in prayer. Around me, a damp, all-consuming wave of emotion swelled and lapped through the massed ranks of dedicated mourners.

I knew later, at the wake, that Annaliese's instructions would be obeyed to the letter. Champagne will be drunk, reminiscences will be exchanged, and laughter will ring through the rooms of Annaliese's home where she had lived so happily with her devoted husband Robert.

I have no doubt Caro will have arranged an almost non-stop buffet of the delicate, delicious finger food of which Annaliese had been so fond.

I know at the tree planting ceremony the poor sapling will be in danger of being trampled under the feet of the attending hordes. Yet now, here, her friends are free to express their feelings in a great amorphous outpouring of sincere love and loss for the woman called Annaliese.

Another hymn, another favourite, *The Lord Is My Shepherd*. More memories of Annaliese curled up before the fire, her head on Robert's lap, softly singing it, low and longingly, her blue eyes consuming the reflected flames. Her comfort song, she called it, only to be sung when one was slightly blue and in need of a spiritual tonic.

The depth of Annaliese's faith had surprised me. Once, I asked how she reconciled her religious beliefs with her life of wild parties and excess. I remember blue eyes turning a surprised gaze upon me. Why were the two so incompatible, she exclaimed. Jesus himself attended at least one celebration we knew of, and not only that, but he had supplied all the booze.

After the hymn, the vicar announced that one of Annaliese's friends and protégées, the young opera singer, Kristina Blackwood, was to sing Annaliese's favourite song. Kristina arose and accepted the sycophantically offered hand of the vicar as he assisted her and all her fame, up the pulpit steps.

The music started, and as I expected, the achingly familiar strains of *Pieu Jesu* soared upwards. Kristina's glorious voice, trembling with emotion, washed over us like finest brandy.

Looking around, I see I am not the only one affected by the breath-taking purity of Kristina's voice as she lingers over and caresses the words.

A fresh wave of sorrow crests and breaks at the foot of the pulpit, as Kristina expertly gathers up our souls in her hands and wrings them dry.

Finally, the never-ending service ends. Robert and Scott, together with two other members of the coterie, Miles, and Ferdie, step forward and gently, oh so gently, lift Annaliese onto their shoulders, carrying her with precisely measured steps out into the bright daylight.

Gradually, reluctantly, the mourners trail after, waiting until the inner circle has filed into the aisle, naturally acceding to them the right to be first in line, as they had been during her life.

Having been at the back of the church, I am among the last of the congregation to emerge, blinking in the glaring sunshine, eyes watering at its brightness compared to the candlelit gloom of the church. The unseasonable warmth of the day sparked the thought that even the weather was on its best behaviour for Annaliese.

I lingered at the back of the crowd, unwilling to venture any closer to where I can see the coffin being lowered into the gaping maw of dark brown earth, surrounded by people all wearing the appropriate expressions of sorrow.

It all seems so obscene, and I swallow down a rising tide of bile. Annaliese hated the dark, she loved light – the warmth of the sun, the gentleness of candlelight. It is utterly and completely wrong to be shutting her away forever in the cold darkness.

I stepped forward, words of denial and outrage almost forcing themselves from my mouth. Almost, but not quite. I come to my senses and shrink back, feeling the rough flint walls of the church through my coat.

I can't breathe. The veil is constricting, blocking out the air and I gasp, turning away. I want no more of this. I have done what I came to do. I have said goodbye to the woman who gave me so much, who gave me my life, the woman who betrayed me.

Silently, I slip away unnoticed. This is our local church; I know it and its surroundings intimately. At the back of the church is a footpath that leads through the woods. A five-minute walk will take you to Annaliese's home, yet if you turned left at the stile, another footpath would lead you to the quiet village street a few minutes away, where I'd left the hire car.

I rounded the corner, my hand trailing idly over the rough walls of the church. A man leans against the back door. A cigarette held to his lips; he inhales a ragged sigh of relief.

It is Scott.

My heart leapt in frenzied panic into my throat. I maintain my composure, paced slowly and carefully by him, head down, contemplating the morning's events. One step at a time, one foot down, then the other. I nearly made it – am almost to the bend in the path, when...

"Eve?"

The name snagged at me. I hesitated; a fatal mistake, the subtle body movement confirming his suspicion. With two strides he is upon me, gripping me by the arm and spinning me round to confront him, his large hand ripping the veil from my face to reveal me, nakedly make-up free, eyes swollen, completely open to his gaze.

"Eve! It is you. Where the hell have you been? We tried to find you! We all did. Didn't you realise how much we needed you? How much she ... for

Christ's sake, Eve, why the hell did you vanish like that?"

"Melissa," I snap waspishly. 'My name is Melissa, not Eve. That was her pet name for me. My real name is Melissa and I'll thank you to remember it. Now, I must go, goodbye Scott.'

I turned. Again, his hand gripped my arm. For a moment we stare each other down, his superior height causing me to crane my neck to meet his gaze, fighting to keep my face impassive.

His dark eyes surveyed me coldly as if I were a stranger to him. I swallow sharp regret that Scott, the man I once loved so completely and unrequitedly, could look at me in such a way.

The awkwardness of the moment stretched between us. Accusations well in my throat and I feel a mad urge to throw myself into his arms, to beg him to tell me why. To plead with him to love me as he once did. Or did he?

That not knowing; that uncertainty, that sting of final betrayal steadied me, reminding me of what I had seen, and what had happened.

The reason I left is still there. Has never been resolved. I returned his stare with one of equal calm. Suddenly, he seemed to relax and smiled. Releasing my arm, he stepped back with a shrug.

"Come on," he said, "I'll walk you to the Hall. Let's beat the crush and be the first to the champagne."

"Don't you want to say goodbye to her?" I asked in surprise, gesturing back to the church.

"She's not there," he replied, his voice tight. "And besides ..." He paused, glancing at me significantly. "I've already said my goodbyes."

A red-hot wave of guilt washes through me, followed immediately by anger. How dare he make me feel guilty, implying I had been the one to let Annaliese down because, in the end, I had not been there for her?

"I'm not going to the Hall," I stated, and his eyebrows shot up in surprise. He says nothing as usual but falls into step beside me as I turn and walk along the footpath.

We walk silently, almost companionably, and I am forcibly reminded of other, happier times, when I'd stretch out my stride to match his loose, long-limbed gait, desperately hoping he'd notice me and realise I was so much more than just Eve, Annaliese's newest little pet. We reached the stile, paused, and I held out my hand to him.

"Goodbye, Scott. It was good seeing you."

He hesitated, then placed his hand over mine. I felt his heat through my skin. Once again, bitter regret and might-have-beens threaten to engulf me. Quickly, I pulled my hand free, turned to go.

"She asked for you ... at the end. She kept asking for you..."

The words are low and calm. Each one penetrates. Poisoned barbs, they spread their toxin through my system, breaking down my defences and smashing through my barriers. I stand, head bowed, and accept the inevitable.

I still loved Annaliese despite what she had done, still loved her as passionately as the day I first met her, and now I mourned her death. I mourned the loss of the most extraordinary woman I was ever likely to meet.

"Was it so very bad?" I need to ask, need to know. "Her end was it ...?"

"Fucking horrendous?" he enquired. "Oh yes, in the end, she didn't know us, any of us. She kept asking for you, not for Robert or Caro who had always been in her life. Not for me or Mimi, who were there for her right up until the end. No, it was you, beautiful, treacherous Eve. You were the one she wanted. God only knows why."

"I'm sorry," I gulped, feeling an unwanted tear slip down my cheek, my body shaking with the enormity of his words. "I'm sorry, I couldn't. I had no choice…"

With a muffled curse he reached for me, his large hand tipping my head back to expose me, vulnerable and open. His face softened and a fingertip traced the path of the tear.

"Eve …" he began.

"Melissa," I insisted defiantly.

He shrugged impatiently, angrily, then enfolding me in his arms he simply lets me cry. I realise it is something I have needed to do for the longest time. Since Ruth's e-mail and all through the long journey home, maybe even longer.

Since that terrible night, when Annaliese took my youthful dreams and confidence and twisted them into something dark and unrecognisable.

Patiently, he waited, until finally I am reduced to a damp hiccupping mess, patting frantically at my pocket to retrieve Dennis's handkerchief.

"Come on."

Taking me firmly by the hand he pulled me down the footpath towards the stile and the Hall.

"No," my protest is minimal, half-hearted. He ignores it and gently and solicitously helps me over the stile as if I were some elderly and infirm spinster, instead of a perfectly capable woman in her late twenties.

Again, we walk in silence, only this time he holds my hand tightly in his, glancing at me from time to time as if unable to believe I'm here and is half afraid I'll try to make a dash for it.

I consider it but am incapable of even completing the thought. Strange complicity floods my limbs, an intense weariness which drains the energy from my very bones rendering me weak and helpless, unable to do anything but allow Scott to lead me, unresisting, along the path to Annaliese's home.

We reach the Hall before the others. I wondered if Annaliese's request that people not linger by her graveside was being honoured, or if her friends were hesitant to leave her alone in her narrow earthen bed, reluctant to turn their faces away from the dead and back to the living.

As we enter, I gesture helplessly at Scott.

"I need to tidy myself. I don't want anyone to see me like this."

He surveyed my ravaged face and his expression softened. Silently, gently, he undid the oversized buttons of my coat as if I were a small child, clumsy and incapable. Just as gently, he took the hat from my head. My hair springs free and he frowns, pushing his hand through the short springy curls.

"You've cut your hair." His voice is almost accusatory. I feel myself flushing, immediately on the defensive.

"I fancied a change."

My tone is challenging, daring him to make an issue of it. He surveyed me a moment longer, then his hand dropped to his side, and he shrugged. There's movement, and noise at the door and I flee upstairs as the first of the mourners arrive.

It has been over a year since I was last here. Nothing has changed. The walls of the landing are still papered in pale golden yellow, glimmering in the strong midday sun streaming through large windows.

Instinctively, I head for the room which for nine years had been mine, pausing in the doorway, looking, and realising that nothing has been touched. It is all as I left it.

I remember when Annaliese had first thrown the door open. "This can be your room," she'd exclaimed, and I'd cried out in wonder at its golden perfection, the beauty of the pale wooden four-poster bed with its sumptuous drapes, the ornate little Queen Anne fireplace and the pair of tall windows open to breath-taking views of the surrounding parkland.

I slipped gratefully into the adjoining bathroom, wincing at the strange woman's face looking back at me from the large, brutally honest mirror over the vanity unit, her eyes wild, her curls crushed from the confining hat, her skin blotchy and ugly from crying.

I opened the under-sink unit, shocked to discover my make-up and skin care products exactly as I'd left them, and take out the expensive foundation, eye shadows and blushers, noticing my brushes and combs are still there, too, arranged neatly by the sink where I'd liked to keep them.

With hands that shook, for the first time in nearly a year I smoothed artificial life onto my skin, applied colour to my cheeks, and outlined my eyes with my signature black kohl.

With a few simple, automatic gestures I shed Melissa and stepped back into Eve, donning her look once again. A look that for so long had been the mask from behind which I had faced the outside world. A world that had seemed so ugly and pointless beyond the golden walls of Annaliese's kingdom.

Outwardly ready to face them, I reluctantly, left the room to go back downstairs and greet my friends. I realised that in my absence Scott must have advised them of my presence and had probably warned them not to mention my gap year from their lives. Perhaps not to blame, accuse, or condemn me for my absence from Annaliese's side during her fatal illness.

Instead, I am greeted with warmth and effusion, Mimi gathering me up in her arms for a hug which leaves me reeling in a cloud of Chanel and French woman chic. Her tiny, birdlike frame is clad in sophisticated and extremely becoming black, yet her immaculately made-up face shows evidence of stress. The same stress, I realise, I can see on all their faces.

It has plainly been a difficult time for them, and I felt ashamed. Not so much that I had not been there for Annaliese, but that I had not been there for my friends.

The champagne flowed. The food is served, as I had predicted, delectable little mouthfuls of pure gourmet delight. Tentative, hushed tones become louder as people reminisce, remember and regret.

Finally, someone laughed at a particularly outrageous Annaliese anecdote, immediately hushing themselves guiltily, but it is too late, the laughter is out. Just as Annaliese would have wanted, the party gets into full swing.

Somehow, I find I have consumed far too much champagne on an empty stomach. I am floating on a cloud of immediacy, unable to think of such mundane things as driving; the fact I have nowhere to stay that night, or even of going to see my parents.

Cocooned in the blanket of my friends' presence, I allow myself, for the first time, to realise how much I have missed them all, and how big a hole their absence from my life has created.

The tree-planting ceremony is beautiful and moving. Every single mourner gathers at the chosen site on the edge of the parkland to watch Henry, the gardener, his face set and solemn, carefully, almost delicately, place the adolescent sapling into its new home, piling earth around its hopeful young roots, rather as the earth had been shovelled into Annaliese's new home.

The silver birch is watered in thoroughly with a bottle of champagne, its cork buried deep in the hole, and we all pause, heads bowed, as the sun begins to set, tipping the slim branches with shafts of gold.

Finally, Robert sighed and walked up to the tree. Tenderly, he touched its papery bark.

"Goodbye, Annaliese," he murmured and set off back towards the Hall.

One by one we all follow suit, some merely patting the tree, others letting their fingers linger on its trunk, seeing in its bright merriness and quivering leaves an embodiment of Annaliese's spirit. I think what a good choice Caro has made.

Caro. She alone has made no attempt at reconciliation. Instead, I feel her eyes, hard and accusing, as she works her way through the crowd, acting as a hostess in Annaliese's place, ensuring all are well fed and the champagne never runs dry.

Just after sunset, I stagger outside onto the veranda for some fresh air. Awash in a sea of good quality champagne and caviar, I feel light-headed and giggly, a feeling I haven't had in so long. An indescribable sensation of intense wellbeing and optimism, the sensation I always had in Annaliese's presence.

As I clung to the stone balustrade, drawing deeply of the chilly September evening, I became aware of a small glowing tip on the steps below me. There's movement, and Scott steps into the dim light, a cigarette dangling from his lips.

"I thought you'd given up?"

I heard my voice, shrill and unfocused, realising I am drunk and how wonderfully, gloriously liberating it is.

"I had," he shrugs, and stubs out the offending cigarette on the wall, stuffing it back into the packet. "I started again a couple of months ago, when ..." His voice trailed away. In my mind, I finished the sentence. He started again when Annaliese reached the beginning of the end.

There's silence as he leans casually against the wall, hands in pockets, staring moodily out into the gloomy park. The quiet stretches and expands. I can almost hear it and feel my heart racing to fill the silent void, thumping against my rib cage in a frenzy of anticipation.

"I had my reasons," I say.

In the darkness, I see his head turn, the glitter of his eyes intense and focused.

"For what I did," I continued. "You know I had my reasons. Good reasons. I didn't just one day decide to leave. Annaliese ... she must have told you she saw me. That I knew and finally understood."

"Understood? Understood what?"

He sounds genuinely confused, and I realise in a flash of understanding that she hadn't told him. He doesn't know. A horrible reluctance to speak of it grips me and I step away from him.

"It doesn't matter," I said, taking a deep breath. "I don't want to talk about it, Scott. I don't want to speak ill of her, not now she..."

"Can't fight back?" he snapped, and I heard the anger in his voice. "Do you have any idea what it did to her when you disappeared, Eve? How worried she was? How worried I ... we all were? Then that pathetic note saying nothing, that you were all right, and that we were not to look for you."

"I'm sorry," I interrupted desperately. "I had to go. I knew..."

"Knew what?" he demanded, then sighed in exasperation at my mutinous silence. "Oh, keep your bloody secrets," he muttered and stomped past me up the steps towards the Hall.

"Scott!"

I clutched at his arm. He turns and I smell him; that achingly familiar mix of expensive aftershave and cigarette smoke.

For a second, I longed for what might have been when I was young and stupid, hoping beyond all hope he could care for me the way I cared for him. But he didn't, he couldn't, and so it wasn't to be.

~31~

There are footsteps above us, and we looked up to see Robert, barely visible in the inky blackness which has crept upon us whilst we've been talking, his pale face appearing aged in the monochrome shadow cast by the Hall.

"Scott, I've been looking for you. It's time," he stated flatly and turned to go.

Scott pulled free from my grasp and moved to follow him. I shrank back against the unforgiving stone, my head a whirl of conflicting emotions. Robert stopped, looking back over his shoulder.

"This concerns you, too, Eve, please come."

He led us to Annaliese's study, a generously proportioned room that during the day is flooded with golden sunshine from large French doors leading out onto a balcony. Now, with the curtains drawn and a small fire glowing in the hearth, it is inviting and cosy.

For a moment I think I see her, sitting at the antique rosewood desk, working at her latest book, writing slowly and methodically with one of her beautiful, old-fashioned, fountain pens, her long hair escaping from its ribbon, a frown of concentration on her face.

I blink away from the vision and look around me, wondering why I am here. Why we are all here, I silently amend, as I see the other members of the coterie already seated.

Mimi, as graceful as ever, poised on the elegant brocade sofa. Miles sat beside her, warm brown eyes crinkling at the edges as he flashes a welcoming smile at us. Ferdie is busy opening a bottle of champagne, and Caro is hovering beside him like a hawk, as if afraid he will somehow get it wrong.

Silently, Scott and I sit side by side on the other sofa, facing Miles and Mimi. Robert hovers near the fire holding out thin cold fingers to its welcoming warmth.

Ferdie and Caro poured champagne into thin, elegant flutes, and efficiently hand them around, Caro's eyes narrowing fractionally as she hands one to me. I murmur thanks, noticing that a television set now stands in the corner of the room where a luscious pot plant used to be, and wonder why it's there.

"I'd like to propose a toast," Robert said, and our eyes swivelled obediently in his direction.

"To Annaliese," he proclaimed, holding up his glass. We all follow suit, taking sips of the champagne's welcoming coldness.

"You're probably wondering why I've called you all in here," he continued and holds up a small remote control. "Well, Annaliese had a message she wanted me to give you on the day of her funeral. A message from her."

Amid our curious mutters, he points the remote at the television. It flickers to life and the next moment she is there on the screen.

Even though the image is two-dimensional, it's as if she is in the room with us. I realise it must have been recorded many months ago, before the final grip of the illness. Although looking closer, it is possible to see the lines of pain around her mouth and the sheen of drugs in her eyes.

"My darling friends," she begins.

It has been a year since I last heard her voice and a lancet of pain stabs through my heart. How could I have forgotten that quick lilting accent? That tone which always seemed to suggest laughter was lurking mere moments away.

"By the time you watch this," she continued, "it will all be over; I will have lost the battle. I have no illusions about the outcome. The doctors have been very honest with me, and I know this is a battle I cannot win, so I hope the funeral has gone well."

We shift uncomfortably, catching each other's eyes in a shared moment of awkwardness.

"Caro, sweetheart, I'm sure you arranged everything splendidly, that it was all exactly as I wanted it to be, and I thank you for performing this final task for me. You have been the most faithful friend and loyal companion and I wish to give you something. My final gift to you, my dearest, is the gift of truth. You will know exactly what I mean by that and will understand I entrust it to you completely. That it is yours to do with what you will."

We turn curious eyes onto Caro, who flushes and looks down at the ground, mouth working furiously as she fights to hold back tears.

"Scott, my angel, last year you asked me for advice. I recommended you be patient, that it was too soon, and told you if you only waited a little while longer you would get your heart's desire. That advice was wrong, and I bitterly regret the consequences, as I know you do. My advice to you now, for what it is worth, is to forget about waiting and being patient and seize the moment. I have learnt to my cost that life is fleeting and simply too short to waste a single second. So, Scott, my dear heart, if it is still what you want more than anything else in the world, and I believe it is, then to coin a familiar phrase, go for it."

I glanced at Scott. My curiosity keenly aroused. His head is bowed. In disbelief, I see the glint of tears in his eyes. He scrubs furiously at them, turning away from me as if he cannot bear for me to see his distress.

"Mimi, my dear friend, I know life has been hard for you and that you've never fully recovered from the tragedy. My message to you is to look beside you, look hard, my darling Mimi. You will see life is not completely over. That there is something precious, something overlooked, waiting for you. Don't be afraid my angel. Grasp it with both hands and you will find true happiness."

Annaliese paused and smiled, a sweet smile of love directly into the camera.

"Miles, dear heart, now is not the time to be timid or a gentleman. You must be positive and assertive. I know what you want, what you have always wanted, but have been too afraid to try for. Don't be afraid, you have so much to offer. Be true to your heart and you cannot fail."

Mimi turned to gaze at Miles, who shuffled in his seat and stared awkwardly at the ground. Then resolve seemed to grip him. He straightened and returned her stare, chin high, his eyes challenging and questioning.

Fascinated, I watched the elegant, composed Frenchwoman blink in surprise, then comprehension flooded her features and she blushed like a teenager. Her breath quickened and I saw a pulse flutter in her throat.

For a long, silent moment they studied each other, then Mimi quietly held out a hand, which

Miles stared at incredulously before a smile of pure joy spread across his face and he grasped it eagerly.

Mimi nodded once as if something had been agreed upon and settled upon between them. Together, they turned their faces towards Annaliese's gently smiling visage.

"Oh, my darlings," she cried, and I wondered in amazement how she could have been so sure, so confident.

"I am so very happy for you both. Now then, Ferdie, for what it is worth, I want to give you my blessing and thank you for being so patient, and so discreet. And before you ask," she went on, as Ferdie's eyes widened and he spluttered into his champagne, "since the very beginning. You may have been able to hide it from everybody else, but I am the person who loves you the second-most in the world. I not only knew but was happy for you. For both of you."

Momentarily united, Scott and I exchanged a bemused glance, looking at Ferdie as he slumped down into a chair, a stunned expression rendering his cheekily handsome face immobile.

"And finally, we come to you, my precious Robert, most wonderful of husbands and best of companions. We have been together for so long, you and I, that there should have been no secrets between us. But there were, weren't there, my love? I want to tell you, Robert, that I know, I think I have always known, maybe even before you did. Oh, I appreciate and understand why you felt you had to keep it from me, although you could have confided in me, my darling. Somehow we'd have found a way to make it work."

The champagne glass slipped unnoticed from Robert's hand to crack in half on the tiled hearth, its contents fizzing as it came into contact with the hot grate. Seeing him sway, Ferdie leapt forward to steady Robert and help him to a chair.

"She knew?" I heard Robert mutter. "Oh my God, she knew, Annaliese ..." In desperation, ashen-faced, he held out a quivering hand to her perfect image.

"My darling," stressed Annaliese, leaning forward urgently in her chair. "I know what you're thinking and feeling right now, but it's all right, truthfully, and honestly, it's all right. You have been the best of husbands. I want more than anything in the world for you to be happy and know that I leave you in the very best of hands."

Ferdie's hand tightened on Robert's shoulder and Robert cast a quick, telling look up at him. Suddenly, everything made perfect, utter sense and I stared, we all stared, as the penny collectively dropped.

Ferdie glared at us, his expression defensive. "Yes, that's right," he stated, his voice low and controlled. "It's true, yet I swear to you we did nothing about it. We couldn't. We'd both rather have died than have caused her any pain at all."

"I have one last favour to ask of you, Robert," the flawless image went on. "You will know what it is when the time comes, and what must be done. Do this one small thing for me and you will have my everlasting gratitude," she smiled gently.

"And now, my friends," Annaliese continued, "love one another and be happy. If you ever think of me, then remember how much I loved you all and that we'll see each other again, soon."

It is all too much for me. Even though I probably deserve it, my exclusion from Annaliese's message from beyond the grave has hurt more than I could ever have imagined. I stumbled to my feet. I needed air and space, I needed to be away from them all, from their cosy little circle.

"Eve," Scott said, but I ignored him, reaching blindly for the door, pain pounding in my chest.

"Please don't go, Eve."

Her voice froze me to the spot, my hand cold on the smooth white porcelain of the handle.

"Please, Eve … stay…"

Slowly, I turned to gaze in disbelief at the screen where she stares back at me, her eyes locked on mine.

I feel the stunned looks of the others and hear Mimi mutter something under her breath in French but am oblivious to them all.

In a dream, I walked to the television, knelt before her image, and placed my fingertips on the screen.

She seems to look straight at me. I see the love in her eyes.

"My darling girl," she murmured. "My little Evie…"

And in a flash, I am back in that day, nearly a decade ago, to page one, chapter one, of the book of my life with Annaliese.

CHAPTER II – GENESIS

"Are you kind?"

The day I met Annaliese, and was first introduced into her magical golden world, started much like any other. Mike, my boyfriend, was still in bed, grumbling as I stomped around the bedroom pulling on clothes, shooting him evil looks, and making as much noise as one nineteen-year-old girl could make and still be considered this side of inconsiderate.

I wasn't resentful, well not much, about the fact he'd lost yet another job that week, making me, once again, the sole breadwinner. I was annoyed he seemed to be making no effort at all, or none that I could see, to find another.

Muttering curses about shiftless, lazy arse men, I located my missing shoe under the ugly sagging sofa still bearing the aroma of last night's chips, pulled a jacket over my shoulders and set off to work, taking great delight in letting the door bang hard behind me.

It was early summer in the year 2010. I turned my face up to the clear blue sky, delighting in the warmth of the morning sun as it peeped coyly over the trees lining the road where Mike and I were currently living in a small flat, barely one step up from a squat. Frankly admitting to myself it was gross, I looked upon it as purely temporary. Somewhere to live, for now, until I figured out what I wanted to do with my life.

And Mike? Well, a small but persistent voice inside was beginning to insist that maybe he too was purely temporary. At school, he had been the boy every girl wanted to be with – moody, lazy, and with a serious attitude that had always got him into trouble. In short, he was every would-be rebel teenage girl's dream. I thought all my Christmases had come at once when, out of all the girls in my year, he had chosen me.

We had been together nearly three years now, had left school together, vowing to make a life together, stick together through thick and thin and somehow, together, achieve our joint dream of a marvellous, rich future. Well, maybe now I was tired of all that *togetherness.*

We both found work easily enough. I found a job at the local newspaper, starting at the bottom of the ladder, determined to work my way up to the dizzy heights of journalist.

Mike was taken on by a local building firm as an electrician's apprentice, with the long-term goal of one day running his own company.

"That's where the money is, Mel," he insisted, as we toasted our success with cheap lager. "Being self-employed and making other suckers do the work whilst I make all the money."

The job with the building firm lasted all of two months, which, bearing in mind the twelve other jobs that had come and gone over the years, proved to be something of a record as Mike ricocheted from job to job, trying out everything possible but never quite finding one that fitted.

As for me, well, I was still with the newspaper but was becoming increasingly convinced I had made the wrong choice. That much as I loved the written word, the dreary restrictive world of a small-town reporter was not the fun and interesting life I had imagined it to be.

And so, we drifted through another year. Looking back, I felt my teeth gritting at the sheer waste of time. This wasn't what I'd planned. I didn't want to keep sitting around waiting for my life to begin; I wanted it all, and I wanted it now.

This impatience, coupled with the financial hole Mike's latest unemployment had landed us in, was the reason I had been moonlighting evenings and weekends, trying out other career options from the safety of a regular wage slip. Despising myself for not being as brave, or was that as foolhardy, as Mike, to take the plunge and leave a job I was beginning to detest.

Instead, I was dipping my toe, afraid of jumping, telling myself one of us must be sensible. That we wouldn't survive if both of us were floating belly up in the unemployed pond.

Of course, I could at any time give up and move back with Mum and Dad. They would welcome me with open arms, especially if I bore the glad tidings that I was no longer with Mike and, my mum's special fear, wasn't pregnant.

My parents despised Mike but were careful to hide it. They feared, probably correctly, that if I was forced to make a choice, then sheer teenage bloody-mindedness would prevail and they would lose me to him, and all he represented.

I guess I come from what you would call a middle, middle-class upbringing. My parents are teachers so earn respectable wages. They live in a nice comfortable house on the nice side of town. They have nice neighbours and get invited around for nice dinner parties and barbecues.

I went to a nice school – not the one my parents taught at, they felt that wouldn't have been fair to me – but still a very good state school where I did very well and got good grades.

Mike was the anomaly. He could in no way be described as nice. He was my rebellion against my upbringing; the stage I was going through, and my parents sensibly treated him as such.

Unfailingly polite to him, they invited him to tea, attempted to converse with him and, outwardly, were the very epitome of modern, tolerant parents.

But I saw the exchanged glances every time Mike grunted a monosyllabic reply, every time he lost another job, every time he drank a little too much of my dad's best beer, and every time he demonstrated to my parents that he wasn't looking after their little girl in the manner to which she was accustomed.

I saw the pained looks and squirmed inside, deeply embarrassed because I knew what they thought of him. I was angry at them for being snobs, and angrier still with myself because, deep down, I agreed with them.

When I moved in with him and we started living together in a series of damply depressing and squalid abodes, the pained looks became more obvious.

Dad even dared to tentatively query if I were sure this was what I wanted, at which point I'd snapped at him, punishing them both by not going around for two weeks. Mainly because I was annoyed at what I saw as interference in my life, but also because I'd wanted to throw myself into his arms and sob, no, this was not what I wanted at all, daddy; please make it all right.

My parents aren't my real parents; I mean, they're not my birth parents. They adopted me when I was a year old, so as far as love and commitment and memory go, they are my mum and dad, and I am perfectly okay with it all.

I've known for as long as I can remember I'm very special; that mummy and daddy couldn't have a little girl of their own so were lucky enough to be able to choose one, and to their great delight and joy got me.

I know some adopted children have a burning ambition to find their real mum, but not me. As far as I am concerned, she gave me up. She had lost any rights over me then and my loyalties were firmly with my real mum and dad; the people who had brought me up; loved me, and always been there for me.

"Hey, Mel!"

Jolted out of my daydream, I looked up as Ally jerked her car to a stop, waving frantically out of the open window.

"Come on, get in," she ordered. "We're late."

Obediently, I wrenched open the door of her old, rusty Ford Escort, marvelling the thing was still going, given the way Ally treated it. It seemed to run on fumes and a prayer, fuel gauge permanently hovering a shadow above red, and I don't recall Ally ever buying petrol. I suppose she must have done – but being as permanently broke as the rest of us – assumed she put in only the barest minimum, enough to keep it rattling from her parent's home in one of the villages to the various part-time and temporary jobs Ally filled her days with.

She stamped her foot to the floor. Dutifully, the little car lurched and shook its way down the road, brakes squealing as she slung us around the corner. Used to Ally's driving, I unconsciously braced myself, too grateful for the lift to object.

Today being a Saturday, I wasn't at work. Instead, I was going with Ally to earn some much-needed cash. The dregs of our money had been blown last night on chips and lager, so Ally's phone call, two days earlier, asking if I wanted to go with her on Saturday up to the posh Hall to do a spot of waitressing, couldn't have come at a better time.

Of course, being a waitress was not on my to-do list, but if I wanted to eat that night, and I did, I had to earn some pennies and fast. Ally glanced at me, noting the neat black skirt and white blouse which she'd dropped off the night before.

"Clothes fit okay?" she asked, expertly managing to change gear, take a corner and light a cigarette, all at the same time.

"Yes thanks," I replied, smoothing down the skirt. I am a good three inches taller than Ally, so the skirt, which on her was decent and staid, on me barely reached mid-thigh.

Beggars, however, cannot be choosers, and as I'd nothing even vaguely suitable in my wardrobe, had been very grateful for Ally's offer of a loan.

"Not sure how comfortable you're going be in those shoes though," she continued, looking down at my spiked heels and pulling a face.

"We're on our feet all day. Flats would probably have been a better idea."

"I'll be fine," I reassured her, not wanting to admit the only other black shoes I had were so scuffed and down at the heel, I would have been too embarrassed to wear them. She shrugged, turning her attention back to the road, and not speaking again until we slowed and turned left.

We drove through large ornate gates standing open to admit a steady stream of traffic. Gravel crunching under four bald tyres, we followed a gleaming Mercedes until the driveway split in two. The expensive car, obviously carrying guests, went one way and the mere hired help, us, drove around to the back of the Hall, scrunching to a halt outside the kitchen door.

Quickly, Ally hustled me out of the car, muttering under her breath at our lateness. Ally quite often helped at the Hall when they had one of their many parties, coming back with tales of the beauty and magnificence of the place, of the rich and famous people she saw whilst handing round champagne and canapés.

Most of all, she talked about the owner of the Hall, the renowned author, Annaliese.

I had read all her books, of course, I mean, who hadn't? We did them at school. They were considered modern classics, and my teacher, who had met her, was so besotted it had been easy to waste a whole lesson by getting him onto the subject of Annaliese.

So, when Ally asked if I wanted to come up to the Hall and help at a party to celebrate her thirty-fifth birthday, I jumped at the chance. Not only to earn some much-needed cash, but also to satisfy my curiosity about a woman I'd heard so much about and have a look at the place she'd lived in for over fifteen years with her husband and agent, Robert Macleod.

Ally talked often about the Hall and its occupants, so I knew Annaliese and her husband lived alone, having no children or any other family. I also knew Annaliese's assistant, the formidable Caroline O'Donnell, lived in the gatehouse, yet also had a room at the Hall where she often stayed. There was a large circle of friends, Ally had told me, and it was a rare night that none of them was staying over.

Annaliese was a very sociable person, she informed me knowledgeably, and had many friends. All this information was gained from Annaliese's housekeeper, Mrs Briggs, who had become fond of Ally over the two years she'd been helping whenever necessary.

So now, as we rushed down a long stone-flagged corridor and into a large, bright, and modern kitchen, I guessed the motherly soul who bustled over to us, flourishing white aprons, and exclaiming at our lateness, was none other than the indomitable Mrs Briggs.

"Sorry, Mrs B," gasped Ally, flipping the apron around her waist and expertly tying it into a neat bow with an ease that came from much practice. "This is Melissa, the one I told you about."

Mrs Briggs shot me a look and pursed her lips, no doubt at my somewhat dishevelled appearance, and I found my hands automatically flying up to try and tame my wild riotous curls. I guessed I was looking even more uncultivated than normal due to Ally's race to get us here, and the open car window.

Ally quickly tied the apron around my waist, flashing me a silently supportive smile, sensing my unease and a sudden fit of nerves.

"Well, no matter, you're here now," said Mrs Briggs, and gestured at trays already loaded with beautiful crystal champagne flutes, all precisely filled with the sparkling golden liquid.

"Take these through to the entrance hall," she ordered. "The guests are arriving, and Robert wants everyone to have a glass of champagne to wish Annaliese a very happy birthday."

I was, I must confess, surprised at the easy way she used their first names, almost as if they were family. Perhaps, subconsciously, I was expecting her to be subservient.

My knowledge of domestic help was limited to period dramas on the telly and the way my mother treated her cleaner – an odd mixture of relief someone else was tackling the housework and middle-class guilt that another woman was cleaning her house.

Later, I would learn Mrs Briggs had been Robert's housekeeper for twenty years, so considered herself family and allowed herself certain privileges; however, should any other lesser member of staff attempt such familiarity, then her matronly bosom would heave with righteous indignation and the saucy young upstart would be left in no doubt as to the impropriety of their actions.

Picking up a tray of glasses, I wobbled slightly, feet already throbbing in too tight, unfamiliar heeled shoes, and a flicker of concern crossed Mrs Brigg's kindly face.

"You will be careful, won't you, dear?"

"I'll be fine." I did my best to give her my most reassuring smile and followed Ally as she expertly sashayed out of the kitchen through a swing door, into the large entrance hallway and straight into a 1920's party.

Grinning with spontaneous delight, my eyes were everywhere taking in the gorgeous, beaded dresses and headpieces of the female guests, and the classically impressive tuxedos of the men.

A jazz band was playing a sedate ragtime tune in the corner, and I could see one or two guests attempting a Charleston.

What were my first impressions of the place that would be my home? Gold and sunshine; early summer light streaming through great double doors thrown open to their full width. The guests were entering with cries of joyful recognition and seemingly genuine pleasure, as they greeted, kissed, and hugged one another.

The wallpaper was a beautiful, brocaded stripe, the colour of old-fashioned guineas, which the light seemed to turn into cloth of gold as I weaved through the crowds, grateful hands removing glasses until at last my tray was empty.

Following Ally, I made my way back to the kitchen for another tray, and another, until every guest I could see had a full glass in their hands.

Melting unobtrusively into the background with Ally, we pressed our backs against the door to the kitchen quarters, only moving when it silently creaked open and Mrs Briggs slipped out, her face wreathed in a bright smile, a glass of champagne gripped tightly in her capable hand.

A man, tall and in his late forties, ran lightly up the beautiful marble staircase and stopped halfway. Facing the guests, he held up a hand until the excited buzz had died away.

"My friends," he began. "I want to thank you all for joining us on this very special day, the day my darling wife and your dear friend, Annaliese, turns thirty-five."

There were cheers from the guests as they turned shiny happy faces up to him, anticipation and pleasure lighting their expressions. Letting my eyes roam, I saw standing at the foot of the stairs a tiny woman, obviously late in pregnancy. Her short dark hair was styled into a sharply angled bob under a black and sequined feathered headdress. I envied her for the control she had over it, and for the chic air, she wore like a second skin.

I wondered who she was and watched silently as she looked up at the tall man standing beside her. He smiled at her, his love and adoration obvious even from the other side of the room. Tenderly, he rested a large hand on her abdomen, and I guessed he must be the father of her baby.

They seemed an unlikely pair, her so slight and dark, her classic chic making me doubt she was English, and him so typically Scottish looking, with his burly physique and red hair. And yet, as she slipped under his arm, fitting exactly against his side, I realised they were a perfect match.

Opposite them, on the other side of the stairs, stood a very tall, untidily assembled woman, short frizzy hair cropped almost regimentally close to the side of her head, eyes blinking through thick-rimmed spectacles as she gazed up at Robert, clutching her glass as if it were a lifeline, mouth silently moving in time to his speech. In a sudden burst of clarity, I realised this must be the assistant, Caroline O'Donnell, and gazed curiously at her.

Ally hadn't been very forthcoming with information about her, only that she'd been with Annaliese for years, since her first book had been published, and ran both Annaliese and Robert's lives with such military precision they'd be lost without her. Ally knew she had been married. She had a son who lived in America and very rarely came home, at least, Ally had never seen him.

Next to her stood a man. He smiled at the pregnant couple, and I felt the breath catch in my throat. He was, quite simply, the most gorgeous man I had ever seen. Dark-haired and tall, he looked to be in his late twenties and was dressed in a cream tuxedo which screamed expensive and made him look the part. He was Jay Gatsby, and every other hero from the Roaring Twenties I had ever read about or seen in a film.

I gaped hungrily at his square-jawed profile, thinking wildly that he looked like old photographs of those men who'd conquered the British Empire and done great deeds of daring-do in the wilds of Africa, or some such place.

Clean-shaven, he had a firm, perfect chin, and a straight nose. Looking up at Robert, head held at a slightly arrogant angle, I realised why he seemed familiar. My father still had all his old Rider Haggard books, and this man could have posed for one of its covers.

"Who's that?" I whispered to Ally, angling my head in his direction.

"Scott," she muttered back, and we rolled our eyes in a mute expression of shared lust which had Mrs Briggs clicking her tongue disapprovingly and beetling her brows at us.

Behind Scott was another man, shorter, slighter, and with blond hair which flopped over a soft, kindly-looking face. He pulled a rueful face at the pregnant woman, and I noted the feminine angle of his chin and the set of his mouth. Probably gay, I said to myself. As he turned further to gaze around at the assembled guests, I amended firmly to myself, definitely gay.

The pregnant woman swayed. I saw concern flicker over the redheaded man's face as his grip on her elbow tightened. He glanced around, seeking support, but before he could do anything, another man standing behind them silently and unobtrusively slipped a chair from the wall.

Without any fuss, he touched the woman on the shoulder, who turned, saw the chair, sank gracefully down onto it, and flashed a grateful smile at her rescuer. Her husband too nodded his thanks in the other man's direction, who smiled, before turning his attention back up to Robert.

Curiously, I studied them, the woman sitting neatly, her legs crossed at the ankles. Her poise and grace made me aware of my slouch, and I drew myself up.

Her raspberry-coloured flapper dress was stylish and suited her, clever draping over the stomach, serving to lead the eye away from the bulge without resorting to the usual tent-like camouflage which women in very late pregnancy seemed to sport.

Beside her stood the man whom I had decided was her husband, tall and solid. Muscular, rather than fat, he stood like a rugby player, his burly body taking on a thin guise of respectability under his well-cut, black tuxedo.

Then, in the position he had assumed behind her chair, was the other man. Not as tall as the redheaded giant, nor as physically intimidating, his soft brown hair was cut into a neat, bank manager style, yet his face seemed kind.

When he looked down at the shining black crown of the woman's bob, his expression softened into tender concern. As if sensing this, the woman glanced up, her small, perfectly manicured hand lightly touching his as though to reassure.

They formed a circle around the foot of the stairs, with the pregnant woman, her husband and their friend on the left, and Caroline, Scott, and the gay-looking man on the right.

I now noticed how the other guests formed an outer ring a couple of paces back, leaving a clear space between them and this charmed circle of six, the air of exclusiveness which hung over them palpable and obvious.

Who were they? I asked myself. Who were these beautiful people whose confidence and attractiveness set them apart from us mere mortals?

I snapped to attention as Robert paused, and into the silence, a rich, highly amused voice resounded in a stage whisper from upstairs.

"For heaven's sake, darling, do get on with it, I want some champagne."

There was a roar of laughter and Robert shook his head, shrugging with comic resignation.

"Ladies and gentlemen," he cried over the mirth, "with no further ado, will you please raise your glasses to the birthday girl, Annaliese."

"Annaliese!" chorused the guests, glasses raised, and there she was.

Poised, charming, she hesitated on the stairs, hand clasped to her chest in mock surprise. Her gorgeously beaded pink flapper dress jingled slightly as she moved, its beads reflecting the late afternoon sun streaming through the open front doors.

Then she descended, laughing, her long golden hair lifting over her shoulders. She took the hand her husband offered her, and the glass of champagne which Scott quickly ran up the stairs and presented her with. Pressing a merry kiss to her husband's beaming face, I saw the love in their expressions and sighed wistfully, understanding the futility of my relationship with Mike.

"My friends," she cried, blue eyes sparkling with fun and happiness. "Thank you so much for coming to my surprise birthday party."

She twinkled at the word surprise, and there was a knowing chuckle from her audience.

"Enjoy yourselves, that is my birthday wish. I want everyone to have the best time imaginable. Thank you."

There was a round of good-natured applause as Annaliese ran lightly down the stairs, pressing kisses onto cheeks, gently dropping a hand onto the swollen belly of her friend, and exchanging a few low words with her, before smiling and being caught up in hugs by the other two men. Scott, I noticed, stayed close to her side, chatting easily with Robert, his eyes constantly straying back to the brightness that was Annaliese.

"Melissa," whispered Ally. "Come on, we need to get back to work."

"Okay," I murmured and was about to follow her when Annaliese looked up. Through a gap in the crowd, our eyes met and locked. She gazed at me for what felt like forever, as my heart pounded and the breath caught in my lungs, stubbornly refusing to come out. She smiled gently, almost wistfully, then released me from her stare and turned to talk to someone else.

Caroline O'Donnell also looked at me, her small eyes narrowed and hostile. Flushing, after all, I was being paid to work, not stare at the rich and famous at play, I quickly followed Ally through the swing door and back into the kitchen.

Later, hours later, and with Mrs Briggs's blessing, I took my poor aching feet and escaped with a plateful of food and a mug of tea out into the back courtyard to have my break.

Carefully placing my plate and mug onto what I assumed was an old mounting block, I eased my swollen feet out of the hateful shoes, catching my breath in a sob of pain at the flesh and blood left behind.

Choosing not to think about how I was going to force my rubbed raw feet back into such instruments of torture, I left the shoes where they lay and wandered away onto the lush grass, seeking somewhere to have my picnic.

Back at the Hall, the party was still in full swing and would continue until the small hours, but Ally had informed me that we hired help were not expected to stay until the bitter end.

Instead, we had about another hour of handing out food and drink and clearing away the empties, then we would help Mrs Briggs tidy the kitchen and load the dishwashers.

A mobile catering unit had been hired which would arrive at four and would begin serving freshly cooked fish and chips, burgers, and pizzas.

"How original," I heard one guest exclaim. "Oh, what fun," another had cried, and I reflected ironically that fish and chips were something of a novelty to these people, not part of their staple diet.

The catering unit would stay all night, dispensing hot food whenever the guests wanted it. In the morning, it would offer a choice of breakfast foods ranging from the traditional bacon and egg roll to waffles, toast, and crumpets. Mrs Briggs would also be back in the morning to make sure there was enough tea, coffee, and juice on tap for all the partied-out guests.

It was like I had been allowed a glimpse of another life, of another world where people thought nothing of spending thousands on a party.

Passing round drinks and trays full of delicious looking, yet unfamiliar food, I caught glimpses of Annaliese opening her presents, contrasting the beautiful jewellery and gorgeous pieces of china, with the thirty pounds my parents had given me in an envelope last month when I'd turned nineteen. Mike, being out of work, as usual, had given me nothing, and my birthday money had quickly gone on food.

Annaliese fascinated me. As I slipped through the guests, silently handing out canapés and topping up glasses, I constantly looked for her, instinctively knowing as soon as I entered a room if she was there or not because of her brightness, that quick silvery laugh, and the fact that wherever there was a crowd of laughing happy people, Annaliese was invariably at its centre.

Now I wandered through the cooling grass, a moan of pleasure on my lips at the relief after the torture of too-high and too-tight shoes.

Finding a weeping willow tree, I eased my way under its concealing branches, dropping down to sit cross-legged on the ground, taking a swig of tea and looking with interest at my plate.

My parents are very plain eaters. Much of the food I had been serving all day was unfamiliar to me. Cautiously, I picked up a small golden-brown pastry parcel and bit into it, flaky bits erupting onto my lips and skirt, as a warm, nutty cheesy taste with the tangy flavour of spinach exploded in my mouth.

Hmm, I thought, not bad. I tried an olive and instantly spat it out, its oily salty taste was unpleasant to my uneducated palate.

The little vol-au-vents filled with anchovies marinated in fresh herbs and lemon juice were nice, as were the triangles of brown bread topped with smoked salmon and caviar. The taramasalata made me feel sick so I pushed it to one side and instead crunched up a garlic and herb breadstick.

I had eaten nothing since a small portion of greasy sausage and chips the night before, so could feel my stomach rumbling and protesting at the richly unfamiliar food.

I sipped my tea, wishing it were champagne. I had had champagne before. When I passed my exams, my parents had bought a bottle, but I suspected its gassy disappointing taste, which had burnt the back of my throat and caused indigestion, was a pale imitation of the golden bubbling liquid I had been serving all day.

I watched in silent envy as the guests gulped it down, the atmosphere fizzing and frothing almost as much as the champagne, voices rising until a bubble of happy sound seemed to encase the whole hall.

I finished my tea, tipping the dregs onto the ground, and placed the plate, with its leftover bits of food, on the ground beside me. Wiggling down, I stretched out on the grass, flexing my feet as the blisters throbbed, dreading trying to squeeze them back into those shoes.

"I'd be careful if I were you."

My eyes snapped open in shock at the male voice which intruded into my sanctuary, and I struggled to sit up, frantically pulling down a skirt that had ridden up to the top of my thighs.

"I'm sorry, what?" I gasped, pushing hair out of my eyes, peering through the fronds of the tree to where a man stood, the sun behind him casting a halo of light around his pale suit. I shaded my eyes and realised it was Scott.

"You should be careful lying there," he continued. 'There's an ant's nest in that tree and the ferocious little buggers will have smelt the food."

I felt a tickle on my leg, and in sudden paranoid fear swiped my hand across my shin, dislodging a probing exploring ant, feelers held high as he searched for food.

Quickly, I scrambled to my feet and hopped out from under the tree, brushing myself down, imagining the scrabble of tiny feet on my body.

"Oh," I exclaimed in disgust, as the remnants of food on my plate heaved and moved under a mass of small black bodies, "What shall I do?"

Scott frowned, cautiously reached down, and tipped the plate over, tapping it on the ground to dislodge food and ants into an angrily vibrating heap, then handed the empty plate and mug back to me.

"Let them have their own party," he said, looking at me curiously. "You're not the girl who usually comes with Ally."

I heard the question in his voice and felt myself colour under his gaze. Oh my, he really was outstandingly gorgeous.

I had always thought Mike good-looking, but compared to this man, he paled into insignificance. Scott so vividly reminded me of one of those heroes from books I had done in English, the Great Gatsby or Sebastian from Brideshead Revisited; that same self-assurance which bordered on arrogance.

I realised he was still waiting for my answer, and that I was gaping at him like a landed trout.

"No," I stuttered. "I'm not. She, that is, Jenny ... umm, the girl who usually comes with Ally, well, she's on her honeymoon, so Ally asked me to come instead."

"Oh," he said, his eyes moving down my long, exposed legs. I saw a flicker of something in them, before he drawled, "Well, you're certainly easier on the eye than the other girl. What happened to your shoes?"

"I took them off," I explained hurriedly. "My feet were hurting so much. I'm not used to wearing heels, but they were the only pair of black shoes I had."

He smiled but didn't answer. Silence stretched between us. I stared at him. I knew I was staring but I couldn't help it. There was something in his gaze that was leaving me hot and breathless, and I could feel the colour mounting in my cheeks.

Suddenly, an unearthly screech sounded from the undergrowth, and I practically leapt into his arms.

"What the hell?!" I yelped, and he chuckled as he steadied me, his hands warm on my arms.

"It's okay," he reassured me. "It's only Humphrey."

"Humphrey?" The screech sounded again, and I gripped his hand in involuntary shock. "What the hell is a Humphrey?"

There was a rustle in the undergrowth and a large peacock strutted out. Surveying us arrogantly, he cried out again and paced by his long tail dragging through the grass.

"That is Humphrey," Scott informed me.

"A peacock," I breathed. "I've never seen one in real life before. He's huge! And that noise he made ... Is he friendly?"

"Not particularly," Scott warned, and gently pulled on my hand to stop me from stepping after the magnificent creature. "He's rather a grumpy sod, so be careful about approaching him."

"Is he?" I looked from Scott to Humphrey, trying to decide which was the most arrogant looking, which was the most beautiful. "Why?"

"His mate died two years ago, and Humphrey has been pining away with a broken heart ever since."

"Oh," I sympathised. "Poor Humphrey. Couldn't another mate be found for him?"

"Sadly, no," Scott replied. "When Annaliese bought the Hall, Humphrey and his mate came with it. The previous owner had acquired them several years earlier, but this particular breed of peacock is now on the endangered list and it's illegal to buy them."

"So, that means poor Humphrey..."

"Is doomed to wander the grounds alone until the end of his days crying out for his lost mate."

"That's so sad," I whispered, almost in tears at his words and looked at the departing peacock in sorrow.

We stood, watching Humphrey leave, and I realised that somehow my hand was still in Scott's hand and that we were standing so close our shoulders were practically touching.

I looked up at him. He turned his head and gazed steadily at me, his dark eyes reflecting the sunlight that danced through the branches overhead.

Gently, almost reluctantly, I pulled my sweaty hand from his grasp.

"I'd better be getting back," I said, breathily. "My break was only fifteen minutes. Thank you for rescuing me from the ants and Humphrey. I hope you enjoy the rest of your party. Goodbye."

I turned and fled from his seductive dark eyes and his sardonically handsome smile.

"Wait," he called. "What's your name?"

But I pretended not to hear and hurried back to the courtyard, my face flaming with embarrassed colour. I rescued my shoes, sat on the mounting block to brush grass and dirt from my feet, and attempted to persuade them back into the cheap, tightly fitting shoes, wincing with pain as blisters tore and bled, rubbing excruciatingly until my eyes watered.

"My word, you've caught the sun," exclaimed Mrs Briggs as I re-entered the kitchen, mistaking my blazing cheeks for exposure to the elements. "Best you have some water. Don't want you collapsing from dehydration now, do we?"

Gratefully, I filled a glass from the tap and gulped it thirstily, feeling the icy-cold water slip down my throat, and taking the opportunity to collect my wildly scattered thoughts.

"All right now?" she asked in motherly concern, and I nodded in response. "That's good," she said and thrust an opened bottle of champagne into each hand.

"Now, go and top up glasses while Ally has her break, then you can both give me a hand taking out the desserts."

I gripped the bottles tightly, feeling their coldness through my palms, and the drops of condensation which oozed their way slowly down the thickened glass necks.

On my way out, I passed Ally entering the kitchen bearing a tray full of empty plates, glasses, and scrunched-up napkins. She pulled a weary face at me, and I smiled sympathetically.

Moving once more through the guests, ignored, and overlooked, I silently refilled any glass I saw, watching as the party sprawled like a living thing, spreading itself through the many rooms of the Hall.

A game of billiards was being played in one, and the spectators, mostly men, waved me away, indicating they were onto the whisky and had no need of my champagne.

The band was playing lively 1920s tunes, and people were moving together. One elderly couple gathered an admiring crowd as they perfectly performed what looked like a tango or something similar.

I refilled glasses, emptied both my bottles, returned to the kitchen, and emerged with two more, wondering how much all this champagne had cost.

I passed through the rest of the rooms, seeing Mrs Briggs laying out elegant trays of tea and coffee things in the conservatory, where some of the older, more sedate partygoers had gathered.

And everywhere I went, there was the sound of people enjoying themselves. I watched in silence as the sophisticated, beautiful guests, laughed and chatted, the level of noise rising in direct relation to the amount of alcohol being consumed.

I am aware that I'm constantly looking for Scott, but I am unable to explain why he so fascinates me. I have never met anyone like him before. He makes all the boys I hung around with at school, all the men at work, Mike, his mates, seem so coarse and rough.

My eyes scan the crowd. With a clutch of excitement, I see him, sprawled on the lawn with the rest of the inner circle.

Lurking in the doorway, I watched as they lazily chatted to each other, and heard the gentle laughter rising like a heat haze in the warm still air.

They are so beautiful, all of them, glamorous and unreachable like kings.

Annaliese is sitting on a covered swing, the pregnant woman lying with her head in her lap, her stomach sticking upright, her eyes closed wearily as Annaliese gently rubbed her temples, one small bare foot pushing at the ground to send them slowly rocking.

The woman's redheaded giant of a husband is lying back in a deckchair, listening in smiling silence to Robert as he expounds on some unheard subject, his hands gesturing as though to emphasise a point.

Of Caroline, there is no sign, but the other two men, the kindly looking one who'd so gallantly found a seat for his pregnant friend, and the blond-haired gay one, are sitting on deckchairs chatting to Annaliese, legs stretched out as they slouched easily.

And there was Scott, sprawled at Annaliese's feet on a tartan rug. Raised on his elbows, he listened to the different conversations around him and watched Annaliese's face.

Occasionally, her eyes would flick down to his and she would smile a gentle, loving smile. I wondered, with a stab of quick hot envy, if anything was going on between them.

Then Annaliese once again seemed to sense my presence and she raised her head, looking directly at me across the distance, her blue eyes serious and intense. She smiled and raised a hand to me in greeting, Scott began to turn to see what had caught her attention, and I fled, cheeks flaming, back to the kitchen to help Mrs Briggs with the desserts.

Carefully, feet now so excruciatingly painful that every step was agony, I hobbled behind Mrs Briggs and Ally as we transported great platters on which resided the most amazing desserts I had ever seen.

A magnificent summer fruit pavlova, a massive cut crystal bowl of succulent strawberries, Mrs Briggs' homemade trifle, a moist and delicious-looking chocolate fudge cake, great jugs of cream, and a huge cheeseboard decorated with grapes, celery, nuts, and fresh figs.

Finally, Mrs Briggs and Ally manoeuvred a massive three-tiered birthday cake into the conservatory, ablaze with thirty-five candles.

Annaliese was quickly summoned to blow them out amidst a rousing chorus of Happy Birthday to You, and For She's a Jolly Good Fellow.

I stood there, clutching a flat wicker basket piled up with juicy apples and pears, watching her try to blow out all the candles, intensely aware of how stunningly vibrant and alive she was.

She threw back her head, laughed with sheer delight, and I thought how she didn't look thirty-five. If I was brutally honest with myself, she probably looked younger than me.

The past year I had eaten a steady diet of junk food and my skin suffered as a result. Embarrassed by my bitten-down nails, I curled them under the edge of the basket, trying to hide them from view, acutely aware that my hair desperately needed conditioning and a decent cut.

Scott stood with her, waiting with a knife to help her cut the cake. I dropped my eyes away from their attractiveness. The contrast between their life and mine couldn't have been more obvious. I wished I hadn't come. All I wanted to do now was collect my money and go home.

There was a surge as the guests swelled forward to congratulate Annaliese, and I felt an intense raw blast of pain as someone blundered heavily onto my foot, crushing the already blistered and mangled toes, causing me to shriek in agony, stumble to my knees and drop the basket of fruit.

Mortified, I watched in frozen fascination as dozens of faces begin to turn curiously in my direction, and apples rolled gaily in all directions, some imperceptible slope in the floor making the majority of them bounce jauntily under the table, thudding to a stop against Scott's feet.

"Melissa!" hissed Ally in horror.

I turned teary, panic-stricken eyes to the birthday girl, stunned when she burst into peals of delighted laughter. Stooping, she gathered up a handful of apples.

"Maybe I should rename you Adam," she taunted Scott, waving them under his nose. "Wasn't he tempted when Eve threw an apple at him?"

There was a ripple of laughter. Ally pulled me up, desperate to get us both back to the sanctuary of the kitchen. I took a step, pain shooting up my leg, and my face crumpled in anguish as an agonised cry was forced from my throat.

The laughter immediately disappeared from Annaliese. The next instant she was by my side forcing me to sit in a chair, kneeling at my feet as she tenderly removed my shoes, her eyes going wide with shock at their raw bleeding state.

"Oh, my goodness," she cried. "You poor darling! Scott..."

Immediately he was next to her, his face registering concern at the condition of my feet.

"Scott. Be an angel and carry your poor little Eve to my room. Those feet need to be tended to."

"There's no need," I gasped, mortified at being the cause of such uproar. "I can walk to the kitchen and it's nearly time for me to go home anyway."

"Nonsense," Annaliese cried her brow wrinkling in distress. "You're not going anywhere until those poor feet have been sorted out."

She arose and nodded to Scott. I squeaked as he swiftly and efficiently swept me up into his arms, pushing his way through the crowds of curious onlookers who murmured in sympathy and silently created a pathway through which he strode.

"Caro, darling." Caroline O'Donnell appeared from nowhere, glaring at me as if I had done it on purpose, small eyes flinty hard with suspicion.

"Please could you supervise cutting the cake and make sure everyone tucks into those yummy-looking desserts. I'm going to tend to poor Eve's feet and then we'll be right down."

Caro's mouth opened to object, but Annaliese swept past, motioning Scott to proceed up the stairs with me still lying in his arms, shocked to the core, yet secretly enjoying the experience immensely. Over his shoulder, I saw Ally, mouth open, eyes stunned, hints of envy lurking within them.

Annaliese's room was a cool shady oasis of cream and palest green. I looked around me in silent, appreciative admiration as Scott gently placed me on a small sofa, set at a right angle to a charming little fireplace in which a basket of white flowers rested. He shook his head as Annaliese hurried through an adjoining door, which I assumed led to a bathroom.

"I know you said your feet hurt," he commented dryly, "but I didn't realise they were hurting that much. Why on earth didn't you say something?"

"They weren't that bad," I mumbled. "At least, they weren't until they got trodden on."

"Scott, my sweetheart." Annaliese re-entered the room, carefully carrying a large china bowl in which warm water lapped. "Could you please go and ask Mrs Briggs for some antiseptic cream and plasters?"

"Of course," he replied coolly and left the room.

Annaliese knelt and eased my feet into the bowl, and I swallowed down my moan of pain as the hot water washed over torn and bleeding skin. She glanced at me sympathetically.

Close to, she was as beautiful as she was at a distance, and although I could see a fine network of laughter lines fanning out from the corners of her eyes, they only served to heighten her appeal.

"You poor thing," she murmured, small hands softly sluicing water over my battered feet. "You should have said something," she gently chided.

"I didn't want to make a fuss. It's your birthday party after all," I replied, and she flashed me a mischievous smile, china-blue eyes twinkling with amusement.

"So instead, you threw apples at poor Scott?"

I flushed, and she laughed out loud.

"Don't worry about it, Eve. The look on his face was simply priceless."

I found myself unable to help returning her smile and she patted my hand.

"That's better," she exclaimed. "Now then..."

She carefully lifted my feet out of the water and wrapped them in a large fluffy towel she had also brought from the bathroom.

"I'll let you dry your feet whilst I find you a pair of shoes to go home in."

"Oh no," I exclaimed in horror. "That's ok, I'll..."

"Now then, Eve," she interrupted with a mockingly stern look, "you don't want to squeeze your poor feet back into those killer heels, do you?"

Sheepishly, I shook my head, watching mutely as she vanished through another door into an enormous walk-in wardrobe, reappearing a few moments later brandishing a beautiful pair of flat, jewelled leather sandals.

"These are probably the best thing," she said, handing them to me. "They won't rub on your toes."

I took the shoes and examined them in delight, running my fingers over the gemstone-encrusted straps. I had never seen anything so pretty and beamed at Annaliese.

"They're gorgeous," I exclaimed, and she smiled with pleasure.

There was a knock at the door, and Scott entered carrying a small red first aid kit. Annaliese held her hand out for it, but he shook his head.

"I'll help Eve put on the plasters," he offered. "You're needed downstairs, Annaliese. Some of the older guests are making noises about leaving. You should go and say goodbye to them."

"Should I?" she sighed in resignation. "You're right as usual, Scott. You take care of Eve. I'll see you both downstairs soon."

Leaning over, she pressed a quick kiss on my forehead, stroking my hair.

"You take care of yourself, darling Eve, and promise me, no more squeezing those poor little feet of yours into horrid uncomfortable shoes."

"I won't," I promised earnestly. "And thank you," I cried as she moved away, desperate to delay her leaving by even a moment.

"Thank you for everything, and the shoes."

"It was nothing ..." she gestured impatiently with her hands.

"No, really, thank you. I promise I'll return them as soon as possible."

"Keep them," she insisted, but I shook my head in horror.

"I couldn't, I mean, it's so kind of you to lend them to me, but..."

"Very well, Eve," she smiled, that bright, illuminating smile already so achingly familiar to me, "return the shoes if you like. At least that way we'll get to see you again."

"Yes," I agreed gratefully. "I'll bring them back soon."

One more smile, a nod, and she was gone, leaving the room dark and strangely empty. Scott knelt by my feet, snapped open the first aid kit and rummaged through the assorted medical essentials until he located a tube of antiseptic cream. I watched in silent fascination as he unscrewed the lid, his large hands making it seem of almost toy-town proportions.

Slowly, he squeezed some onto his finger and I swallowed, unable to tear my gaze away from his hands. Reaching out, he cupped my foot in the palm of his hand. The shock of contact seared up my leg and stabbed me in the groin, and I choked back a groan, squirming at his touch.

"Sorry," he apologised, mistaking the motive for the intake of breath and sudden flinching, as he slowly and gently dabbed the cream onto the broken skin. "This might sting a little."

"Just a little," I muttered, looking down at his dark shiny hair, feeling the strongest of urges to run my fingers through it.

My hand rose, hovered mere inches away from his head and then I caught sight of the broken nails, the rough chapped skin, and resolutely pulled it back.

Our worlds were light-years apart. He was rich and years older than me, probably used to sophisticated and beautiful women, not grubby little waitresses with wild hair and spots.

He was a daydream. A gorgeously unobtainable daydream. I felt small and incredibly stupid for even thinking for one second that he could ever be interested in a silly kid like me because that was all I was to him, a child.

"It's okay." Embarrassed, I pulled my foot from his grasp. "I can do that, really, you don't have to... I mean, it's... it's just, I'll do it."

"Suit yourself."

In one fluid movement, he lifted the china bowl and took it into the bathroom where I heard him tip the contents down the sink. Desperately, I wrapped my toes in plasters, the inane thought occurring about how toes are so unattractive – short squat sausages on the end of our feet.

"Thank you," I muttered, as he re-entered the room. "You've been very kind, you and... Annaliese." I stumbled over her name, and he smiled as if understanding my discomfort.

"Kindness should be Annaliese's middle name," he replied. "I don't know how she does it. I mean, I've never heard her say an unpleasant word about anyone."

"And you?" I heard myself say. "Are you kind?"

He paused, as if considering my ridiculous question, then shrugged again. "Sometimes," he replied. "When it suits me."

He left me alone then in Annaliese's room, after telling me firmly to rest for a few moments then come down to the party for a glass of champagne, seeming to forget I was merely staff, the hired help.

I leaned back against the sofa, closing my eyes in weary confusion. Emotionally drained, I felt like I had been abducted by aliens and carried off to a beautiful but strange new world; a place of grace and elegance and extreme kindness to total strangers.

I liked this world. I wanted to stay in it.

Cautiously I stood up, Annaliese's shoes felt cool against my swollen feet. As she had hoped, the open-toed shoes avoided the blisters. Apart from the unattractiveness of having a plaster stuck on every toe, my feet felt the best they had all day.

I left the room, easing the door shut behind me, and made my way back to the stairs, letting my hand trail down the silky softness of the wooden bannister, my shoes clicking slightly on the beauty of the marbled stairs.

Halfway down, the stairs took a sharp right turn. Up until that point, anyone coming down the stairs was hidden from the view of people in the hall below, and I realised this was where Annaliese had waited to make her grand entrance earlier.

I paused and imagined her standing there, listening to her husband's admiring speech, the laughter of her friends waiting for her, and then I heard them – strangers, two party guests. They were standing on the stairs, hidden from my view by the bend in the wall.

"Splendid party." The voice was male, bluff, and hearty, his tone speaking of a lifetime of wealth and gentlemen's clubs.

"Yes, well, Annaliese always does throw a good bash. But I say, how about that embarrassing scene earlier?" The other voice was female, catty, and shrill.

"You mean when the little waitress dropped the fruit basket? Rather funny, I thought, though I don't know why Annaliese had to make such a fuss over her."

"You know Annaliese and her little charity cases. I think she enjoys playing Lady Bountiful, but honestly, it doesn't do to treat the staff as equals, gives them ideas above their station."

"You're absolutely right, of course. Anyway, shall we go and find some more champagne?"

They moved away, back down the stairs, and their voices mingled, disappearing into the wall of sound below. Stunned, I leaned against the wall, bile rising in the back of my throat.

Charity case? Was that how Annaliese saw me? And Scott? Their actions, which had seemed so kind and natural, now took on a more condescending element, and my face burned with humiliation.

Carefully, I moved, stumbling upstairs, unable, and unwilling to face them. In a daze, I wandered along the landing past the door to Annaliese's room, finally found a small staircase hidden behind a corner, and made my way down, hoping I'd found the old servants' stairs which would lead me back to the kitchen, bypassing the party and its snobby, patronising guests.

I didn't want to see them, any of them, ever again, and felt a wave of profound relief when I finally emerged at the end of the corridor which led to the kitchen. I entered the room to find Mrs Briggs and Ally, their faces concerned and, was it my imagination, more than a little annoyed.

"Melissa, where on earth have you been?" cried Ally, her voice sharp and accusing.

"I'm sorry," I mumbled. "I got lost and it took me ages to find my way back to the kitchen."

"It's a big house," agreed Mrs Briggs and handed me a white envelope. "Thank you very much for your help today, my dear. Next time, make sure you wear comfortable shoes."

"Thank you," I replied, taking the envelope gratefully. "I will."

I smiled reassuringly at her but knew that even if I was offered a million pounds I wouldn't be coming back. I had seen a glimpse of their world, of Annaliese's world, where they ruled with the supreme confidence of kings of old.

For a while I had been dazzled by it, blinded by the easy luxury, their soft voices, and correct manners. Yet a few thoughtless words by total strangers had quickly snatched the blinkers from my eyes and showed me their world for what it really was – indolent and careless, their kindness the mere patronage of the very wealthy to the very poor.

It sickened me. I wanted no more of it, but a part of me could not shake the way I had felt when I looked into her laughing blue eyes; the thrill of feeling part of their circle, even for a moment; the exciting, unfamiliar emotions that Scott, with his nonchalantly privileged attitude and confidently firm touch, had awakened deep within me.

I sighed, accepted my old shoes which Ally passed to me, her lips tight with barely suppressed jealousy, and followed her out to the car to make our silent way home.

Driving away, I craned my neck for one last look at Annaliese's kingdom, glowing golden in the afternoon sun, its windows shining like mercury. Partygoers, all dressed in their finest, spilt out of its doors onto the veranda, and a part of me ached to be accepted within that world.

Resolutely, I turned away. Once again, I faced the real world, my world, and I determined to post Annaliese's shoes to her as soon as possible, rather than take them back as promised. That would be an end to it. My brief brush with the elite would be over, and I would settle down and get on with my life.

CHAPTER III – KINGS

"You're a part of the group now."

Two weeks later I was still smarting over the experience and had done nothing about returning Annaliese's shoes. They lay like a nagging reminder, wrapped in tissue paper at the bottom of the wardrobe. For days after the party, I had been half-convinced Annaliese would somehow contact me, jumping every time my mobile rang.

Logically, I knew it was impossible; she didn't even know my real name let alone my number. Still, a small part of me feared, hoped, I would hear from her again.

Much to my surprise and concern, Mike got himself a job, yet was so smugly secretive, I worried what he had gotten himself into. I was even more concerned when friends told me they had seen him hanging about with Wayne Jones.

If Mike had been the bad boy at school, then Wayne had been the antichrist. Violent, thuggish, and cunning, Wayne bunked off school pretty much all the time. He got away with it, not only because he was so disruptive the teachers' lives were easier without him, but because they were afraid of him.

Large, strong, and unpredictable, rumour had it he carried a knife. Although no one ever claimed to have seen it, the mad glint in his eyes and the company he kept left no doubt in anyone's mind it was probably true. When we all left school, he had dropped off my radar, and apart from the odd sighting of him sloping around town, I had not seen him for over a year.

So, when Mike told me he had accepted a job working for Wayne, I stared at him with dismay.

"What kind of job?" I demanded and he shrugged, a furtive gleam appearing in his eyes.

"None of your business," he replied, slamming out of the flat moments later, off to do a bit of 'business' with his new boss.

I watched and worried, knowing only too well the kind of business Wayne would be running; I feared what Mike was letting himself be dragged into, worrying even more when he came home later that evening and thrust a hundred pounds into my unwilling hands.

"There you go, Mel," he declared, pride shining on his face. "Payback for the times you've bailed me out. It's for you to spend on whatever you like, and there'll be more, you'll see."

With a sinking heart I stared at the notes in my hand, knowing I should give it back, refuse to take it, and yet ... and yet, I so desperately needed money. In the end, I blew most of it on a facial and a trip to the hairdressers for a decent cut and deep condition, the rest being spent on a ton of fresh fruit, salad, and vegetables.

The situation at work deteriorated. Every morning I awoke, dreading the day, literally forcing myself to make the too short ten-minute walk from the flat to the newspaper office. When I was there, I found myself shrinking inwards, away from the others, their small, narrow minds, and their obsession with everyone else's lives.

I watched, disinterested, refusing to participate in their routine character assassinations every morning over coffee, knowing full well, that when I left the room, I was the subject of intense gossip and speculation.

The days drifted and I drifted with them, only half-awake most of the time, aware I'd reached some sort of monumental crossroads in my life, but unsure what to do next or which way to go.

Instead, I absolved myself from everyday life, finding even the smallest, most inconsequential decisions beyond my capabilities.

Mike was out most evenings, so I spent my life curled up on the sagging sofa which smelt of takeaways past and present, staring at the new TV that had mysteriously appeared one day. I watched, without seeing, an endless round of soaps and reality shows, none of them as real as the life being played out constantly in my head, where scenarios and entire scenes paraded behind my eyes, with myself at the centre of them, myself, and them.

Crazy as it seemed, I was missing Annaliese and Scott and their friends, even though I had never met them and didn't even know their names. Most of all, I missed being Eve. For a few precious moments, I had been someone else, not Melissa, the quiet boring girl who was shacked up with Mike. No, I was Eve and I liked being her.

I liked the fact that as Eve I could be anyone I chose; could reinvent myself in any image.

My day at the Hall opened my eyes to what life could be like. Not so much from the money point of view, although it would be nice not to have to worry about it all the time. No, the quiet envy coursing through my heart and brain was of Annaliese. Of her sunny, almost too perfect outlook on life, and her kindness and generosity.

Had it been charity? The disembodied voices had claimed it was, and at the time, over-sensitive and prideful, I had been only too ready to accept it as such. Yet, when I was in their company, Annaliese's, and Scott's, I hadn't felt as if I was being condescended to, nor had there been any patronage in their manner or attitude. It had felt more like they were genuinely concerned and worried about me, and I had basked in the warmth of their attentions.

But most of all, I envied Annaliese her friends – the hundred or so who had attended the party and the six – that charmed inner circle whom I'd instinctively known were her special companions, her confidantes.

I saw the easy affection which existed between them, the way they all fitted together so neatly and so perfectly, and I wished for such friends.

I didn't have any friends, not really. Oh, there were friends from school I still occasionally went out with, but they didn't approve of Mike. I could sense in their attitude, by what wasn't said, that they all felt I should have left him far behind when I'd left school. That by insisting on staying with him, I somehow lowered myself to his level.

There was Ally, but she was so busy with all her various jobs I hardly ever saw her. Since the day at the Hall, I hadn't heard from her and suspected she was a little annoyed and jealous, that in a few short hours I'd achieved a degree of acquaintance with Annaliese she'd failed to reach in two years of working for her.

No, I had no friends. Not real, pour your heart and soul out, trust them forever type friends, and a quiet envious longing consumed me.

My mood was not improved by the fact the weather, so balmy and perfect for Annaliese's birthday party, had turned damp and miserable. Days of non-stop torrential downpours mirrored the bone-deep lethargy that gripped me, and which I could not seem to shake off.

After two weeks of lonely evenings at home, and even lonelier days at work, I was depressed and irritable, ready to snap at the slightest thing. My mood not improved when Wayne and Mike turned up one evening after dark, complete with a van load of sealed boxes which they proceeded to stack in the corner of the minuscule lounge.

Holding my tongue whilst Wayne was there, something about the maniacal glint in his eye and the way his gaze travelled over my body, his mouth wet and slack, made the words of protest freeze in my throat. I saved my terrified concern until he left, after pushing an envelope bulging with notes into Mike's greedy hands.

The row lasted all night, until exhausted and sick with worry, I dragged myself off to work to endure eight hours of comments on my red-rimmed eyes and hangdog expression.

"Lovers tiff?" they teased, semi-maliciously, until I wanted to scream at them all.

Walking home through yet another monsoon-like deluge later that afternoon, I found my feet dragging slower and slower. I didn't want to go home. I didn't want to face Mike and his stubborn determination to not admit he'd gotten himself deeply entrenched in something dishonest. Something with the potential to spell disaster, not only for himself but for me, too.

Reluctantly, I turned the corner of the street and immediately flattened myself to the wall, the rough brick snagging at the sopping material of my jacket. Wayne's van was pulling up outside the flat. As I watched, he jumped out, locking the van behind him before strolling into the building.

That settled it; I wasn't going home whilst he was there. Resolutely turning my back on the flat, I set off back into town. I had no idea where I was going and groaned as my cheap boots gave up in the face of floods of biblical proportions, and cold water oozed its way between my toes.

Muttering curses, I hunched into my inadequate jacket, blinked raindrops from my eyelashes, and wondered whether I should go and see my parents. I didn't want to alarm them by arriving unannounced but desperately needed somewhere to shelter. I dithered on the corner of the road, unsure whether to take the turning which led into town or carry on out into suburbia land where Mum and Dad lived.

I'd taken a step forward, thinking sod it, I would go and see my parents, even their inevitable twenty questions were better than drowning, when a car, long, sleek, and red, suddenly tore round the corner of the road too close to the kerb, ploughed straight through a massive muddy puddle, and drenched me from head to foot in freezing water.

Stunned and dazed, I looked down in angry dismay at my sodden clothes, shook my fist at the retreating car, alarmed when brake lights flashed red. It skidded to a halt a few yards away and the driver's door flew open. I stepped back, shocked, as a tall, dark-haired man holding a waxed green coat over his head, jumped out and hurried towards me.

"Eve?" I blinked stupidly, the name rendering me paralysed. I realised it was Scott, his face concerned when he saw my drowned rat status.

"Oh my God, I'm so sorry, I took the corner too fast, and you were there. Shit, you're soaked."

I wiped a hand across my face, staring at the mud which came off on my fingers, feeling cold wetness trickling down my cleavage. I was quite literally soaked to the skin. Tears of despair pricked my eyes. It was all too much, I'd had enough. I glared at Scott angrily.

"What on earth are you doing out in this, Eve?" he asked, oblivious to the fact I wanted to kill him. "Can I give you a lift somewhere?"

"No, I wasn't going anywhere," I replied. "I was just out ... walking."

"Well, you shouldn't be out in this, you'll catch your death. Come on, get in the car." He held out a hand to me and I backed away suspiciously.

"No, honestly, I'll be fine..."

"Don't be silly. Come on, I insist." Somehow, I found myself allowing him to lead me back to the car where he laid his coat on the passenger's seat, lining side down, and helped me to sit on it before shutting the door and hurtling back round to the driver's side.

Once inside the car, I realised how heavy the rain was, watching with fascination as it lashed at the windows and flooded down the windscreen. Scott wiped a hand over his wet face and grinned at me.

"It's really something, isn't it? I keep expecting to see an ark come floating by."

I smiled feebly, rendered speechless by how utterly and completely gorgeous he was. It was as if over the past fortnight I had forgotten, and now, being face to face with him again was struck anew by how very male he was.

"So," he began, turning the key in the ignition. "Where can I take you?"

"Nowhere," I replied without thinking, and in the unnatural gloom of the car, felt his surprise.

"At least let me take you home," he pleaded. I quickly shook my head.

"I don't want to go home, because, well, it's complicated, I can't go home right now."

I felt his confusion but didn't look at him. I couldn't bring myself to explain I didn't want to go home, because my possibly criminal boyfriend and his definitely criminal boss were there.

"Okay," he said slowly. "Well, we can't sit here all night, and I'm certainly not letting you wander off by yourself in this weather." He paused. "Tell you what, you can come with me."

"With you?" I stuttered. "Where?"

"To Annaliese's," he replied jauntily. "Mrs Briggs is away for a few days and Annaliese phoned and invited me over. She asked me to pick up a Chinese on the way, although judging by the amount of food I've collected, either the entire population of China is also invited, or the others are round for the evening."

For the first time, I noticed several plastic takeaway bags, filled to the brim with cartons, standing in the footwell by my feet.

"I couldn't possibly arrive unannounced," I protested, my heart doing a nervous little dance inside my rib cage.

"You would probably be saving my life if you came," he stated.

"What? Why?" I frowned.

"Because if Annaliese hears I half-drowned you, then drove away and left you to die of pneumonia, she will kill me. So that's settled then, you're coming with me. Everyone will be thrilled to see you. I know Annaliese was disappointed when you vanished from her party. There's plenty of food in case you're worrying..."

He paused and my stomach, empty since a small bowl of cornflakes that morning, caught a whiff of delicious food smells and emitted a monstrous rumble.

"Especially as it sounds like thunder," he finished and smiled innocently at my small squeak of embarrassment.

Ten minutes later we pulled up outside the Hall, the rain so heavy now it had been like driving underwater. I had been impressed with how competently and calmly Scott handled the wheel, feeling safe in his hands, cocooned in the cosy small world of the car.

In that short ten minutes, the daydreams crowded over me, and I remained silent, indulging in the pleasant fantasy that we were a couple going to see friends, together. Afterwards, at the end of the evening, we would go home together, where we...

Scott turned off the engine and I snapped back into reality, shooting a nervous look at his oblivious profile, thankful the thoughts in my head were private. Quickly, we dashed from the car to the door, Scott holding his coat over us both whilst I carried the bags of Chinese. Once inside, I squelched across the tiled entranceway which was as stunning as I remembered.

My eyes flicked up the stairway, recalling how I had stood there, listening, as I was dismissed as a mere charity case; the hired help getting above herself.

Scott hung our dripping coats on a rack and headed off down the hall where a patch of light shone, a chatter of voices indicating that this was where the rest of the group was gathered.

He pushed the door open, and several voices exclaimed at once, admonishing him for taking so long and commenting on the rain. I heard a voice, female, French, and sexy.

"At last, I am so hungry. It is not good for the baby to go without food for so long."

I realised it must be the dark-haired pregnant woman speaking, and the deep male voice with the slight Scottish burr which followed must be her redheaded husband.

"That's right, sweetheart, it must be all of ... oh, an hour, since you last ate." There was laughter, and Scott grinned, before pulling me deeper into the room.

"Look who I nearly drowned on the way here."

"Eve!"

I heard Annaliese's joyful cry, saw the genuine pleasure which leapt into her eyes, and realised, no matter what I had overheard, she, at least, did not consider me a charity case. She jumped to her feet and crossed to me, her face registering shock as she realised how wet I was.

"Oh, my goodness!" She exclaimed. "You weren't kidding, were you? What on earth did you do, Scott? Take her to the nearest pond and throw her in?"

"Something like that," Scott agreed. Annaliese took the bags of takeaway from me, handed them back to him, and took me by the hand.

"Well, all questions later," she declared firmly. "First, we need to get you out of those wet things. Will you stay and eat with us?" she asked, an almost pleading note in her voice.

"Umm, well, if that's all right with everyone," I replied shyly, gratified by the chorus of affirmatives that rang out from the others.

"Well then, that's settled isn't it," stated Annaliese, and beamed at me. I was instantly bathed in a warm glow of happiness, inexplicably feeling as if I had come home.

Twenty minutes later, after a quick shower to warm me up and clean all the mud off, I emerged dressed in clothes borrowed from Annaliese, surprised they fitted.

Despite her assurances we were the same size, I hadn't seen how that could be. I felt so large and cumbersome next to her petite slightness – a carthorse next to a thoroughbred. The same species but points apart in every respect.

I smoothed on wisps of coffee-coloured silk underwear, which flattened my stomach, and so cleverly moulded my breasts it looked as though I had some. Pulling on jeans so soft and well-cut they felt like a second skin and running my hands with pleasure over the butter-yellow cashmere sweater, I reflected how nice it must be to have the money to buy such beautiful clothes.

I surveyed myself in her mirror, relieved that despite my experience I didn't look too bad. A lot better, anyway, than I had at the party. Two weeks of good healthy food, and the facial, had worked wonders. There was not a spot to be seen, and the hot shower had brought a quite becoming flush to my cheeks.

The new haircut was holding up well, my hair falling naturally into pretty, damp curls down to my shoulders. I hadn't bothered with the hairdryer Annaliese had left out, my hair being the sort best left to its own devices. Any heated appliances tend to reduce it to a pile of frizz.

Making my way downstairs, I wondered whether I should phone Mike to let him know where I was. I didn't want to talk to him, not now, not here, didn't even want to think about him, but reluctantly decided I had to do something.

The last thing I wanted was for him to call my parents and set them worrying, something he might very well do if I failed to come home from work. In the end, I took the coward way out and sent him a text – 'gone 4 dinner with m8s' – and left it at that, moments later receiving an equally brief 'ok out all nite, cu 2mrw' reply. Relieved, I switched off my phone, slipped it back into my bag, and went to join the others.

They were lounging in the smaller, less formal reception room to the left of the stairs. A fire had been lit to ward off the unseasonable chill and a TV screen flickered in the corner of the room.

As I entered, Annaliese beckoned me over, patting the sofa next to her and taking in my now dry appearance with satisfaction before handing me a plate and a napkin.

"I'm afraid we started without you," she said. "We didn't think it was a good idea to make Mimi wait any longer for her food."

"I'm eating for two now," Mimi complained, a heaped plate balanced on her bump, as she expertly and quickly ladled noodles into her mouth with a pair of chopsticks.

"This is Mimi," Annaliese confirmed, then waved a hand at the burly redheaded man with the kindly face sitting beside her. "And that is her angelic husband, Andrew." We murmured pleasantries to each other. Annaliese's husband, Robert, sitting on the other side of the room, waved a hand as Annaliese introduced him.

"Sitting next to you is Miles," she continued, and I smiled at him, recognising him as the man who had fetched Mimi a chair at the party.

"Scott, you already know." Annaliese worked her way around the room. He looked up from his plate and we exchanged grins.

"So, that leaves my dear heart, Ferdie, and that's everyone."

I accepted with thanks the glass of icy cold white wine, which Ferdie, who was absolutely, definitely gay, handed me.

Mimi struggled to sit up to reach for more Chinese, and I smiled when she gave up and swapped her empty plate with Andrew's full one. He sighed in resignation before helping himself to more food.

"I have him well trained," she smirked.

"When are you due?" I asked shyly.

"Another three weeks," she sighed in resignation. "I shall be the size of an elephant, my skin all stretched and wrinkled."

She huffed in mock disgust as her husband patted her on the thigh, before holding a mini spring roll out to her which she delicately ate, kissing his fingers as she finished it.

"Tuck in, Eve, there's plenty," urged Annaliese, gesturing towards the oversized coffee table on which a long line of warming trays stood, piled high with dozens of cartons all full of wonderful-looking food.

As I said, my parents are extremely plain eaters and I'd never really eaten Chinese food before. Sure, Mike and I occasionally had a takeaway, but because we were always broke, our sole excursions had tended to be of the chicken ball and chips variety.

So now I ploughed in with anticipation, trying a little of everything, and finding it all utterly delicious. I carefully watched the others out of the corner of my eye, observing that first, you smeared the dark sauce over the pancake, then piled on shredded duck and vegetables and rolled it into a pancake, before picking it up with your fingers and biting into a food paradise.

"Eve," began Annaliese, then a slim hand flew to her mouth. "Oh, how silly of me," she said. "That's not your name, is it? You must think I'm dreadful. What's your real name?"

"It's Melissa," I replied shyly. "But I don't mind you calling me, Eve, I quite like it."

"All right," she said, smiling at me, her blue eyes warm and friendly, "Eve it is. It's so wonderful to see you again. Where did you disappear to last time?"

"Oh," I began awkwardly, aware of the curiosity of the others. "Ally wanted to go home. As I was getting a lift with her, I felt I should go."

She nodded thoughtfully, then seemed to accept my words and dropped the subject, turning to face Scott as he gestured at the TV with a chopstick.

"What are we watching?"

"Oh, Miles brought it, it's fascinating," replied Annaliese. 'It's about a woman who is abandoned by her husband for a beautiful famous actress and decides to exact her revenge."

"I know this, I've read the book. It was amazing," I declared in excitement, paying the screen attention now the more urgent need for food had been addressed. "I usually hate it when they adapt a book I've loved into a film or TV programme." I turned to Miles. "Please tell me they haven't completely re-written it?"

"They haven't," he promised. His soft brown eyes lighting up with pleasure, he leaned forward and refilled my glass. I absent-mindedly spooned more food onto my plate, envying the way the others ate so easily with chopsticks whilst I was left ladling it up with a spoon, watching in awe as Mimi waved her chopstick about to emphasise a point, a single pea held daintily mid-air.

"She hates this bitch so much," she stated, her accent making me think of the Eiffel Tower, accordions, and cigarette smoke wafting up from men in black polo necks and berets as they philosophised on existentialism and the bleakness of life.

"She hates her," she continued, "for taking everything she has, so sets out to destroy her."

"No, you're wrong," I interrupted. Mimi raised a brow at me. "What I mean is," I hastily continued, "yes, she destroys her, but there's more to it than that. She takes back everything the other woman stole from her, but goes further. She becomes this woman. If she only hated her, she wouldn't have done that, she'd have been satisfied with ruining her life. Yet she becomes her. That's not hate, that's envy."

There was silence, and I took a large gulp of the most delicious wine I had ever had, feeling rather stupid and wishing I had kept my big mouth shut. I glanced around, Annaliese was looking at Mimi, their faces thoughtful; Andrew and Ferdie seemed preoccupied with their food.

Robert was gazing at Annaliese, his expression concerned. Scott, his face unreadable as usual, smiled at me and gave one of his characteristic shrugs, as though he didn't care one way or the other. Beside me, Miles nodded, beaming as if I had correctly solved a complicated puzzle.

"Well done," he said. "You're right, Eve. It is a book about the powerful force jealousy can be, and the desire to become that which you envy. A lot of people fail to understand this, believing it is purely about hatred, but, as you so succinctly put it, if it were merely about revenge then why put yourself through so much to become the person you are supposed to despise."

He nodded again, obviously pleased, and I felt as though I'd been awarded a medal, smiling at Annaliese when she patted me on the shoulder.

"You've made Miles very happy," she whispered. "He teaches English Literature at

Queens and feels we're a desperately illiterate bunch. It's nice he has someone to talk to."

"But ..." I stammered in surprise. "You're an author, can't he talk to you about books? I mean, you ... you write such awesome ones, I would have thought ..." My voice trailed away, and Annaliese blushed with pleasure.

"Bless you, Eve, what a lovely thing to say, but I'm afraid it's true. I write from the heart, and although I do enjoy dipping into the odd novel, I'm afraid my tastes are for fun and frothy women's fiction, and not the great classics which Miles keeps insisting I should read."

"You should at least attempt them, Annaliese," he protested half-heartedly, and I sensed this was a dispute of long-standing.

"I can't get into them," Annaliese insisted, a twinkle in her eyes. "And life is simply too short to waste time doing something I don't like. I'd rather be having fun with my dear friends."

Miles sighed in exasperation, but I could tell from the tender look he gave her that anything Annaliese did was fine by him. He was as much under her spell as the rest of us.

How can I describe that evening? The light-hearted conversation which lapped and swelled around the room; the amiable teasing that spoke of an easy familiarity amongst them that I envied, like the wronged wife in the DVD. Although, far from wishing to destroy them or become them, I wished merely to be allowed to be a part of their elite; to feel I was one of them, to be fully accepted as a member.

I knew Melissa could never aspire to such heights, but I hoped maybe Eve could.

They made it easy, so easy, for me to like and admire them, all of them, although I realised Caroline wasn't there and wondered at her absence. Ferdie, obviously the group jester, kept the level of humour topped up with his outrageously witty comments, reducing us at times to helpless hand gestures, clutching at stomachs aching with laughter, Mimi begging him to stop because all this laughing was making her need to go and pee, again.

Robert and Andrew were the most serious of the group, yet contributed stability, calming Ferdie's more giddy excesses, their eyes constantly straying to their respective wives. Again, I felt envy at such quietly unassuming, totally unassailable, love and affection.

Miles chatted to me eagerly about books and authors, keen to discover my tastes and experiences in the field of literature. I realised how isolated I had become in terms of reading.

At school I had absorbed myself in the world of A-level English, also belonging to several book clubs and the school library. I missed not only consuming books at a frantic rate but also having the chance to discuss and analyse them with other like-minded people.

Since leaving school, although I continued to read, it had become a solitary and guilty pleasure. Mike never read anything more complicated than the TV guide, and as for discussing what I was reading with him, I may as well have attempted to explain open-heart surgery to a Mongolian goat herder.

Annaliese, of course, was her usual sunny self. Sitting back on the sofa, a glass of wine in hand, she watched with obvious pleasure as the evening unfolded around her, dropping the odd comment into the mix to ensure it never lapsed or ran out of subject matter.

I was at first unsure of Mimi. Being a woman, I was automatically more suspicious of her, feeling her acceptance of me into their charmed circle was not as effusive as that of the men, and that she had reservations about me. I wondered what was going on behind that flawless façade and the carelessly correct French manner.

She looked up, caught me watching her, and to my surprise lowered her eyelid in a deeply conspiratorial wink. She glanced at the others busy piling up plates and cartons, shot me a wickedly mischievous look, then placed a hand on her stomach and let out a moan.

Instantly, the whole room was by her side.

"What is it?"

"Darling, was it a contraction?"

"Are you in pain?"

"Oh, God, someone rip up some sheets, quick." The last was from Ferdie and earned him a mildly reproving look from Annaliese.

"Ferdie," she murmured, and he mumbled an apology, looking shamefaced. I was later to discover you could swear as much as you liked around Annaliese and she wouldn't bat an eyelid, but blaspheming was a different matter.

"I've eaten too much," exclaimed Mimi, eyes wide and innocent.

The others groaned in disgust.

"She's crying wolf again."

"You have got to stop doing that!"

"One of these days it really will be the big L and nobody will believe you," chided Scott mildly, dark eyes amused. Mimi shrugged and smirked at me, slugging a mouthful of wine from Andrew's glass.

"Sweetheart," he cautioned.

"Pah!" She gestured irritably. "I have been so good, given up all the things that make life worthwhile – shellfish, brie, pate, alcohol – so I've decided to work on the principle of happy mother, happy baby. Besides, this close to the finishing line I hardly think one sip of wine is going to have a drastic effect."

Andrew said nothing but merely continued to hold out his hand. Mimi pouted moodily, handing him back his glass, and scowling at the glass of tonic water he gave her in return.

And then there was Scott. I couldn't read him at all. He took taciturn to new levels, spoke only when necessary yet appeared to be an integral part of the group, the others seeking his opinions as if used to interpreting and expanding on the sparse replies he gave. Often, I would glance up to find his gaze resting thoughtfully upon me, his expression closed and inscrutable. I wondered what emotions if any, brewed and churned behind his still façade. Mostly, I wondered what he thought of me.

Later, when I raised my eyes to him again, he was gone. Before I could wonder where, he casually sauntered back into the room, a glass of coke in hand, and raised his eyebrows at me.

"Your clothes had finished," he said, "so I put them in the tumble drier for you."

"Oh, thank you," I mumbled, mortified to the core at the thought of Scott handling my threadbare fraying bra, and baggy grey pants.

There came a point in the evening when an apex was reached. When bonhomie and goodwill had steadily swelled, forming a protective golden bubble around them. I saw, for the first time, how well they came together, meshing and merging to become almost machine-like; an intricate, beautifully crafted device in which each cog and part appeared incompatible and diverse, yet worked in harmony, each playing his or her part to perfection, the whole becoming so much more than the sum of its parts.

I sat back, gazing in stunned wonder, half in love with them all. I believed them to be royal-like, but now saw they were so much more.

They were kings, but not as our modern royals are, feet of clay firmly planted in mortal soil, but as kings of old used to be – worshipped by their people as being one step removed from the gods.

A door slammed and the bubble burst, Caroline O'Donnell stalked abruptly into the room, running impatient fingers through her short hair which had frizzed unbecomingly, and glistened damply. Bringing the fresh smell of rain with her, she shook droplets of water from her jumper, eyes blind behind the steamed-up windows of her thick glasses.

"Caro, darling, how was your evening class? Look, isn't it lovely? Scott practically ran Eve over and brought her round for the evening."

Was it only me who heard the faintest beseeching note in Annaliese's voice? Caro flicked a quick hard glance in my direction which suggested my presence was anything but lovely, though she said nothing, only murmuring a vague hello to the room in general.

"Any wine left?" she barked in her gruff masculine voice with its strong Irish flavour. 'It's pissing it down out there, didn't think I was going to get through at one point, half the bloody field is across the road at Shaw's Corner."

"I'll go and get some more," offered Annaliese, and quickly left the room.

"Not for me," sighed Mimi. Caro dropped a hand on her shoulder, her stern face softening.

"I'll put the kettle on. Mint tea?" she offered.

Mimi blew her a kiss. "Angel," she murmured, and Caro, too, left the room.

The DVD had finished, and the men began debating fiercely about which one to put on next. Murmuring to Mimi about needing the loo, I slipped silently from the room. My excuse was only half true, in that, yes, too much wine had finally caught up with me, but I also had a vague need to check on Annaliese, concern tingling my spine at the subtle underlying threat I'd fancied I'd read in Caro's body language. She had left me in no doubt that she resented my presence, although why I couldn't begin to imagine.

Silently, I walked down the side of the stairs. Glancing through the bannisters I could see Annaliese and Caro framed in the open kitchen door. They were talking. At least, Annaliese was talking in a low, urgent whisper inaudible to me, her hand clutching at Caro's sleeve, her face a mask of agonised pleading.

Caro shook her head once, a sharp jerky refusal of Annaliese's intense request. I watched, confused, and concerned, as Annaliese's body slumped in despair, her blue eyes mutely begging for Caro's agreement to something. Finally, Caro sighed, briefly closing her eyes as though in pain, before slowly, reluctantly, nodding her head. Annaliese's face lit up and she hugged Caro fiercely, before releasing her and dancing away down the hallway.

Thinking she was alone and unobserved, Caro removed her thick-rimmed spectacles and rubbed a shaking hand across her face, eyes sombre and downcast. She looked oddly vulnerable and naked without the usual barrier of her glasses.

She replaced them and looked up, straight through the bannisters and into my eyes, her expression hardening into a hostile resentment that knocked me back a step. Then she turned and stalked into the kitchen, her back rigid and implacable.

Shaken, I quickly visited the loo and hurried back to the others, needing the reassurance of their presence. When Annaliese and Caro rejoined us, bearing wine and tea, it was as if the intense exchange I had witnessed, that brief confrontational moment between Caro and I, had never occurred. But for the first time, I had the unsettling sensation that this was a house of secrets.

"Favourite novel?"

The evening had turned, and Miles and I were once again discussing books, his eyes warm with interest.

"Umm …" I considered his question, tipping my wine around in the oversized glass, thinking, casting my mind over the vast number of books I had digested in my short life.

"That's a tough one. I'm re-reading Bleak House. I love it, with all the complicated twists and turns, and I've reached the point where Lady Dedlock is telling Esther she's her mother."

"Yes," he agreed enthusiastically. "Dickens at his best, very Victorian, all those family secrets just waiting to come bursting out of the woodwork..."

"And of course, The Woman in White. I keep going back to that one."

"Again, family secrets, and again the lengths someone will go to, to hide their shame of having had an illegitimate child..."

There was a sudden commotion on the other side of the room; Annaliese had spilt a full glass of wine. She pulled a rueful face as the others leapt at her brandishing napkins, apologising as they dabbed at her skirt and carpet.

"Sorry to make you all jump, darlings," she laughed. "Thank heavens it's white and not red."

"What happened?" asked Robert, topping up her glass again.

"It slipped from my hand," she replied.

I turned back to Miles and our conversation.

"There seems to be a pattern emerging in the books that have struck a chord with you," he commented, taking a sip of wine, and frowning into the firelight. "They all deal with secrets buried deep in a family's past. Are you an avid seeker of the truth, Eve?"

"In my career, maybe," I replied slowly. "I want to be a journalist and I guess going after the truth is part of the job description, but in my private life? No, I wouldn't say I'm particularly keen on rooting out secrets best left uncovered. Hell," I laughed, "I'm not even interested in finding out who my real mother is."

There was a fascinated silence in the room.

Scott moved to sit beside me. "What do you mean? Are you adopted or something?"

"Yes, my parents adopted me when I was one."

"And you've never felt the need to know?"

"No, absolutely not. As far as I'm concerned, my birth mother gave me away. She didn't want me, so now I don't want her."

"Very black and white," murmured Scott, brushing a stray curl off my cheek. 'Tell me, young Eve, is there room for shades of grey, or is everything in your life so cut and dried?"

I flushed, sure he was mocking me in some way, uncertain how to respond. Miles saw my discomfort and came to my rescue.

"Leave the poor girl alone, Scott. Just because you get piles from sitting on the fence, it doesn't mean to say everyone else must as well."

"I do not sit on the fence," Scott retorted, yet a smile tugged at his mouth. "I'm cautious, I like to weigh up all my options before making a decision, and I don't jump straight in with both feet, unlike some I could mention."

Several eyes swivelled towards Ferdie, who held up his hands and laughed.

"Guilty as charged, I'm afraid I'm one of those people, Eve, who simply love to rush in where angels fear to tread."

"A strategy which has got you in deep doo-doo on more than one occasion," remarked Annaliese dryly, and Ferdie shrugged carelessly.

"It's more fun that way," he retorted flippantly, then bounded over to put on another DVD.

Finally, the evening began to draw to a close and I could hardly keep my eyes open. Looking around, I saw a sleepy Mimi being helped to her feet by Andrew.

"Goodnight, Eve," she murmured from the safe harbour of her husband's arms. "I hope we see you again soon."

"Goodnight," I replied, and watched as Annaliese tenderly kissed Mimi on the cheek.

"Sleep well, darling, I'll see you in the morning."

Mimi nodded and they left the room, I realised they must be staying the night. Miles and Ferdie pressed friendly kisses to my cheek and wished me goodnight, before heading in the direction of the stairs.

Coldness gripped me. In the euphoria of the evening, it had slipped my mind to wonder how on earth I was getting home.

"Come on, Eve." Scott reappeared with our now dry coats. "I'll give you a lift back."

"Oh, thank you," I cried with relief. "I'd better go and change back into my clothes."

Shedding Eve, along with Annaliese's beautiful clothes, I felt like a snake sloughing its skin, or maybe a chameleon changing its appearance to blend in with its surroundings. Reluctantly, I put Melissa back on and trailed despondently downstairs to find Annaliese and Scott waiting for me.

"Darling, Eve!" exclaimed Annaliese, enfolding me into a warm, friendly hug. "Don't wait for an invitation next time. Please feel free to drop in whenever you want. If you can't get here, just call." She pressed a piece of paper with various phone numbers scribbled on it into my hand. "There'll always be someone around to come and collect you."

"Thank you," I replied, hugging her back with enthusiasm. "Thank you for a wonderful evening and the food. It was all lovely. Sorry I haven't returned your shoes yet."

"Bring them with you next time." Dismissing them, she turned to hug Scott. "Now, you drive carefully," she admonished.

Outside, it had finally stopped raining and the wind had blown away the clouds, leaving the stars burning in an endless, inky black sky. I tipped my head heavenwards, the night air cool on my flushed cheeks, and tried to remember the last time I had felt so good. In the car, the blanket of contentment still surrounded me, and I beamed at Scott as he started the engine and pulled on his seatbelt.

"Had fun?" he asked.

I nodded in enthusiastic assent.

"Oh, yes, it was marvellous. You're wonderful, all of you," I declared. "I love everyone, Miles, Mimi and Andrew, Ferdie, and Robert, and of course Annaliese, I love them all."

"And me?" he asked, amusement in his voice.

"Of course, you as well," I exclaimed, realising how very drunk I was. Also realising I didn't care. "Tonight, well it was like a dream come true, like something out of a fairy tale."

"Well, come on then Cinderella," he answered, putting the car in gear, and pulling away into the darkness. "It's time your pumpkin coach got you back to reality."

"Oh, but I don't want to go home," I pouted in the darkness. I felt, rather than saw, his considering look.

"You'll be back," he finally said, and for a moment I thought I heard something buried deep beneath his normal calmness. "You're a part of the group now, so you'll be back."

"Part of the group," I echoed his words. "I want to be, but..."

"But what?"

"I'm not sure I'm good enough. You, Annaliese, all of you, you're all so beautiful, glamorous, and sophisticated and so ... well, so grown up."

There was a long silence and then he sighed. "How old are you, Eve?"

"Nineteen," I replied, sulky at the condescension I fancied I heard in his voice.

"Nineteen," he laughed. "You're so young and have a lot of growing up to do. If you use Annaliese as your role model you won't go far wrong."

I was silenced by the love I heard in his voice as he spoke of her, feeling a hot jolt of jealousy and the tiniest twinge of resentment towards Annaliese. I huddled on my side of the car and tried to understand the conflicting emotions which warred inside.

The bright lights of town all too quickly bathed the car in a yellow glow. Scott glanced at me, his profile chiselled in the unnatural light.

"Where do you live?"

Quietly, I gave directions, until we pulled up outside the dingy run-down Victorian house that had been converted into six flats, one of them ours. I flinched, seeing it through his eyes, comparing it with the perfect gorgeous home we had just left, and jumped out quickly; wanting it over with now, wanting him to go as fast as possible.

I felt the last vestiges of Eve slip away as his window glided down and he called to me.

"Eve."

At the doorway, I turned. His face was in the shadow of the building, the permanently broken streetlight plunging this part of the road into darkness.

"Yes?"

"Come back to us. Don't be put off by your insecurities. I … we all liked you, and I know Annaliese is already very fond of you. Please don't hurt her by disappearing again."

I hesitated, nodded, and then realised he probably couldn't see me, so replied quietly.

"Okay … goodnight."

"Goodnight, Eve, take care of yourself."

I let myself into the building, hearing the low purr of the car's engine as it pulled away. My hands shook as I unlocked the flimsy door to the flat and entered.

In the darkness, I walked straight into a pile of boxes, muttered curses as I rapped my shin on a sharp corner and fumbled for the lamp. Light flooded the squalid room, and I realised the pile had grown quite considerably since morning.

Getting ready for bed, I looked at the girl in the mirror; at the light dancing in her eyes, her flushed cheeks, her mouth parted on a breathy sigh. Who was she? Eve or Melissa? Who was I?

It occurred to me that to get what I wanted, to become part of Annaliese's world; Melissa had to die. I had to reinvent myself as Eve.

A woman who took things in her stride and could hold her own with Annaliese's friends. No, I corrected myself, with my friends. A woman who wasn't afraid to face up to facts, not bury her head in the hope bad things would go away.

I wandered back into the lounge, bare feet silent on the matted and threadbare carpet. I curled up on the sofa, no longer tired, instead thinking and staring at the whorls and shapes in the faded carpet until my eyes swam.

The sink in the little kitchenette was piled high with frying pans and crockery. Mike had had a fry-up at some point and left it all to soak, a thin scummy crust of fat staining the already disreputable washing-up bowl. I decided to clean up first.

Coward, taunted Eve. No, I'm not, Melissa retorted, I want the place to be tidy.

Pulling on rubber gloves, I swallowed down my distaste and gingerly pulled the slippery plates from the cold slimy liquid, scrubbing them in hot soapy water until they gleamed.

I dried them carefully, put them away in the single cupboard, made myself a cup of tea and sat down on the sofa, my bare feet cold beneath me, sipping slowly at its hotness, delaying the inevitable until I'd finished. I rinsed and dried the cup up, and then had no further excuses.

I chose the sharpest knife I could find, and stood for a moment, listening. Do it, ticked the clock on the wall. Do it, hissed the silence. I stepped forward, galvanised into action, chose the box in the furthest corner, hesitated, returned to the kitchen, and pulled back on the gloves.

Carefully, I slit along the taped edge and eased open a gap big enough for me to see through. The gleaming silver front of a bubble-wrapped laptop stared back at me and what I half suspected and feared was confirmed.

Carefully, still wearing the gloves, I took a roll of tape from the drawer and re-sealed the box, smoothing it down so there was no sign it had ever been tampered with. I returned the knife and gloves to the kitchen, and then went to bed.

Just before dawn, Mike crawled into bed beside me. I could smell he had been drinking and shrank away from him, hoping he had had so much he would fall asleep, but with a sinking heart felt rough hands pushing up my nightgown.

I mumbled and rolled over, pretending I was still asleep, ignoring his whispered declarations of love and praying he would give up and leave me alone, but the hands became more insistent.

Eventually, I surrendered, parted my legs, and gave him Melissa. I allowed him to do what he wanted to her, separated myself from it, listening with detached amusement to his grunts and groans whilst Eve went far away and made plans. Wonderful, glorious plans for her future.

Finally, he finished, rolled off Melissa and dropped into sleep like a stone. I slid from the bed and into the bathroom where I washed every trace of him from my body and got dressed for work.

Slowly, I pulled on my best trousers and top, half clipped my hair up at the sides and paid careful attention to my make-up. I applied lip liner and mascara – frowned at the bluntness of my black eyeliner and rummaged at the bottom of my make-up bag for a sharpener – wondering how come, no matter how carefully you sharpened them, eyeliners were never as good again as they were when first new.

I crept back into the bedroom. Under cover of Mike's earth-shaking snores, I eased Annaliese's shoes from the wardrobe and placed them carefully into the bottom of my largest handbag, into which I also tipped my few pieces of jewellery.

I left the flat, silently closing the door behind me, leaving Mike still sleeping. It was so early. I wandered easily into town, stopping at the café for a cup of tepid coffee and a bacon sandwich, and opening the local paper which I found lying on the table.

'Thieves get away with thousands' screamed the headline. I smiled, a thin smile of amusement, before I paid for my breakfast and slowly made my way to the nearest phone box.

Afterwards, I went to the park and sat amongst the flowers. I heard the silence, felt the birdsong, and knew I was late for work but didn't care. The heavy rain of the night before had swept away the bad weather, and the sun was hopeful in the sky. It warmed my chilly blood.

Eventually, I got up, dropped the newspaper into the nearest bin, and ambled through town to work because I could think of nowhere else to go. At the entrance I stopped, the mid-morning sun now hot on my cheek.

My hand was on the door when something inside snapped. Life is too short to waste time doing something you don't like, Annaliese's words echoed in my head and my hand fell slowly back to my side.

Then, abandoning Melissa and all she stood for at the door, I turned and walked away. Now brisk and purposeful, my footsteps rang out with focused determination on the pavement.

It was done. It was time for Eve to go home.

CHAPTER IV - ESTHER

"Where's the fucking ambulance?"

Gradually, my pace slowed, and I looked around, enjoying the sensation of not being at work. Usually, at that time in the morning, I was entrenched in a large, open-plan office which never saw the light of day, in which you had no privacy and nowhere to escape, not even for a few minutes.

I raised my head, gazing with interest at a very different town from the one I was used to. It was quieter and less frenzied than lunchtime, when everyone charged in and out of shops and sandwich bars with set, 'don't bother me I'm in too much of a hurry', faces.

Now it appeared the domain of mothers, pushing small children in mud-splattered buggies, with rain hoods and covers folded back in case this sudden burst of fine weather turned out to be a temporary state of affairs.

I walked on, leaving the town centre behind, crossing confidently at the lights, knowing where I was headed and not caring that it was quite a walk, seeing it almost as a symbolic journey from my old life, to my new.

I walked through the suburbs, looking with interest at the ranks of neat identical houses, observing the various ways in which their occupants had attempted to personalise them.

I smiled with pleasure at a garden ablaze with summer perennials fresh-faced from all the recent rain and stooped to stroke a friendly black cat which left its lookout point on a wall and jumped down to weave between my legs.

Eventually, I left the town behind, and walked along country lanes, made dangerous by the absence of pavements, and the speed at which the regular flow of traffic roared down them.

I knew somewhere there was a bridle path leading over the fields and through the woods, finally spotting the wooden signpost pointing the way, relieved to be off the roads and into the calm, quiet greenness of the countryside.

The morning passed and still, I walked, not knowing what the time was and not caring, enjoying the rarest sensation of freedom and gladness of spirit which I had never felt before. Rabbits leapt about and I stopped for a moment and leaned on a fence, watching as they played in the midday sun.

I entered the woods, its cool shadiness a welcome relief after the heat of the day. I marvelled at how changeable weather could be – torrential downpour one day, balmy summer weather the next.

A piece of gravel had worked its way into my shoe, and I rested for a moment on a fallen tree to remove it, amazed I felt no weariness and remembering the bone-numbing tiredness I would be experiencing right now were I at work.

I wondered if anyone had missed me or even asked where I was. It surprised me that I felt no fear at the thought no one knew where I was. Instead, the sensation of having stepped outside of normal time and space liberated me.

I travelled on, leaving the woods, and skirting the edge of a cornfield, before turning back onto the road and passing through the large ornate gates which stood welcomingly wide open. The Hall slumbered before me, its windows glinting blindly in the sun, and my heart leapt at the thought of seeing Annaliese again.

For the first time, I wondered if I'd done the right thing, turning up unannounced, but it was too late now, I'd journeyed too far to turn back. I pulled resolutely on the brass bell, heard the loud jangling echo through the Hall, and waited.

Long minutes later I pulled the bell again and heard its demanding tone as it informed them of my arrival. Still, no one came. It dawned on me that the Hall was empty, and no one was home.

I sank onto the step and felt the cold marble clutch at my skin through the thin material of my trousers. Not once in the whole journey had it occurred to me that I would arrive to find the Hall closed and empty.

Perhaps I so associated Annaliese with her home that the thought of her leaving it was incomprehensible. I wondered what to do next.

Tears of disappointment pricked the back of my eyes and I decided, for want of a better plan, to wait for a while.

Time passed. I squirmed uncomfortably on the step, my bottom numb from the hardness of my seat, intensely aware I would soon have to go to the toilet. I wondered what to do and stood up, once more trying the bell in the vain hope that this time someone would come, but there was nothing. I decided to walk around the Hall and try the kitchen door.

It was a long walk. By the time I reached the stout oak door which led to the kitchen quarters, my need to pee had become more pressing. I looked around the parkland, deciding a shady tree might be my only option. A screech sounded from the trees and Humphrey swaggered into view, staring at me as if questioning my right to be there, and the idea lost its appeal.

Because I was there, not with any real optimism, I tried the kitchen door. To my surprise, it was unlocked. Slowly, I creaked it open and called out.

"Hello, anybody home? Annaliese, it's Eve, hello?" There was silence. I had the absurd idea the Hall was holding its breath, watching, and waiting. I entered and closed the door behind me. I decided to use the facilities, knowing Annaliese wouldn't mind, and would probably find it funny.

Gratefully, I used the cloakroom off the kitchen, washed my hands with expensive rose hand soap, and rubbed matching hand cream into my dry skin. My nose tickled from the almost overpowering scent, and I smiled when I had to wrap a piece of tissue around the door handle to turn it because my hands were slippery. I wandered down the hallway, unsure what to do, and perched on the bottom stair.

The next moment I stiffened as a sound, far away and almost imperceptible, touched the very edges of my hearing. I listened hard, straining to hear. There was nothing beyond the pulsing silence and my pounding heartbeat.

No, there it was again. I climbed a few steps and listened, turning my head, trying to pinpoint its exact location. It was definitely there, a yell maybe, coming from upstairs.

I hesitated, not wanting to pry, yet something in that cry snagged at me, dragging me up more stairs. The cry came again, muffled, as if behind closed doors. It was unquestionably human and coming from somewhere upstairs.

Quickly, I climbed to the top of the stairs and hesitated, casting about for the right direction, before setting off purposefully down the landing as the yell sounded again.

Going through another door at the far end, I made my way cautiously up a shallow flight of stairs, paused outside a door, and listened as a scream echoed through the wood, gripping my emotions, and drenching me in a cold sweaty panic, my heart jackhammering with fear at the inhuman gasping and sobbing wails.

"Hello, is there anyone in there?"

Tentatively, I knocked at the door and heard an answering groan and a faintly whispered plea for help. Quickly, I threw the door open and entered the room. It was a bedroom, subtly sophisticated in silvery blues and creams.

It was at the back of the house, so the bright midday sun bathing the front of the Hall in glory had yet to penetrate through the thick curtains draped over the full-length windows.

A gasp, a sigh, an agonised groan of pain that choked into hoarse rattling pants came from the other side of the vast bed. Cautiously, I tiptoed across, holding my breath in dread of what I might find.

It was Mimi, crouched on the floor amongst blood-splattered bedclothes, back arched, mouth open in an animalistic wail of pain. I knelt beside her and touched her shoulder, feeling the clamminess of her skin through the thin silk of her sheer white nightgown.

"Mimi! What's happened, what is it?"

As the words left my mouth, I realised how stupid they were. Even I, with my limited knowledge of such things, could see that she was obviously in labour. I looked around the empty bedroom, my mind shying away from the thought of the empty Hall all around us, completely devoid of people, and help.

"No-o-o-o!"

The scream was dragged from a body wrenched reluctantly into another contraction as she clutched at me, dragging me down to her level. Perfectly manicured nails ripped and tore at my flesh. Her eyes, wild and crazed, looked right through me.

I could do nothing but watch and wait as Mimi battled it, screaming, flailing in its throes before she beat it. It passed, and a faint gleam of recognition entered her eyes.

"Eve?" she gasped. "Help me, something's wrong, please, get help."

"All right," I readily agreed and prised her fingers from my arms.

"No, don't leave me," she cried in sudden panic, and I felt her adrenalin-fuelled strength as she gripped me tightly.

"Oh shit, oh no, here it comes again..."

Her head dropped. An incomprehensible stream of French poured from her mouth as another contraction ripped into her, and I was powerless to help in any way. It passed.

Desperately, I fumbled in my bag for my phone, seeing with relief that the signal was strong, and with shaking fingers dialled 999.

"I need an ambulance quickly," I gasped. "The baby's coming, she's in so much pain. There's blood, so much blood! You must help her. What? Oh yes, the address ..." I gathered my wits enough to give them our location amid Mimi's earthshattering screams.

"I have to push!" she yelled, and grabbed at me, sending the phone spinning from my hand. I crawled after it, hearing the faint tinny, "hello, hello?" of the emergency operator.

"What do I do?" I demanded, voice high and panicky. "She wants to push."

"We need to know if the baby's head is there," stated the calmly reassuring voice on the other end. "Is it possible you could take a look?"

"Umm, okay," I gulped nervously. "I'll have to put the phone down for a minute. Please ... please don't go away."

"I'll hold on," she promised.

Carefully, I crawled back to Mimi, crouched on all fours like a dog, her head hanging, ragged pants being ripped from her poor straining body.

"Mimi..."

I gently pushed her to the ground and tried to roll her onto her back. She fought me, hissing, and snarling like a cornered wild cat, then seemed to simply give in and laid still, her stomach sticking up obscenely into the air.

~113~

Trying not to think about what I was doing, I lifted her long nightgown, recoiling as a fresh gush of blood pulsed from between her legs, drenching the already soaked bedclothes. I parted her legs, wincing at her raw and bloodied state, a rush of sympathy flooding over me.

She would hate this. I knew that elegant, beautifully sophisticated woman I laughed with last night would detest this degradation, this stripping away of any vestige of dignity.

There was so much blood it was hard to see anything else. Quickly, I sprinted to the en suite, snatched up all the towels I could find, wadding one and gently patting it between her legs, frowning at the painfully swollen vulva underneath. I grabbed the phone.

"I've looked," I gasped. 'It's swollen down there, but it doesn't look …" The word sprung to mind courtesy of endless episodes of Casualty and ER, "dilated at all, and there's certainly no sign of the baby's head. In fact…"

I frowned again, trying to look closer as Mimi screamed and bucked up off the floor.

"All I can see is what looks like bits of raw liver coming out of her, and blood, lots of blood, there's just so much blood. Please, tell me what to do?"

By now I am sobbing, clutching the phone as if I'm drowning and it's my only lifeline. On the floor Mimi rolled onto her side, doubling up and clutching at her abdomen, screaming, and shouting that she had to push! She must push!

"Under no circumstances let her push," ordered the voice. "It could seriously harm the baby, and her. If you say she doesn't appear dilated at all and there's no sign of the baby's head, then she absolutely must not push."

"All right, but what shall I do?"

"If you can, you need to angle her onto her left side and support the right buttock with pillows, then you need to elevate the legs in some way. Can you do that?"

"Yes," I gasped, and gently manhandled Mimi into position. She fought me again, but so feebly this time I realised her strength was almost completely depleted. I wedged pillows under her right buttock cheek. Some far away part of my mind registered how trim and compact she was and how small she seemed to be labouring to pass such a huge obstacle.

Finally, I piled pillows under her ankles, tried to raise her feet as much as possible and crawled up to lay beside her, the phone still clutched in my clammy grasp. Mimi clawed at me, her face drawn and haggard, her lips stretched back over her teeth in a grimace of absolute agony.

"She's in position," I shouted down the phone, heart pounding with adrenalin and fear.

"Right, now I want you to help her breathe. Encourage her to breathe with the pain. Pant with her if that helps, short little pants."

"I want to push!" screamed Mimi again, and I cried out at the perfect crescent moon of cuts her elegantly manicured nails left on my arm.

"No," I yelled. "Don't push, you have to breathe into the pain." A further stream of rapid French was the only response as another contraction seized her by the throat and shook her.

"Pant!" I shouted, putting my face close to hers and panting for all I was worth. Her eyes were glazed and blank and I wondered if she could even hear, let alone understand.

"Like this, Mimi," I encouraged. "Pant, pant!"

"Fuck off!" she screamed in perfect English.

"Where's the ambulance?" I pleaded down the phone. "Please, where is it? She can't take much more of this ... oh shit!" I shrieked in alarm as blood gushed out of her, bright red and flecked with raw, glistening lumps of flesh.

"She's bleeding to death!" I screamed in terror. "Oh fuck, oh shit! Where's the fucking ambulance?"

"It's on its way," she reassured me, but a black wave of panic crashed over my head as the awful possibility dawned that Mimi could die. That she could bleed to death right in front of me and there would be nothing I could do to help her.

Then, I heard it – the sound of a siren as the ambulance tore through the gates, raced up the driveway, and scrunched to a halt, gravel spurting from beneath its wheels.

"They're here," I cried out in relief. "Oh, thank God, they're here!" I rushed to the door, crossed the landing, and threw up the heavy sash of a window that I could see overlooked the driveway.

"Up here!" I screamed.

One of the paramedics, tall and competent looking in his green coverall, looked up, shading his eyes from the sun.

"How do we get in, love?" His voice was calm and steadying. I felt my panic abating. Mimi will be all right. They're here with their boxes of medical miracles and their life-saving drugs.

"Drive around the back," I ordered them. "The kitchen door is unlocked, then up the stairs, I'll come to meet you."

I rushed back to Mimi. She was lying so still, so quiet. For a split second, a wild fear gripped me that in my brief absence she'd died. Then I heard her draw a ragged breath and my chest hurts as I released the lungful of air, I hadn't realised I'd been holding.

"The ambulance is here, Mimi," I said. "You'll be all right now. The ambulance is here."

She gave no sign she had even heard. Gently, I knelt beside her, stroking the hair back from her face, and patted her cheek reassuringly.

"I'm going to show them the way, Mimi; I'll be right back, okay?" She moaned slightly, and I ran from the room, nearly tumbling down the stairs in my haste to get the paramedics.

They entered that room of blood and suffering, took one look, then hastily and competently fastened her to a chair-like contraption and carried her downstairs. Her sharp little cries of distress bounced off the walls as they manoeuvred her through the doors, round the corners, and out into the bright sunshine.

I blinked stupidly in the glare. I had forgotten it was such a gorgeous sunny day. Somehow, in that dark and gloomy room helping Mimi fight for life, it had felt like the middle of the night.

I scrambled into the back of the ambulance with Mimi and one of the paramedics. Huddled in a corner, instinctively trying to stay out of his way, I watched as he placed a clear mask over her face and expertly inserted a needle into her arm. I had no idea what he was doing but trusted it was the right thing.

Mimi's eyes flickered open, and for almost the first time she appeared lucid.

"Eve?" she murmured drowsily. "Where's Andrew? I want Andrew, please, get him for me, please." Tears trickled down her face and I slid forward, grasping her hand.

"Of course, I'll get him for you," I reassured.

She smiled with relief, a knowing look sliding onto her face. "Darling," she muttered, eyes rolling back up into her head. "I love what you've done with your make-up." Then she was gone, back into another contraction.

The paramedic looked at me. "Is Andrew her husband?" he asked. I nodded, swiping at the tears which welled. "He needs to get to the hospital," he commented. I nodded again, my mind frantically racing as I wondered how on earth, I could get in touch with him.

Suddenly, I remembered the sheet of numbers Annaliese had given me which I had transferred that morning into my bag. I dragged it out and scanned the numbers.

I knew there was no one in the Hall so it was pointless phoning that number. Annaliese's mobile. With shaking fingers, I dialled, and it went straight to voicemail. Trying to stay calm, I left a message and then dialled the last number on the page, Scott's mobile.

"Hello?" The speed with which he answered shocked me. I gaped at the phone, unable to speak. "Hello?" he repeated, his tone tinged with annoyance.

"Scott," I gasped. "It's Eve!"

"Eve? Oh, hi, is everything okay?"

"No, no it's not, can you get hold of Andrew? I'm with Mimi. We're in an ambulance on our way to the hospital the baby's coming and something's not right she's bleeding so much I had to look for the baby's head only it wasn't there, and I'm really scared and Mimi's in so much pain and she wants Andrew, and I didn't know his number so I thought you might!"

I throw all the information at him in one breathless sound bite, my voice getting quicker and shriller the further into the story I went.

There was a split second of silence when I finished, as though his brain was translating and assimilating my words, and then he spoke, his voice calm and steady.

"Okay, Andrew's in the shop with me, so I'll bring him straight to the hospital. We'll meet you there as soon as possible."

"Thank you," I gabbled, relief nearly making me incoherent. "Thank you. I'll see you soon," but he had already hung up.

We reached the hospital. Mimi was wheeled down endless corridors, where a doctor met the paramedics, her white coat automatically instilling trust and confidence. Then they took Mimi away through double doors and I was left in the waiting room, not knowing what to do, worried sick about her, feeling by not going with her I was somehow letting her down.

Moments later, a nurse came to take details from me, information which I struggled to give, not knowing Mimi's address or her surname.

"Her husband is on his way," I said. My voice quavered, and the nurse looked sympathetic.

"I expect this has all been a bit of a shock, hasn't it?" she stated, her voice calm, soothing.

"Yes," I agreed, clutching at the strap of my handbag. "I've never seen anything like it before. Will Mimi be all right? What's happening?"

"She's suffering from a condition called placenta praevia," explained the nurse. Seeing my blank look, she expanded. "It's a condition where the placenta is lying across the neck of the cervix, blocking the baby's way out. Your friend is being prepped for a caesarean section. The anaesthetic has taken effect so she's no longer in pain, but she's asking for her husband."

"He'll be here ..." I promised again.

The doors burst open and Andrew, closely followed by Scott, dashed into the room, his expression concerned, his red hair intense next to the unnaturally drained pallor of his face.

"My wife?" he gasped to the nurse.

"Follow me," she ordered and led him through the double doors.

Left alone, Scott and I gazed at each other, his expression concerned and curious. Under his coolly level regard I gradually, almost imperceptibly, felt the tightly wound spring of adrenalin begin to uncoil.

I'd done it. I'd looked after Mimi, got her to the hospital, and managed to get her husband. My role was over. I no longer had to keep it all together. I gulped, shaking, as the enormity of the experience finally hit and delayed reaction kicked in.

"Oh fuck," I heard myself gasp. My knees buckled and I slid down onto one of the primary-coloured chairs. Scott sat beside me and took my hand. He said nothing, yet I felt his support and sympathy and was strengthened by it.

For almost a full minute I shook quietly to myself; then took a deep breath, squared my shoulders, and turned to face him.

"Better now?" he asked simply, and I nodded.

"Yes, sorry about that, it was ... well, you know." He nodded thoughtfully, and I was grateful no further words were necessary.

"Coffee?" I marvelled at a man who could say so much in so few words. "Milk, sugar?"

"Just milk, please."

He rose and strode off down the corridor. I took advantage of his absence to whip out my mirror and check my appearance, tutting at my deathly pallor, wide-eyed stare and eyeliner smudged halfway down my face. I had finished repairing the damage when Scott returned, two plastic cups in hand, one of which he handed to me. He sat and peered at my face.

"That's better," he commented, then frowned. "You do something different with your eyes?"

I flushed that he had noticed and buried my nose in my coffee, wincing as the scalding liquid burnt a large blister onto the end of my tongue.

"It was lucky you could get hold of Andrew," I murmured into the silence. "You don't know how relieved I was when you answered so quickly."

"Well, Andrew and I do work together," commented Scott. "So, I usually know where he is during the day."

"Oh, you work together?" I asked curiously. "I didn't know that."

"Why should you," he shrugged. "You've not known us very long."

We drank our coffee in silence, and I reflected on his words, thinking how right he was that although I felt I knew them intimately I didn't know them at all.

I sipped cautiously, wondering what was happening to Mimi, hoping she was ok, and feeling a kind of connection with her after all we had been through together that day. I glanced at Scott as he silently and competently drank his coffee and wondered what would happen next.

The doors to the waiting room opened. Annaliese entered, face concerned, closely followed by Robert and Caro. Scott and I stood, and Annaliese simply held out her arms. Beginning to shake again, fighting down a ridiculous urge to bawl like a four-year-old, I crept into her embrace, letting her soothe and pet me, stroking my hair and murmuring quiet reassurances.

"Now then," she said, leading me back to the chairs and sitting us down. "Tell us everything."

"Well," I wiped my damp eyes, reflecting I had picked a bad day to be more daring with my eye makeup. "I rang the doorbell and there was no answer, so I decided to walk round the back and try the kitchen door..."

"What were you doing at the Hall in the first place?" demanded Caro, her tone almost, but not quite, accusatory.

"I came to return your shoes," I sniffed, fumbling in my bag, and drawing out the tissue-wrapped parcel.

Annaliese smiled gently. "Bless you," she said. "I didn't expect you to bring them back the next day, but go on, what happened next?"

"I knocked on the kitchen door but there was no answer there either, so on the off chance, I tried the handle and was surprised when the door opened."

"So, you decided to waltz in did you?" There's no mistaking Caro's implication now, and Annaliese shot a firm look in her direction.

"Caro," she murmured.

"I'm sorry," I gasped. "I wasn't prying or anything, it was, well, I'd walked all the way from town and was desperate for the loo. I didn't think you'd mind if I used the downstairs one."

"Of course, we don't mind," Annaliese reassured, patting my hand. "Caro's being her usual, dear protective self."

"Then I heard screaming coming from upstairs, so I went to see what was wrong and found Mimi on the floor and knew … knew she was in labour and that the baby was coming, but she was in so much pain and there was blood … blood everywhere. I'm afraid it's made a dreadful mess."

"It doesn't matter," Annaliese said. "But how scary for both of you. What did you do?"

"Well, I phoned for an ambulance, the operator told me what to do, and then the ambulance came. Luckily, I had the numbers in my bag, so I tried yours, but got voicemail."

"We were at a silly charity lunch," explained Annaliese, pulling a face. "Scott called to tell us he and Andrew were on their way to the hospital, so could we please pick up Mimi's hospital bag on our way here."

For the first time, I noticed Robert was clutching a trim, navy blue weekend bag and shot Scott an admiring look. In the middle of a headlong, panic-stricken dash to the hospital with a worried father-to-be, he had stayed calm enough to think of such practicalities.

"So how is Mimi?" Robert asked. "Has there been any news?"

"They were prepping her for a C-section," I explained, slightly proud of my insider knowledge. "She has something called placenta praevia. That's where the placenta is lying across the neck of the cervix and stopping the baby from coming out."

"Goodness!" exclaimed Annaliese, shooting Caro a telling look. "It sounds like Mimi was very lucky you picked today to pay a visit."

We settled down to wait. Time ticked by, nearly forty minutes, before the double doors opened and Andrew emerged, broad face splitting under the weight of a huge grin that stretched from ear to ear, his red hair incongruous with the blue scrubs straining to fit over his sturdy frame.

"It's a girl!" he declared proudly. We clustered around him, exclaiming and congratulating, kissing cheeks and shaking hands, our relief manifesting itself in loud, good-natured teasing.

"How's Mimi?" we asked, and Andrew nodded his head.

"She's still woozy from the anaesthetic, but the doctor has told me she's going to be fine," he replied, and we all exclaimed in relief.

"When can we see them?" Annaliese enquired eagerly.

"As I said, Mimi's sleeping and even when she wakes, she'll need to get cleaned up and changed," Andrew said. "But I know she'll want to see you, so perhaps you could come back at visiting time this evening so we can introduce you properly to the newest member of the group."

"Of course," smiled Annaliese and gestured to Robert to hand over the bag. "We brought her things with us."

"Bless you, Annaliese," Andrew took the bag gratefully. "I know she'll be pleased to have them. Now, I'm going to go and see my daughter." He paused, the grin flashing across his face again. "My daughter," he repeated wonderingly. "I'm a dad, it doesn't seem real. I'm a dad."

"And a wonderful one you'll be, too," Annaliese reassured him, laughing. "Now, you give them both a big kiss from all of us and we'll be back later."

We all turned to go, but Andrew's voice quietly called me back. "Eve?" I looked at him, brows raised in enquiry, and he held out his hand. "Can I talk to you for a moment, please?"

"Of course," I muttered, surprised, and glanced at Annaliese as though asking her permission.

"I'll wait outside for you," she said and followed the others as they left the room. I glanced up at Andrew, who smiled, and to my surprise caught me up in a big bear hug.

"Eve, thank you," he said. "On the way here in the car, Scott told me what happened, and the doctor said if you hadn't come along when you did it could have been a very different story. Thank you so much. You saved them both."

"Well, I don't know about that," I mumbled, flushed with embarrassed pleasure. "I only did what anyone would have done."

"Maybe so." Andrew dismissed my objections impatiently, "but the fact remains you did it. You're the reason my wife and daughter are alive and well. So, thank you, Eve, I'll never forget what you did today."

Outside, I found Annaliese waiting for me, her warm smile and undemanding presence a welcome tonic from the rollercoaster day of emotional highs and lows. It seemed a hundred years since I had left the flat that morning. I wondered what had been happening in the real world.

"All right?" Annaliese asked. At my somewhat wobbly nod, her smile softened, and she slipped an arm easily around my shoulders. "Hungry?"

I stopped to consider and realised I was famished. "Very," I agreed, and she laughed.

"The others have gone down to the car," she informed me. "We're planning on having an early dinner somewhere before coming back here this evening. Want to come?"

"Yes please," I replied, grateful for anything which would extend my time with them. Arm in arm, we made our way through the hospital and out into the car park where the others were waiting by a large 4x4.

"I know, ghastly isn't it," laughed Annaliese. "But it's so useful for carting everyone around. Scott came with Andrew in his car, so you two will have to come with us."

We drove to a nearby village whose trendy gastro pub had been mentioned in the Sunday Times. It had just opened, and the sulky teenage waitress was unsure if the kitchen was cooking yet until the manageress recognised Annaliese and bustled excitedly from the kitchen. Rushing to us with menus, she agreed that, yes indeed, it was a beautiful evening, and of course, it was all right if we ate in the garden.

Robert ordered champagne and we drank to celebrate the safe arrival of the baby. Miles and Ferdie alerted to the situation by Annaliese's various phone calls, tracked us down and joined us, their faces both concerned at Mimi's dreadful experience and relieved at the happy outcome.

As the day's events were related to them, I basked in the glory of being the hero of the hour.

The day had settled into a balmy, sunny evening, and we sprawled at our table as the garden slowly filled with other diners.

Blinking in the sunlight which slanted through the trees, dappling us with moving shade and patches of warmth, I was aware we were the noisiest, and by far the most glamorous people there. I hoped I wasn't letting the side down, pleased I'd decided to wear my most sophisticated clothing that morning. How long ago it seemed. It felt a million years had passed since I had crept from Mike's bed for the last time.

As I ate the amazing food, I mentally calculated whether my bank account would explode when I presented my card to pay for my share, but in the end, the bill was appropriated by Robert who gave the waiter a piece of plastic, my feeble offer to contribute being waved away.

Relaxing over coffee, completely mellowed by food and wine, I determinedly thrust from my mind all thoughts of what would happen later, after we had been to see Mimi and the baby in the hospital. Where should I ask them to drop me off?

My instincts told me to stay away from the flat, and I reluctantly decided it would have to be my parents. I looked up and found Scott studying me, his eyes still and impenetrable. I stared back until at last, he smiled.

"Are you coming to the hospital with us?"

"I'd like to," I replied, "If that's okay?"

"Fine by me," he shrugged. "I told Robert I'd drive so he could have a drink, so you'll have to tell me where you want dropping off afterwards."

"Do you not drink?" I stalled, fiddling with a coaster.

"Very rarely," he replied, and Annaliese, who was listening, leant closer.

"That's Scott's only bad point," she pouted. "He won't drink. Only occasionally at birthdays, weddings, and bar mitzvahs, he might indulge in a little champagne."

I looked at Scott in interest. "Don't you like the taste?" I asked.

"Not particularly, and I don't like not being in control," he answered, then with bulldog-like tenacity returned to his original question. "So, where shall I drop you? Same place as before?"

"Umm, well, I don't think I can go back there…" I stuttered. "I think there's been some trouble and I don't want to get involved."

"Trouble?" he asked, his head rising like a tracker dog's, picking up an escaped prisoner's scent. "What sort of trouble?"

"There's this guy, Mike," I began. "He was, well, he was sort of my boyfriend, only not really, not anymore, and we were living together, although I was thinking about trying to find somewhere else, and he, well, he got himself into trouble with the police and I think they may raid the flat and I don't want to be there when they do."

"Quite."

"Eve, how terrible," exclaimed Annaliese. "What on earth are you going to do?"

"I don't know," I admitted. "Move back in with my parents, I guess, only I don't want to." I gave a little laugh. "It doesn't help that I lost my job today. Well, let's say I finally decided I couldn't stand working there anymore."

"You poor thing," Annaliese squeezed my hand in sympathy. "So, you're homeless and looking for a new job?"

"That about sums it up," I replied, and gave a devil-may-care shrug worthy of Scott himself.

Annaliese looked thoughtful. "What sort of work would you be looking for?" she asked.

"Well, anything to do with words really; I wanted to be a journalist, but now I'm not so sure. I love facts. I love finding out things and writing about them, but how many jobs are around that involve that?"

"I know of one," Annaliese stated in excitement. 'You could come and work for me! I've been thinking for a while, that I could do with a research assistant, you know, someone to do all the tedious checking up of facts and making sure I don't get things wrong. I really can't be bothered to do it, so I need someone who enjoys, well, research."

I stared at Annaliese in shock. "Work for you?" I gasped shrilly and Annaliese's face fell.

"Well only if you want to, sweetie," she replied.

"Want to? Oh my, it's like a dream come true! Are you sure? Oh, thank you, thank you so much! I can't believe it."

"You're welcome," she laughed, sharing in my enthusiasm.

"Now, I've just got to find somewhere to live," I declared. "Then I'm all set."

"Oh, well that's easy," she replied. "You'll come and live with us of course."

"With you?" Again, my mouth gaped open in shock.

"Why not? It'll be fun," Annaliese declared.

"But ... but I can't ..." I spluttered.

"Of course, you can," she stated firmly. "It's the easiest option all around. You get a home and I get a new friend and a research assistant. Oh, Eve, it'll be wonderful having you live with us."

I was speechless and simply hugged her tightly, nodding my agreement into her shoulder, hearing her rich chuckle in my ear, and the excited chatter of the others. Then, I opened my eyes and looked straight into Caro's grimly hostile gaze, feeling the waves of antagonistic mistrust which seemed to ooze from her very pores, and knew one person, at least, who didn't think it would be so wonderful.

After dinner, we all went to the hospital to visit Mimi. I insisted the others visit with her first, so was the last to make my way down the corridor to Mimi's private room.

"Hello," I whispered, hovering in the doorway. She glanced up and smiled. I marvelled at how her hair had fallen neatly back into its chic bob, no sign that not so long ago she had been tearing it out in handfuls.

"Eve, please come in." She gestured towards the chair by her bedside. Nervously, I shuffled further into the room, noticing the tube that snaked out of her hand and up into one of those drip thingies, and the lines of stress that pulled at the skin around her eyes and mouth.

"How are you?" I asked, and Mimi gave one of those shrugs only French people can do, her face pulling down in a moue of distaste.

"I have felt better," she confided. I smiled in shared sympathy, then stiffened as Mimi went to hand me her precious bundle.

I'm not very good with babies. I am an only child and so are my parents, so I'd not had much experience with them. I'd never held one; and certainly not one less than four hours old. Apprehensively, I sank into the chair and took the baby from Mimi, settling it into my arms, my heart thudding with anxiety.

She was asleep, her enviably long eyelashes lying perfectly arranged on peachy-coloured cheeks, eyes shut fast in the slumber of absolute innocence. Her little mouth was puckered into a rosebud kiss, and one small fist protruded from the blanket, clenched firmly around the hem.

I marvelled at her fingers, so perfect, so incredibly tiny. A tuft of red hair stuck up like duckling fluff and I wondered if it would stay that colour.

"She's beautiful," I breathed in awe, glancing up at Mimi's lovestruck eyes, and besotted expression as she gazed in total rapture at her little miracle.

"She is," agreed Mimi. "And it's all thanks to you, Eve. What you did today, you saved her life and mine as well, and I wanted to thank you. I will be eternally grateful to you, Eve. If you hadn't found me when you did, I would have been there all day and could have bled to death."

I smiled, blinking back tears at her earnest tone. "What are you going to call her?" I asked, needing to change the subject before my emotions completely overwhelmed me.

"Esther Annaliese Eve," Mimi replied, and I blinked in surprise. It seemed an impossible number of names for such a small scrap, but then I realised the significance of the last name.

"You're naming the baby after me?" I gasped, touched beyond belief. "I don't know what to say, that's awesome, thank you..."

"No, thank you, Eve," said Andrew, as he stooped and lifted Esther from my arms. "We won't forget what you did today, ever."

"I should go now," I stuttered. "Let you get some sleep. You must be exhausted." I stood, wincing as the chair leg screeched over the tiled floor.

"I am," Mimi agreed wearily. She snuggled the baby back into the crook of her arm, and tenderly adjusted the blanket as Andrew stroked a large finger gently down one soft tiny cheek. Watching the newly formed family bonding, I swallowed down the lump in my throat and quietly slipped away, eager to re-join the others.

CHAPTER V – ACTS

*"he frightened me,
the way he looked at me."*

We returned to the Hall. My new home, I reminded myself with a thrill of intense exhilaration, remembering when I was a child the almost unbearable anticipation of Christmas, how I would be sick with excitement. I felt that way now – jittery, over-stimulated, emotions riding high on adrenalin after one of the most extraordinary days of my life.

Champagne was opened and we drank to the health of Esther Annaliese Eve, Annaliese's eyes going dewy over the names. Esther was the name of Mimi's mother, she informed me, who had unfortunately died of cancer when Mimi was ten.

Later, Annaliese took me upstairs to show me my new domain. "This can be your room," she exclaimed, throwing the door open.

I gasped at the perfection of the room. Positioned at the back of the Hall, the late evening sun was pouring forcefully through the pair of floor-to-ceiling windows, bathing the whole room in golden light.

"Do you like it?" Annaliese asked anxiously.

I blinked at her in stupefaction. How could anyone not like such a glowingly gorgeous room?

"It's beautiful," I gasped, noticing the four-poster bed, the ornate Queen Anne fireplace, and the sophistication of the furniture. A door led from the room into a bathroom, and here everything was sleek and modern.

"Are you sure this is all for me?" I breathed.

Annaliese threw her head back and laughed, a richly amused laugh which set my spine-tingling, warmth flooding through my veins.

"Of course, it's all for you," she reassured. "I hope you'll be very comfortable here, but if there's anything you need, make sure you ask."

The private celebration had become a party. As news spread and phones never stopped pinging, others began to arrive, flushed and excited, eager to wet the baby's head.

I struggled to remember names, feeling the curious gaze of the newcomers, people who had known Annaliese far longer than I, yet were still in the outer circles. Some seemed to accept this. Others, I felt, were resentful, perturbed that a nobody had managed to penetrate the clique.

Finally, I escaped outside for some air, breathing easier as I perched on the stone steps, and drained my glass dry, wishing I'd had the foresight to bring a bottle out with me.

The sun was beginning to set, a molten glowing ball that turned everything it touched into gold, and long shafts of sunlight lay like fingers over the park, brushing tree tips with glitter. I sighed with pleasure.

"That's some sunset," remarked a dry voice behind me. I looked up, shading my eyes, to see

Scott standing at the top of the steps, a champagne bottle in one hand and a lit cigarette in the other.

He climbed down and sat next to me, holding out the bottle in wordless enquiry. Murmuring my thanks, I let him fill my glass, watching the bubbles fizz and gush to the rim.

"So, you've decided to take Annaliese up on her offers, have you?"

I gulped champagne, slightly shocked at his forthrightness. "Umm, yes," I turned to look at him. "Do you mind?"

"Mind?" he enquired mildly, raising his brows. "Why should I mind?"

"Well, because none of you has known me very long, and perhaps feel you don't know whether I can be trusted or not..." I floundered, not knowing how to put into words my vague unease.

"And I know Caro's not very impressed with the idea," I finished weakly.

"Ah, yes, Caro," he mused. "Let me tell you something about Caro. She didn't particularly like any of us in the beginning. She's very protective of Annaliese and is always convinced that people are going to take advantage of her generous nature. But Annaliese is an excellent judge of character and I have never known her to be wrong about anyone, yet."

"She's amazing," I agreed. "I've never met anyone like her. I still can't believe she's asked me to live here and has offered me a job."

"Well, get used to it," Scott replied, "because that's what Annaliese does. She adopts people. Anyone who needs her help. Annaliese loves to feel needed. I think it makes up in part for not being able to have children of her own."

"Why can't she?" I asked curiously.

"I don't know," Scott shrugged. "Some medical reason, that's all I know."

I nodded and fell silent, gazing out over the darkening countryside. From the Hall, I heard shrieks of laughter and shouted conversations. There was a blast of music as someone put on a CD and I knew dancing would soon follow.

"How long do you think the party will go on for?" I asked.

"God knows," Scott replied, stubbing his cigarette out on a step. "All night probably. If you're tired, go to bed, no one will mind. After all, you have had a busy day."

"Hmm," I agreed, realising he was right. I was tired, too tired to go back into the Hall and face the nameless crowd of revellers. I sighed and struggled wearily to my feet.

"I think I will," I murmured. "Would you tell the others I'll see them tomorrow?"

"Of course," he agreed smoothly. "Goodnight, Eve."

"Goodnight," I replied, and ran lightly up the steps. At the top I paused and looked down, hoping for a last glimpse of him, but he had already gone.

I slipped quietly through the open front doors, noticing that furniture had been pushed back to form a dance floor in the formal drawing-room. Melodiously soft, jazzy music was oozing from the state-of-the-art stereo system.

I paused by the door, unseen and unnoticed, and saw Scott re-enter the room through the veranda doors and cross the room to where Annaliese was dancing with Robert.

He bent, said something, and Annaliese moved easily into his arms as Robert stepped to the side and accepted a glass from Ferdie.

I watched them dance together, a perfect match. Scott, tall and classically handsome; Annaliese, barefoot, feminine, and petite, her flower-strewn dress floating round her calves, and her long golden hair lightly kissing the back of his hand as he clasped her waist.

From my onlooker position, I had the strangest feeling that nothing was real; that I was watching a play, with Scott and Annaliese as the hero and heroine, and the others standing around being the supporting acts, waiting in the wings for their moment of fame centre stage. I was the audience – an audience of one.

A pang of something, I didn't know what shot through me. Jealousy. A feeling of being excluded, of being outside the glass bubble unable to get in.

Scott looked up over Annaliese's shoulder, directly into my eyes. Something flickered in his expression. Was it my imagination, or did his arms tighten imperceptibly around her waist?

What was he trying to tell me? Were he and Annaliese lovers? I turned my gaze to Robert who was watching them dance. I saw Ferdie glance at Scott and Annaliese, then back to Robert.

For a moment there was the strangest expression on his face, a furtive concern, a glimpse of secret worry, then it was gone. It was just Ferdie's funny face again as he said something to Robert and made him smile.

I was tired and emotionally exhausted. So much had happened in one short day, was it any wonder I was seeing things that didn't exist?

If Robert *was* watching his wife dancing with her lover then he was remarkably cool about it. Or maybe he didn't know. Maybe he did know but didn't care. Maybe Ferdie suspected, but...

Or maybe you're overreacting Melissa, I told myself firmly. You're tired and you need to go to bed. You're reading too much into one dance, and looks you thought you saw. Go to bed. Things will seem different in the morning.

I took my champagne glass back to the kitchen, filled a clean tumbler with water from the tap, drank it down whole, and then filled it up again. A champagne headache was already creeping up on me, and I didn't want to start the first day of my new life with a raging hangover.

The next day I slept late, not waking until gone ten. I was horrified at having slept so long and afraid of what everyone would say.

Creeping downstairs in a mortified scurry, I soon realised that apart from Robert and Scott, I was the first one up.

"Good morning," beamed Robert, when an unsurprised Mrs Briggs – I assumed she'd already been informed of my change in status – directed me to the morning room where I discovered them having breakfast.

"Eve," said Scott quietly, and held aloft the coffee pot, his brow quirked in enquiry. I nodded gratefully and settled myself into a chair.

"Where is everyone?" I asked in surprise.

"Annaliese was still asleep when I last looked," replied Robert. "Ferdie never emerges before noon on a Saturday, and I would imagine Miles has already gone. Didn't he have a meeting or something this morning, Scott?"

"I believe he did," Scott murmured, pouring strong black coffee into my cup, and pushing the milk jug towards me. "Milk, no sugar, right?" he said. I nodded, touched he had remembered.

"Help yourself to breakfast," commanded Robert, waving his hand expansively towards the sideboard where rows of covered dishes sat on heated trays.

I murmured my thanks, and wandered across to investigate, a smile pulling at my mouth, feeling as if I was in a Noel Coward play or something. I hadn't realised people still lived like this – bacon and kedgeree for breakfast, sipping coffee in the morning room, discussing the contents of their respective newspapers. It all seemed so unreal, contrived, an act.

My mobile rang as I was sitting down. Quickly, I fumbled it out of my trouser pocket, frowning as number unknown flashed up.

"Hello?" I cautiously enquired, aware of the barely concealed curiosity of Robert and Scott. The call was brief, my answers sparse. When I disconnected, I could feel the fear on my face.

"Eve?" said Robert. "What's the matter?"

"That was the police," I replied, breathless with apprehension. "Mike was arrested yesterday, and they want to talk to me."

"What was he arrested for?"

"Robbery," I answered miserably. "I think he got so sick of never having any money, and then he met Wayne..."

"Wayne?"

"Wayne Jones. We knew him at school. Even then he was evil. When Mike said he was going to work for him, I knew ... I knew what kind of work it would be, and ..." My voice trailed away, and I stared silently at the two men.

"And that's why you didn't want to go home," finished Scott. I sighed and nodded.

"I'm so sorry," I said to Robert. "They wanted to know where I was, so I told them I was here. I didn't know what else to say."

"That's fine," he said, instantly dismissing my concerns. "This is your home now so what else could you have said?"

"When are they coming?" enquired Scott.

"Soon ... now." I stared miserably at my plate.

"Then you'd better finish your breakfast," he said practically. Obediently, I sipped at my coffee and struggled to eat the food I'd piled so gaily onto my plate only minutes before, but my throat closed in protest and eventually I pushed it away, anxiety quelling my appetite.

"I think I'd better wake Annaliese," murmured Robert, and slipped from the room before I could beg him not to worry her.

That left Scott. Under his direct, almost knowing gaze, I dropped my own eyes to the table and fiddled with my napkin.

"Poor Eve." He dropped a hand lightly over mine. "Not a great start to your new life, is it?"

"What do you mean?" I asked, defensively.

"I mean, I understand you were hoping for a clean break, to walk away from your old life as Melissa and start a new one as Eve, but I'm afraid it's never that simple. Ghosts from your past have an annoying habit of popping up and reminding you, just when you thought you'd managed to leave them far behind."

I frowned, wondering whether he was referring to ghosts in my life, or in his own.

The police arrived twenty minutes later, official, and stern. I looked at the car parked outside the Hall and gulped in guilty misery. On my very first day here, I had brought trouble to the golden kingdom.

Annaliese swept downstairs, resplendent in coffee-coloured silk, as they rang the doorbell. She paused, gave me a reassuring smile, and winked at me before she threw the doors open and launched into her act.

Later, years later, I would finally come to realise Annaliese had many personas; many different components to her character; and that they weren't an act, weren't pretence. They were all Annaliese, all angles of a complex and multifaceted woman, and she could draw on them at will, selecting which personality best suited which situation.

But I had not yet learnt that, so could only watch in stunned admiration as she assumed what she would later tell me she called her Lady of the Manor act – gracious and helpful, ever so slightly patronising. Not enough to offend, just enough to leave the police in no doubt she was in charge and was bestowing an enormous favour on them by even seeing them. She did it so charmingly, and with such a natural, unassuming manner, they completely fell for it.

There were two of them. The younger one was as I imagined a policeman to be. Dressed in uniform, he was introduced as PC Mulholland and stood by the door, his inferior rank to the other evident from his body language.

The other, Detective Inspector Sanderson, was older, dressed in a rumpled brown suit, and his mild face looked kind, almost fatherly, yet his eyes were sharp. I shivered. He would be more difficult to fool.

Annaliese insisted on serving them coffee in the drawing-room. Even the keen-eyed older one unbent enough in the face of such full-on charm to accept a cup, whilst the younger one was plainly beside himself with admiration.

His round, honest, boyish face gazed at Annaliese in awe as she fussed and fluttered, handed round biscuits, and made sure everyone was settled and comfortable before seating herself beside me on the sofa, facing the man with the knowing eyes.

"Now then, Melissa," he began, setting his cup on the table and leaning forward. "Do you know why we're here?"

"Well," I faltered nervously. "You said on the phone Mike had been arrested for robbery, but I don't know why you need to see me."

"It's routine, Melissa, nothing to worry about, but I do need to ask where you were the night before last. Thursday night."

"I was here," I was able to reply honestly, my gaze locking directly onto his.

"Was anyone else here?" he asked.

"Gracious, yes," Annaliese answered before I could speak. "Both myself and my husband, and four other friends who were also spending the evening with us. We all watched a DVD and had a Chinese takeaway. Scott and Melissa picked it up in town for us on their way here."

"I see," he replied slowly. "What time was that?"

"Scott, darling," Annaliese languidly turned, "what time did you pick up Melissa?"

"Straight from work," he replied smoothly. "We didn't want to eat too late, so I picked up the Chinese first, and then collected Melissa at 5:30."

"So, you hadn't been to the flat since you left for work that morning?"

"No." I shook my head. "Not since the morning."

"I see." Detective Inspector Sanderson looked thoughtful. "And what time did you return home?"

I hesitated, unsure of what the correct answer should be.

"I ran Melissa home at about 2:00am."

Again, someone else answered for me. My eyes flicked up to meet Scott's coolly steady ones, as he smoothly slid his answer in front of the Detective Inspector for his examination.

"Okay," said the Inspector, looking directly at me. "I want you to tell me in your own words, Melissa," his eyes darted almost imperceptibly in Annaliese and Scott's directions as if warning them not to intercede on my behalf again.

"When you returned to the flat you were sharing with your boyfriend..."

"He isn't my boyfriend," I interjected hastily.

"Well, he seems to think differently, Melissa."

"Yes, well, we were in a relationship, but it's not been right for ages, months. I was planning on finding somewhere else to live but was waiting until he was back on his feet, workwise, that is."

"I see," he replied, and his tone implied he did, all too clearly. "Anyway," he continued. "When you returned to the flat you were living in with Michael Tate, was he there?"

"No," I replied. "But then, I wasn't expecting him to be. He'd texted me earlier in the evening that he was staying out all night, so I knew he wouldn't be there when I got back."

"Tell me about the boxes, Melissa."

The question was direct, almost brutally so, and I knew he was trying to catch me out. I had been expecting it though, so was prepared. Keeping my features even and my voice steady, I looked him straight in the eye.

"Mike put some boxes in the lounge last week. I asked him what they were, but he told me to mind my own business."

"And just like that you did?" enquired the Detective Inspector casually, stretching out a hand for his coffee. "I wish my wife was as obedient."

I flushed angrily at the implied accusation hidden beneath the words.

"What do you mean?" I demanded hotly.

"It seems a little strange to me that you weren't in the least bit curious to know why he'd dumped so many boxes in your small flat, and precisely what was in them?"

"Well of course I was curious," I stated firmly. "And worried. I was very worried about what he was getting himself into, especially as he'd been seeing so much of Wayne Jones. But when I asked him, he got angry. We fought about it, and I was too scared to push anymore..."

"Scared of Mike?"

"No, scared of Wayne. He frightened me, the way he looked at me, as though..."

I broke off and looked away, across the room I was aware of Scott turning from his position at the window, his eyes still and thoughtful.

"Why did he frighten you, Melissa?"

The Inspector's voice was gentler.

"I knew him from school, knew the reputation he had and what he was capable of. I was so scared he was dragging Mike into something dodgy. I tried to warn Mike, but he wouldn't listen. He's weak, easily led."

I looked pleadingly at the Detective Inspector.

"He's not a bad person," I continued. "He's finding it hard to settle to a job and he hates not having any money."

"Tell me what happened that night, Melissa."

"I came here for the evening," I stuttered, not wanting to admit that I had seen Wayne turn up at the flat and had known they were up to something. "Scott ran me home at about two."

"What did you find when you got home, Melissa?"

"More boxes..." I paused and swallowed. "I was angry with Mike and decided to have it out with him when I saw him."

Scott's gaze was still on me, rock steady, unwavering. Annaliese gently slipped her hand into mine. Somehow, they gave me the courage to draw back my shoulders, look the Detective Inspector straight in the eyes, calmly and coolly lie.

"He must have come home sometime during the night though because when I woke up, he was in bed fast asleep. I didn't want to have an argument before going to work, so I left him sleeping, thinking I'd talk to him when I got home."

"So, you left him asleep in bed and went to work."

"Yes."

"Only, you didn't go to work did you, Melissa?"
"No, I didn't."
"Why not?"

"I'm not sure really. I got to the door and realised I'd had enough. I don't like my job, and yesterday it all seemed too much. I decided to take the day off and visit Annaliese instead."

"Did you phone to let her know you were coming?"

"No."

"Why not?"

"I don't know," I shrugged. "It didn't occur to me."

"How did you get here?"

"I walked."

"From town?"

"Yes."

"That's quite a step, Melissa."

"It was a lovely day, I felt like walking."

"What time did you get here, Melissa?"

"I'm not too sure. About one, I think, certainly not much later."

"Can you confirm that, Ms Macleod?" turning the spotlight on Annaliese.

"No, Inspector. Unfortunately, I was out at a charity lunch."

"I see. Is there anyone else who could confirm what time you reached here, Melissa?"

"No, no one was in."

"So, you'd walked all that way only to find the Hall empty and locked up?"

"No, the back door was unlocked, I let myself in."

"Is there a point to all of this, Detective Inspector?" Annaliese questioned, sweetly. "I mean, Melissa has already told you she knew nothing of her ex-boyfriend's nefarious goings-on, so unless you are accusing her of something, do you need to interrogate her in this manner?"

"Merely gaining background information, Ms Macleod," the Detective Inspector replied calmly. "Trying to see the whole picture, as it were."

"Well, it was a jolly good thing Melissa did decide to pay me a visit yesterday, Detective Inspector," Annaliese retorted hotly.

"Oh, why was that?"

"Because she saved the life of our friend, and her unborn baby's life, too!"

The Detective Inspector raised his head and regarded me with interest.

"Is that so?" he commented mildly.

"Well, I don't know about saving their lives," I mumbled.

"Oh, don't be so modest, Melissa," insisted Annaliese, and proceeded to tell him exactly what had happened.

The Detective Inspector drained his coffee cup, placed it carefully back into his saucer, and nodded his head thoughtfully.

For a moment there was silence in the room, and once again, I had the feeling I was watching an act, a play, with the policemen, Scott, Annaliese, and even myself, all acting out pre-determined roles.

"Thank you, Melissa." The Detective Inspector rose to his feet. "You've been most helpful."

Annaliese and I rose to our feet.

"That's it?" I couldn't help but exclaim.

"That's it," he agreed and smiled, looking almost human when he did so. He made his way towards the door. PC Mulholland was reaching for the handle when the Detective Inspector abruptly stopped and turned.

"Just one thing, Melissa," he said.

"Yes, what?" I replied.

"You didn't ask how we knew."

"Knew what?" Relief at his imminent departure made me careless.

"How we knew the boxes were in the flat, and what aroused our suspicions about Mike."

"I ...umm... I thought, that is..."

I stopped, feeling my face flame, and saw the knowledge in his eyes. The recognition and confirmation.

"We had an anonymous tip-off," he said, his voice surprisingly gentle. "Someone phoned us early yesterday morning and told us where to find the goods stolen from two electrical warehouses in the area over the last fortnight."

"Oh?" was all I could think to say.

"Whoever it was," he continued, looking straight at me, "was very brave, because even though it was the right thing to do, considering the kind of people we know Wayne Jones and his associates to be, it was also quite a risky thing to do."

"How risky, Detective Inspector?" Annaliese's voice was casual. "I mean, this anonymous informer, are they in any kind of danger?"

The Detective Inspector's gaze met hers over my shoulder. I sensed something passing between them, some message received and understood.

"They shouldn't be," he replied slowly. "The police won't inform anyone there was a tip-off. So long as they don't learn about it from any other source, the informer should be safe enough."

"What a relief," said Annaliese brightly. "For the informer that is."

"Thank you for your time, Melissa," the Detective Inspector's eyes flicked back to mine. "You've been very helpful, thank you."

"What will happen to him?" I blurted out guiltily. "To Mike, I mean?"

"It's his first offence," replied the Detective Inspector smoothly. "So, I imagine the magistrates will be quite lenient with him, although I doubt Mr Jones will fare so well. We know him of old and have been watching him for some time now."

I nodded, not knowing what else to say.

We followed them out to the porch, mouthing formal goodbyes as we watched them climb into their car and drive away down the long sweeping driveway.

"You did very well, Eve," Annaliese murmured in my ear. "They won't be back."

The next hurdle to overcome before my new life could begin was my parents. Somehow, by tapping into the information network all parents seem to have direct access to, they had heard about Mike's arrest by that afternoon and phoned me.

I was sitting in Annaliese's office, trying to absorb the nuances and details of my new job, and feeling a rising tide of excitement at the realisation that I could do this. Finally, I had found an occupation that would stretch my abilities; something stimulating and interesting; a job which I could do and do well.

When my phone rang, I answered it automatically, my face falling at my mother's panicked voice, interspersed by the slightly calmer, enquiring one of my father.

Annaliese waited patiently, pulling a sympathetic face as I attempted to explain and placate them. Of course, I wasn't involved in Mike's misdemeanours. Of course, the police weren't going to arrest me. I'd already spoken to them. Yes, I'd been as helpful as possible. Yes, I appreciated they'd always had their doubts about my now ex-boyfriend. What was I going to do now? I was of course moving home.

I took a deep breath and began to explain that I'd got a new job. A new job? What about my job with the newspaper? Wasn't that what I had always wanted, to be a journalist?

Patiently, I tried to tell them the truth. I had been unhappy at the newspaper. It wasn't what I wanted after all, but my new job was everything I'd ever dreamt of, and more.

Well, what was it, what was I doing? What on earth was I thinking of, giving up my job and moving in with strangers? Did I have no concept of the potential dangers? My mother's voice became shrill, my father's strident. Both vied to be the one to hammer home to me the recklessness of my actions.

My reassuring words got twisted, my tongue tripping over itself as I attempted to calm and mollify. My sentences became short and choppy, disconnected, meaningless phrases and words stammered and stuttered down the line.

Annaliese took the phone from me and beamed a big smile down it, almost as though my mother could see her.

"Hello? Mrs Stephens? Hello, yes, this is Annaliese Macleod. I think it would be best if

Melissa and I came to see you so we can discuss the matter calmly. Yes, yes, I quite agree, of course, you're worried. I would be too, in your position. Yes, Melissa is young and of course, it's completely understandable you have certain responsibilities. Absolutely, right, ok, shall we say we'll be there in an hour? Wonderful, I look forward to meeting you both, goodbye."

She flashed me a reassuring smile and handed the phone back. I stammered a goodbye, disconnected and stared at her in dismay.

"I'm so sorry," I gulped, feeling like a naughty child told off in front of her friends by her mother.

"What on earth for?" asked Annaliese in obvious surprise.

"For my parents, the police, so much trouble. You must be wishing you'd never met me."

"Don't be silly," retorted Annaliese hotly. "Of course, they're worried about you, any parent would be. If I were in their position and you were my daughter, I would want to know where you were going to be living, and exactly who you were going to be living with."

"I suppose," I sulked. "They seem to think I'm still a child though." I heard the whine in my voice, realised how like a child I was behaving.

"Well, then," Annaliese replied gently, "you'll have to prove them wrong, won't you?"

When we arrived at my parents, it was obvious my mother had done the quickest tidy-up job ever and my father, who was an English teacher, had realised who Annaliese was.

Instead of the near-hysterical ranting, I had expected, my parents greeted us at the door, the very model of calm rational human beings, hugging me and shaking hands with Annaliese. My father's eyes even showed signs of awe at having such a famous author, and one whom I happened to know he very much respected, in their home.

Once again, before my admiring eyes, Annaliese slipped effortlessly into another persona, acting out her role perfectly as the reassuring and understanding employer, anticipating their concerns, and answering them before they could even be voiced.

I watched in silent wonder as she completely charmed and won them over, eyes wide and guileless, manner pitched so perfectly my mother thawed enough to offer tea, bustling into the kitchen to return with a tray laden with her best china, having even unearthed a packet of chocolate biscuits.

Who was this woman, I thought, and of all these different facets, which one was the actual Annaliese? All of them, none of them, or had I yet to encounter the real one?

Somehow, Annaliese encouraged my parents to open up to her. I listened, toes curling in embarrassment, as my mother regaled her with endless tales of my antics as a toddler, before finally going upstairs to bring down the dreaded albums, which Annaliese assured her she would love to look at.

"This is Mel aged thirteen months," my mother proudly told her, as Annaliese opened the pink embossed book at the first page and gently turned over the protective tissue paper.

"You have none of her as a baby?" enquired Annaliese innocently, and my mother tensed.

"We couldn't have children," she replied, shades of stiffness in her tone. "We adopted Mel. She was thirteen months old when we finally got her. That picture was taken on the day we brought her home."

Annaliese stared at the photo for the longest time, her finger gently touching the pink ribbons which twirled down the side of the page.

"What a beautiful little girl," she finally said, and I looked at her curiously. For a moment there, I heard something in her voice, wistfulness, and regret, and I wondered... But her next words seemed to explain it.

"I can't have children either," she confided to my mother, whose face twisted in a womanly expression of sympathy, and she patted Annaliese on the arm, a shared look of understanding passing between them.

"More tea?" asked my father, obviously uncomfortable with the rising level of female hormones in the room. Annaliese smiled and nodded in agreement, slowly turning the pages of the album, lingering, absorbing, almost drinking in every picture, and questioning my mother about each one.

How old was I in this one? Where had that one been taken? Why did I have such a grumpy expression on my face in this one?

By the time she closed the final album, with obvious signs of regret there were no more, my mother was completely and utterly won over.

There was no longer any doubt I would be moving into the Hall and would be accepting the job as Annaliese's assistant with the approval and, indeed, the blessing of both my parents.

I silently marvelled at Annaliese's cleverness. She had seemed to know precisely how to sway my parent's opinion and had manoeuvred with such charm and tact that only I, watching the act from the outside, suspected her of any duplicity at all.

Following my encounters with the police and my parents, my first day at the Hall could hardly be described as a smooth one, but within a week, I could barely remember what it had been like to live anywhere else, so completely had my new life absorbed me.

The quiet sophistication, the understated luxury and elegance, were things I very quickly grew accustomed to, as I did to my new career.

Within my role as Annaliese's researcher, I finally found the stimulation and job satisfaction that I had been searching for, enjoying enormously the experience of being immersed in the worlds which Annaliese created.

I relished being a small but integral part of helping her bring her rich characters and plot lines to life, although sometimes was forced to ground some of her more fanciful notions in the reality of fact.

My transition from Melissa to Eve was a simple and smooth one. No protracted labour or agonising birth pangs for me. As easily as a snake sheds its skin, I left boring, middle-class Melissa behind, and gladly embraced my new persona of Eve – young, talented, and blessed with friends the like of which I'd never in my wildest dreams imagined possessing.

Gradually, I honed and perfected the act that was Eve. Melissa had drunk any old coffee, not bothering herself with make or blend. Eve only drank freshly ground or not at all.

Melissa had made do with cheap perfume and supermarket makeup. Eve learnt fast and well which colours suited her skin tone best, finally settling on good quality, kind to animals, range – such things mattered to Eve – and choosing a subtly sophisticated perfume which she wore every day; her signature scent with which she signalled to the world that Eve was a stylish and confident woman.

Annaliese insisted on advancing me some of my extremely generous salary and had taken me to London for some shopping. Her maternal act was so convincing, that more than one shop assistant commented quietly to me how lucky I was to have such a young and attractive mother.

Eve moved confidently amongst the rich and beautiful, rubbing shoulders with the great and famous, and grew accustomed to mingling with people so far above Melissa, she would have been struck dumb at even the mere thought of being in the same room as them.

As Annaliese's researcher, I tried my wings under her proudly anxious eyes. When she considered me ready, I offered my skills to other authors, slowly gathering a reputation as someone who paid meticulous attention to details, and always, without fail, got the facts right.

I squirrelled away my earnings and watched in stunned astonishment as my savings grew, yet I continued to live at the Hall. Whenever I mentioned getting a place of my own, Annaliese would protest I mustn't leave, that she enjoyed having me there too much to let me go.

My parents watched my growing success, at first with sceptical disbelief, then gradually with ever-increasing pride. I knew their clever daughter, who commanded such respectable fees and who mingled with the elite of the land, was the topic of conversation at many of the nice dinner parties they attended.

The façade of Eve grew so engrained, that at times I almost believed in her myself, yet two people grounded me. Two who never let me entirely forget who I was and where I had come from.

The first was Scott. Somehow, with him, I could never be anything other than who I truly was. One look from those calm steady eyes and I would drop any pretentious act I had been fooling everyone else with and was simply myself.

And even though he called me Eve, it was almost as though he did it to humour me, as if he regarded it a secret between us. That although I might convince everybody else, I could never pretend with him for he could see right into my soul.

I knew this and I didn't care. To me, he was Scott, the man I loved absolutely and completely with every fibre of my heart and body. I would have walked over hot coals to the ends of the earth for him, yet he remained oblivious to my love, treating me with the same amused friendliness he afforded the others.

Gradually, as days ticked into weeks into months into years, I stifled my love, suffocating it beneath layers of moments of friendship and shared memories of innocent fun, and accepted, albeit sadly and with many a pang of regret, that he would never feel that way for me.

No, I was his dear little friend, Eve, the woman who could make him laugh when one of his silent moods came upon him. The woman who would persuade him to drop daily duties and join her on some spontaneous madcap excursion.

The woman who knew he sneaked out of the Hall at the same time every evening to have an illicit cigarette – knew, covered up for him and often joined him for a stolen ten minutes – that, unbeknownst to him, she cherished and remembered for the whole of the next day.

I had to be content with this and I was, most of the time. Sometimes, when looking after Mimi's perfect baby, whose grand list of names had been shortened to merely Essie and to whom I'd completely and irrevocably lost my heart, discovering hidden maternal depths within me, I would feel his gaze upon me and glance up.

His look almost fooled me into thinking maybe, just maybe, his feelings for me ran deeper than I thought. Then he would make a blasé comment, his manner as tightly controlled and contained as ever, and the moment would pass by, unremarked upon.

I wanted to learn how to drive, and he taught me, his unfailing patience and quiet stillness making him a good teacher. I don't remember him ever losing his temper with me, not even when I lost mine and railed at him over the difficulties of driving, and not even when I mangled the gears of his beloved sports car.

He wasn't a monk of course. During my years of living with Annaliese, a few women passed through his life. These I barely tolerated, hiding my jealousy beneath an impeccable act of smiling friendliness, breathing sighs of relief when they vanished from the scene, and he was once again my Scott.

And, of course, neither was I a nun. Men featured occasionally in my life, all to a type – good-looking, suave, sophisticated, rich, and successful. Gradually, I realised they were all clones of him – imperfect, unsatisfactory copies of a masterpiece, good for sex and not much else.

The other person not fooled by Eve was Caro.

Her simmering resentment at my newly found position of favour within Annaliese's court steadily bubbled and brewed, like molten lava, gradually building up to an explosion of volcanic proportions.

I was constantly aware of her eyes watching me, forever watching me, critical and condemning. I avoided her as much as possible. Her bitterness both confused and alarmed me.

All of Annaliese's other friends had accepted my place in the inner circle and Annaliese's affections, yet Caro's antipathy to me was so thinly veiled, so barely concealed, there were moments when the others registered it, too. On more than one occasion, Annaliese and even Scott would step between us, acting as a buffer, absorbing the venom from a slyly barbed remark or action.

One day, a month after I had moved in, I found myself alone in the kitchen when Caro entered and set about making herself a cup of tea.

I watched her warily. Long weeks of implications and hinted accusations had made me mistrustful and suspicious of Annaliese's much-valued assistant.

She glanced at me, small flint-like eyes hard and unyielding behind thick glasses.

"So," she began, her voice heavy with Irish sarcasm. "Comfortable, are we? Feet well and truly under the table, are they?"

I flushed at her words, immediately feeling guilt at their meaning, then a sudden wave of quick, hot anger flooded over me, and I glared at her with dislike.

"Did I wrong you in a previous life, Caro?" I demanded. "What have I ever done to you that you hate me so much?"

"It's not what you've done," she spat, her loathing now openly naked. "It's what you'll do."

"What?" I was confused and taken aback by the tone of her voice. This woman didn't just dislike me, she hated me. "What do you mean? What am I going to do?"

"You're going to hurt her."

"Who?"

"Annaliese."

"No," I protested hotly. "I love her, I'd never hurt her, never."

"You might not mean to," she insisted, "but you will. One day you will destroy her."

"No, you're crazy," I all but shouted. "Why on earth would I ever want to hurt Annaliese? After all, she's done for me, I'd never do anything like that, never."

"You won't be able to help yourself," she replied.

I stared at her in bewildered dismay. Her eyes softened and an expression, unfathomable and unreadable, crept into them, and she looked at me with something akin to contemptuous pity.

"It's not anything you will do," she said slowly. "It's what you are that will hurt her, and you can no more change what you are than the earth can stop revolving."

"I don't understand," I began. "What do you mean?"

"There's no point saying anymore," she snapped waspishly. "What's done is done. You're here now, the wheels have been set in motion, and it's too late to stop them." She stomped from the kitchen, leaving me angry and more than a little fearful.

Of course, in one sense Caro's bleak prediction was realised. In the end, I did hurt Annaliese. I hurt her when I left without a word or a trace. When I stayed away for almost a year, only coming back when it was too late, when she was dead, and it was too late for apologies and explanations.

But my self-imposed exile was self-defence. It did not come about through any desire on my part to hurt Annaliese.

No, I was forced to leave. The monumental and devastating blow Annaliese dealt me first, left me with no other option than to run as fast, and as far, as I could.

CHAPTER VI - CHRONICLES

*"Everyone's in love
with the wrong person..."*

At this point in the book of my life with Annaliese, maybe I should take a step back and examine the supporting acts. Her friends. The inner circle. That small group of people who, in the apparent absence of any blood relations, stood in as her surrogate family.

Not until I left the narcotic and addictively soothing presence of Annaliese did it occur to me how strange it was that she did not possess a single family member. No parents, living or dead. No siblings, no aunts, or uncles, not a single cousin, or at least none I ever heard of.

It was as if Annaliese had arrived on the planet, fully formed and perfect at the age of seventeen; her first novel completed, and on its way to winning the Booker prize, her second novel in the draft stage.

She was truly a woman of mystery; her origins shrouded in secrecy and ignorance.

The way Annaliese came to the attention of Robert Macleod, the solidly successful agent some fourteen years her senior, was a modern-day fairy tale. Magazines were forever rehashing the story of how the seventeen-year-old had merely walked into his agency one day and charmed the secretary into taking the handwritten draft of her first novel.

The secretary, who'd worked for Robert for many years and perhaps believed herself more competent than he at discovering new talent, had taken the manuscript home that weekend, wanting to read it for herself before taking a chance on passing it on to her employer.

Rushing back into work the following Monday, after having sat up until three that morning, weeping copiously and unable to put the novel down, the secretary had enthused about the sparkling new author with the innocent, untouched air, and the sweetly shy smile. The writer whose very first novel touched the heartstrings with its simple, homespun characters, and subtly sophisticated plot.

Intrigued, knowing his secretary was not one to get excited over nothing, Robert had read the novel himself that day, sitting quietly in his wood-panelled office, his secretary fielding all calls and rescheduling appointments whilst he turned the pages, the naivete of the words somehow emphasised by the gently sloping handwriting of the author.

When he finished the final page, after having read uninterrupted for six hours, he emerged, blinking, back into the real world feeling a frisson of excitement creep down his spine as he realised this new author was going to be huge and was going to revitalise his flagging agency.

Controlling his enthusiasm with difficulty, he buzzed his secretary for the author's details, and the awful truth dawned upon the hapless woman. Apart from the large, neatly written pile of papers containing the feelgood tale of love and family loyalty which had so bewitched them, the young girl had left nothing else – no address, no telephone number, not even her name.

A month passed and the manuscript sat on Robert's desk, inert, but by no means forgotten about. Occasionally, Robert would flip through the bundle of papers, scanning the neat schoolgirl-like writing, seeking some clue previously overlooked.

Then, one drizzly February evening, the phone rang as his secretary was applying lipstick for the tube journey home. After all, one never knew where or when Mr Right would show up.

Briefly, she contemplated leaving it, but thought Robert, still in his office, would probably take a dim view of that, so she snatched the phone up, dropping the lipstick in the process.

The next moment, as the softly lilting tone which invoked sensations of flower-strewn meadows and babbling brooks drifted down the line, the secretary sat bolt upright in her chair, the lost makeup dismissed, as she realised it was *her*. The missing author. The elusive girl they had been trying so hard to find.

"I'm sorry," interrupted Robert's secretary, desperately grabbing her pad and pen. "What did you say your name was? Annaliese?"

There was a long pause, and she felt her heart thud at the thought she might have once again lost her.

"Yes," agreed the girl slowly. "That's it, that's my name, Annaliese."

Taking the precaution of carefully writing down a contact telephone number and her address, just in case, and barely able to contain her excitement, the secretary placed the call through to an unsuspecting Robert.

She then loitered, pink with anticipation, until a good ten minutes past the end of the working day, until the twin realisations of the train she'd now missed, and the ever-increasing downpour outside had made her reluctantly put her coat on and go home.

The next day Annaliese came to the office, as beautiful and charming as the secretary remembered, and the romantic heart beating under her sensible grey suit throbbed with vicarious pleasure at the bemused and stunned expression on Robert's face, as she'd ushered Annaliese into his office.

Later, taking them coffee, she observed the look on his quietly handsome face when he offered Annaliese a cup, the pretty blush which appeared on the shy young girl's face, and the thrilled secretary felt she'd stepped straight into the pages of Jane Eyre.

An hour later they emerged, eyes not quite meeting in the agony of instant attraction. Robert had chivalrously helped Annaliese on with her coat, and his secretary beamed pinkly with pleasure as he explained he was taking the young lady out to lunch to discuss 'terms', and could she please leave any messages on his desk as he was unsure how long he would be.

A month later, two days after Annaliese's eighteenth birthday, they were married, leaving immediately for a month-long honeymoon in the Caribbean.

Upon their return, the secretary noted with satisfaction that Annaliese had matured and developed, money and grooming making her appear older than her age and that Robert looked almost a decade younger. Love and relaxation made him appear so near his new bride in years, that no innuendoes or snide comments were forthcoming at either Annaliese's youth or the disparity in their ages.

The following year, her first novel was published under the name of Annaliese Macleod. It was the instant and massive success that Robert had predicted.

Twenty-seven years and some twenty novels later, the marriage was still as solid as a rock, Robert's eyes lighting up whenever Annaliese entered the room, and in the nine or so years that I lived at the Hall, I never heard a cross word exchanged between them.

Magazines held them up as a true example that celebrity marriages could last and be happy, and until the night of my desperate flight, I never saw anything to contradict this premise.

Caro, I suppose, is the person I should deal with next – Annaliese's bulldog. Where Robert's background and introduction into Annaliese's life was a matter of common knowledge, very little was known of the woman who had controlled and managed Annaliese's affairs since she was eighteen years old.

All I knew, all anyone knew, was that Annaliese had hired Caroline O'Donnell on her return from honeymoon to aid her with correspondence and research. Gradually, as Annaliese became successful and rich in her own right, Caro helped her with her various charities and worthy causes, especially the string of orphanages that Annaliese founded.

In time, Caro ceased to be Annaliese's researcher and instead concentrated on deploying her not inconsiderable administrative skills in the practical side of Annaliese's life.

She had been married, many years previously, to an American named Edward Shayne. Rich and powerful, he owned a travelogue magazine, but although their relationship seemed cordial, Caro never travelled to America to see him and, to my knowledge, he never came to see her.

I knew the marriage did not last long, a year or so at most, and that they had been divorced for almost as long as Annaliese and Robert had been married.

During their brief marriage, they had a son, Luke. He worked as a photographer for his father's magazine, travelling around the world to take stunning, award-winning pictures of the world's most inaccessible regions.

I never met him. He lived with his father; a situation I found so unutterably alien it further biased my feelings towards Caro. How could any mother allow her only child to be taken so far away from her, to be raised by her ex-husband?

No matter how loving or wonderful a father he was, it still felt wrong to me; unnatural and unwomanly. I would sometimes look at Caro and wonder what precisely went on behind that hard-as-nails exterior. Could any woman be so devoid of emotion as Caro appeared?

I knew she loved Annaliese with a passion bordering on obsessive, including Robert within that obsession as an extension of Annaliese.

She also seemed to have a great affection for Mimi, and sometimes I saw her watching Essie when she believed herself unobserved, and her face would soften into an expression almost approaching love.

Towards the rest of us, she was cold and detached, tolerating the others, and positively detesting me. Her antipathy was constant and unwavering, even though I lived for many long and happy years with the Macleod's, and despite her gloomy predictions, had so far done nothing to hurt or damage them at all.

Mimi's real name was Marie Clare, and she was the next friend to join the charmed circle, becoming Annaliese's closest female friend soon after Annaliese and Robert had bought the Hall and moved away from the increasing stresses of London life.

Born to a French father and an English mother, Marie Clare's first nine years of life had passed normally enough in a small village located to the south of Paris.

Following the tragic death of her mother to cervical cancer, ten-year-old Marie Claire and her father moved to Paris to live with family, and it was there her father met Sophie. She was to become Marie Clare's stepmother and would have a profound effect on her life.

Stylish, chic, and beautiful, Sophie ran a small and exclusive boutique in the heart of the first city of fashion, and Marie Clare became fascinated by the heady, exciting world her stepmother occupied.

She would rush directly to the boutique every day after school, working there during the holidays, absorbing, and learning everything she could about the clothing and retail industry.

She wished to enter the industry immediately upon finishing university, yet Sophie persuaded her to take some time out to travel and see a little of the world before settling in one place, even if that place was Paris, which in Sophie's opinion was the only place in the world.

Gradually becoming excited at the thought of stretching her wings, Marie Clare decided to go to England, her mother's homeland, which she had never even visited, to look up relatives who were merely names on Christmas cards.

She boarded the Channel train one sunny June day, planning on spending a few short weeks having a brief holiday, before going home and commencing the start of the rest of her life.

She was never to return.

Upon reaching the small market town where her mother had been born and raised, Marie Clare wandered down to the park and sat neatly on a bench, admiring the massed banks of colourful blooms.

Looking in dismay at the women who passed by, dressed in ugly, unsuitable, and ill-fitting clothing, she muttered depreciating comments in French, longing for the stylish sophistication of the friends she'd left behind.

There was a snort of laughter from the bench next door, and Marie Clare had raised mortified and curious eyes to meet the laughing blue gaze of one of the most radiantly beautiful women she had ever seen. Sleek and sophisticated she was not, yet she had a certain something about her and Marie Clare itched to tell her how to dress to maximise her assets.

Embarrassed, and shy, instead she mumbled a hasty apology and hurried from the park.

Wandering around the town, trying to find her way back to her hotel, Marie Clare had taken a wrong turn and found herself drifting down a charming street where a small bistro had tables and potted trees outside. A second-hand bookshop invited you in, and there, sandwiched between the two, she found her shop.

Not knowing at first, that it was her shop, Marie Clare had merely paused, her trained eye noticing the potential of its twin, deep bay windows, and the appeal of the pretty stained-glass panels above the door.

Pressing her nose against its grimy glass, she noted with approval the depth and generous proportions of the shop's interior.

The next day, her feet somehow found their way back to the street and the shop, and she stood and looked and thought and considered.

A week later it was a done deal. She'd signed a year's lease on the shop, arranging with her stepmother's suppliers to establish a direct line into the UK, realising there would be teething problems and that it might take time to get established, but confident with her skills and knowledge that she would succeed because this town and its women needed her.

The first month was sketchy, the second month worse, and Marie Clare despaired. She needed sales to pick up or else she would be going home with her tail between her legs.

After all her grand plans and reassurances to her father and Sophie, she was determined that was something that could never happen.

Then, one day, the shop bell tinkled and in walked the woman from the park, eyes widening in gleeful recognition, and Marie Clare's life once again changed.

She was an author, the woman explained. A magazine was doing a centre page feature on her, so she needed new clothes, but was unsure what suited her. Would she be able to advise and help?

Of course, Marie Clare was only too delighted to help, relishing the chance to dress this oh-so-beautiful and unusual English woman in clothes that made the most of her elfin slim figure, and long golden hair.

Skilfully, she put together a capsule wardrobe to take her from a simple lunch date to a night at the opera, showing her how to wear the outfits and with what accessories.

The woman listened seriously, her blue eyes intent and absorbed, caught up in the passion the tiny fiery French woman felt for her subject.

In the end, she handed over her credit card for more money than Marie Clare had taken in a month, with a careless abandon that had Marie Clare biting her lip in admiration, and then gasping as she recognised the name.

The feature was a great success, the simple elegance and style of the outfits Marie Clare had chosen for her enhancing Annaliese's ethereal beauty and otherworldliness.

At Annaliese's insistence, the magazine had given the name and address of Marie Clare's shop as the place where Annaliese bought all her clothes. The business never looked back.

Stunned by the woman's generosity, Marie Clare sent her a stylish card offering a discount on all future purchases and thanking her for what she had done for her fledgeling business.

Squinting to read the illegible spidery handwriting, Annaliese misread the signature, believing the abbreviated Mme to be the name Mimi, and proceeded to address Marie Clare as such when she'd telephoned to invite her for supper at the Hall with herself and her husband.

Unwilling to correct her, Marie Clare left Annaliese in ignorance of her mistake until many months had passed and they were firm friends, the name too securely entrenched to be changed.

With the discovery of Annaliese, the fortunes of Robert's agency had taken a significant turn for the better. Even after they moved to the country, Robert still spent a few days a week in London, constantly searching for the new and exciting talent his agency had gained a reputation for being able to spot.

Influenced by Annaliese, Robert became more daring; more open to new authors whom many agencies would have rejected out of hand as not being commercial or mainstream enough.

Gradually, he built up a stable of fresh and original talent, somehow managing to tap into new trends and to always have a finger on the pulse of the moment – to be of the zeitgeist.

Very often, Annaliese would travel to London with him, staying at their comfortable apartment and filling her days whilst he was at work with writing, shopping, and visiting friends.

One day, deciding to drag her husband out to lunch if it was the last thing she did, Annaliese slipped into the office, noticing his secretary was absent and that a young man was sitting on the sofa, an air of nervousness hanging about him, his soft floppy brown hair showing clear signs of being anxiously tugged at.

"Where is everyone?" she enquired, and the young man turned worried brown eyes to her.

"Mr Macleod's secretary is off sick and he's running a bit behind on his appointments. I said I'd wait, but I'm afraid I've no idea how long he's going to be."

"Oh, no!" Annaliese exclaimed, biting her lip in annoyance. "I was hoping to see him."

The young man looked at her and his face softened. "Why don't you sit down?" he asked and patted the sofa next to him.

Intrigued, realising he had no idea who she was, Annaliese sat beside him. "Why are you here?" she asked, and the man flushed.

"The usual," he explained. "I've written a book and was hoping Mr Macleod might be interested in it. I have tried other agents but been rejected so many times I was about to give up, then saw an article about Mr Macleod in the Writers Magazine. It said he often gives chances to authors nobody else will even look at, so I thought, well, let's give it one more go."

"What is your book about?" Annaliese asked, feeling herself warm towards this intense young man with kindly brown eyes.

"Poetry through the ages and how it's reflected upon the society in which it was written, giving us an insight into the hearts and minds of the age," he replied, and Annaliese smiled at the fervour she saw in his eyes.

"Poetry is something you care very deeply for," she suggested, and the man coloured again.

"Yes, well all literature really; I lecture at Queens College, Cambridge." Annaliese started, hoping he hadn't noticed her instinctive reaction to the discovery that he lived so close to the Hall.

"Tell me about your book," she pleaded.

His eyes lit up and he talked. Believing her to be a fellow struggling author, he explained the ideas and thinking behind his book, and then got side-tracked into favourite poems and poets.

Annaliese listened, spellbound, caught up in his enthusiasm, thinking to herself how this man could talk to a group of inner-city kids about Byron and hold them enraptured in the palm of his hand by the power of his passion.

His voice was rich and melodious, like plum cake or finest malt whisky, and Annaliese felt tears spring to her eyes as he finished the final line of the poem.

"... and miles to go before I sleep..."

"That was so beautiful," she breathed and laid a hand on his arm. "You must get your book published, you simply must."

He dipped his head, obviously pleased.

"Thank you, you're too kind. But what about you?" he demanded. "I've spent all this time talking about myself and haven't even asked you about your book."

"Oh," Annaliese began casually. "It's nothing really, a silly little novel about how small women's lives can be."

"It sounds fascinating," he replied. "Can you tell me more?"

"I will," she promised, then stood at the sound of Robert's office door being opened. "But first, you must go in there and sell your book. Tell him all about it, exactly the way you told me."

"But..."

"Go on, now's your chance," and she gave him a gentle push. Robert turned from saying goodbye to his previous appointment, acknowledged his next, and Annaliese had slipped quietly out the door.

As he was ushered into the office, the man glanced back, feeling a pang of disappointment that the vivacious and bright young woman he had so enjoyed talking to was gone.

That evening, Annaliese persuaded her husband to give him a chance. Unsure, but trusting his wife's instincts, and too much in love to refuse her anything, Robert finally agreed, and Annaliese rejoiced that the young man, whom she insisted on calling her Miles-to-go-man, would finally be given the opportunity she firmly believed he deserved.

Annaliese's instincts, as usual, were correct. The large, beautifully illustrated, coffee-table book shot straight to the top of the Christmas bestsellers list, its author being invited onto a late-night art show as a latter-day champion of the dying art form of poetry.

Impressed by his personable nature and charismatic way of speaking, a BBC4 producer invited him onto the panel of judges for Young Poet of the Year. Then, after receiving scores of letters from children expressing how much they enjoyed the way he talked about poetry, and how he talked *to* them and not *at* them, he was invited to do a short programme about poetry in schools.

It was a surprise hit, and the young man's career was launched. Remaining true to his college though, he increased his appeal by limiting his TV appearances to one six-part series of his Poetry In... programmes and maybe a couple of guest appearances per year.

Thrilled by his new client's success, and urged on by Annaliese, Robert invited him to dinner, and the young man's face had been a picture when he discovered his agent's wife and bestselling author, was his sweet little friend who'd encouraged him that day in Robert's office.

Annaliese had hugged him with delight, exclaiming she had always known her Miles-to-go man would turn out to be a great success, and so another friendship was formed.

Miles's real name was William, yet somehow Miles suited him better and it was a name he adopted, happily joining Annaliese and Robert's ever-increasing circle of friends, his gentle good nature enabling him to get along with everyone.

Right from the moment they met, though, his heart was lost to Mimi. Sadly, the passionate and forthright Frenchwoman never had an inkling that buried deep beneath Miles's staid and buttoned-up academic exterior, beat a true and abiding love for her.

Desperately shy, constantly waiting for a sign of returned affection which never came, Miles resigned himself to forever being a friend. A much loved and appreciated one, but still, nonetheless, just a friend.

Andrew was the next to come along. Annaliese met him at a charity dinner she and Robert were attending in London. Bored rigid with the never-ending after-dinner speeches, and feeling her fixed smile wavering, Annaliese slipped unnoticed out of the function room and into the beautiful courtyard garden of the luxury hotel in which the event was being held.

Sighing with relief and believing herself alone, Annaliese thankfully pulled her shoes off and let her cramped toes stretch out in reprieve on the cool red-brick pathway. Sinking gracefully onto a low bench, she let the peace of the evening, and the harmony of the garden, wash over her.

"Feeling better?" a deeply amused voice had enquired in a rumbling Scottish burr.

Annaliese jumped in surprise, turning to peer into the darkness as a tall, burly, redheaded man sauntered into view clutching a bottle of whisky.

"Much, thank you," she replied, equally amused as he perched himself on the bench beside her. "Although I will pay good money for a swig of that," she continued, tapping his bottle with an elegantly manicured nail.

"Lovely lady, you may have some for free," he gallantly replied, holding out the bottle. Annaliese gulped it down, not even flinching as the neat alcohol hit the back of her throat.

Andrew would later comment it was this single act that made him realise they were going to be the best of friends. Annaliese handed him back the bottle with a sigh of relief and wiped her hand across her mouth, feeling the burn in the back of her throat.

"My word, that's better," she gasped, and in the moonlight, he beamed at her.

"You're a lady after my own heart," he exclaimed. "What's your name?"

"Annaliese, Annaliese Macleod."

"Ahh, the writer lady?" he enquired, and at Annaliese's nod of confirmation had smiled. "My mother loves your books, but I'm afraid I've never read them."

"That's okay," she shrugged carelessly, "Probably not your thing."

"No," he agreed and took another pull at the bottle, before handing it to Annaliese, watching in amused admiration as she matched him – swallow for swallow.

"So," she gasped, handing it back to him. "I've told you who I am, are you going to tell me exactly who it is I'm sharing whisky with?"

"That depends," he replied obscurely.

"On what?"

"On whether you want me to tell you my real name, or the name my friends know me as because believe me, my real name is one I'd rather forget."

"Okay," replied Annaliese slowly. "I'm sure it can't be that bad, why don't you tell me both?"

"Well, my surname is Oates, which is bad enough given that the only other Oates in history is the South Pole guy who decided to go for a walk in the snow. Also, it may have escaped your notice, but I'm Scottish ..."

"No?" interrupted Annaliese, an amused smile tugging at her lips.

"I'm afraid so," he continued. "So, no jokes about porridge-oat eating Scots please, because I've more or less heard them all."

"All right," agreed Annaliese. "So, the surname is not great. It's not the worst I've ever heard, but it's not the best either. You going hit me with the first name?"

"Hamish Malcolm Macduff."

"Ouch," said Annaliese in sympathy, and patted his arm reassuringly. "Don't worry; I'm sure your parents loved you really. So, what do your friends call you?"

"Andrew."

"Andrew?" At his nod, she shrugged. "Okay, boringly normal compared to that lovely trio. Any particular reason why Andrew?"

"Because I live in St Andrew's."

"Fair enough," Annaliese agreed, taking another slug of whisky. "So, what are you doing so far away from home, Andrew?"

"I've been staying with a friend, my best friend, for a couple of weeks and his godmother had tickets for this do and asked us to accompany her. She's a real character. We both enjoy her company, so said we'd come. I was hoping it would take my mind off the fact I've got to go home tomorrow."

"Why don't you want to go back? Don't you like your home?"

"I love it, it's ... well, my father's a solicitor and it's always been his dream I'd become one, too, and go into partnership with him, you know, Oates & Oates, that sort of thing. I've done all my legal training, put in the time, and learnt what I needed to know because at the time I couldn't think of anything else I wanted to do. I knew it would mean the world to him and I wanted to please him, so I did it ... but now..."

"But now you've realised you don't want to be a solicitor after all?" guessed Annaliese, and Andrew nodded mournfully. "So, what do you want to do?"

"That's just it, I don't know. I mean, it's crazy, isn't it? I've done all the training and have a guaranteed job and top-whack salary waiting for me, but the thought of being a solicitor for the rest of my life is making me feel physically sick. I don't know what else I want to be, I only know what I don't want to be, and that's a solicitor." He paused and pulled on the bottle.

"I know if I tell the old man it's going to break his heart, so I don't know what to do. These past couple of weeks were supposed to help me get things clear in my head, but if anything, they've made things worse."

"In what way?" asked Annaliese gently, as he passed the bottle back to her and she tipped it elegantly to her mouth.

He glanced at her, noticing the way the moonlight reflected off the slim white column of her throat and set her golden hair aglow. Christ, he thought blearily, she sure was a looker. He wondered how old she was, certainly not many years older than him.

"Well, I've been staying with a friend. He's stuck in a job he hates as well, working for an auction house. I know he's miserable in London where he doesn't know anyone. He, well, doesn't make friends easily, and finds it very hard to talk to people. They tend to think he's arrogant and aloof, but he's not, not really, he's a very deep and reserved person. I see him struggling on, day after day, gritting his teeth, getting on with it, and wonder if I should do the same. But then I keep thinking there must be more to life than that, putting up with shit because you can't see a way out. There *must* be more."

"There is more to life than that," agreed Annaliese, putting her small white hand over his large capable one. "Don't stop believing, Andrew. Something will come along when you least expect it, and it'll be right, and you'll know it's right. As for your father, well, all any parent wants, is for their child to be happy. Talk to him, Andrew, and explain your feelings. Give him a chance to understand. He may surprise you."

"Maybe," agreed Andrew uncertainly. They both looked up as the sound of prolonged applause erupted from inside the hotel.

"I suppose we'd better get back inside."

"Yes, I suppose so," said Annaliese with obvious reluctance and handed him back the bottle. "Give me your number, Andrew. I'd like to stay in touch if that's all right."

"Sure," confirmed Andrew, and watched as she programmed it into her phone.

"I'd better go," murmured Annaliese, and pressed a quick kiss onto his cheek. "It was wonderful meeting you, Andrew. You'll see, things will work out."

"Yeah, right, thanks Annaliese, you take care of yourself."

She quickly slipped her heeled evening shoes back on and floated into the hotel. He realised after she left that she had made no attempt to give him her number, and he wondered if he'd ever hear from her again.

But he did. Three weeks after he returned home and faced the music, finally finding the courage from somewhere to tell his father that his dreams of a brass plaque stating Oates & Oates were not to be.

To his surprise, his father merely gave him a long dour look, remarked dryly it'd taken him long enough to realise what he'd suspected years ago, and what the bloody hell did he want to do with his life now he'd wasted years of it training to be a solicitor?

Stunned, Andrew mumbled how sorry he was to let him down, to which his father's expression softened. He told him not to be so bloody daft, that all he wanted was for Andrew to be happy.

Of course, if Andrew had decided he truly wanted to be a solicitor his father would have been delighted, but as he'd decided he wasn't cut out for it he needed to get off his arse and decide what it was that would make him happy.

Andrew thought of Annaliese and wished he had some way to get in touch with her to tell her what he'd done. A fortnight later his phone rang, and it was her.

She was giddy with exciting news. Her local wine merchant was retiring and was looking to sell his business as a going concern, and she wondered if he was interested.

Taken aback – becoming a wine merchant was not something he'd ever considered – he thought about it, feeling a frisson of excitement as she talked to him about the business and the area.

He was interested enough to fly down, staying with Annaliese and Robert at the Hall for a few days, meeting with the wine merchant who was a close, personal, friend of Annaliese's, and looking around the business.

He spent hours checking out the market town in which it was based, hiring a car to explore the surrounding countryside, pouring over the wine merchant's books, and spending a day in the small shop attached to the business which sold wines and spirits. He realised it was already a good, steady business, but had the potential to be so much more.

Raising the money to buy the business had been surprisingly easy. His savings, a loan from his father who flew down to fully investigate the business into which his son was asking him to invest, and a small investment from Annaliese, had been enough to secure himself a new career as a wine merchant.

Business was good from the start, with Andrew taking great care to offer existing clients the same excellent care they'd become accustomed to, as well as seeking out new clients and constantly looking for ways to improve and expand on the services he offered.

The business thrived until finally he went to see Annaliese one day and told her he was thinking of taking on a partner.

"That's wonderful news," she enthused. "Who did you have in mind?"

So, Andrew told her about his friend. They met on their first day at university and sat next to each other in their first class. Andrew had nodded and said a friendly hello to the classically handsome young man sitting next to him, only to be dismissed with a curt nod and blank expression. Well sod you then, Andrew thought angrily, just trying to be friendly mate.

Concentrating on what the teacher was saying, he was amazed when he was called upon to answer a question and even more amazed that he got it right, the teacher nodding thoughtfully.

"Yes, that's an interesting point... I'm sorry, first day of term, I haven't had a chance to get familiar with everyone's names."

"It's Oates, sir," Andrew had replied, and there was a small snigger in the class.

"Oates, eh?" enquired the lecturer, then glanced at the chisel-jawed stony countenance of his neighbour.

"So, if he's Oates, I guess you must be Scott?"

The class had erupted into good-natured laughter. Andrew saw the flush that briefly stained the young man's face, the panicked look that flashed into his eyes, and realised he wasn't the arrogant prick Andrew had dismissed him as but instead seemed cripplingly shy.

Andrew felt a twinge of sympathy and a pang of interest. Was interested enough that after the lecture he invited Scott for coffee, refused to take no for an answer, and so the deep and abiding partnership of Oates and Scott had been born.

Scott's difficult to get to know, he explained to Annaliese, concerned she might not like his friend, but worth the effort because once you got to know him and he decided to trust you, then you had a friend for life. One who was constant, and loyal, and would do anything for a friend.

And so, Scott had come for a visit. Achingly unhappy with his life in London and missing his friend more than he liked to admit, even to himself, Scott looked at what Andrew was offering – half share in a business which intrigued him, and which Scott could see would be more fun than work.

A relaxed lifestyle in a friendly town surrounded by beautiful countryside, and the companionship of his best friend. His only friend if Scott was brutally honest with himself. Add to that the fact his godmother lived only an hour's drive away and Scott was halfway to agreeing on the first day of his visit.

Then Andrew took him to meet Annaliese. They drove through the tall ornate gates, Scott's eyes impenetrable and unreadable as he looked at the great imposing Hall, its windows flashing gold in the morning sun.

They parked, wandered around the back, and found Annaliese curled up on a swing, one small bare foot flat on the ground giving an idle push now and again to set it swaying. Her long golden hair was flowing over her face, and a glass of fresh lemonade was cold in her hand, beads of condensation misting its frosted surface. She looked up at their approach, the sun shining directly into her eyes and setting them on fire like flaming sapphires.

"Darling," she exclaimed, jumping to her feet and hugging Andrew, before turning to examine Scott with interest, tilting her head to look up at his superior height; noting the proud lift to his chin and the supercilious lift of his eyebrow.

But her keen eye also noted the slight tic at the corner of his mouth, the brief flash of anxious anticipation in his eyes, and the fact his hands were ever so slightly shaking.

Instantly, she saw what it had taken Andrew months of patient digging to discover. This was a man who didn't trust easily or open to people lightly yet was one who craved human contact and companionship. She wondered what had happened to make him so mistrustful of people.

As for Scott, he would later tell me he took one look into Annaliese's eyes and fell completely, and instantly, in love. A deep and sincere friendship was formed that day, one which lasted for over twelve years with never a disagreement or a cross word, until the day she died.

Scott told me the story of his introduction into Annaliese's life one summer's evening as we sat outside on the steps, him smoking his guiltily illicit cigarette, and me keeping him company in an agony of unrequited love.

He was quite open with that story, yet no matter how I pushed, I could never get him to go any further back in his life than the day he met Andrew. It galled me that the man I loved trusted no one with his origins. Not even Andrew, his best friend, knew for certain where he came from, or who his family were. Like Annaliese, he appeared to have sprung fully formed into adulthood, his childhood a secret.

"So, what is your real name?" I asked curiously and he hesitated, quirking his brow at me in obvious reluctance.

"Nigel," he eventually said, and my lips twitched with amusement.

"Nigel?" At my snort of laughter, he glared at me sourly, before a reluctant smile crept onto his face. "I prefer Scott," I remarked, and he shrugged, stubbing out his cigarette on the step.

"So, do I," he said, holding down a hand to heave me to my feet, the tone of his voice indicating the subject was well and truly closed.

Mimi, as the first of Annaliese's close little circle of friends, had been accepting and charming to Miles, appreciating his intelligence and gentle humour. She also liked Scott, understanding his reticence on some basic level, his reluctance to trust, and maybe in one respect, admiring him for his self-control. She watched the quiet understated way he conducted his business and his life, finding nothing to condemn or criticise in his behaviour.

But with Andrew, it was a completely different story. Right from the beginning she hated, loathed, and detested him for his red hair and large muscular body, preferring the sophisticated slim elegance of Frenchmen or men like Scott.

He was too loud, too confident, too brash, and too Scottish. His devil-may-care attitude to his career made her snap at him for being reckless and flippant, not seeing that beneath his brash exterior there lay a canny mind, a loyal heart, and a generous friendly nature.

Refusing to look any further than the surface, she clashed royally with him, her fiery French spirit making sparks fly every time she took on his volatile Scottish temperament.

In vain, Annaliese begged her to cease this endless hostility. As far as Mimi was concerned, Andrew was a bluff, arrogant bore with no finesse or manners, his simple, unassuming personality the complete antithesis of everything Mimi found attractive in a man.

At first, amused by her constant sniping, then perturbed, then annoyed, Andrew railed about the tiny Frenchwoman to Scott, who listened in amusement, wondering when Andrew and Mimi would stop all this nonsense and acknowledge the truth the others had known all along.

He was completely amazed that his usually observant friend could be so blind to the sexual chemistry which churned and bubbled between him and Mimi.

That the reason she gave him such a hard time was that she found him intensely attractive and was angrily fighting against it, refusing to believe she could go so off type, and desperately denying her feelings.

Things finally came to a head one sunny day in late July.

In the centre of the park surrounding the Hall was a large and peaceful lake, the habitat of swans and ducks. In the middle of the lake was a small, wooded island, perfect for picnics, and it was to this island an even more silent than usual Scott rowed Andrew and Mimi one day.

They were meeting the others, and he watched with wryly amused eyes as they studiously ignored each other, furious the others had gone ahead, and they were stuck in the same boat.

They landed at the small shingle beach, Andrew holding out a hand to assist Mimi, a hand which she slapped away, her long brown legs flashing in the midday sun as she climbed nimbly out of the boat and splashed through the shallows onto dry land.

Carrying bags and rugs, they made their way to the normal picnic spot, a beautiful clearing in the middle of the island, surprised to find it empty. It was clear someone had been there from the spread-out rugs, baskets of food, and the large tin bucket already full of cold lake water in which rested several bottles of champagne.

"Where is everyone?" demanded Mimi in surprise, surveying the deserted clearing and glaring evilly at Andrew as if he were somehow responsible for their absence.

"Don't know," Scott shrugged. "I'll go and get the rest of the stuff from the boat. Why don't you two go down to the other beach and see if they're there? Maybe they've gone for a swim."

And before Mimi could complain at being left alone with Andrew, or demand she accompany Scott instead, he slipped away quietly through the trees, leaving the two protagonists staring at each other in mutual distrust.

"Do you think they're at the other beach?" demanded Mimi, and Andrew shook his head, puzzled. The island was small. If the others were already on it then unless they were keeping unusually silent for some reason, they should be able to hear them.

"This is ridiculous," Mimi began. "They must be…"

Andrew tensed, holding up his hand for silence. Furious, Mimi was about to let rip, then heard what had caught his attention; the sound of oars being dipped into the water.

They looked at each other puzzled. Then the same thought struck simultaneously, and they hurtled back through the trees, skidding to a halt at the lake's edge, staring in disbelief at Scott rowing determinedly and unhesitatingly away from the island.

"Scott!" bellowed Andrew. "What the hell do you think you're doing?"

"Come back!" screamed Mimi, angrily. "Don't leave me here with this imbecile!"

"Sorry, guys." Scott's voice was toneless. "You're there until you sort out whatever your problem is because we're sick and tired of you two constantly sniping and bickering like a pair of six-year-olds."

Speechless with shock, Andrew and Mimi looked at each other in a shared mutual horror before bellowing orders to come back in Scott's direction, Andrew's voice deep with indignation, and Mimi's shrill with incensed rage.

Studiously ignoring them, Scott reached the other side as Annaliese slipped through the trees and helped him tie up the boat.

Waving to her stranded friends and blowing them a kiss, she waited as Scott climbed out of the boat, slung an easy arm around her shoulders, and then the pair of them set off for the Hall without so much as a backwards glance.

"Swim across and bring back a boat!" Mimi demanded, her tone imperious, her dark eyes haughty.

Andrew looked at the deep, icy cold water of the lake with distaste and shook his head.

"There's no way in hell I'm going in there," he'd stated mildly. Mimi screamed in disbelief before launching into a stream of French which she loosened in his direction, accompanied by much gesturing and hand waving.

Andrew's French was strictly of the schoolboy variety, but he comprehended enough that his brows shot up at some of the crude, violent, and downright anatomically impossible insults Mimi was subjecting him to.

He listened patiently for a while, but when it seemed she was never going to run out of steam, he simply picked her up and ignoring the blows her small fists rained down on him, walked with her to the water's edge.

"Lady," he stated flatly, "you need to cool down." And he dumped her in the lake, turned his back on her outraged howls, and made his way back to the picnic site.

By the time Mimi heaved herself out, drenched and covered in duckweed, and stomped furiously after him, almost beside herself with rage, he was sitting in a deck chair sipping champagne, and showing evident signs of enjoyment as he listened to her crashing and cursing her way through the trees.

"You bastard!"

"Champagne, my sweet?"

"Fuck off!"

"My, my, little lady, that's real pretty language coming from such a classy woman."

A further stream of French came in response, and Andrew raised his brows, lips quirking into a smile.

"What's so funny, you great, dumb ox?"

"I was thinking how amazingly beautiful and sexy you look right now."

Completely wrong-footed, Mimi's jaw dropped, and she stood quietly, chest heaving with exertion, eyes wide and disbelieving as Andrew slowly rose and walked across to her, running his large thumb across her bottom lip.

Their eyes clashed. Mimi found she had problems breathing and Andrew swallowed as heat, devastating for its unexpectedness, roared down his body leaving him stunned and quaking.

"Don't ..." she said as he bent to her, and he shook his head in disbelief.

"I can't not ..." he murmured.

She moaned as his mouth closed hungrily onto hers and his large hands slid over her damp body, feeling her tremble as she kissed him back, hesitantly at first, then with growing need and desperation. Hands pulled at clothing, mouths sought and greedily consumed, limbs shook with unbearable desire.

Urgently, they pulled each other down onto the already spread rug and the peaceful clearing filled with the sounds of their passionate, long overdue, lovemaking.

By the time Scott rowed back hours later, they had admitted to each other and themselves that they were violently, passionately in love, always had been, but had both been too stubbornly blind to realise it.

They spent the afternoon making love, stunned at the blissful ecstasy they found, and Andrew had quietly decided that this was the woman he was going to marry.

As Scott pulled the boat up onto the beach he looked warily around wondering if one, or both, were going to attack him.

Calling out to warn them of his presence, he hesitated, a small, satisfied smile playing over his lips at the unmistakable sounds of people getting hastily, and hurriedly, dressed.

He pretended not to notice the buttons on Mimi's dress now done up incorrectly, her kiss-swollen lips, or the love bite perched jauntily on the side of Andrew's neck.

Helping them carry everything back to the boat he merely asked, "All right now?"

Seeing how they looked at each other, he realised with disconcerting surprise, that it wasn't just a sexual itch they'd needed to get out of their system. His best friend was in love.

And judging by the way Mimi was clinging to his hand, her body moulding itself fiercely to his side, the way their eyes met and held, she loved him back every bit as passionately.

Nobody was surprised a few months later when Andrew and Mimi announced their engagement, marrying the following year, and setting up home together in a delightful little Georgian former rectory on the outskirts of town.

Their relationship was always going to be volatile and passionate, yet their friends rejoiced they found such happiness in each other. One of their friends though, Miles, nursed a secret heartache that it wasn't him Mimi had chosen.

But his generous soul was happy for her obvious delight with her husband, and he genuinely liked and admired Andrew, so quietly buried his feelings for Mimi deep under layers of friendship and tried to think no more of them.

The last of the inner circle to join, apart from me of course, was Ferdie. The group clown, his outrageous comments and explosive sense of humour masked a more sensitive and troubled side to his nature, and I wondered how he'd become a member of the *coterie*, later learning he'd been introduced to the group by Miles.

Miles had long known about Ferdie, he lectured English history at the college where Miles worked, but other than on a professional basis their paths had never crossed.

Miles knew little about him other than the students adored him, and other members of staff were constantly muttering about his outlandish manner and eccentric teaching methods.

One evening, Miles was making his way to the staff car park, relieved it was the last day and the long summer holiday lay before him, and looking forward to the end-of-term party Annaliese was throwing in his honour that evening.

Turning the corner, he was surprised to see Ferdie perched on a bench, his usually smiling countenance bleak and sorrowful. Miles paused, keys in hand. He was running late and didn't really know the man, yet it went against his nature to walk away from someone as clearly troubled as Ferdie appeared to be.

"Is everything all right?" he asked.

Ferdie looked up, startled, and Miles had noticed with concern his pale and drawn face, the hands which were shaking, constantly twisting, and pulling at the strap of his briefcase.

"No, not really," Ferdie had replied, flashing Miles a watery smile. "I've been dumped," he'd confided. "By text, which somehow makes it so much worse, and now I don't know what to do."

"Oh," said Miles, uncomfortably. "Bad luck, did she give a reason?"

"No, the bastard said he needed his space and that it wasn't me…"

Miles blinked, his brain busily assimilating the information he had been handed, remembering the rumours about Ferdie he'd previously dismissed as vicious gossip.

"I mean, needed more space," Ferdie had continued, apparently oblivious to Miles staring open-mouthed, in awkward silence.

"What exactly does that mean? I would have given him space. He could have had all the bloody space he needed. Shit, he could have gone to the moon for a long weekend if he wanted. And it's not me? Why say that when it quite plainly is me? So anyway, there it is, my dilemma in a nutshell. He's back at my flat packing his stuff so I don't want to go there, and I can't think of anyone else to inflict my hurt pride on."

"Come to a party," Miles had blurted out, then could have chewed off his tongue for his stupidity. "I mean, if you want to," he stuttered, as Ferdie stared at him in surprise. "Some friends of mine are throwing an end-of-term party for me. You're welcome to come if you like."

"All right," Ferdie had agreed eagerly and scrambled to his feet. "Only, I'll have to come in your car, the bastard's borrowing mine to move all his stuff. I'll get a taxi back later. Thank you, I think a party will be just the thing to take my mind off it all."

Miles led the way to his car with Ferdie leaping about him, chattering excitedly like a hyperactive leprechaun. As they got in, he frowned.

"I've realised I don't even know your name?"

"Well, it's William, but my friends call me Miles."

"Why?"

"Umm, it's a long story, I'll tell you later."

"Okay," agreed Ferdie affably. "By the way, I'm Ferdie."

"I know."

"Tell me about these friends of yours," demanded Ferdie, so Miles did.

It wasn't until they were driving through the ornate gateway to the Hall and Ferdie squealed in ecstatic pleasure as the Hall and its breathtaking surroundings came into view, that Miles had a sudden thought.

"Ferdie?"

"Yes?"

"I'm not ... I mean ... well, that is ... what I'm trying to say..."

"What are you trying to say?"

"I'm straight," Miles blurted out, and Ferdie grinned wickedly at him.

"Well of course you are, sweetie," he agreed innocently. "I never for a moment thought you were anything else."

Ferdie was an instant hit with the group, wickedly funny and yet genuinely sweet. Annaliese adopted him as her jester, granting him access to her inner circle of friends, who in turn were amused by his unfailing good nature and flippant attitude to life.

Underneath all the jokes and humour lay a troubled side to Ferdie, a black dog of depression that sometimes perched on his shoulder.

During these periods he clung to his friends, needing their understanding and love to pull him out of the pit; to support him until it had passed, and he was once again their dear Ferdie, naughty and bright, the life and soul of the party.

Ferdie adored Annaliese and laughed when he told her he would cheerfully lay down his life for her, but something in his eyes left no doubt that it was how he felt.

After Annaliese, Ferdie was closest to Miles, perhaps remembering it was through Miles he'd been allowed access into Annaliese's world, or perhaps it was because with Andrew and Mimi being a definite couple, Scott being difficult for Ferdie to understand, and Caro quite plainly having no patience with his outrageous ways, Miles was a sympathetic loner in the group, just like him.

So, there we were, our merry little band of nine, including me. Always together, we were bound by invisible threads of need and commitment. Although our personalities were diverse, somehow, we came together and worked in perfect harmony, with Essie the child of the whole group.

Thrilled to be one of her godparents, along with Annaliese and Scott, I felt we were all her surrogate parents and that her upbringing was a joint effort.

Of course, I learnt all this gradually over long years in which nothing much happened, other than the fact I was happy and successful. And I had no idea as I sat with Annaliese in the garden, watching the others play a haphazard game of cricket almost exactly eight years after I'd first met them, that this was the last weekend we would all be together like this, happy and innocent.

Beside me, Annaliese watched, and we both shivered as a large cloud obliterated the face of the sun, plunging the garden temporarily into darkness. She said something, something which I heard, but when I asked her what she meant she laughed and dismissed it as nothing; something silly which had popped into her head for no apparent reason.

Later, I would remember her words and wonder.

"What a strange group we are," she quite clearly murmured. "Everyone's in love with the wrong person..."

CHAPTER VII – RUTH

"The boy's head over heels in love with you,"

"What are you doing today, Eve?" At Scott's question, I looked up, blinking in the strong sunlight pouring through the windows of the morning room. Breakfast had long since finished and we were alone. Ferdie and Miles, who had both stayed the night, had already left for work.

Annaliese had not been feeling well and was still in bed and Robert was closeted in his study, apparently working, but I knew he would probably be worrying too much about Annaliese to get anything done.

Annaliese, never normally ill, was being plagued with mysterious blinding headaches which seemed to descend for no discernible reason, leaving her weak and nauseated.

We were all concerned, despite her protests that she was fine and that it was probably old age creeping up on her.

Scott repeated his question, and I realised my attention had wandered away from him, gazing in blind intensity through the large windows at the blue skies and large billowy clouds which were massing high up in the heavens.

"Sorry," I said. "Daydreaming. Umm, what am I doing today? Well, not a lot. I'm sort of in-between jobs; Annaliese has no work for me, and I can't decide between these two latest offers which have come in the post."

"Who are they from?" he asked in interest, pouring himself a cup of coffee, and wincing at its coldness.

"Well, one's from Lady Constance. She's writing another of her bodice rippers and wants me to check out a few things. That's only a day or two's work. And there's Sebert Foxton..."

"Oh?" Scott's eyebrows rose. "And what does he want?"

"Apparently ..." I paused and surveyed the letter, "he's re-writing the Jack the Ripper story and wants me to go back to all the primary sources to see if anything fresh and exciting leaps out at me."

I pulled a face at Scott. Sebert Foxton was a much-loved and popular historical author, even if his writing was a little overblown and florid for my taste. I had worked for him several times but, after the fiasco of our last encounter, was reluctant to place myself within his grasp again.

"What happened?" Scott asked, and I realised I had voiced my concerns aloud.

"Oh, nothing too drastic," I replied casually. "He somehow got the idea I was a rampant little filly desperate to be taught a thing or two by a sensitive man of more mature years and ended up chasing me around the library."

"Randy old billy goat!" exclaimed Scott in horror. "How did you manage to convince him that no, really did mean no?"

"Hit him in his more mature years with the Oxford English Dictionary."

"Ouch," winced Scott. "I guess that did the trick?"

"Hmm," I agreed. "So, you can see why I'm not keen to repeat the experience."

"I'm amazed he had the cheek to ask you."

"Yes well, he says, and I quote ... 'I am hoping, dearest Eve, that we can put the regrettable incident in the past and continue the bright path of friendship our feet had so jauntily begun'."

I dropped the letter and raised my brows at Scott, who smiled and shook his head.

"Well, as you're not doing anything, would you'd like to come out with me for the day?"

"Ooh, yes please," I cried. "Where are we going?" I reflected how not long ago I would have been rendered speechless at the thought of spending a whole day alone with Scott. Back in the days when I was passionately, madly, and completely head-over-heels in love with him, I schemed to find ways to be on my own with him. Thank heavens I was over that crush.

Not once had Scott ever given any indication that I was anything other than a much-loved friend. Gradually, over the years, I had successfully managed to bury my feelings so deeply only the occasional pang would surface when I would look at his face and sigh a little at what might have been.

"I'm going to visit my godmother and see a client who runs a hotel quite close to her. Then I thought I might take you out to lunch somewhere," he said.

"That sounds great!" I beamed at him in delight. "When do you want to leave?"

"Whenever you're ready," he replied, leaning back in his chair with patient amusement as I squeaked with excitement and rushed from the room to change.

It was a glorious summer day. Running lightly down the steps of the Hall, I saw with pleasure he'd put down the top of his sports car. He looked up, the sun glinting off his dark eyes and for a moment I fancied something stirred within them.

My heart stumbled in my chest. Then, whatever it was, was gone, and he was Scott again, smiling in gentle approval at my outfit.

"Very nice," he commented. "Is it new?"

"It is," I agreed, climbing carefully into the low-slung car, and making sure my green, linen shift dress was arranged neatly over my suntanned thighs, as he courteously closed the door for me, jumped into the driver's seat and we were off.

Scott's a good driver. I always relax when he's at the wheel, and now I tipped my head back as sunlight flickered on my face. Stretching out on expensive leather seats, I felt his gaze brush over the long silky brownness of my legs.

I'm curious, even anxious, about meeting Scott's godmother. I knew nothing about her, due mainly to the fact that Scott never talked about her. But then, Scott never talked about anything, his complete lack of small talk both at times a welcome relief, and an annoyance.

I did know he went to see her regularly. She seemed to be the only family he had, at least the only family he ever mentioned. Until now, he visited her strictly on his own so my curiosity about her had remained unsatisfied.

"Where does your godmother live?" I asked, as Scott expertly joined the A road and put his foot down, the car bucking like an unbroken mustang beneath us.

"Southwold," he replied, and I nodded. Southwold was a charming little town on the coast an hour's drive away, and my spirits rose at the thought of spending a day at the coast.

I pulled on my sunglasses and leaned back, enjoying the sensation of the wind rushing through my hair and the sun warm on my bare arms and legs. Scott glanced at me and smiled.

"You look like a cat stretched out in the sun."

"Hmm, I love the heat," I sighed blissfully, flexing my legs, aware that my dress had ridden even further up my thighs. Scott's gaze briefly flicked over their tanned, well-toned length before his eyes swivelled firmly back to the road, hands tightening ever so slightly on the wheel.

A smile pulled at my lips. Was it possible he wasn't as indifferent to me as I thought? Hmm, I mused, definitely a very interesting notion, and one which required a great deal of thought.

The rest of the journey passed uneventfully, and it wasn't long before we reached the outskirts of Southwold. I looked about in interest as Scott indicated right and turned off the main road onto a small lane which grew progressively narrower as we crept along it. Overgrown shrubs brushed the side of the car, and I took my sunglasses off, flinching away as a long snagging branch brushed up and over the windscreen, flopping down onto my shoulder.

"Sorry," remarked Scott. "I keep telling Ruth she needs to employ someone to sort out the garden and this lane, but she keeps forgetting."

"Is that your godmother's name?" I asked curiously. "Ruth?"

"Yes, Ruth Amberson-Smythe. You may have heard of her," he added casually. "She writes books."

My head snapped around and my mouth dropped open as incomprehensible squeaks emitted from me, which Scott listened to in evident amusement.

"Ruth Amberson-Smythe is your godmother?" I finally managed to gasp. He nodded. "*The* Ruth Amberson-Smythe?" He nodded again, and I sank back into the seat in stunned silence.

Ruth Amberson-Smythe was something of a British institution. Seventy years old and a dame, she was one of the most respected and best-loved historical authors. Her many novels had been translated into practically every language on Earth and were constantly on the bestsellers list. Her attention to detail was legendary. So precise were her historical facts, her novels had long been regarded by history teachers everywhere as essential tools for inspiring interest in their students.

I loved her books. I think I had read practically everything she had ever written and knew Ferdie would have traded a kidney to be where I was right now. I chortled a little at how jealous he would be when I told him.

All this time, Scott's godmother had been a woman whom I respected and admired more than any other author. All this time and he had never even so much as hinted at the fact. I glared at him with hostility.

"Why," I began through gritted teeth, "did you never tell me Ruth Amberson-Smythe was your godmother?"

"You never asked," he shrugged.

I clenched my fists, struggling valiantly not to hit him. "There are times," I ground out, "when I really, *really* hate you, Scott."

"I've recommended you, to carry out some research work for her into sugar plantations in Jamaica. She's going there soon and would want you to go with her," he continued.

"And there are times," I squealed, "when I really, *really* love you! Me? She wants to take me to Jamaica?"

"Well, that depends," he answered, bringing the car to a halt outside a huge, gorgeous, but completely run-down Edwardian villa set in the middle of rambling, equally run-down gardens.

"On what?" I asked curiously, clambering out of the car, following him up the steps and through the ornate front door.

"On whether she likes you," he replied bluntly. "I'm afraid if she doesn't, she will tell you so to your face. Ruth's not big on tact, sees it as hypocrisy, and as she doesn't like many people, tends to be rude on a regular basis."

I smiled, but fingers of nervous anticipation rattled up and down my spine, and my feet dragged a little, as I followed Scott into a large and dusty hallway which felt cool after the brilliant sunshine outside. I shivered, and Scott glanced at me in concern.

"You okay?"

"I'm fine; it's chilly in here." He nodded, pushed open a door on the right, and I followed him into a large shady room that was only marginally warmer than the hallway due to the sun streaming through a pair of extremely dirty French doors, out of which could be spied lush green foliage and old terracotta pots filled with an overgrown collection of perennials.

I looked around curiously, eyes widening as I realised that apart from the large fireplace and the massive oil painting above it, every other square inch of wall was taken up by books, masses of them. They marched in uneven ranks from floor to ceiling.

A glance showed no order to their arrangement, and I saw a tatty and much-read copy of War & Peace rubbing shoulders with a Harry Potter, piled on top of which were about half a dozen Mills & Boons.

My head swivelled, noticing the large portrait above a fireplace still heaped high with ash from its last fire. I recognised it as one of Ruth. Painted in the mid-1960s, it showed her reclining on a sofa. Pale pouting lips and kohl-lined eyes stared at me from the face of the woman who had been as much an "It" girl of the swinging sixties as Twiggy and Mary Quant.

"I was considered quite a looker then," drawled a voice behind me. "But of course," it continued, as I turned to see Ruth herself, resplendent in a large, winged armchair, "I was only 20, and any woman who can't fool the world into thinking she's a looker when she's young is either a ninny or so monumentally ugly there's no hope for her."

"This is my godmother, Ruth," began Scott, crossing to her and planting an affectionate kiss on her lined cheek. "And this," he continued, waving a hand in my direction, "is my very good friend Eve."

"So, you've finally brought her to see me have you?" demanded Ruth waspishly. "Well, come here then, let me have a look at you. Let's see why you're all I ever hear about when my godson visits me."

I stepped forward into the sunlight, noting with satisfaction that Scott seemed flustered by her words. So, he talked about me a lot, did he? Good. That too was worthy of later consideration.

There was a loaded pause as the elderly author studied me, her light blue eyes keen with intelligence. She looked me over, rather as one might a horse one was thinking of buying, then waved her hand dismissively at Scott.

"All right, you've brought her to me, now make yourself scarce while your Eve and I get acquainted, and I decide whether she'll suit."

"But, Ruth, I ..." began Scott, and she quelled him with a single glance.

"Go," she ordered. "Come back later. If I like her, I'll let you take us both out to lunch."

"I'm sorry, Eve." Scott looked helplessly at me.

"Don't worry." I smiled at his consternation. "We'll be fine."

"All right," he sighed in resignation. "I'll go and see my client and be back in a couple of hours."

There was a long silence after he'd left and the throb of his car's engine had faded back into the stillness of her house, the only sounds being the ponderous ticking of an antique clock, cheerfully telling the wrong time on the mantelpiece, and the busy chirping of birdsong floating in through the open window.

"So," she finally said, "you're Eve. I've heard a lot about you."

"Yes," I agreed, cheerfully, "I'm Eve. I'm afraid I've heard absolutely nothing about you."

She nodded thoughtfully. Her hair, piled in a large messy bun at the base of her neck, made a sudden bid for freedom and she absentmindedly pushed it back into place, jabbing hairclips randomly into the greying strands.

"It may have escaped your notice," she began, her tone dripping with irony, "but my godson is not one for idle chitchat."

"I'd say that's a bit of an understatement," I replied. "I think in the eight years I've known Scott, I've probably had longer conversations with my hairdresser, than with him."

She snorted, eyeing me with interest.

"I expect you'd like coffee," she snapped.

"Only if it's not too much trouble," I shrugged.

"Well, it is too much trouble," she barked, and my brows raised in reluctant admiration of such blatant rudeness. "I really cannot heave myself out of this chair and trudge down to the kitchen," she continued. "Besides, once I got there, I'd have no idea where anything was. Mary, my woman who does, is not here today. So, you have a choice, Eve with the long legs whose got my poor godson in such a tizzy, you can go down to the kitchen and forage for yourself."

"I can do that," I agreed mildly. "Can I bring you back a cup?"

"No, filthy stuff," she shuddered dramatically. "Never could bear the taste. Or you can open that rather nice Merlot standing on the desk."

"Wine, please," I answered immediately.

Her face creased into unexpected lines of mirth. "Good girl," she replied, obviously highly delighted with me, and watched as I crossed to the large writing desk standing at an angle to the window, removed the foil from the neck of the bottle and deftly opened the wine.

Turning over two glasses from a tray of half a dozen beside the bottle, I poured two glasses and handed her one, before sitting in the chair opposite, sipping at my wine with pleasure. She was right, it was rather nice, and I pulled an appreciative face.

"Now then," she commanded, taking a very unladylike gulp of her wine, "tell me about yourself."

So, I told her about the authors I'd worked for, the historical periods I'd already researched, and because by this point I'd had two glasses of wine and I thought it would amuse her, I told her about Sebert Foxton.

Her parchment face screwed up with merriment as I confided how I had dampened down his quite considerable ardour with a rather hefty wallop from the Oxford English Dictionary.

"Sebert always was a complete idiot," she chortled. "Glad to know you can take care of yourself." She stopped and looked at me in silent contemplation.

"I like you," she stated. "You seem less of a ninny than most, you're bright and funny, you enjoy wine which is a big plus, and my godson has personally recommended you." She paused, swigging at her wine as though it were water.

"Do you want to come to Jamaica with me?"

"Yes please," I said, and she visibly brightened, "When?"

"Next week."

"Okay," I replied slowly, my mind zipping through my appointments for the week ahead, none of which couldn't be changed. "It's my goddaughter's birthday a week next Friday though. I must be back for that."

"We fly back the Wednesday before," she reassured, draining her glass, and holding it out for more, "so that's all right. Oh," she exclaimed in disappointment as I upended the bottle into her glass and a dribble came out. "dead soldier. Best you open another bottle."

By the time Scott came back, Ruth and I had almost finished the second bottle and he looked at us in amused exasperation.

"Maybe it wasn't such a good idea introducing you two complete lushes to each other," he commented wryly, and I beamed at him, stumbling to my feet.

"Scott," I exclaimed, tripping over the corner of the threadbare rug and launching myself tipsily into his arms, nearly emptying the contents of my glass down his front. I looked up into his face and felt his arms tighten as he took my full weight.

"Hello," I giggled. "Ruth's taking me to Jamaica."

"That's nice," he replied, hauling me upright and taking the glass from me. "But now I think it might be a good idea if I take my two favourite ladies out and get them some food to keep their wine company."

"Marvellous idea," agreed Ruth, getting slowly to her feet, sober as a judge. "The pub in the village has a very impressive wine list. Food's not bad either," she added as an afterthought.

"I don't think Eve should drink anymore," Scott decreed, picking up my handbag and attempting to thread it onto my arm.

"Spoilsport," I pouted, the room revolving very pleasantly around my head.

"She's a big girl," barked Ruth. "She can decide for herself."

"Yes, I can," I agreed solemnly, the effect somewhat spoilt by my wobbling.

"I don't want her to be ill," Scott snapped, putting an arm about me, and turning me towards the door. He glared at Ruth. Much to my surprise, she flushed and bit her lip, coarse brick red colour washing her lined cheeks.

A look passed between them, a look I couldn't understand, a look which later, when my hangover had passed and I tried to remember and analyse the events of the day, I couldn't even be sure I'd seen at all.

Working for Ruth was certainly an experience, although I made sure whenever I joined her to share a bottle, or two, of wine, my stomach was well and truly full of food. I'd never seen anyone drink as much as she could and remain lucid.

Admiring her stamina, I was concerned as to what it was doing to her brain cells and liver, yet when I dared bring up the subject, she dismissed my fears with a resolute, "I'm seventy-two years old, I've been drinking red wine since I was eleven, what's it going to do? Kill me?"

Jamaica was a revelation to me. It was stunningly beautiful, and I couldn't get enough of the heat and the sun. When Ruth took to her air-conditioned room, wilting from the temperature, I gladly visited the library and archives in Kingston, bringing back my findings and impressions to her each evening.

I also visited an old sugar plantation, listening and filling page after page with notes as a local historian, whom Ruth had arranged for me to meet with, talked about what life would have been like for the unfortunate souls forced to work on it. In all, it was a magical week.

On our last evening, we ate dinner on the terrace overlooking the sea, Ruth consuming almost double her normal quantity of red wine as well as native rum punches, which she had taken a liking to. It was late and I supposed we should have been getting to bed, mindful of the long journey home, but I couldn't bring myself to leave my view of the sea. Ruth too seemed happily settled in her spacious armchair, sipping at rum punches, now and then her head lolling back in her chair.

"Shame you're not here with your young man instead of a crusty old bird like me," she commented. I opened my eyes and smiled at her.

"Well, it would be if I had a young man," I replied dreamily, reluctant to break the beauty of the evening with talk.

"No, I mean Nigel, or Scott as I know he likes to be called."

"Scott's not my young man."

"Why not?" she snorted, "What's wrong with him?"

"Nothing," I laughed. "He doesn't think of me in that way..."

"Don't be such a ninny," she scoffed. "The boy's head over heels in love with you. Has been for years."

Carefully, I pulled myself upright in my chair and turned to look at her. She sipped her drink and stared steadily back.

"What do you mean?" I asked slowly, my heart stuttering inside my chest.

"Exactly what I said," she stated firmly, and I shook my head in confusion.

"But he's never said, never even hinted that he might," I broke off and bit my lip, shock making me incautious. "All this time I've waited and hoped, but he's never ... no!" I shook my head again. "You're wrong. If he has feelings for me why hasn't he said something, done something?"

"Well, why haven't you?" Ruth answered my question with another question.

"Because he's never given me even the slightest reason to hope," I cried hotly. "Because he's so emotionally constipated, I seriously doubt he's capable of love, let alone is in love with me."

"He has good reasons for being that way," Ruth stated.

"Well, I wish you'd tell me what they are," I exclaimed bitterly, throwing myself back in my chair in exasperation. She fell silent, staring thoughtfully at me over the rim of her glass. I rubbed at my eyes in weary despair, aware of the faint crashing of the sea on the shore, and the breeze wafting across my face drying tears that had barely had a chance to form.

"All right," she said. "I'll tell you, and then you'll understand."

Ruth had been an old friend of Scott's family since long before he was born. She was best friends with his mother. We went to university together, she explained, and stayed in close touch, even after their lives diverged onto completely different paths.

Ruth became an author, remaining resolutely single, and gaining more fame and fortune with every successful novel. Scott's mother married late in life, a marriage which Ruth strongly advised her against, having heard through the grapevine what a cold fish her fiancé was, and how the gossip mills were buzzing over the fact he was only marrying her for her money.

Scott's mother came from money, new money. His father came from an old title but was practically penniless. It was not uncommon, Ruth said, and, if both parties are aware of the terms of the marriage, then it can work out reasonably well for all concerned. But if one partner is in love and believes themselves loved in return, the truth can come as a violent and shocking blow. Scott's mother, unfortunately, did not become aware of the state of affairs until the ink had dried on the marriage contract and she had passed over great chunks of her fortune to her husband.

Ruth watched with angry frustration as Scott's father turned a loving and bright girl into a quietly miserable woman, slowly dying by degrees, trapped in a cold and loveless marriage. Ruth constantly urged her to leave her husband and was stunned when her friend announced her pregnancy and the net tightened around her.

Being an older mother there were, quite naturally, concerns about her health, especially when it was discovered she was carrying twins. Twins? I sat bolt upright at this point.

Yes, continued Ruth firmly. Scott was the oldest of twins, born five minutes before his brother Samuel, and never had two brothers been as close as those two, even to the extent that they had their own language. Extremely disconcerting it had been too, listening to them babbling away to each other.

Anyway, Scott's mother asked her to be their godmother, and for a while, it looked as if things would turn out all right after all. Scott's father had been softened by the birth of the heir and the spare, and Scott's mother had her two little boys to love and fill the emotional void in her life.

Then, disaster struck. Scott's mother complained one day of not feeling well, before collapsing halfway through a charity lunch in aid of the local hospice. She never regained consciousness, dying at age thirty-eight of an aneurism. The boys were only three years old.

Ruth did the best she could, but her career was skyrocketing and the demands on her time were many. She did help find the boys a nanny though, a loving yet practical woman whom Ruth felt confident leaving in charge of two little devastated and lonely boys. With the loss of their mother, their world, quite understandably, had collapsed around them. Their father, always a distant figure, retreated even further into his thoughts and paid them no attention at all.

Things limped on for a few years, the boys clinging more and more to each other and communicating only with one another, their nanny, and Ruth during her occasional visits. Their exclusion from the outside world grew so complete that they rarely spoke English anymore, conversing with each other easily in their private twin talk.

Then, Ruth received an emotional phone call from the boys' nanny. She had been let go. Their father had decided the boys needed to go to school. Horrified to hear them jabbering to each other like a pair of monkeys, he had enrolled them in a boarding school eighty miles away.

In vain did Ruth fly home and plead with him to change his mind. The boys were only seven years old, she raged, far too young to be sent so far away from home. If they must go to school, and she agreed they probably should, then could they not attend the excellent local primary school so they could at least come home each evening?

But his mind was made up and Ruth was abruptly reminded of the limits of her power as godmother. She went to visit the boys in their new school before sadly flying back to America to finish the book signing tour she was contracted to complete.

Scott didn't mind school so much. More confident and outgoing than his brother, he would have settled in easily if he had been alone, maybe would even have enjoyed having his keen intelligence stretched by such a rigidly structured educational institution.

Although he missed his home, his nanny, and the freedom he had to roam about the grounds and do as he pleased, he had the sense to understand the situation could not have continued forever. The absence of his father meant nothing to him. Neither boy understood what it meant to have a loving parent, having only had a brief taste of a mother's love and none of a fathers.

Samuel hated school. Backwards, insecure, and shy, he clung to his brother, depending on him to protect and buffer him against the rough and tumble of an all-boys private boarding school, crying himself to sleep every night, and becoming more and more introverted.

Speaking only in twin talk, he desperately tried to get back to the world where he and his brother had freedom, peace, and solitude.

Observing this, the school, with the heedless cruelty of adults in authority and with their father's permission, separated them, placing them in different houses and classes, hoping this would sever the cord that tied Samuel so tightly to his brother.

Scared and alone, missing his brother and worried about how Samuel would cope without him, Scott, too, went into a decline. His schoolwork suffered. Teachers who had previously been happy with his progress now held emergency meetings to discuss the worsening problem of the twins.

No one seemed to understand that if they let Scott see Samuel, talk to him, reassure him everything was going to be all right and reassure himself Samuel was coping, the problem would have resolved itself.

Stubbornly, they persisted in their agreed policy. The twins had been separated for their own good, and apart they would remain until they worked their way through this nonsense.

One night, Scott awoke, groggy with sleep, his brother's distress and cries for help ringing in his head. He crept from his bed and silently slipped from the room making his way down darkened corridors looking eerily different in the dim light.

Emerging into the night, he stopped for a moment to gain his bearings and saw a light flash someway ahead of him, down by the river. Without thinking he made his way towards it, almost sleepwalking, believing Samuel was waiting there for him.

He was almost to the river when he stumbled and came to his senses, snapping out of his dreamlike state to stare around at the silent moonlit world in dismay. Disorientated and scared, all thoughts of trying to reach Samuel fled his confused thoughts. All he wanted now was to find his way back to his dorm and get into bed before someone found him.

"Who's that?"

"Quick, grab him!"

Suddenly he was surrounded, hands reaching out and grabbing him, silencing his yells with big clammy palms. They seemed like giants but were a small group of older boys, sneaking out to meet in the old boat house, where they kept their illicit supply of booze and cigarettes.

"Who is it?"

"Dunno, one of the small kids."

"Bring him with us. Quick, keep him quiet or he'll wake the whole school."

Frantically struggling, scared beyond belief, Scott was carried into the old boathouse and dumped on the floor, staring in wide-eyed terror at the three boys who were already sitting there, recognising one as Wilkinson, rugby captain and hero of practically the whole school.

"What's this?" Wilkinson asked mildly, blowing an impressive ring of smoke and eyeing Scott curiously.

"Found him wandering around outside," one of the others explained, and Wilkinson leant forward for a closer look.

"It's one of those twins," exclaimed another.

"So, it is." Wilkinson's eyes narrowed thoughtfully, and he prodded Scott's trembling body with his foot. "Which one are you?" he demanded. "The quiet one, or the weird one?"

Scott stared in mute terror. Wilkinson frowned in annoyance, prodded him again, and repeated his question. When Scott still sat in petrified silence, one of the other boys roughly shook him.

"Answer his question."

"The ... the quiet one ..." stammered Scott, and felt the burn of guilty disloyalty, as if by his words he had somehow betrayed his brother and was agreeing with them that, yes, Samuel was weird. His cheeks scorched with shame, and his mind soared outwards as if seeking his brother, begging forgiveness for his treachery.

"What were you doing roaming around outside?" demanded Wilkinson, pulling on his cigarette, and blowing smoke into Scott's face.

"Looking for my brother ..." Scott stuttered.

"Well, you won't find him here, that's for sure." Wilkinson snorted. "The thing is ..." He paused, lifting a can of beer to his lips, and swigging thirstily, eyeing Scott over the rim.

"The thing is." He smiled nastily. "What do we do with you now?" There was an uneasy movement amongst the other boys. Scott saw the two sitting with Wilkinson exchange worried glances behind his back.

"You've seen us. You could tell on us..."

"I won't, I promise!" interrupted Scott, his eight-year-old heart pumping frantically, now convinced Wilkinson meant to kill him.

"That's not good enough though, is it?" commented Wilkinson mildly.

"Steady on Wilkie," pleaded one of the others. "He's just a kid."

Wilkinson glared at him. The boy swallowed, licked his lips nervously, yet stood his ground, and Scott gazed hopefully at his champion.

"He's just a little kid," the boy repeated. "Can't you see he's scared shitless?"

There was a long pause. Scott felt the tension emanating from the others as the power struggle raged silently in the intense stares of Wilkinson and the other boy. Then Wilkinson shrugged, smiled, and the tension broke.

"You're right, Mitch, of course, you're right, he is just a kid." He turned and smiled at Scott, a mirthless smile that had Scott shrinking back as if from a rabid dog. "We're not going to harm you," he reassured and gestured expansively with his can. "And to show there are no hard feelings, someone get the kid a drink."

"I don't want one," Scott squeaked.

"You don't want to offend me, kid." the smile tightened. "I said you'll have a drink with us."

"But Wilkie ..." protested Mitch. Wilkinson gave him a long, narrow-eyed gaze that had Mitch reddening and stumbling back, mumbling an apology, as another boy handed Scott a can.

"Drink," ordered Wilkinson.

"But I don't want..."

"I said drink!" roared Wilkinson.

Shaking with renewed terror, Scott put the can to his mouth and drank. The first swallow was foul. Scott fought to keep it from coming straight back up, choking and spluttering, as the other boys laughed and clapped him on the back.

"Swallow it down, kid, that's right," demanded Wilkinson, highly amused with Scott's discomfort. "We'll make a man of you yet."

What happened after that was the stuff of nightmares that would haunt the man he became for the rest of his life.

He was held down and forced to drink. Wilkinson poured beer down his throat, laughing when it bubbled back up. Sitting him upright and thumping him on the back until he swallowed, forcing him to drink more and more until Scott felt he would burst at the seams, his small body couldn't possibly hold it all.

He desperately needed the toilet, but they wouldn't stop. Finally, shaking in shame and terror, he wet himself, and the spreading stain on his pyjamas caused them to laugh even more.

Dimly, through his tears and the jeers of the others, he could hear the nice one, the one called Mitch, begging them to stop, his voice shrilling with fear they were going to kill him.

Finally, Scott's body could take no more and began to void itself. Endlessly and helplessly, he writhed in agony as his system fought to reject the huge quantities of alcohol it had been forced to consume in such a short space of time.

The boys drew back, watching as his body bucked and retched, then fell silent, the frightening realisation dawning on them that they had gone too far and nervously looking to their leader for guidance.

When Scott at last lay still, Wilkinson knelt beside him, gingerly avoiding the sticky splattered piles of vomit and diarrhoea. He grabbed Scott's hair and forced his head up so Scott had no choice but to stare into Wilkinson's cold grey eyes, his vision blurry through a sea of tears and terror, panic, and pain.

"Now listen, kid," ordered Wilkinson. "You tell anyone, anyone, about us or this place, I'll know. You even think about talking, I'll know, and do you know what'll happen?"

Numbly, Scott shook his head. Wilkinson leant closer, his voice a whisper.

"Someone will die," he stated flatly. Scott's eyes rolled back into his head in terror, and he passed out, the sound of Wilkinson's laugh ringing in his ears.

What happened after that, Ruth couldn't say for sure, but Scott had been found unconscious and seeped in his own waste, dumped outside the nurse's office. He had been rushed to hospital where excessive alcohol consumption had been diagnosed, the doctor's lips pursing in disgust at such a thing in so young a boy.

The next thing Scott knew, he was waking up in the hospital, cleaned and in fresh pyjamas, suffering from the hangover from hell and shaking from his experience. Remembering Wilkinson's final words to him, and the threat he had made, it all seemed like a bad dream.

Scott shifted uneasily in his narrow bed. He had to tell, didn't he? After all, the school would want to know how he'd got into such a state. Scott wasn't sure he could hold out against what would surely be intensive questioning.

No, he would tell. Wilkinson couldn't do anything to harm him. As for the threat that someone would die, Scott shivered and resolutely made up his mind. He had been trying to frighten him. No one would die. He would tell. When they came for him in the morning, he would tell. Relieved, his mind made up, he snuggled down under the covers to try and sleep.

The cry echoed in his head, ripping him from sleep and forcing him bolt upright in bed, his heart jackhammering with fear. It came again, resounding through the corridors of his brain, and Scott's hands flew to his head.

"Samuel!" he screamed in terror.

Lights snapped on in the ward as others awoke and complained. Nurses came running, shocked to see him scrambling out of bed like a boy possessed, running for the door, his eyes wide and blank at some invisible terror.

"What's the matter?" One of the nurses tried to hold him, feeling his thin body strain out of her embrace, his head lashing violently.

"Samuel!" he screamed again. The nurse would later tell Ruth all the hairs on the back of her neck had stood upright at the horror in his voice and the look in his eyes.

"It was as if he was hearing and seeing things I couldn't," she tried to explain, her kind face creasing at the memory. "He was so young, so small, no meat on him at all, but it took all my strength to hold him. He fought me like a wildcat. I was afraid he'd do himself an injury."

Alerted by another nurse the doctor came running, took one look at Scott and ordered he be sedated, alarmed by the blind panic in the boy's eyes, and the frenzied, maddened way in which he resisted all attempts to calm him.

It took two nurses to wrestle him back onto his bed, whisking curtains around to stop the curious gazes of the other children. Nurses rushed to bedsides to comfort and reassure, whilst all the time Scott fought and raged, screaming again and again.

"Samuel, Samuel, Samuel!"

"Who is Samuel?" they begged, as the doctor slipped the needle into his arm. "Who is he? Perhaps we can bring him here to you?"

"My brother!" he finally gasped, "he's my brother." As the sedative took effect, pulling him under the encroaching waves, he grabbed the doctor's arm, his face twisting with anguish.

"It's too late," he cried, "he's gone!" and he flopped, unconscious, onto the bed.

Later, much later, the doctor and nurses would discover that at the same moment they were trying to restrain the frenzied boy, his twin brother Samuel was losing his fight for life in intensive care two floors above them; his twin feeling the instant his other half slipped away from him, unable to stop him from going and unable to be with him at the end.

"Samuel died?" I breathed in horror. "Did Wilkinson kill him?"

"No, no, no," huffed Ruth in exasperation. "Don't be such a melodramatic ninny. No, Samuel died of meningitis."

When Scott regained consciousness, he knew Samuel was gone. That he was alone. He could feel the gaping hole in his soul that had been his twin. Guilt burned in his gut.

It was his fault. Wilkinson warned him, and he hadn't believed. He had thought about telling someone, had been going to tell them what had happened, and now, because of that, Samuel was dead. His twin, that which made him complete, was gone. It was his fault, all his fault.

Released from the hospital and sent back to school, Scott retreated into a world of guilt and silence. His plan to talk had cost Samuel his life, so now Scott determined to never speak again.

At first, teachers put it down to understandable grief, exclaiming their surprise and disapproval that no one had come to take the bereaved little boy home. Let him stay at school, had been his father's orders and so, at school, Scott remained.

The other boys avoided him, made uneasy by his silence and the way his eyes, dark and haunted, looked right through them as if they weren't there. Almost as if, they whispered amongst themselves, he was seeing something they couldn't. His twin's ghost, the scared mutterings continued, after all, twins were known to be special; to be linked. Maybe his brother was communicating with him from beyond the grave.

But no one was communicating with Scott. Although he would have given his soul for one word from his brother, he heard nothing, felt nothing. Samuel was gone, and Scott ached with the burning conviction it was all because of him.

If someone had known, and realised, the psychological damage that had been inflicted on such a little boy, then maybe with immediate professional care and counselling he could have been pulled back from the brink.

But no one knew or cared enough to find out. Scott was left to fend for himself; to attempt to deal with the situation alone. He coped, by totally retreating into himself.

When his father eventually bothered to let Ruth know what had happened, she flew home immediately, her heart grieving for the loss of Samuel, and worrying about the effect it would have upon Scott.

By the time she reached the school, and someone went to find Scott, it was too late. The damage was done. Scott hadn't spoken a single word to anyone in over a month.

Two months later his father died, too, a life filled with bitterness and hatred for all finally culminating in a heart attack. According to the will, Scott inherited everything, and Ruth was named as his guardian.

Thankfully, she sold the house which echoed at every corner with memories, bought an old rambling villa on the east coast, took Scott away from the school which had so devastated his young life, and dedicated herself to healing him.

Gradually, with patience, understanding and professional guidance, Scott emerged on the other side of the silence. Ruth still remembered the heart-gladdening day he looked at her and spoke for the first time since Samuel's death.

He remained a quiet and thoughtful little boy who made not a single friend at the local primary school Ruth enrolled him in, but at least he would talk, if necessary. Ruth watched in concern and sadness as Scott grew from an abnormally quiet and mistrustful little boy, into a taciturn and friendless man.

She told me how relieved she had been when he met Andrew, how much she liked the bluff hearty Scotsman who had seen through Scott's diffident exterior to realise that what lay underneath was worth the effort. Through

Andrew, he had met Annaliese, the others, and me. She paused and looked at me, her eyes crossing, finally feeling the effects of the amount of alcohol she had consumed.

"He loves you," she stated firmly. At my negative murmur, her face tightened.

"Oh, yes, he does," she insisted. "I know Scott better than anyone else. I've seen the look in his eyes when he talks about you. He loves you more than life itself but will never say. He won't risk loving someone again."

"So, what can I do?" I cried in despair, and she fixed me with a steely glare.

"Do you love him?" she asked.

"Yes," I sobbed in despair. "I've always loved him, right from the start."

"Then you must be the one to go to him and make him believe you do. It's up to you, Eve. He is too afraid of losing someone else he loves to ever make the first move. It is up to you."

Later, after I helped a booze-soaked Ruth to bed and packed our cases ready for the early flight, I wandered back out onto the terrace, thinking about the story she had told me.

Hot tears welled for the loss of his twin, for the scared and abused little boy Scott had been, and the scarred and damaged man, he had become.

My man, I decided, knowing I wanted no other. I wiped away my tears, smiling at the chance Ruth had given me. A chance to make things right so Scott and I could be together, as fate had always intended us to be.

We were flying home tomorrow. I would see him. Somehow, I would get him alone and would let him know I loved him and would find out if Ruth was right and he loved me too.

I drew back my shoulders, determined to see it through, quite how I would go about it still unclear to me. Maybe I should seduce him. I grinned and felt a quick hot stab of lust at the thought of us making love. Oh yes, my cheeks flamed, and my heart raced, that was a plan.

As it turned out, my plans were all for nothing. I didn't consider that upon returning home jet lag would seize me and I would sleep around the clock. That I wouldn't wake until late Thursday evening when everyone was gathered in the house excitedly making plans for Essie's eighth birthday party the next day.

That other than casting longing looks at Scott, I would barely have a moment to exchange more than a few cordial words with him about my trip.

Never mind, I consoled myself, maybe it was better this way. Get the frenzied madness of Essie's birthday out the way and then, oh, yes, it would be our turn.

Nothing would stop me from taking Scott away somewhere private, leaving him in no doubt as to my feelings for him.

But it was not to be. Thinking back on my long, lonely year of self-imposed isolation, I often wondered if things could have been different.

If I had had the chance to talk to Scott before Essie's party, if we had made the connection then, and were already bonded to each other, would my life have taken a very different path?

It was impossible to know. Life beats out its own rhythm and we have no choice but to dance to the tune it dictates.

CHAPTER VIII – LAMENTATIONS

"Sometimes Eve, you can be a thoughtless bitch,"

It was dawn. Thin fingers of light were oozing through chinks in the curtains and birds were greeting the new day with an enthusiastic burst of song, when I heard the silent, yet unmistakeable, sound of my bedroom door being opened. I felt the presence of an uninvited intruder and knew I was not alone.

I lay still, listening with bated breath, and biding my time as stealthy footsteps crept ever closer to the bed. I waited, coiled and ready until they paused by my bedside, and I sensed hands reaching toward me.

Then, like a jack-in-the-box, I sprang upwards, grabbing the trespasser, and wrestling them onto the bed using the element of surprise to pin their hands and launch a merciless attack.

"Auntie E-e-e-v-v-v-e," stuttered Essie, helpless with laughter as I tickled her without mercy. Thrashing around like a slippery eel, she slithered from my grasp and swarmed across the bed, disappearing headfirst over the side and landing with a thud on the floor.

"Essie?" I cried in semi-alarm at her silence.

Then it was my turn to shriek as she catapulted upwards, grabbing one of my pillows on her upward trajectory and walloping me round the side of the head with it.

"Why you ..." I gasped, ear still ringing from the blow, and then it was all-out war as I grabbed another pillow and retaliated, catching her a blow across the bottom which sent her giggling across the bed, long colt-like legs flashing under her Disney princess nightshirt.

The battle was long and not without injuries, but finally, I had her pinned down under my duvet, gasping for air, our sides hurting with too much laughter.

"Happy birthday, brat," I said, planting a wet raspberry kiss on her cheek which had her shrieking with disgust.

Laughing, I slithered into bed beside her, dropping my pillow back in place and collapsing breathlessly onto it. I caught sight of the time on my bedside clock and groaned in disbelief.

"5:30? Essie!"

"Present," she demanded.

"What makes you so sure I've got you one?"

I raised my brows in amused disbelief. She smirked as if such a comment was unworthy of an answer, and I sighed with resignation.

"You can have one small one now," I replied. "But the rest are for the party this afternoon."

She wiggled with anticipation, holding out her hands as I reached under my bed and drew out a gaily wrapped, oddly shaped parcel.

With a small squeak, she ripped the paper off to reveal a pretty, little tiara, its fake diamonds glittering in the dim light.

"Your birthday crown to wear at your party, Your Highness," I said.

She grinned and pulled the tiara on, flopping back onto the pillows and pulling the duvet up to her chin. We lay quietly for a few minutes.

I could feel sleep tugging at me and hoped Essie would doze. She had a very busy day ahead, and I knew Mimi would probably appreciate her being as rested as possible.

"Auntie Eve?"

"Um huh?"

"Will you tell me about sex?"

Instantly jolted awake, my eyes flew open, and I turned my head to gaze at my goddaughter's suspiciously innocent face.

"Umm," I began helplessly. "What do you want to know, Essie?"

"Everything," she replied. "The girls at school talk about it, but I don't think they know much because some of the things they say seem gross and, quite frankly, impossible. I'd like to know the absolute truth."

"Why don't you ask your mother?" I began hopefully, but Essie shook her head vehemently.

"I can't," she stated flatly. "It would be just, like, too embarrassing."

I sighed, painfully aware of how quickly girls seemed to grow up now, then remembered when I'd been about Essie's age looking at my Barbie and Ken dolls, examining their bodies minutely, and longing to know exactly what went where and how, frustrated, and confused because nobody would tell me anything.

"All right," I agreed slowly, and Essie squeaked with joy. "But not today," I continued. "I don't want to go into the whole thing right now..."

"But Auntie Eve," she began desperately, and I shook my head.

"No," I replied, on firmer ground now. "It's complicated, Essie, and you'll have loads of questions. I want us to have the time and privacy to talk about it properly."

"You mean that?" she begged. "You're not fobbing me off?"

"No," I reassured her. "I'll tell you whatever you want to know if you're sure you're ready to deal with it." She looked thoughtful, her young face seeming infinitely older and wiser than her eight years, then smiled at me and nodded.

"I really do want to know, Auntie Eve, and I promise you I can deal with it, whatever it is."

"One other thing you must promise me," I continued, and she nodded eagerly. "For heaven's sake, don't tell your mother..."

The rest of the day passed in a blur of preparations. Andrew took Essie to school, much to Mimi's relief, for as Essie's over-excited levels of hyperactivity had risen through breakfast, so had her long-suffering mother's stress levels.

Being in the last week of the summer term, Mimi had asked Essie if she'd rather have her party the following week once school had broken up, only to be met with an incredulous stare.

How could her mother even think of depriving her of the status of being at school with an impending party granted her?

Once we waved her goodbye, a sigh of relief swept through the group, and we rolled up our sleeves and got down to it.

Andrew and Scott had gone to work, Scott promising to leave off early to help with any last-minute preparations and Andrew reassuring Mimi that no he hadn't forgotten he was to collect Essie from school and bring her straight to Annaliese's.

With exams over, the university had already finished for the summer, so Miles and Ferdie had been roped into being gofers, running errands for us exhausted and stressed women.

Finally, it reached three o'clock and everything was ready. We stood on the veranda and surveyed the pink paradise that had been created, and I felt a little spark of anticipation at how much Essie was going to love it.

A pink marquee had been erected, its sides rolled up and secured with bunches of pink and silver ribbons to allow a breeze to roll through to cool the twenty little princesses who would be attending.

The long table was already laid with a pink cloth on which silver party favours, hair accessories, and glittering necklaces and bracelets had been scattered. Pink and silver balloons bobbed on the back of every chair, and at the head of the table was a huge pink and silver throne fit for a princess.

Pink bunting was strung from the marquee to the house and a large, pink, bouncy castle wobbled invitingly. The mobile disco was being set up in the hall ready for dancing after dinner, and the caterers were hard at work in the kitchen preparing a feast fit for royalty. As indeed Essie and her friends were for this most special day.

A buffet was being laid on for the parents, and the garden was littered with little groupings of tables and chairs. Waiters were preparing the bar set up on the veranda, bottles of champagne and soft drinks were chilling, and glasses were lined up like ranks of sparkling soldiers.

Flowers were banked everywhere. Sitting back in a garden chair, gratefully accepting a glass of champagne from Ferdie, I could smell the richly gorgeous scent of pink roses arranged in a large display behind me.

It all looked amazing. We beamed smugly at each other as a red sports car growled its way up the drive. With a catch at my heart, I realised Scott had arrived.

He parked and climbed out, a smile briefly touching his face as he saw the transformed garden. As he walked towards us, Mimi came rushing out of the Hall clutching her phone, panicked annoyance on her face.

"Martha called," she exclaimed shrilly. Martha was her housekeeper. "Andrew's been home to change, but he forgot to pick up Essie's party dress. Honestly, I told him so many times and hung it in the hallway, how could he have forgotten?"

She glanced at her watch. "I'll have to go home and get it," she stated, looking around wildly. "Has anyone seen my car keys?"

"I'll go and get it," offered Scott mildly. "It won't take me long."

"Angel," breathed Mimi thankfully, and blew him a kiss. "I'll phone Martha and tell her."

"No problem," reassured Scott. He clambered back into his car and roared off as Mimi hurried away muttering into her phone.

Ferdie and I exchanged glances. He danced after Mimi, gathering her up and waltzing her down the veranda, before forcing a glass of champagne onto her, flirting so outrageously that a smile appeared on Mimi's face and the worry lines on her forehead smoothed themselves out.

"I must change," she exclaimed, draining her champagne. "The guests will be arriving at half four and it must be nearly that now," she added, and then hurried away into the house.

I sighed and brushed a hand lightly over my new pink silk dress, feeling with pleasure the rasp of expensive material over my thighs and the answering jolt of desire.

Ever since my return from Jamaica with the decision to let Scott know how I felt about him, I'd walked around in a cloud of arousal, hardly able to look him in the eye, feeling the buzz of a heady secret not yet divulged, and enjoying the sensation of possible, soon-to-be-requited, lust.

The warmth of the afternoon intensified. Robert, Miles, Ferdie, and I, relaxed like cats in the sun, swigging champagne, enjoying the calm before the storm, and waiting for things to begin.

Caro had not yet walked up from the lodge, so I didn't even have to contend with her usual glare of disapproval. Annaliese, too, had not yet emerged, presumably still changing, or dealing with last-minute details indoors.

Robert pulled himself up and shaded his eyes as one of the catering staff, a young, pretty, blonde girl, came out clutching a large bunch of pink glittery balloons, followed by a young man carrying jugs of sparkling iced juice.

Together, they wandered down to the marquee as we heard the familiar roar of Scott's car and looked to see him turning into the drive, followed by a police car.

Puzzled, we glanced at each other.

"What do you suppose ...?" murmured Robert, and got up, wandering down the steps as Scott drew to a halt and got out of the car.

Behind him, the police car also stopped and two policemen, looking hot and solemn in sober blue uniforms, climbed out.

I rose with Miles and Ferdie and watched, unease dancing down my spine, as Robert reached Scott and exchanged quick, unheard words with him.

We saw him blanch and stagger back, holding out a hand as if in denial.

Scott shook his head. They both glanced at the house and, I felt, at me. Dread oozed thickly through my veins.

Robert turned to the policemen, gestured for them to follow him into the house, and Scott walked slowly up to us.

"Scott?" I heard myself cry, my voice thin and shrill. "What's happened?"

"There's been an accident," he replied.

His eyes were blank and shuttered, his words precise and careful as if he were having to think before he spoke.

"The police were at the house when I got there. They were trying to find Mimi to tell her, to tell her ..." He paused, looked down and swallowed.

"What's happened, Scott? Why were they trying to find Mimi?" Miles quietly asked.

"Andrew," he replied flatly.

I went icy cold all over.

"A tractor pulled out of a concealed entrance and Andrew went into the side of it."

"No!" I gasped in horror. "Is he all right?"

Before he could answer a sudden thought gripped me. "He was on his way to pick up Essie, someone needs to go and get her. She'll be standing at school wondering where he is …" My voice trailed away at the look in Scott's eyes.

"Eve," he began gently, placing his hands on my shoulders. "He'd already collected Essie. She was in the car with him."

"Is she all right?" I demanded, panic pounding in my temples and my heart. "Scott, are they all right? How badly hurt are they?"

I saw the truth in his eyes, but couldn't … wouldn't … accept it, and backed away from him with a low moan of denial.

A scream sounded from the house, coarse and guttural, like the death cry of an animal.

I felt the blood drain from my cheeks and saw the answering looks of horrified realisation on the faces of Miles and Ferdie as we stood, petrified and helpless, listening to Mimi's pain.

"Mimi!" I cried and started forward, but Scott held me fast.

"Don't, Eve," was all he said.

"I must go to her!" I twisted in his grasp.

"No," he said simply. "She has Annaliese and Robert. That's enough for now."

"I want to help!" I screamed. "I can't stand here and do nothing! Scott … Essie!"

I started to shake as the true horror of the situation began to sink in.

"Andrew ... Both of them? No, it's not true! Both of them?!"

I saw Ferdie's eyes well, his hand scrubbing futilely at his eyes and the frozen horror on Miles's face. I slapped furiously at Scott's hands, unable to bear his touch.

"The guests," Miles exclaimed. "They'll be arriving at any minute expecting a party. We can't ... they can't..."

"No," agreed Scott. "Go and stop them at the gates," he ordered. "Tell them what's happened and send them away. Ferdie, get Caro, we need her. She can help us get rid of all ... this ..." he gestured helplessly at the marquee, bouncy castle, and pink bunting.

"If Mimi sees this, it'll make it worse."

The two men nodded and loped off, plainly relieved at being given tasks to do, anything to help them delay having to think, or feel. Scott and I were left alone staring at each other.

"How can you just stand there?" I demanded in sudden anger. "Don't you care? Oh God, oh no, Essie!"

I pounded on his chest in impotent anger at a world in which such things could happen.

Patiently, he waited until my rage collapsed into dry howls that ripped at my chest and throat, then gathered me up in his arms, quietly holding me as I trembled in shocked disbelief.

Over his shoulder I saw the caterers, supremely oblivious to the tragedy which had occurred, laughing together in the marquee. She was trying to fasten the balloons to the throne, and he was distracting her, whispering things in her ear that had her blushing furiously and pushing him half-heartedly away.

They were young, plainly in love, and it seemed so obscenely wrong I wanted to scream at them. I watched with a growing sense of disjointed inevitability as the string of balloons slipped through her fingers, and sailed away from her outstretched hands, escaping out the side of the marquee.

My eyes tracked their progress. Eight sparkly pink balloons, one for every year of her short life, soaring ever upwards into the heavens...

It was later. The longest day of my life had ended. I was alone in my room, sitting on the edge of my bed, knowing I should try to sleep and realising the futility of even trying.

Mimi had slept, at last, sedated by the doctor summoned when Mimi's screams became hysterical. Her wild cries filled the Hall with outraged denial as she struggled to understand how life had so turned. Why her passionately adored husband and beloved daughter were never coming home again?

We crept in shock about her grief. Not knowing what to do, struggling to comprehend. Powerless to help Mimi, or ourselves.

Annaliese had dealt with her, until white-faced and in the grip of a savage headache, she'd collapsed into Robert's arms, and he'd carried her off to bed, leaving a grim and stony-faced Caro to sit by Mimi's bedside in case she stirred in the night.

I'd slipped away at that point, unable to cope with such sustained grief any longer, desperate to be alone. Yet, once I reached the privacy of my room, I found myself longing for the companionship of others.

Apart from those few wild dry sobs in Scott's arms, I had yet to weep and could feel a sea of tears locked up tight in my chest.

Unable to escape, they brewed and fermented, creating a painful ball that choked and strangled me. I clasped a palm to my heart, knowing no amount of antacid could cure this heartburn.

Dusk began to creep across the room yet still I sat, motionless and silent on the edge of my bed, feeling my eyes grow still and wide, focusing intensely on a single spot on the carpet until it seemed I could almost see each individual fibre.

A knock sounded at the door. I blinked, struggled to regain reality, and then slowly turned my head to stare, unable to move or react. The knock sounded again, more insistent this time. Still, I could not answer.

I watched as the handle turned. The door gently creaked open and Scott's concerned expression appeared around it.

"Eve, are you okay?"

I looked at him, slowly shook my head, and then continued my study of the carpet. I felt the bed dip as he sat beside me and placed an arm around my shoulders. We waited in mutual silence until finally, he sighed.

"You should try to get some sleep."

"No," I murmured, "I'm not sure I'll ever sleep again." I looked into his still, dark eyes.

"How could such a thing have happened, Scott? What had Andrew ever done to harm anyone, and Essie, she was only a little girl, what had she done wrong?"

"Sometimes there is no reason why bad things happen." His voice was neutral. "Sometimes people you love are simply not there one day and you never know why. They're just gone."

I knew he was thinking of his mother, his nanny, and Samuel. I ached to comfort him but was unable to. Numb and disbelieving, my plans to declare my love and seduce him seemed inane and compared to what had happened.

"Try to sleep," he advised, and eased me down onto the bed, pulling the comforter up and over me, tucking it around me, his face oddly gentle.

He stood as if to leave, and I heard my voice, small, like a little girl's.

"Please stay. Please stay with me; I don't want to be alone tonight."

He paused, looked at me in the gloom. "Okay," he agreed. "I'll sleep on the sofa."

"No," I insisted. "Please come and lay next to me so I can feel you're there. I need someone to hold me tonight."

Again, he hesitated, then seemed to capitulate and sat on the bed to remove his shoes. I moved across to make room for him and he slid under the comforter with me, his warmth and presence immediately making things more bearable.

I groped under the cover to find his hand and clutched it tightly.

"Thank you," I whispered, snuggling closer.

"Glad to be of service," he whispered back.

We lay like that, side by side, holding hands until the emotions of the day finally caught up with me and I dropped like a stone into a deep and dreamless sleep.

When I awoke sometime the next morning, he was gone, only the faintest trace of his cologne on the pillow beside me bearing testament to the fact he had ever been there at all.

I rolled over in bed, unwilling to get up and face the day, wanting nothing more than to stay tucked tightly in my cocoon and not have to deal with the tragedy which awaited me downstairs.

But I knew I had no choice. It would have to be faced. Reluctantly, I sat up, swung my legs out of bed, and my feet touched something cold and foreign lying on the floor, half under the bed.

Puzzled, I reached down and found Essie's tiara, forgotten and unused, lying where she had dropped it the previous morning. It twinkled in the sun streaming in through the open curtains.

I stared at it until my chest heaved and finally, finally, the tears came.

How do I tell of the seconds, minutes, and hours that followed? How do I write of the days, weeks, and months? Where are the words that can describe the funeral, when we stood in rows and watched in still-eyed mourning as the two caskets, Essie's heartbreakingly small, were carried out into the sun which obscenely shone down as though on a wedding day.

How can I write of Mimi, bereft and devastated, her life ripped apart by a whim of fate and a farmworker in too much of a hurry to wait?

Growing thinner and paler as the days wore on, we worried about her and about Annaliese, on whom the brunt of caring for her had fallen.

I tried to help, I did, yet lacked the certainty of always seeming to know the right thing to say and do that Annaliese so naturally possessed.

Dealing with my own shock and grief, I found it hard to even look at Mimi and did not know how to be with her anymore, feeling awkward and clumsy in her presence.

The seasons turned, and time passed. Christmas was upon us – a pale imitation of Christmases past. We were a kingdom that had lost its princess, and we mourned.

I had been working for Ruth, craving the distraction it offered, losing myself in the complexities of the job and only too pleased when my fact-finding missions for her took me away from home for a few days.

I dreaded being in the Hall; Mimi's grief was all-encompassing. At times I resented her for it and then hated myself for being so self-centred.

Ruth never mentioned Scott or the conversation we'd that night. I wondered, given the amount she'd drunk, whether she even remembered it.

I had yet to act on her advice, and the longer I left it, the harder it seemed to get. I would watch him. His patience and forbearing with Mimi filled me with admiration, but in the five months since Andrew and Essie's deaths, I had not seen him grieve at all.

His coldness made me doubt myself, doubt whether Ruth could have been correct when she claimed he loved me.

In December, following gentle urging by Annaliese, I escaped, flying to Jamaica for a much-needed holiday.

Desperate to get away from the stifling and claustrophobic atmosphere at the Hall, I felt my spirits lift as the plane took off and carried me far away to the other side of the world where it was hot and sunny, and where I could lie on a beach all day, mindless and solitary, with no one to please but myself and nothing more strenuous to do than work on my tan.

I returned ten days before Christmas, feeling the best I had since the tragedy, but immediately found myself sucked back into the morass of despair at the Hall. I longed to escape. Most of all, I longed for something, anything, to break the monotony of grief.

Two days later I received a phone call from Ally, of all people, wondering if I would like to meet, exclaiming she hadn't seen me in ages and that it would be good to catch up.

To say she hadn't seen me for ages was a massive understatement. It was over six years, and I felt a guilty flush at the thought.

I'm ashamed to admit that after I moved into the Hall, I quietly, but determinedly severed all connections with friends from my old life, wanting to leave Melissa and everyone who knew her far behind and concentrate on becoming Eve.

So now, Ally's phone call was a shock, and strangely a relief. It was an excuse to leave the Hall and get away from my normal circle of friends, all of whom knew of the tragedy, and to spend time with someone oblivious of it.

To enjoy an evening of aimless small talk was a temptation too great to resist and I agreed to meet Ally the following evening.

Feminine pride had me ensuring I looked my best. As I pushed open the restaurant door and caught sight of myself in its reflective glass, I knew I looked amazing.

I refused to cover up my long legs tanned golden by the hot Jamaican sun, despite the freezing temperatures, and they were showcased nicely between a scandalously short pleated red skirt, and long black leather boots.

A white silk blouse billowed under a very expensive fake fur jacket and was cinched around my hips with a designer leather belt which matched my horrendously over-priced, postage-stamp-sized bag.

It was small-minded of me, I know, to deliberately set out to create an overwhelming impression of how successful I was now. I had no excuse for it other than being a woman.

Ally was already there. I caught the flash of envy in her eyes when she first spotted me, the tinge of malice in her tone when she kissed my cheek and we exchanged insincere greetings.

The restaurant was busy with pre-Christmas revellers, its cosily decorated interior, and the wine we ordered helped me to relax and drop my guard, becoming less Eve and more Melissa, during the evening.

Later, as we were pulling our jackets on, she suggested that the evening continued.

"How about you come back to mine, and I'll make us a cup of tea? You can wait there for a taxi. It'll be ages before you can get one, being a Saturday and this close to Christmas."

"Okay," I agreed. "Where do you live now?"

"Not far." She named a nearby street, and I nodded, following as she led the way out of the restaurant's warm interior and into a frosty, frozen, white world outside.

I shivered in the below-zero temperatures, cursing my stupid feminine pride and wishing for thick tights and a long warm coat.

It was still reasonably early and the fair which came to town every Christmas was ablaze with lights and glitzy glamour, the old-fashioned carousel with its brightly painted wooden horses whirling around and around.

We stopped for a moment, watching as children clung tightly and waved to parents who dutifully waved back. It was charming.

I felt a lump in my throat at the thought that back at the Hall we didn't even have a Christmas tree this year. None of us had liked to suggest having one, feeling it would have been insensitive to Mimi. Now I was struck by the thought that maybe we should instead have clung to the old traditions, that perhaps she would have found a little comfort in them.

Ally lived on a street that led away from the hill and its cheerful reminder that Christmas was so close. We were soon entering the small, terraced house, grateful for its welcoming warmth as Ally firmly closed and, to my uneasy surprise, locked the front door behind us.

"Go through," she urged, gesturing towards the lounge. I entered the room, reeling back in shock at the gaunt, steely-eyed man sitting in the armchair, eyes narrowing with grim satisfaction at my discomfort as I glanced nervously back towards the door.

"Hello, Mel," said Mike.

"Mike," I replied, my calm tone hiding the frantic pace of my heart. "What are you doing here?"

He smiled. It wasn't a nice smile, not the happy-go-lucky grin I remembered.

"I live here," he answered.

I looked at Ally's still, watchful face, and saw the whole evening had been a set-up. A ploy to get me here, although for what purpose I couldn't begin to imagine.

"I see," I replied slowly, my mind racing. I raised my brows at Ally. "Something you forgot to mention during our catch-up session?"

She flushed, then glared at me.

"I bumped into Mike two years ago," she said, her tone hostile and defensive. "He was out of prison and desperate to see you, to see if maybe you could pick up where you'd left off, even though you'd never made any attempt to visit him inside. He didn't know, you see, Mel..."

"Didn't know what?" I asked casually, my heart hammering with sudden fear.

"Didn't know it was you who shopped me," he replied.

"That's ridiculous," I insisted. "Why on earth would I have turned my boyfriend in?"

"Because you'd got in with Annaliese and her crowd and we weren't good enough for you anymore," Ally answered, eight years of fermented jealousy bubbling behind her eyes.

"No," I said as calmly as I could. "It wasn't like that, I came home, and you were gone, then the police came. They questioned me, wanting to know what was in the boxes ..." I paused and allowed a pitying look to slide onto my face.

"Oh Mike," I said. "How could you have been so stupid? Storing the goods in our flat, was that Wayne's idea?"

"No," he replied petulantly, uncertainty on his face. I pressed home my advantage.

"I didn't know what you were up to, Mike, and even if I had I wouldn't have shopped you because I could have got myself into trouble. It was only through luck I had an alibi for the nights of the robberies. As it was, my parents got to hear about it and were furious with me. They ordered me to have nothing to do with you, even though I was so worried about you."

I injected a small catch of my breath into the speech, as though fighting with old emotions.

"Do you have any idea what it was like for me, Mike? My boyfriend had been arrested, I wasn't allowed to visit you, and everyone thought I'd had something to do with it. In the end, I had no choice but to get on with my life."

"Huh!" snorted Ally. "If you believe that, you'll believe anything."

"Shut it, Ally," ordered Mike, and looked at me, considering.

I gazed back in wide-eyed innocence. Then he smiled a genuine smile, and I knew I had pulled it off. He believed me, even if Ally didn't.

"It's good to see you again, Mel..."

"I don't fucking believe this!" exploded Ally in rage and Mike glared at her, his good humour vanishing in a flash. I saw a glimpse of what prison had done to him, of the violence simmering below the surface, and shivered.

"Go make that tea you promised," he ordered, eyes narrowing to slits and I prayed for Ally's sake that she obeyed him.

She opened her mouth to argue further, then closed it again, her hand straying to rub distractedly at her cheek as if remembering an old injury. I wondered if he ever hit her.

"So, Mel..." Mike turned to me once Ally had flounced from the room. "What are you doing with yourself now? You're looking amazing."

"Thank you," I replied calmly. "I'm working as a freelance research assistant."

"Very posh." He pulled a face. "Used to the finer life now then, are you?"

"You could say that." I shrugged, brain racing, wondering where this was leading. If he was going to touch me for money, or if he had something else in mind.

"Tell you what," he said. "I've got something better than tea, Mel, something I'm sure you'll appreciate a lot more."

"Oh yes?" I replied, voice disinterested. "What's that?"

To my horror, he pulled a small plastic bag from his pocket, containing what I guessed wasn't talcum powder. He smirked at me and cleared a space on the coffee table.

"I'm okay," I reassured him. "Not for me, thanks."

He looked at me. I saw the crafty cunning beneath his friendly smile and realised all the while I thought I had been fooling him he'd been fooling me.

"No, no, Mel, I insist," he replied, his smile growing fixed and steely.

"Okay," I shrugged. "Though I know you, Mike Tate, and it better not be any cheap shit. As you said, I'm used to the finer stuff in life now, you know."

His grin broadened, and he leant back in his chair, staring at me in grudging admiration.

"It's good stuff," he assured me.

"Okay, but I need to pee first," I replied. "Upstairs is it?"

"Yeah," he agreed. "Second door on the right. Oh, and Mel," he said, as I turned to go, "leave your bag. We don't want you phoning the police or anything silly, do we?"

I raised my brows as if offended by the accusation, shrugged, and dropped my bag onto a chair, slowly walking from the room and making my way upstairs.

I found the bathroom. Quietly, but firmly, I shut and locked the door behind me, not allowing my control to slip until I knew I was alone.

I rummaged desperately in my jacket pocket for my phone, thankful I had been unable to fit it into my tiny leather bag, so had slipped it into my pocket instead.

With hands that shook I dialled Scott's number, almost sobbing with relief when he answered.

"Scott," I whispered frantically. "Scott, you have to help me!"

"Eve? What's up? What's the matter?"

"I'm hiding in the bathroom and he's downstairs, and he's got drugs, I think it's cocaine and he's going to make me take some and I'm so scared, Scott, I can't get out, the front door's locked and I know if I try to make a run for it, he'll catch me."

"What? Eve, what are you talking about? Who's going to make you take drugs?"

"Mike Tate, my ex."

"I see," his voice was cold and distant. "Where exactly are you?"

Quickly, I whispered the address knowing it wasn't far from his apartment, blood pounding thankfully in my head when he sighed.

"Okay, I'll be there as quick as I can, just be careful, Eve."

I stuffed the phone in my pocket and used the loo. Tension and too much wine with dinner had played havoc with my bladder. I took my time washing my hands and then sauntered casually back downstairs.

Ally was sitting in the lounge, mugs of tea on the table in front of her. She glared at me as I came in. My eyes flicked to my bag. I could see from the fact it was half undone, that they had taken the chance whilst I was upstairs to go through it.

"Better?" queried Mike. I nodded.

Turning to Ally, I adopted one of Annaliese's best lady-of-the-manor poses.

"Ally, dear, I couldn't trouble you for a glass of water, could I? That wine has left me dry."

I kept the sweet smile on my face until she flounced off again into the kitchen, then pulled a superior face at Mike.

"Oh dear, I think I've upset her," I said, deliberately trying to get him to side with me against her.

"She'll get over it," he replied abruptly, watching as she re-emerged and thrust a glass into my hands.

Slowly, I sipped at it, listening as there were determined footsteps on the pavement outside, followed by a sharp knock at the door.

"Expecting company?" I asked, putting my glass down. Mike jerked his head at Ally, and she sidled into the hallway. I heard her unlock the door and ease it open.

"Yes?"

"I've come to collect Eve."

Scott's voice was familiar and welcome. I gathered up my bag and gave Mike a dazzling smile.

"Who?" Ally replied, puzzled. I stepped into the hall behind her.

"He means me." I pushed past her. "Goodbye." I glanced back at Mike who hadn't moved, and my smile became grim.

"You ever try to contact me again, either of you." I shot Ally a warning glare. "I really will turn you in."

I stepped out into the chill evening air, smirking at the disbelieving look on Ally's face as I tucked my arm into Scott's and walked away from the pair of them.

"Oh crap," I gasped, beginning to shake now I was no longer in any danger. "So pleased you were home tonight. I don't think I've ever been so scared…"

I broke off at the disdainful look he gave me as he pulled his arm free of my grasp.

"What the hell were you playing at, Eve? You go out with a man you know is a burglar and has been in trouble with the law, then you must expect this sort of thing to happen."

"I didn't,' I retorted, stung by his accusation.

He snorted and strode off. I hurried after him, my heels rapping sharply on the pavement.

"I swear to you I didn't, Scott. Ally called. She said she hadn't seen me for ages so could we meet up for a meal. I had no idea she was seeing Mike. I mean, why should I? I haven't even thought about him in eight years. After the meal, she offered me a cup of tea back at her place. I didn't know he was living with her, not until she locked the door behind me and there he was."

Scott stopped, turned to look at me, and sighed wearily.

"Okay," he said. "Come on, I'll make you a coffee back at mine and then I'll run you home."

He held out his arm again. Gratefully, I tucked my hand through it and allowed him to lead me up the hill onto the street where his apartment was located.

I loved Scott's apartment. Topmost one in a block which had been converted from offices, the views from his floor-to-ceiling windows out over the whole town were spectacular.

Silently, he let us into the apartment, leading the way to the ultra-modern, spacious kitchen, flicking the switch on the kettle, and getting down the coffee pot and mugs from the cupboard.

I slipped off my jacket and slung it over a chair, watching as he efficiently spooned coffee into the pot.

"What I don't understand," he said, his back still to me, "is why you met with Ally? I thought you'd left that life far behind you and didn't want to be reminded of Melissa anymore?"

"I didn't," I agreed, then hesitated. "I had to get away from the Hall, Scott. I feel so sorry for Mimi, of course, and was devastated by what happened, but sometimes I have to escape, get out of it. When Ally phoned and suggested a meeting it seemed too good an opportunity to miss. It's all right for you. You can get away by coming here when it all gets too much – if it ever does..." I muttered under my breath.

"What's that supposed to mean?" he demanded, swinging around to glare at me.

"Nothing ... well, I suppose it's because it doesn't seem to have affected you ... not like the rest of us, and I guess, sometimes, I don't understand how you can be so cold and uncaring..."

I broke off, afraid of the look in his eyes.

"Sometimes Eve, you can be a thoughtless bitch," he declared flatly. "I don't know why I ..." he stopped and rubbed his eyes.

"Andrew was my business partner, my friend, my best friend. His death has left such a hole in my life I doubt it can ever be filled. As for Essie, she was my goddaughter, I loved her, but if you can't believe that because I didn't weep and wail and fall apart like the rest of you, well then, I'm very sorry, Eve, but that's the way I am."

He turned away and threw coffee into the pot almost savagely. I stared at him, brain churning at the sudden realisation that if it weren't for the Scotts and Caros of this world, who quietly coped and dealt with everyday details during a crisis, then people like Mimi, Annaliese, and myself, wouldn't have the luxury of being able to completely fall apart and let everything go.

Something else occurred. Essie had been the same age as Samuel when he died.

I took a hesitant step forward, noticing the imperceptible trembling of his hands.

Another step and I stood beside him, gazing at him intently, watching the tiny muscle that pulsed at the corner of his mouth.

He glanced at me, his expression once more shuttered and unreadable.

"What is it, Eve?" he demanded warily.

I shook my head and made a tiny movement that brought me so close to him our arms brushed as he laid the coffee spoon down and pushed the pot towards the kettle.

Then, surprising us both, I reached up, locked my hands behind his neck, and pulled his head down to mine, pressing startled lips onto his beautiful mouth.

It was like kissing an icicle, rigid and unyielding.

I despaired, persevered, pressing my body to his, standing on tiptoe as I wound my arms about his body, pouring heart and soul into the kiss.

Suddenly, his arms grabbed at mine and pulled me away. I gazed into his stunned dark eyes.

For a moment I feared he was going to push me away. Then something broke in his expression, he bent his head and feasted greedily on my lips.

It was like kissing a volcano, hot and demanding.

His mouth moved hungrily over mine. Desire and need ricocheted between our bodies. Hands closed over my waist, lifting me onto the counter, sending mugs skidding as I wrapped my legs around him, pulling him closer, feeling his heat rub against me, groaning with desire as his large hands undid the buttons on my blouse, struggling with the zips on the inside of my boots.

His touch was scalding hot on my bare legs as he ran his fingers up my thighs, pulling off the boots and tossing them heedlessly away, his eyes widening at the long black socks I was wearing underneath.

"Let me take them off," I muttered hastily, embarrassed, but he stopped me.

"Leave them on," he ordered, his breathing ragged. "With the pleated skirt, they make you look like a schoolgirl."

"Perv," I gasped, as he pushed my shirt off and his hands closed over my breasts. I was rewarded by the sound of his rich chuckle, the first time I had heard him laugh since the tragedy.

"Scott," I groaned, as his mouth closed over my nipple, suckling on it through the silk of my cream lace bra.

"I want you. I want you so much."

I moved my hips, rotating my pulsing throbbing centre onto the bulge in his trousers, and heard his breathing catch as he thrust back.

"I could make love to you right here and now," he gasped.

"Then why don't you?" I bent my head and nibbled at his jaw.

"Because I've waited too long to have you in my bed for it to happen anywhere else."

His arms tightened around me, and I shrieked as he lifted me bodily off the counter, carrying me through the lounge and into the bedroom.

Gently, he deposited me onto his super-king-sized bed and reached to undo the buttons on his shirt, but I knelt up and pushed his fingers away.

Need making me clumsy, I tugged them open, before finally being rewarded with his bare, superbly toned flesh. I flattened my palms over his chest, feeling the heat of his skin and the thud of his heart.

Slithering down, I fumbled with the laces on his shoes, finally getting them undone and helping him to kick them off, pulled off his socks, then crawled back up his body and undid his zip, easing his trousers down over his hips, breath catching in my throat as I saw him for the first time.

Long and hard and firm, he was gorgeous, and I couldn't help myself but took him deep into my mouth. He cried out, hands fisting in my hair as I tasted and teased, starting slowly, then gradually becoming faster, relishing the hoarse cries being forced from his throat.

Finally, he pulled me away, his eyes dark, glittering with lust and need, hands shaking as he undid my skirt. It dropped to the ground, leaving me in matching cream lace underwear which he quickly disposed of, stepping out of his trousers, and following me down onto the bed.

We lay, heartbeat to heartbeat, skin to skin, our mouths joining in a frenzied kiss of ownership.

"Please," I begged. "Now, I want you now!"

He shifted me onto my back and knelt between my thighs. I felt him, hard and ready, and groaned with delight, raising my hips to meet him as he rubbed himself between my swollen lips, easing in the smallest way, mouth closing firmly over mine.

Then he paused and pulled away to look at me.

"Are you on the pill, Eve?"

"What?

I was incapable of rational thought, struggling to focus on his words.

"No, no, I'm not."

I felt the effort it took for him to pull back, away from me.

"Don't stop!" I begged, clutching at him. "I'm sure it'll be fine, please, don't stop."

"It's okay," he reassured. "I've got some condoms somewhere."

He rolled over and yanked open the top drawer of his bedside cabinet, frantically sifting through its contents, growling with frustration as he struggled to find them.

I rolled over behind him, running my hands over his perfect body, pressing kisses and small teasing bites down his spine and over his hips.

"Eve," he groaned. "You're not helping…"

My fist closed over him and began to move, and he gasped and jerked, the drawer flying out and upending its entire contents onto the floor.

"There they are," I exclaimed, pointing at a small cellophane-wrapped packet entangled in a mobile charger cord.

He snatched them up, fumbling helplessly with the packaging, glaring at me when I giggled, rolling onto his back, his movements clumsy.

Finally, it was on, and he rolled back, gathered me up in his arms and simply thrust in one smooth glorious movement.

Now it was my turn to cry out, head back, eyes closed to preserve the perfection of the moment in my memory.

Yes, cried my body. At last, sighed my heart.

I pulled him to me, mouths meeting in a kiss of such tenderness I wanted to cry for the love I fancied I felt behind it.

We began to move together, perfect harmony, perfect rhythm, as he plunged and thrust, deep and even strokes which quickly brought me quivering to the edge of orgasm, then he stopped, held still, and I grasped him with dismay.

"Don't stop!" I begged. "Please don't stop."

"I have to," he gasped. "I want you so badly and I've waited for so long, I can't hold back. It'll be over too quickly for you."

"No, it won't," I panted. "I'm there, too, with you, come with me, oh yes!" I groaned as he began to move again.

"Yes, that's it, oh Scott, my Scott..."

I clutched at him, my head thrashing from side to side, feet planted firmly on the mattress as my body thrust up to meet him, stroke for stroke. The world stood still for a glorious, infinite moment.

Then the orgasm crashed down, and I felt him jerk, push deep inside me, throb, and pulse in faultless tempo with my climax, one word only being ripped from his throat.

"Eve!"

Gradually, we slowed and lay still, our ragged breathing the only sound in the dimly lit room.

I longed for him to say the words, ached to say them back to him. But because he couldn't, I wouldn't, and so the moment passed.

He rolled onto his back, taking me with him so I flopped in a state of fluid contentment, my head on his chest, realising with a twist of amusement that I was still wearing the socks.

He removed the condom with a grimace of distaste and deposited it into a tissue. I laughed at his face.

"Looks like I need to try taking the pill again," I murmured. He looked at me in concern, gathering me closer in his arms, drawing the duvet up and over us.

"Why did you stop taking it?"

"Oh, my blood pressure went through the roof and the doctor said I needed to come off it, but that was years ago, I'm sure..."

"No," he interrupted fiercely. "You're not taking it, not if there's a chance it could hurt you. We'll manage with condoms."

"But they're pretty gross…"

"We'll manage," he insisted firmly, and I realised it was the end of the matter.

We lay quietly, sated and content, firmly clasped in each other's arms. I didn't think I'd ever been so happy.

We kissed, tenderly and gently, yet there was fire brewing beneath the kisses, and I knew, with a thrill of anticipation, that it wouldn't be long before we made love again.

Beside me, Scott stretched and made to get out of bed. I groaned and reached after him.

"Don't go," I pleaded.

He chuckled and kissed me firmly. "I won't be long," he promised. "There's something I want to get."

He pulled on his trousers, leaving them unbuttoned so they rode low over his slim hips, and I growled with approval, making him glance at me, amused.

"Down girl," he teased. "I'll be back, soon."

I watched him go, realising I had never appreciated how truly gorgeous his body was. I'd seen him in shorts and swimming trunks, knew he took care of himself, worked out and so on, but it hadn't been until today, seeing him completely naked, that I'd realised how perfect it was.

I waited patiently for a few moments but missed him, so I slithered from the bed, tried to find my blouse, and then remembered it was probably still lying on the kitchen floor.

I pulled his shirt loosely over me, doing up only the middle two buttons, padding into the lounge in search of him.

The sound of a champagne cork being pulled in the kitchen made me smile, but the amazing view from the wall of glass caught and pulled me over to gaze out across the town.

I could see the fair, its twinkling, coloured lights looking like a distant magical kingdom. I watched as the big wheel revolved, the people on it waving their arms in the air and wondered if they could see me.

I waved, no one waved back, then forgot about them as a pair of arms, warm and strong and already achingly familiar, crept about me and Scott pulled me close, pressing kisses into my neck.

"I wondered where you'd gone to," he murmured, and I leant back into him.

"I was watching the fair," I replied dreamily. "How magical it looks."

"Do you want to get dressed and go to it?" he asked.

I turned to look him in the eyes, rubbing my thumb over his bottom lip, watching as his gaze clouded over with desire.

"The only place I want you to take me," I murmured, "is back to bed."

He took me by the hand and led me there. I smiled to see a bottle of champagne resting in an ice bucket, and a pair of delicate crystal flutes beside it on the bedside cabinet.

He poured out two glasses and handed me one. I sipped at the delicious golden liquid, eyeing him archly over the rim.

"I didn't think you drank," I murmured, and he smiled at me, a shy and sweet smile, so unlike his usual sardonic smirk that I blinked in surprise.

"I'll have a glass of champagne on really special occasions," he replied, and I ran my fingers lightly down his bare chest.

"So, is this a special occasion?" I asked.

He moved closer, his free arm slipping around my waist, holding me firmly.

"Oh, I think so, don't you?" he murmured, nibbling at my lip, his breath tasting of champagne.

My heart thudding against my rib cage, I ached for him to go that final step and tell me what his true feelings were.

He looked at me, his heart in his eyes. I held my breath, hoping, waiting...

"Eve ..." he began hesitantly.

"Yes?" I breathed, heart-thumping painfully with hopeful anticipation.

"Eve, I..."

His phone rang, and the moment was lost. He sighed, and picked it up, frowning at the caller ID.

"It's Annaliese," he said. "Annaliese, hi, oh, I see, no, no, Eve's with me, she had dinner with a friend in town and we met up afterwards for a drink."

I smiled at his telling of the literal truth and all it was concealing, lightly tracing my fingers up and down his bare chest.

"No, no, that won't be a problem, I was about to run Eve home anyway."

At my narrow-eyed look of enquiry, he frowned and slightly shook his head.

"Yes, yes, I quite understand, no, you're right, it is worrying, so we'll go there right now, and I'll call you to let you know everything's ok, right, bye."

"What was all that about?" I asked, as he tossed the phone onto the bed and began to hastily fasten his trousers.

"Annaliese and Robert are still in London, Miles and Ferdie have gone to some university do, and Caro's out at her evening class. Annaliese realised Mimi's completely on her own so tried to ring her, but she's getting no answer."

"She's probably gone to bed," I replied, reluctantly giving him back his shirt.

"I know," he said, sitting on the edge of the bed to pull back on his socks and shoes. "But Annaliese is worried, so I said we'd go check Mimi's okay."

I pouted and he smiled, pressing a hasty kiss onto my nose.

"Bring the champagne," he ordered. "I promise I'll help you finish the bottle."

"Okay," I reluctantly agreed and picked up my underwear. "Have you seen my blouse?" I asked, wiggling back into my underwear as he watched in evident enjoyment.

"Kitchen, I think," he replied, "I'll get it."

When he came back, I was picking something up off the floor.

"What are you doing?" he asked.

I held up the pack of condoms.

"Packing for you," I replied and smirked, enjoying the head rush of power at the desire which leapt into his face.

"How fast can you drive to the Hall and still be safe?" I purred.

"Very fast," he gasped, snatching the condoms, and stuffing them into his pocket.

I attacked him in the lift, and again in the car, leaving him erect and groaning with frustrated need, his hands roaming up under my short skirt, long clever fingers arousing me to an achingly painful want, the sharp tang of sex evident as we flopped back in our seats, flushed and panting.

"Can't we have one here?" I begged. "Just to tide us over."

"Eve," he groaned, obviously tempted. "I promised Annaliese we'd be quick."

"Oh, believe me," I gasped, "it'll be quick."

I straddled him, rubbing myself onto his firm maleness. For a moment he succumbed, hands clasping my waist, thrusting upwards in evident desire. Then he groaned, reluctantly pulled me off and deposited me back onto the passenger's seat.

"Bad girl," he gasped, pulling on his seatbelt. "Let's sort out the whole Mimi thing as quick as possible and then the only question will be..."

"My room or yours?"

I finished his sentence, laid my head back on the rest, my eyes huge with promise, as he started the engine and we shot out of the car park.

"My room has a fire ready laid," I murmured, hands delving between his legs, stroking and caressing. "And I have a yearning to seduce you in front of a roaring fire, before taking you to bed and doing it all over again."

"Eve ..." he moaned, only just stopping at a red light in time and narrowly missing hitting the kerb.

I laughed, low and throaty, thoroughly enjoying myself, wishing I'd had the nerve to do this years ago.

We made it to the Hall in record time, the car squealing to a halt, sending gravel flying in all directions. I jumped out, impatiently waiting as Scott climbed out and locked the doors, before grabbing and kissing me fiercely.

"Now behave yourself," he murmured, "It's probably best if we act like everything's normal in front of Mimi."

"Okay," I promised, my hands roaming over his body. "I'll try, oh oh..." my head lolled back as his hand cupped my breast, catching the nipple between his fingers.

"You keep doing stuff like that though, and I'm afraid I'll simply take you there and then, Mimi or no Mimi."

He laughed and pulled away. I thought about how I had never known him to be so carefree, then he glanced up at the Hall and frowned.

"That's odd," he remarked. "There are no lights on."

I looked up at the dark and imposing façade of the Hall, realising he was right. It was in total darkness.

This was unheard of. Annaliese tended to leave lights on all over the place and we had all fallen into the same bad habit.

But now, not a glimmer of light could be seen anywhere, the only illumination coming from two carriage lights on either side of the door.

Holding hands, we hurried up the steps and through the heavy front door. Inside, the entrance hall was almost pitch dark and I stumbled slightly, Scott's hand tightening on mine to steady me.

"Mimi?" he called, his voice echoing into the blackness. "You stay here," he ordered, "I'll feel my way across to the light switches, perhaps a fuse has blown or something. I hope not, I don't fancy trying to find Mimi in the dark."

"Eve?"

There was a soft rustle from the direction of the stairs, and I fancied I saw a shape creep softly upwards in the darkness.

"Mimi?" I called. "Is that you? Why is it so dark?"

"I switched the lights off," she replied, her voice low and toneless. "They hurt my eyes."

This had been one of the most bizarre symptoms of Mimi's grief – her extreme sensitivity to light. Ferdie had claimed, in one of his rare insightful moments, that it was because she didn't want to see real life anymore so hid away from it in the shadows.

"Please," she murmured. "Please don't turn them back on yet. Could you sit with me for a while, I don't want to be alone, and I'd like to talk ... about what happened and about them..."

Beside me, I felt Scott tense. Throughout the past five months, Mimi had rarely spoken about the accident, or about Andrew and Essie.

Various experts had told Annaliese that in their opinion, until Mimi snapped out of this denial and fully acknowledged they were gone, she would never be able to move on, or reach, to use that dreadful American phrase, closure.

"Of course," Scott spoke, his voice low and reassuring. "We'll sit here on the stairs with you,

Mimi, and we can talk about whatever you want to."

I felt a pang of disappointment but shook it off. Scott and I had the rest of the night, indeed, the rest of our lives together, and this was important.

If Mimi was finally prepared to talk about what had happened, then we had to put all other concerns to one side and be prepared to listen.

Carefully, we felt our way over to the stairs and began to climb. I stifled a gasp as Scott's hand slid under my skirt, briefly caressed my bottom, and then slithered down my thighs.

"Where are you, Mimi?" he asked. I marvelled that his voice could sound so flat, so normal, especially as I knew how aroused he was.

"Here," came the reply, quite close, only a couple more steps up from where we were standing, and I realised she was hidden from view around the corner. Gently, Scott sank onto a step, pulling me down with him, his presence reassuring in the almost total darkness.

The icy marble was shocking against my bare legs, and I shivered into my jacket, goose-bumps sprinkling my flesh. After a brief pause, Mimi began to talk.

I quickly understood our role was to be silent listeners, only being called upon to interject occasional, quiet agreements, as she rambled through her memories of her time with her husband, and her short, too short, time with her daughter.

We listened and were there for her. All the time I was achingly aware of him, could smell his cologne, hear his calm even breathing, and gradually inched my fingers across the stair until they collided with his.

For a while we sat, silently holding hands, giving Mimi our undivided attention as she talked and talked, her voice slightly slurred and thick as if she were drunk or drugged. I wondered if she had taken a sleeping pill that evening.

Scott raised my hand to his mouth. In the darkness he silently kissed my fingers, his tongue rasping into the palm of my hand, and I bit my lip to stop myself from sighing out loud.

I felt for his other hand, so chilled from contact with the step it seemed almost damp, and pressed his palm to my heart, trying to convey to him the depth of my feelings for him, attempting to tell him, without the need for words, that I loved him.

His fingers splayed between my breasts. Then he reached for my hand and mirrored the movement, pressing my hand to him, to where I could feel the thump of his heart. His other hand crept to my face. Tenderly, gently, he cupped my chin.

My breath caught, desperately trying not to read too much into it, but wanting, oh so badly, for it to mean he loved me, too.

I reached for him, found his shoulder in the darkness, and pulled him to me, quietly pressing kisses over his face and neck, his breath quickening beneath my lips.

I wondered how much longer we had to wait before Mimi stopped and we could put her to bed, could go to my room and lock the door.

I became aware Mimi had stopped talking and pushed Scott away, turning my head to where I knew Mimi was in the darkness.

"Mimi?" I questioned, but there was no reply.

"Mimi?" Scott echoed. "Are you still with us?" Again, there was nothing but silence, and he murmured into the darkness.

"I think she's asleep."

"I think so," I agreed. "Maybe we should help her to bed."

"Yes, and then I think I'll turn in, too," he said, his voice so calm and logical I wanted to burst into hysterical giggles.

"Stay here," he said. "I'll go back down and switch on the lights."

I stroked a hand down his thigh as he rose, heard the slight intake of breath and felt a rush of exhilarated anticipation, listening and laughing at his painstakingly slow progress downstairs, muttering curses under his breath as he misjudged the number and fell down the last two steps.

"Are you all right?" I called and smiled at his exasperated agreement. He reached the switches and turned on the lights.

I closed my eyes against the sudden brightness, feeling a little of what Mimi meant when she claimed the light hurt her eyes.

I grinned through the bannisters at Scott; then frowned in horrified disbelief.

A red handprint, smeared but quite distinct, was plastered across his chest.

Scarlet blotched his shoulder.

He stared back at me, an equally appalled expression on his face. I looked down – blood, fresh, red, and sticky. A large handprint stained my blouse, its vividness standing out obscenely on the sheer white silken fabric.

My hands were bloody. The marble steps on which I sat were splotched and splattered, a milky way of red. Following the pattern, my eyes turned upwards.

I rose, stumbled up the stairs on hands and knees, barked my shins as I tripped and fell, followed the pattern around the corner and saw, but couldn't comprehend what I was seeing.

Mimi slumped against the wall; face chalk-white in stark comparison to the blood which dripped from her wrists. It had left its trail down the stairs to the step where we had sat, rose red against snow-white marble.

The scream clawed its way out of my throat.

Scott was running up the stairs, crying out in horror, and rushing to Mimi, his foot kicking the small blade lying on the step beside her. It bounced and trembled, glinting in the blinding light.

"Eve!" he shouted. "Phone for an ambulance, quickly!"

I couldn't move.

Her blood was on my hands, was indelibly printed over both our hearts, we were both soaked in it. My precious new love, tentatively unfolding from its shiny new bud of creation was spoiled and tainted, washed away in a sticky tide of red.

CHAPTER IX – LUKE

"Have you ever lost someone you loved?"

She lived, in that she did not die, but an essential part of Mimi passed away that evening. The part belonging to Andrew and Essie, that segment of her which had loved passionately and completely, was lost forever, drained away with her lifeblood spilt down a marble staircase.

My memories of that evening are dim. The events leading up to the switching on of the lights remain sharply etched in my mind, but the precise sequence of events after that point, I am still, to this day, unclear.

I know that Miles and Ferdie arrived at the same time as the ambulance, following it as it screamed through the park gates, exchanging glances of trepidation, and wondering what latest catastrophe had befallen us.

I have a vague recollection of Scott desperately ripping strips off his shirt to bind her wrists, on which the wounds gaped like open mouths, red and raw. I couldn't bear to look at them but was unable to look away.

I heard his voice, dim and distant, as he shouted at her to stay with us. He slapped her face and held her arms above her head. He shouted at me, too, his face tight and alarmed.

I heard his concern but couldn't respond. I was incapable of movement and sat, gripping the bannisters, like a child afraid of monsters.

He gabbled an explanation at Miles and Ferdie as they crowded through the door, expressions horrified at the sight of Mimi on the stretcher, so pale, so small.

Miles immediately insisted on going to the hospital with her, his normally mild-mannered tone becoming belligerent and unrelenting. He was going with her and that was that.

In the end, both Scott and Miles went, leaving Ferdie to deal with me. Twittering with concern, he gently helped me to my room and into the bathroom. I saw myself in the mirror, the blood – her blood – daubed my face like a brand where Scott had held my chin. I choked on the thought and vomited up the memory.

Ferdie undressed me as if I were a child, tenderly and gently. He put me in the shower where I scrubbed until I was raw, desperate to wash away the blood staining my skin.

He bundled me into a thick robe and combed my hair, crooning nonsense the whole time until I began to shake, and the reality of the situation hit home. Then he held me as my teeth chattered and I shivered in delayed shock, tutting his concern at my extreme distress; not realising the depths of my torture.

It was all spoilt. My beautiful, innocent love affair which had barely had a chance to begin was over, washed away in a tide of Mimi's blood. I was selfish enough to despise her for it and shuddered with self-loathing at the thought.

I felt dirty. Unclean. We'd held and touched each other and the whole time, mere feet away, Mimi's life had been slowly ebbing from her body. We'd been oblivious, desperate for each other, caught up in the newness of our affair.

Ferdie put me to bed, force-fed me a sleeping tablet, and rocked me until dark waves closed over my head and dragged me under.

Unused to taking them, I slept until late the following day, waking with a muzzy head and a dry mouth, disorientated, unable to comprehend where I was and what had happened.

I struggled to sit up in bed. Blinking in the gloom, I reached out to snap on the bedside lamp. There was movement from the sofa and Scott stood, his expression relieved when he saw me sitting up, rubbing at eyes crusted with sleep.

"Eve," he breathed. "I was beginning to think you'd sleep forever…"

"Mimi?" I interrupted urgently.

"She's going to be all right. They had to give her a blood transfusion, and she needed surgery on her wrists, but she's going to be okay." He paused and pulled a wry expression. "Well, as okay as you can be after something like this."

I let my head drop to my chest, relieved, but disconcerted by his presence. He crossed to the bed, sat beside me, and reached for my hand. I pulled away. I couldn't let him touch me, could hardly bring myself to look at him. I saw wariness enter his eyes.

"Eve?" he began. "Is everything okay?"

"Well," I mumbled, voice croaky and dry, "you said Mimi's going to be all right, so I guess everything's okay."

"No, I mean with us?"

"There is no us," I stated flatly, and his eyes narrowed in disbelief.

"How can you say that?" he demanded. "After last night I thought..."

"If Mimi hadn't nearly bled to death all over us, there might have been an us," I cried. "If she had done it at any other time and in any other place, then, maybe, perhaps, we might have had a chance. But not now."

"Don't say that." I heard panic under his words. Frantically, he grabbed at my shoulders and tried to pull me into his arms. I remained stiff and unyielding, bile rising in my throat at the memories his touch invoked.

"I'm sorry, Scott," I whispered into his shoulder and felt his instinctive clutch of denial, "I can't do this. Every time you touch me, I see her. I think about her blood on us, and it makes me feel sick and unclean. It's ruined everything."

"You'll feel differently," he insisted hotly. "In time, you'll get over this and we can be together."

He pulled back, cupping my face in his hands. I shrivelled inside, imagining her blood there again, staining and tainting.

"Eve, please..."

I said nothing, merely stared at him in numb misery, adamant in my rejection.

Looking back, I believe if he had persisted, had refused to take no for an answer, had told me he loved me, maybe he could have broken through to me and things would have been different.

Such behaviour was totally alien to Scott and completely beyond his capability. Slowly, he moved from me. I saw the barriers which had tentatively begun to lower for me, slam back up, and knew it was over. Without saying another word, he rose and left the room, and I wept until I had no more tears to shed.

Christmas was a subdued and mournful experience that year, with no Andrew and no Essie, and Mimi still incarcerated in the hospital. Annaliese's headaches grew worse, exacerbated, I believed, by the stress of the situation, and the constant, ongoing concern she had for Mimi.

Caro, too, vented her worry for Mimi by snapping and snarling at anyone who got in her way. The rest of us were silent and withdrawn.

I was aware I'd hurt Scott beyond measure and knew it was apparent to everyone how much he'd retreated within himself. He began staying late at work, barely talking to anyone, and using Andrew's absence as a feasible excuse, but I knew it was because he was avoiding me.

I both longed for his presence and recoiled from it. Confused and alone, I, too, began spending more time away from home, visiting my parents and accepting work which necessitated travelling and staying away for days, sometimes even weeks, on end.

Time limped on. Eventually, Mimi came home, a pale, silent shadow of her former feisty, vibrant self, and the whole Hall tiptoed around her fragile hold on sanity.

I found it hard to look at her. I wondered how much she remembered of that evening; wondered if she'd heard us. If she had, she made no mention of it, in fact, she rarely spoke at all.

I knew Annaliese was beginning to despair of ever pulling her through the dark forest and out into the sunlight on the other side.

One evening I couldn't sleep and slipped downstairs to fetch a book from the library. The room was empty, a green-shaded lamp casting warming shadows over the room. I pulled out a copy of Bleak House then heard the door handle creak, and instinctively ducked down into a high-backed winged chair.

I didn't know who I was hiding from, only knew I wasn't in the mood to deal with Mimi's dead-eyed sorrow or Scott's curtly dismissive manner. I curled deeper into the chair, hoping whoever it was would leave quickly so I could escape back to my room.

"Mimi?" I heard Annaliese call from the hallway outside; and then came Mimi's low answer so I knew she was in the room, over by the desk, mere feet away from me.

"Darling," Annaliese said softly. "What are you doing in here all alone?"

"I couldn't sleep," Mimi replied, her voice vague and uncaring.

"Would you like me to make you some hot chocolate?" offered Annaliese, and I almost heard Mimi's indifferent shrug.

"If you like..."

"No, if you'd like," replied Annaliese, yet I fancied for the first time I heard a ring of impatience in her voice.

"I don't care," said Mimi.

There was a silence that stretched on for so long I wondered if they'd quietly left the room.

"Mimi," said Annaliese, her voice crisp. "This has to stop you know, it can't go on forever."

"What can't?"

"This self-indulgent mourning."

"What?" Mimi sounded shocked at Annaliese's words.

"I know you didn't mean to die. I understand it was a cry for help."

"A cry for help? I slashed my wrists!" exclaimed Mimi hotly, her voice animated for the first time since the death of her family.

"Not very effectively though," retorted Annaliese. "You and I both know, Mimi if you'd meant it, if you'd intended to die, then you'd have gone somewhere alone and done a much better job of it."

"How can you say such a thing?" cried Mimi in outrage.

"Because you cut across your wrists," replied Annaliese calmly. "And we both know the wrists must be cut upwards to the elbow to get the job done. Also, you knew you wouldn't be left alone for very long, and that someone would find you."

"I wanted to die," insisted Mimi. "I wanted to be with my husband and daughter."

"I know," replied Annaliese gently. "But this isn't the way to go about it. Even if you had succeeded Mimi, you still wouldn't have been with them."

"Why not?" cried Mimi, a sob catching at her throat.

"Because there's a natural order to things," answered Annaliese firmly. "And suicides upset that natural order. You would have gone to a different place Mimi, and never have seen them again. You must wait until it's your turn."

"But I miss them so much," sobbed Mimi. "I want them back. I want to be with them. You have no idea what it's like to lose someone you love, to lose a child."

"Sometimes our children are taken from us, and we have no idea why," Annaliese replied softly, and I frowned at her words, wondering what she meant. "It's all part of God's plan," she finished, and Mimi cried out at her words, rounding on her in full-blown anger.

"I care nothing for your God," she screamed. "How can I believe in something that would take my little girl away from me, my Andrew?"

"Because he's the one who gave them to you in the first place," Annaliese stated firmly. "Because you had Andrew for twelve happy and healthy years, and you watched your daughter grow into a beautiful and strong eight-year-old. That is so much more than some get, believe me."

"It wasn't enough," Mimi gasped. "I wanted them forever. Andrew – I expected us to grow old together, and Essie – no one should have to bury their child! You speak of the natural order. Is it the natural order that she died before me? It should have been me who died, not her, it should have been me!"

Her sobs became wild and reckless. "Why wasn't it me?" she demanded brokenly, and I heard Annaliese soothing her.

"Maybe God has other plans for you," she murmured. Peeping around the corner of my chair, I saw her rocking Mimi in her arms, holding her until her sobs had abated and she gasped for air, struggling to breathe through a blocked-up nose. Annaliese pulled tissues from the box on the desk and gently wiped her eyes.

"Is everything all right?" Caro's gruff tones demanded from the doorway. I froze in my hiding place, unwilling to face her censure if I was discovered eavesdropping.

"Caro, darling," said Annaliese, "could you possibly take Mimi to the kitchen and make her a big mug of your wonderful hot chocolate."

"Of course," agreed Caro readily, her voice surprisingly gentle. "Come on, lovey," she coaxed, "I think I can even find some extra cream and marshmallows, just how you like it."

"That ... would be ... nice," Mimi whispered.

"Annaliese, shall I make one for you?"

"Yes, please," agreed Annaliese. "I'll be there in a minute." She waited until the door closed behind them, before saying, "It's all right, they've gone. You can come out now, Eve."

I popped my head up from behind the chair.

"How did you know I was here?" I demanded.

"Jean-Paul Gaultier?" she laughed, lifted my wrist, and sniffed, as my eyes went wide with surprised agreement. "I could smell it, was surprised Mimi didn't notice it, but then, she did have her mind on other things."

"Will she be all right?" I asked, worried.

Annaliese's smile slipped. She squeezed into the chair's broad expanse next to me, placing an arm about my shoulders and pulling me close.

"I think she will be now," she replied, slowly. "I hated having to be so harsh with her, but sometimes the people we love cannot see that what they need is a good hard jolt of reality."

I did not reply, but dropped my head onto her shoulder, enjoying the moment of closeness, the physical intimacy.

"Annaliese?"

"Yes?"

"Have you ever lost someone you loved?"

There was a long silence. Annaliese absently traced her finger around the embossed letter B on the cover of my book. Round and round. I wondered if she was going to answer. Then she rested her cheek on the top of my head.

"Yes, I have."

"Who was it?"

"Oh, someone," she said vaguely. "It was a very long time ago and it doesn't matter now." She slipped out of my embrace, "I'd better go and check on Mimi," she continued, and I had the feeling she was escaping from the question.

She paused, took my head in her hands, and pressed a soft kiss to my forehead.

"Sleep well, my dear little Eve," she murmured and was gone.

To say Mimi improved from that moment on would be over-simplifying things. Rather it seemed she made up her mind at that point to get better. Gradually, day by day and week by week, we began to see tiny improvements.

The day she allowed Robert and Annaliese to take her for a drive in the country; the day she popped into the shop to see how her frighteningly efficient, yet over-stretched manageress was coping; the day Scott took her to the coast; the day she came out to lunch with me; the evening Miles took her to the theatre, and the day she smiled, for the first time in months, at one of Ferdie's jokes.

These were all monumental milestones for Mimi. We noted and silently applauded her upon achieving each one.

The weather grew warmer, the seasons turned, and the fresh days of April were upon us.

It had been four months since that frenzied, passionate encounter in Scott's apartment.

In all that time he'd not exchanged more than a dozen words with me, words so impartial and casual, that they could have been mere small talk uttered at random by a passing stranger.

I deeply mourned the loss, not only of my lover but of my friend. Reflecting bitterly on how if I had known there would be such a heavy trade-off for the ecstasy I found in his arms, I never would have taken that fateful step.

Instead, I would have stayed his friend forever. Wistful, maybe; regretting what might have been, possibly; but still his beloved little Eve. His friend. To be looked at in amusement and with affection, not someone to be dismissed as though of no importance, no regard.

It was my fault, I knew that, but could see no way to rectify it. I'd had my chance and pushed him away. Maybe it was because I was reeling with shock over Mimi's attempted suicide, but for Scott, this was not an acceptable excuse. He opened himself up to me, only to be rejected. I knew he would not take that chance again.

I came upon him once, huddled in a corner and talking in urgent, hushed whispers with Annaliese, hand grasping her arm, mouth close to her face, his expression anguished. At my entrance, they had sprung apart guiltily.

I'd quickly murmured my apologies and left, heart pounding at what I'd seen, convinced they'd been discussing me, and yet ... thinking about it, remembering the looks on their faces when they saw me, I wasn't so sure.

More time passed and summer burst upon us. The anniversary of Andrew and Essie's deaths came and went. Mimi visited their graves to lay flowers and weep at their memory. Yet her blank-eyed days of mourning were over, and it was a healthy sorrow, her tears cleansing.

The summer passed, as summers do. Then, into this house of still reflection and sombre thoughts came a stranger. Someone who would change everything and would act as a catalyst for the explosion which had been quietly building.

What happened wasn't his fault. Instead, it was a combination of my unhappiness and loneliness, of Scott's mistrust and old and festering secrets finally forcing their way to the surface after being buried too long underground.

His name was Luke, and he was Caro's son.

The first I heard of his visit was when I came across Annaliese following Mrs Briggs into one of the spare rooms, a heap of bedding and towels in her arms.

"Company?" I asked, and she turned to face me, her expression animated.

"Yes, isn't it exciting? Caro's son Luke is coming to visit so I'm sprucing up a room for him."

"Oh?" I replied, feeling a spark of interest. "When's he coming?"

"Tomorrow, Robert's picking him up from Heathrow on his way back from London."

Over the next twenty-four hours, I found myself thinking often of the stranger who would soon be staying amongst us. I wondered what he was like and tried to imagine how I would feel to have a grown-up son of twenty-five coming to see me for the first time since he was a child.

I observed Caro closely, yet if she was apprehensive at his impending visit, she gave no sign of it, going about her normal business with her usual air of efficiency, scowling at me when she noticed me watching her.

At last, the moment arrived. When Robert's car pulled up outside the Hall, I was lurking at an upstairs window curious to catch a glimpse of him. I was surprised to see Scott climb from the car, then realised with a jolt it was a stranger, yet so like Scott from behind it was uncanny.

As tall as Scott and almost as dark, his tanned lean body looked dangerously masculine in chinos and a casual shirt.

He stretched, looking around in interest, his eyes flicking upwards and meeting mine. Embarrassed, I ducked back, but not before I saw his keen blue eyes crinkle with amusement, his hand half rising in a salute of greeting.

Quickly, I ran downstairs to join the others, nonchalantly assuming a casual position on the sofa next to Annaliese, as if I'd been there all the time. But it didn't fool him for a moment.

When he entered the room behind Robert, his eyes twinkled in my direction, and then he was greeted by Caro, sweeping her up in a hug which left her flustered and groping for words.

I liked him, at least I thought I did. He was very American, confident and brash, so sure of himself and his place in the world and ruggedly handsome. Dark hair framed a strong tanned face in which blue eyes sparkled with humour.

His tight shirt showcased a well-muscled torso and there was an air of toughness about him. I knew his work often took him to dangerous regions of the world, and he certainly appeared a man who could take care of himself.

He shook hands with the men, was courtly to the women, and downright flirtatious with me. As Caro grudgingly introduced us, his hand held on for slightly longer than necessary and his eyes locked onto mine, registering his interest.

It was a shock to be looked at with desire. After eight months of Scott's stony disapproval, I had forgotten the head rush it could cause to be looked at that way by an attractive man.

Flustered and confused, not daring to look in Scott's direction, and feeling Caro's glare of disapproval, I stumbled backwards and sat on the sofa.

I listened with interest as he answered Annaliese's questions about his journey, his work, how long he intended to stay, and what his plans were. All the time, I was aware of his glance occasionally flicking my way.

We all had dinner together. Mrs Briggs surpassed herself with a stupendous meal, which Luke praised to the skies, making her flush with pleasure, and ensuring he got the lion's share of pudding.

As I looked around at the happy smiling faces, I realised Luke's presence had almost jolted us back in time to the way we were before the tragedy. When an evening spent together would always be a time of much laughter and shared pleasure in each other's company.

I felt myself relax, thinking how nice it was for Caro that her son had seemingly turned out so warm and friendly, so normal, given his mother had abandoned him when he was only one.

I beamed at her, got a suspicious glare in return, and hastily looked away, catching sight of Scott's face. He stared at me. It was as if someone had painted a disapproving face onto a slab of granite. I looked at my plate feeling a prick of tears, my previously good mood deflated.

Luke stayed a week with us. During that time, I found my emotions going through abrupt three-point turns. He'd flirt outrageously with me, and I'd find myself enjoying it, then catch sight of Scott, or he'd pop into my head, and I'd pull away feeling confused and guilty, although over what I wasn't too sure.

Not that we saw much of Scott. The pressure of work, he urbanely explained to Annaliese when she questioned him about his absence.

Long hot days … Luke spent a lot of time with his mother. I fancied I saw a softening in her manner, and once or twice caught her looking at him with an expression of wonder, as if marvelling that such a man could be her son.

Annaliese, Mimi, and I took him to lunch in town and showed him around. He took photos of things that caught his eye; things I'd seen before, dozens of times, but never taken any notice of until Luke showed them to me through the lens of a camera.

And still, the temperature rose … It went beyond being pleasantly warm to being unbearable. Sightseeing was abandoned, heat bounced at us from broiling pavements, and we increasingly sought refuge in the cool of the Hall, its shady woodland, or on the island, dangling feet in the coldness of the lake, filling buckets with chilled water to keep our wine cool.

It grew steadily hotter. As the temperature rose, so did the confusion within my heart. I knew Luke liked me a lot. Given the slightest encouragement, I knew he would make a move, his admiration and blatant lust were intoxicating and heady, especially as he kept it so well hidden from the others.

In front of them, he behaved himself, yet if he ever caught me alone his voice would drop to a husky murmur, his eyes would intensify and his hands would touch me in innocent, suggestive ways.

He would brush a stray hair off my cheek, gently grasp my wrist to check the time on my watch, drop his hand to the small of my back as I preceded him through a door, and I would feel it burning through my dress, branding my skin.

The days slipped into one another. My confusion grew as Luke's flirting became more blatant. I liked him, I did. It was immensely flattering to have such a handsome and personable man so interested in me. In any other circumstances, I probably would have succumbed to his advances. After all, I was young, free, and single. I had no ties or commitments, except ... Scott.

It had been eight months since we made love. Eight long, lonely months since that amazing, frenzied, hurried coupling. I thought about it all the time.

He may have completely withdrawn from me to a point I could barely label him a friend anymore, but still, I ached for him. My heart burned with a longing to be his beloved Eve again. A tiny portion of me continued to hope, and it was that hope which stopped me from giving in to Luke.

Luke's last day came. Temperatures reached record-breaking levels. It was like being inside a pressure cooker. We arranged to meet for a picnic on the island and I wandered to the shore a little early, desperate to reach the cool shadiness of the island, and maybe swim in the lake's icy waters.

Luke was there, looking at one of the boats with interest.

"Jump in," he ordered at my approach. "I'll row us across."

"Are the others already there?" I asked, reluctant to be alone with him, knowing with a strange clutch of excitement, what would inevitably happen if I was.

"Yeah, they've already rowed across," he replied. I scrambled into the boat, laughing as he took the oars and competently rowed us over the short expanse of dark green water.

"You look pretty expert at that," I commented, as we landed on the other side and splashed through the shallows, pulling the boat behind us up onto the beach.

"I guess you could say I've turned my hand to pretty much everything," he replied and held out a hand to me. I hesitated, then placed my palm within his, feeling as if I had sealed my fate.

We walked to the clearing. As I had somehow been expecting, no one was there. I looked at him in brow-raised silence and he shrugged sheepishly.

"You've caught me," he confessed. "I wanted to be alone with you, Eve, and this seemed the only way to do it."

"Oh?" I mumbled through dry lips. "Why?"

"I think you know," he replied. Gently, he pushed me against a tree trunk, his arms enfolding me, his mouth moving hungrily over mine.

I resisted, briefly, but was so tired of waiting and hoping, of being rejected and looked at as if I were less than nothing. A moan rose in my throat, and I was kissing him back, lust exploding in the pit of my belly.

"Eve," he groaned. "I've never met anyone like you. I want you, now, here…"

Did I agree? I can't remember. All I know is when his hands moved over my breasts, stroking and arousing, I cried out from the pleasure of it, making no move to stop him as his large hands undid the buttons of my sleeveless blouse. Maybe I even helped him.

He slipped the blouse from my shoulders, and it fell to the ground. I shuddered as he bent his head and pulled down the bikini I wore underneath. His mouth closed over one erect nipple, gently biting, and pulling on it, all the while massaging the other into a throbbing, wanting peak.

My head fell back against the tree, its bark rough against my spine. I closed my eyes, savouring the explosion of need and lust, my hands fisting in his hair, urging him on. I would do this. I deserved this. I would make love with Luke and to hell with Scott.

I opened my eyes and looked down at Luke's dark head at my breast. He was so like Scott. I knew it was no good. I couldn't go through with it.

"No," I whispered, bringing my hands up to push him away. "I'm sorry, no, Luke, please stop."

He raised his head, eyes intense with lust, and stared at me in disbelief.

"What?"

"I'm sorry, I can't do this, I'm so sorry Luke, but you have to stop."

Gently, I moved away from his grasp and pulled my bikini straps back over my shoulders.

"But, Eve, I don't understand, what's wrong? You wanted it, too, every bit as much as I did."

"I know, and I'm sorry, I should've stopped you earlier, shouldn't have come to the island with you, I'm so sorry, Luke, I really am ... but there's someone else, and I can't have sex with you while I'm still in love with him."

"You picked a hell of a time to remember you have a boyfriend," he snapped angrily, and I flushed with shame.

"I know. I'm sorry ... he's not a boyfriend, at least, we're not a couple. I don't think he even loves me anymore, but I still love him, and until I stop loving him, I can't be with anyone else, and ... and I'm sorry," I finished miserably, picking up my blouse from the ground and attempting to pull it back on.

"I see." Luke's expression softened. He stepped back, rubbing away the sweat that beaded on his forehead. "Tough call," he commented, and I heard a rough kind of sympathy in his voice.

"Yeah, tell me about it," I nodded. "I'm so sorry, Luke."

"Aw hell." He stuffed his hands in his pockets and for a moment looked about twelve years old. "It's ok, I guess I understand, my pride's just a little wounded"

"I'm sorry," I said again helplessly.

"Will you please stop saying you're sorry."

He grinned at me, and I realised he was joking, that the moment had passed, and he was okay with it and with me.

"You know," I began slowly. "You are a nice man, Luke."

"I am," he agreed with false modesty. "Look me up when you're over this other guy, who, by the way, is a first-class loser for ever letting you go."

"No, he's not a loser," I replied. "The situation's ... complicated."

"A situation's only as complicated as you make it," he said, then a thoughtful look crossed his face. "Look, this may be a completely off-the-wall suggestion, but when I leave tomorrow, why don't you come with me?"

"What?" I gasped.

"Sure, why not?" he said, warming to his idea. "I'm flying out to meet a camera crew in New Zealand. Come with me."

"I'm not sure that's such a good idea," I replied slowly.

"Sure, it is," he insisted. "Look, Eve, I won't lie to you; I want you. If you ever decide you're bored of waiting for this other guy to make up his mind, then I'm quite happy to be a means of mending your broken heart. Hell, I'm not proud; I'll take what I can get. But it would be your decision, Eve. I like you, really like you. You're interesting and funny and I enjoy your company. If you tell me you'll come with me for a holiday and that it's to be separate rooms, I'll respect that."

"I don't know what to say," I murmured, stunned by his offer.

"Say yes," he suggested. "Or at the very least, say you'll think about it."

I smiled and finally nodded. His face cleared in a big beaming smile and when he stepped forward and pulled me into a brotherly hug, I went easily, drawing strength and comfort from his embrace, laughing when he whispered suggestive nonsense into my ear.

I opened my eyes and looked straight into Scott's gaze, realised what it must look like, and what he must think.

Hastily, I pulled away from Luke's arms as Ferdie came crashing through the trees, his eyes widening as he took in the situation.

"Well, well," he exclaimed in delight. "What do we have here?"

"Nothing," I stuttered guiltily, colour staining my cheeks, stumbling over tree roots in my haste to move away from Luke.

"You naughty people." Ferdie wouldn't let it go, his face screwing up in a chortle of mirth.

"Who's being naughty?" asked Mimi, arriving in the clearing behind him, closely followed by Miles, Robert, and Caro. "It's far too hot to be naughty."

"Our little Eve and your big strong son, Caro," declared Ferdie. "That's who."

Several pairs of eyes swivelled to look with interest in our direction, Mimi, Miles, and Robert were laughing, obviously not taking Ferdie very seriously, although I fancied Mimi's gaze narrowed thoughtfully as she took in my flushed face.

Caro's expression was one of complete and utter fury. As she stared at me in blazing-eyed contempt, I was very grateful looks really couldn't kill.

As for Scott, I couldn't even bring myself to look at him, and was intensely aware of him, frozen at the edge of the clearing, staring at me as if I were something disgusting, he had found on the bottom of his shoe.

"Give us a break, guys," Luke protested, laughing as Ferdie made kissing noises in his direction. "It was a hug, in a sort of brother-sister kind of way."

"Is that so?" exclaimed Ferdie, his eyes wide. "Then why," he insisted innocently. "Is Eve's blouse on inside out?"

Everyone stared at me with renewed interest.

"So it is," remarked Robert mildly, and I shot him a furious glare.

"Where's Annaliese?" I asked, desperate to change the subject. Instantly, the amusement left his face to be replaced with anxiety.

"She's got another one of those headaches," he replied, and I frowned in concern.

"Again? You really must persuade her to go to the doctor, Robert. It's not right, all these headaches; she needs to get them checked out."

He nodded in agreement and turned to help Miles unload the bags. Thankfully, attention then turned away from me and Luke onto more important things, like wine and food.

The day progressed. The heat showed no signs of abating if anything it grew hotter. The whole time I could feel Caro staring at me, her expression one of tightly controlled fury. I was also miserably aware of Scott ignoring me, his face still and unreadable. Guilt crawled along my spine.

Although we were protected from the worst of the heat by the dappled shade offered by the trees on the island, we could still feel its power. Several times we went down to the lake and dived in to cool off, staggering back to the clearing, shaking with cold, only to be bone dry and too hot again within twenty minutes.

"This heat," moaned Mimi, lying back against a cushion, her face flushed. "It's too hot. What is the matter with the weather? This is crazy."

Miles fanned her with a rolled-up newspaper, glancing up at the darkening sky.

"I think we may be in for a storm," he replied thoughtfully. "It's not possible for things to get this intense without there being an explosion."

How right he was.

All too soon, Robert decided he was going back to the Hall. Concerned about Annaliese and worried about leaving her for so long, he began to collect things to take back. Ferdie, Miles, and Mimi, too, staggered to their feet, declaring their intention of going with him.

I helped them load up the boat and they rowed to the other side. I stood, gazing over darkening waters, unable to shake the sense of impending doom. Then I wandered along the lake's edge, unwilling to return to the clearing, sensing even Luke's friendliness wouldn't be enough to offset the blatant hostility of Caro and the monolithic disdain of Scott.

I walked slowly, stumbling over the tree roots rising in my path, confused thoughts colliding in my brain. Why had I rejected Luke? As for his offer to go away with him, tempting though it was, I knew I wouldn't be taking him up on it.

I stopped, feeling sudden anger at myself. What was the matter with me? Did I have no pride? I was wasting my life, eating my heart out for a man who wanted nothing more to do with me.

A man who maybe, once upon a time, had had feelings for me, but now regarded me as a heart-breaking tease, and after today, probably considered me little better than a slut.

By now I had walked the entire circuit of the island and was approaching the beach from the opposite side. I sank onto its pebbly surface, pulled my knees into my chest, rested my cheek on them and tried to think what to do.

"Eve?"

I looked up as a shadow loomed from the darkness, saw it was Scott and scrabbled to my feet to face him. I was unable to read his expression in the gloom but knew from the unyielding stiffness of his posture he was still angry with me. A chill wind gusted across the lake. I heard the ominous rumbling of thunder and shivered.

Miles had been right, there was going to be an explosion.

"Where are the others?" I asked.

"Caro wanted to spend some time alone with Luke on his last night, so they've gone back to the gatehouse. I said I'd wait for you."

"Oh," I replied, and turned towards the boat, then gasped in shock when he stepped forward and violently grabbed my arm.

"Just what game do you think you're playing, Eve?"

"Game? What do you mean? I'm not playing any *game*." I cried out in pain as his grip tightened.

"Scott, let go, you're hurting me!" He released me with an exclamation.

"You and Luke!" He spat the words in disdain. "It was pretty obvious to everyone what you two had been up to. How could you, Eve?"

"How could I what?" I demanded hotly, my temper flaring. I was sick of it, sick of tiptoeing around him and his crippled emotions.

"I don't owe you an explanation, Scott."

"The two of you pawing at each other, it was disgusting."

"How dare you! You have no idea what happened."

"Well, your blouse had been off at some point, so you tell me, what did happen?"

"That is none of your bloody business," I snapped.

"Oh, I think it is…"

"Why?" I demanded crossly. "What business could it possibly be of yours how many men I've slept with?"

"Have you?" he snapped.

"Have I what?" I replied in confusion, having lost the thread of my argument. Thunder rumbled again, almost directly overhead, followed seconds later by lightning, its brief flash showing me the steely set to his jaw.

"Slept with him?"

"How dare you," I shrieked, shaking with outrage. "I'll sleep with whoever I please, and if I decide to have sex with Luke then that's what I'll bloody well do!"

"So, you haven't then," he stated. If I hadn't been so entrenched in my tantrum, I might have heard the relief in his voice.

"Not yet," I yelled defiantly. "But he's asked me to go away with him to New Zealand tomorrow, so I'll have plenty of opportunities to have sex with him then!"

"You will not go away with him," he stated flatly, and I flailed at him with my fists, my anger spilling over into a frenzy.

"Don't you dare tell me what I can and cannot do," I screamed.

"You're not going with him," he declared, grabbing my arms, and dragging me to him.

His mouth closed furiously over mine. The kiss was brief and savage, his teeth scraping over my lips as I fought him, struggling like a trapped wild animal in his grasp.

My heart was breaking as I realised there was no love behind the kiss, only possessive passion. I fell away from him, crying out at my shattered dreams, wiping at lips that bled from his roughness.

"You bastard!" I shrieked.

"Eve," he began and held out a hand to me which I slapped away in fury, my temper matched by the crash of thunder and the crack of lightning.

"You bloody, bloody bastard! You fucking dog in a manger!" My anger was uncontainable. "You don't want me, but you don't want anybody else to have me. Well, you know what, I'm sick of being in love with you, Scott, sick of wanting you so badly I die a little more inside every day knowing how much you hate and despise me..."

"What? Eve?" Was that despair in his voice, confusion? If it was, I was too far gone to recognise or respond to it.

"I can't take this anymore!"

Sobs clawed their way from my chest and erupted into the storm. I turned and ran, away from him, away from the travesty we had become.

I dimly heard his voice as I plunged into the lake and struck out strongly for the other shore, knowing he couldn't follow. I'm a very strong swimmer, whereas Scott had never really learnt. My body knifed through the water, confident and able. I felt its chill, and then on my head, the slice of rain. There was a hiss as the heavens opened and finally, finally, the heat wave of the past week broke.

I reached the other side and clambered out, hearing his shouts from across the water. I ignored them and fled into the woods.

My chest heaved with loud ragged gasps as I ran, tripping and stumbling through the gathering gloom between the trees, their branches offering scant protection from the driving rain, until finally I sank into a tiny ball within the protective tangle of an oak tree's exposed roots and screamed my fury to the raging heavens, my heart cracking with pain.

A sheet of lightning splintered overhead. Aeons later I returned to my senses and rose to my feet to get my bearings, realising I had run almost to the gates. I set my jaw determinedly, I would go to the gatehouse and find Luke, would tell him when he left in the morning that I would be going with him.

Damn Scott and his shrivelled emotions, I couldn't and wouldn't waste another second of my life fretting for him.

Shivering with cold, wrung out from the maelstrom of emotions I had been through; I stood on the porch and knocked at the door. It flew open and Caro stood there, mouth pursed, eyes grim as she took in my drenched, bedraggled appearance.

"I want to talk to Luke," I announced, and she shook her head.

"You can't," she declared and went to shut the door in my face. In an angry reaction, I barged past her and into the small lounge.

"Luke?" I called out but was greeted by silence.

"He's not here," she replied. "He's gone back to the Hall." I turned to go, but she blocked my way, her expression stony.

"He told me he'd asked you to go away with him." Her tone was hard and accusing, yet I stood my ground, lifting my chin in defiance of the anger in her eyes.

"Yes, he did," I agreed.

"You're not to go with him," she interrupted abruptly.

"If I want to I will," I retorted.

"Oh no you won't, I forbid it," she replied, and I blinked in astonishment.

"What is it with people today?" I demanded hotly. "Everyone seems to think they have the right to tell me how to live my life. Well, I'm sick of it, and I'm not going to take it anymore. Luke's asked me to go away with him and not you or anyone else can stop me from going."

"Have you slept with him yet?" she demanded.

"What?" I spluttered, outraged. "I don't see how that's any of your business."

"Have you slept with him yet?" Her eyes narrowed to serpentine slits.

"No, I haven't," I raged.

"Good. I don't want you anywhere near my son."

"I think that's rather up to Luke, isn't it?" I pushed wet hair over my shoulder, shaking with a delayed reaction. "What is it with you, Caro?" I wearily demanded. "Why have you always been so hostile towards me? I've never done you any wrong so why this obsessive hatred?"

"You stay away from him," she ordered. "Do you hear me?"

"I hear you," I replied calmly, drawing myself up to my fullest height and facing her squarely in the eyes. "And let me tell you what I'm going to do now. I'm going back to the Hall to have the most amazing, mind-blowing sex with your son and there is nothing you can do to stop me."

"You stay away from him you little whore!" she screamed and slapped me viciously across the face. I reeled back, shocked and saw an expression of horror cross her face.

"Eve," she began, her voice twisted and choked. "I'm sorry, I didn't mean to..."

"Oh yes, you did," I retorted wearily, rubbing my stinging cheek. "Let's be honest here, Caro, it's what you've been longing to do ever since you met me."

And I walked away from her without another word, out into the night to begin the long walk home up the driveway.

It was dark, so dark. The rain stung my sore cheek, and the storm still raged and rumbled. I thought it was moving away, but as I trudged across the gravel thunder sounded again – louder this time. It scared me, the elemental savagery of the storm.

I was tired... bone-achingly tired. I wrapped my arms chilled to goose flesh around my cold, wet body. The last thing I felt like doing was having a rampant sex session with a man I barely knew.

I wanted a long hot shower and a mug of hot chocolate. I wanted Annaliese, I wanted to put my head on her shoulder, have a good cry, and tell her everything. I wanted to ask her for advice.

It was an instinctive reaction, I suppose. I was hurting, alone, and confused. My hopes and dreams lay in shredded pieces at my feet. I had made a mess of everything.

Like a child, I began to cry, great gulping snotty sobs. I needed my mother, I needed Annaliese – the two were indistinguishable...

CHAPTER X – REVELATIONS

"It will always be you, Eve."

There was silence in the study almost a year to the day later, as I crouched before a television screen and stared at her face. "Eve," her voice, soft as a whisper, pulled me back to the present.

I looked into her eyes and almost believed she could hear me, could see me; forgetting for a moment that she was dead, and I'd never had the chance to say goodbye; to ask her why.

"Eve," she continued. "There is so much to tell you, so much you need to know … it's hard to know where to start. Perhaps I should begin by telling you my real name. I was born in a small village in County Cork forty-five years ago, and my name was Anna Louise Kennedy."

I shrank violently back, away from the screen and her kindly, knowing eyes. Patiently she waited, plainly knowing the consternation her statement would cause.

"Eve?" said Scott. He knelt beside me and touched my shoulder. "What is it? What's the matter? You look as if you've seen a ghost."

"I have," I murmured through clenched teeth. "That name ... Anna Louise Kennedy ... that's the name on my birth certificate ... Annaliese was my mother!"

"What?"

The shock in his eyes mirrored my own. Without thinking, I slipped my hand into his, drawing courage from his quiet presence, and allowed him to help me to my feet. He led me to the sofa, sat me down and perched beside me; his eyes never leaving my face.

"Annaliese was your mother?"

I nodded, seeing the looks on the faces of the others. Robert's mouth had dropped open, and he was gaping, first at me, then at the image of Annaliese on the screen.

He frowned, his lips moving as if about to speak, but then a thoughtful look crossed his face and his mouth snapped determinedly closed.

Miles and Ferdie simply looked stunned, yet Mimi was nodding slowly.

"I knew there was some kind of connection," she murmured. "Something to explain the bond there was between you, right from the start, but not this, no, I never suspected this..."

Only Caro's face was impassive and unmoved. As I glanced at her, the idea flashed through my mind that this wasn't news to her. She already knew.

"Eve."

Our attention was instantly drawn back to the screen where Annaliese was smiling gently, her brow creased with concern.

"I understand this will have come as a great shock to you. You'll probably be wondering how it can be true, yet it is, mine is the name on your birth certificate ..." She paused, a wistful look on her face.

"You were the most beautiful baby, Eve. When I lost you, it was the worst thing that ever happened to me. And I want you to know from that moment until the day you walked back into my life, there wasn't a day that went by I didn't think about you."

A great shuddering gasp burst from me. Scott's hand tightened over mine as the tears broke free and I stared at the face of the woman who had been my best friend, who'd broken my heart, and who now claimed to be my mother.

"You were, and always will be my little girl, Eve. I loved you from the very instant I laid eyes on you, all red and shrivelled, your little fists bunched up to take on the world. I know you must have many questions, questions I wish I could answer, but I'm afraid you'll have to take my word that whatever I did, I did it for you. Maybe I made the wrong choices and did the wrong things, but it was with the best of intentions, even if it did have devastating consequences."

She paused, her eyes roaming the room as if she could see us, her gaze resting on every one of her friends before finally seeming to settle on me again.

"I can only pray, my darling girl, that you came back. That at the end you were unable to stay away and came back to say goodbye. It's what I'm counting on, what I'm pinning my hopes on, this last chance to say goodbye, Eve, and I love you."

There was a click, the screen went blank, and she was gone, leaving us staring at one another in shell-shocked amazement, our worlds completely turned upside down.

"Eve? Eve?"

Scott's concerned voice finally penetrated, and I realised he had been calling my name for some time. Slowly, I turned to look at him, shaking my head in confusion.

"She was my mother? I don't ... can't ... believe it."

"Are you all right?"

"I don't know, I'd like to go to my room now, I need some time alone to think about this..."

I pulled my hand free and stood up, moving away from the others, their shocked faces, and murmured concerned agreements.

I left the room. Closed the door behind me and leaned against it.

The wake was in full swing. Music blared from somewhere and loud raucous laughter echoed through the Hall. Annaliese's last request was at least being honoured – her funeral was turning into one hell of a party.

I passed through it, giving tightly controlled smiles to those who greeted me, moving, always moving, until I reached the bottom of the stairs. I paused, my lungs painfully struggling to re-inflate and take in much-needed air.

Gripping the bannisters, my eyes slid up the stairs bright marble surface, the blood pounded behind my eyes, and suddenly it was a year ago.

It was my dream.

It was reality.

Memory and nightmare merged, blending into one shockingly vivid truth.

I needed my mother, I needed Annaliese…
Thankful to be out of the storm, I reached the Hall and slipped silently through the door. It was late. I had been in the woods longer than I thought. There was no sign of the others and I realised they must have gone to bed.

Wearily, I pulled my body up the stairs. At the door to Scott's room, I paused, hesitated, struggling with my instincts before I gently tapped on the wood and waited. Long minutes passed with no answer.

Finally, I eased the door open and peered inside. The room was empty. Lightning flashed through the open curtains illuminating the perfectly made bed, which had not been slept in.

Worry sliced through me. I had left him on the island, alone in a storm, and he wasn't a strong swimmer. My imagination saw him capsizing the boat in his haste to follow me; saw him flailing desperately in the water, slipping beneath its inky black surface.

I swallowed down panic, unsure what to do. Yet that urge, that desire which had propelled my shaking legs up the long driveway, still prevailed. I needed Annaliese.

Quietly, I crept down the hallway to her room, knowing Robert would be sleeping in his room tonight because of her earlier headache. Water oozed from my sodden sandals and their swollen leather straps chafed against my cold numb feet.

Like a scene from a horror film, the storm which had been moving away came crashing back. Thunder rumbled ominously and lightning flickered through the landing window, causing my heart to stutter with inexplicable fright.

The door to Annaliese's room was slightly ajar. I held out a hand, then hesitated, unwilling to disturb her if she slept. But my need for her overrode any consideration and gently, carefully, I pushed it open and waited on the threshold, straining my eyes to see in the darkness.

The thunder rolled again, so close it seemed on the very roof of the Hall. Seconds later the lightning flashed, revealing the room for a split second and I froze, unable to believe what I had seen, my heart missing a beat at the scene glimpsed before me.

Impatiently I waited.

Thunder banged. Once again, lightning flashed, a triple explosion of light which lit up the room brighter than a spotlight, and I saw, but couldn't believe what I saw.

Annaliese, her beautiful golden hair spread over the pillow, body arching off the bed in ecstasy, her head thrown back, the long column of her throat gleaming white in the glare.

Her hands clutched at the shoulders of the man who moved steadily and firmly inside her, his well-muscled arms braced to take his weight as her feet pressed firmly on his buttocks, urging him in, deeper and deeper, her thighs spread wide, taking all of him.

I saw his dark hair and his perfectly toned body. A body I, too, had clung to in mindless ecstasy. A body I knew almost as well as my own.

I staggered back.

My cry of horrified denial was swallowed up in the ear-splitting thump of the thunder. In the flash of lightning, I saw her eyes, open and fixed upon me over his strongly muscled shoulder, saw the expression in them, a mingled look of triumph and apprehension, and saw the cat-like smirk of satisfaction.

At last, I knew; I understood. Right from the very start, I had suspected, but I had dismissed my insecurities as mere baseless jealousies.

I had seen enough. I turned and fled...

I reached the sanctuary of my room. It was my dream, and it was the truth. I *had* gone to Annaliese's room that night, needing her so badly, desperately wanting her calm, steady, maternal love which had been such a constant in my life.

Instead, I found betrayal and treachery.

The woman I considered inviolate. The woman I loved as fiercely as my mother, possibly more if I was completely honest.

This woman, who should have instinctively known what my feelings were for Scott, had betrayed me, so utterly and completely there had been no coming back from it.

As for Scott...

I stared at the stranger in the mirror, her eyes wide and blank in her tanned face, her short curls springing out around her head like a halo.

I had loved him. It was the simple, inconvenient truth. I had loved him.

Had believed for a short, wonderful time he might return my feelings, but he hadn't. He couldn't.

The whole time it had been her he wanted, her he needed, her he loved.

My dream always ended at this point, freeze-framed at the couple on the bed, but now, unbidden, another memory, the continuation of that other night arose before my eyes. I gripped the edge of the sink and let it wash over me, taking me back, drenching me with remembrance.

Scott and Annaliese? Annaliese and Scott! I couldn't ... wouldn't believe it ... and yet, and yet I'd seen them, together, in Annaliese's bed, seen their beautiful naked bodies moving together in perfect harmony, heard their soft cries of pleasure...

I shuddered and ground the heels of my hands into my eyes to block out the awful picture branded on my vision.

I stripped off my sodden clothes, tossing them heedlessly into the laundry basket. I'd ached for a shower but there had been no time, so had simply rubbed feeling back into my numb body with a towel, then quickly pulled on clean clothes, doing up my jeans buttons with shaking hands, swallowing down the tide of bile which burnt the back of my throat, my breath gasping in ragged pants.

I pulled down my weekend case and randomly tossed things in – nightwear, underwear, odd articles of clothing.

I stopped, frowned, tried to think logically, then snapped shut my laptop and threw it in, along with my bank and savings account paperwork, some toiletries, and my passport.

The rest I simply left – walked away from it all without a second glance.

The Hall was silent when I slipped from my room and turned left, headed for the narrow back stairs which led to the kitchen quarters rather than go past her room again.

The back door had already been locked so I quietly eased the key round and let myself into the night, thankful the storm had moved away, although I could still hear vague rumblings of thunder, the sky still flickering with occasional flashes of lightning. Along with the full, bright moon and the stars, my way was lit along the long gravel driveway.

I reached the gatehouse and paused. It was in darkness. I wondered if Caro was asleep, or if she was still up, unable to sleep, staring into the darkness and picturing me, the unworthy slut, screwing her beloved son. A wry grin flickered at the thought.

I turned to cast one last look at the Hall, frowning as I saw a small pinprick of light move among the trees to the right.

Briefly, I wondered what it was, then dismissed it from my mind and turned my back on what had been my home for eight years.

Hurrying through the gates I made for the main road where I could phone for a taxi to come and collect me and take me somewhere, anywhere, so long as it was far away from here.

I went to Jamaica, instinctively heading to a place I could remember being happy, to somewhere completely removed from the Hall and its inhabitants. Now I shivered, missing its warmth, my bones and blood so used to the Caribbean that I felt cold, even though I appreciated that for England it was a warm September day.

I noticed there was a fire laid in the grate and a basket of logs standing ready on the hearth. Fumbling a match from a box on the mantelpiece, I knelt on the rug and lit the kindling. Tinder dry, it roared through. Within minutes I could feel its welcoming warmth and held out hands chilled to the bone.

Sitting back on the sofa, I dropped my head in my hands, the shockwaves of Annaliese's announcement still reverberating inside my skull. She was my mother?

Surely, I had been told that Annaliese was incapable of bearing children? Annaliese herself had told me some medical condition prevented her from ever conceiving.

I frowned, had she?

Or had someone else told me that?

I couldn't remember.

Had she lied, or had there been complications following my birth that had rendered her sterile?

I rubbed my forehead wearily, feeling the beginnings of a champagne hangover. I was thirsty yet had nothing to drink and was reluctant to venture out from the safety of my room.

Memories crowded, thick and fast.

Annaliese's face, so sorrowful, saying she had once lost someone she loved very much, right after that strange statement she made to Mimi that sometimes children were taken away and you didn't know why.

Had she meant me?

I remembered how interested she had been in the photos of me as a baby; how avidly she studied them. Were they poignant pictures of the baby she had given away, growing into a sturdy toddler, a child, a teenager?

Further back still, I remembered the first evening I spent with them all when we ate Chinese and watched DVDs.

A snapshot memory flashed in my mind, Miles and I had been talking about... oh, what had we been talking about, yes, The Woman in White and Miles had made the comment it was a novel that dealt with secrets, illegitimate children, and Annaliese had dropped her wine.

I had forgotten about the incident, yet now could see the glass drop, hear her soft exclamation and her hurried excuses.

At the time it had meant nothing, but now...

Other moments in our years together, her enjoyment of the fact shop assistants would take her for my mother.

So many incidents and comments, unremarkable at the time, all now fell into place like a vast complex puzzle, presenting me with a solidly indisputable fact.

Annaliese was my mother.

It explained so much.

It answered nothing.

I slipped onto the sofa, cradled my poor aching head in my arms, and closed my eyes. Overriding everything though, all the happy memories of Annaliese caring for me and loving me, were the images of the last time I saw her.

I couldn't get it out of my head. That brutally shocking vision of her writhing on the bed with Scott, strong arms braced to take his weight, her long nails raking over the tattoo on his shoulder.

My eyes flew open, I sat bolt upright on the sofa, hands flying to my mouth in horror.

"Oh my god," I moaned aloud. "What have I done?"

I buried my face in my hands and then jumped out of my skin at the low knock at the door.

For a moment I considered ignoring it, but then pulled myself together, rose and opened the door.

It was Scott.

I stared at him, head still whirling with memories and sudden revelations. He looked concerned and half smiled at me.

"I thought you might like some tea."

Looking down, I saw he held a tray prettily laid with a lace cloth on which rested a delicately small bone china teapot with two matching cups, saucers, and a small jug of milk.

Touched at his thoughtfulness, I stepped back to allow him access to the room.

"Thank you," I said as he carefully laid the tray down on the low table beside the sofa. "I was thinking how thirsty I felt."

He smiled, poured out two cups, added a splash of milk the way I liked it and handed me a cup before sitting in the armchair beside the fire, stretching his long legs appreciatively to its warmth.

For a while, we did not speak but drank our tea in companionable silence. It was hot and fragrant. I drank it gratefully, feeling it revive and refresh me.

"Where did you go, Eve?"

I looked up at his question and saw the flicker behind the steady gaze of his dark eyes. Not for the first time, I wondered at his powers of self-control.

Any other man would surely have raged at me by now, shouting, demanding answers, but Scott sat there, coolly, and calmly drinking his tea, dropping the question into the silence between us as though merely commenting on the weather.

"Jamaica," I eventually replied. "I went to Jamaica."

"Of course," he said smoothly. "I should have remembered how much you liked the place. Have you been there the whole time?"

"Yes," my voice was as controlled as his. "I flew back two days ago."

"I see," he nodded thoughtfully. "I searched for you," he said, eyes never leaving my face. "I questioned your parents, went to Ally and Mike, and interrogated them ..." He paused. "I even turned Wolverhampton upside down looking for you."

"Wolverhampton?" I enquired puzzled, and he frowned.

"Yes, the note you sent a couple of weeks after you left, was postmarked Wolverhampton."

"Oh!" I exclaimed, remembering. "I gave that note to a young couple I met out there on their honeymoon. They ate often at the bar I was a waitress at. They were kind to me, and I liked them. Before they left, I asked them to post it for me when they got home. I remember now, they said they were going back to Wolverhampton."

"So, you were never there?" he asked.

"I'm afraid not," I replied. "I've never been there in my life."

"Damn," he commented mildly. "I took that bloody town apart looking for you."

"Sorry," I said.

He shrugged, and once more the silence descended.

"Why did you leave?" he asked slowly.

I knew he had been building up to the question all day; had burnt to ask, ached for an answer, to know, to understand; yet he'd held back, waiting for me to volunteer the information. Only now, finally, did his self-control slip enough that he had to ask.

So, I told him. I told him everything, right up to and including, that blinding moment of revelation when I stood at the door to Annaliese's room and had my faith smashed in the blinding glare of a lightning flash.

"I thought it was you," I said, and saw him pale under his tan. "I thought it was you," I said again. "And I couldn't bear it, so ran away. I couldn't stay, not after that, not after seeing you and Annaliese."

"It wasn't me," he broke in, an edge of despair in his voice. "I don't know what I can say or do to convince you I'm telling the truth, and I don't know who it was, but it wasn't me."

"I know," I replied resolutely. "I realise that now ... the man had a tattoo on his shoulder. I didn't remember seeing it before. Perhaps I always feared that you and Annaliese ... maybe it's why I was so ready to believe. But being here again, in this house, it's as if the mist has cleared from my mind and I've finally let myself remember ... everything. All the things I blanked out, wouldn't even allow myself to think about. All this past year, I've tortured myself, but now I know ... it wasn't you."

I paused, remembering the events of a year ago. My mad heedless flight into the night, the taxi that took me to the station, the train that took me to London, to the airport.

I remembered sitting in the departure lounge with a one-way ticket to Jamaica in my hand, my teeth clenched against an endless scream. How fated it had seemed – the available seat on a flight leaving for the island.

"But what did you do in Jamaica for a whole year?" he asked.

"I wrote a book," I replied.

"Did you?" he asked, surprised. "Is it any good?"

"Well ..." I smiled at him. "Ruth's agent felt it showed promise, but I think I need to re-write the ending now."

"Ruth?" His smile slipped. "You mean Ruth knew where you were? But she knew how worried I was, how worried we all were..."

"No," I quickly reassured. "She knew nothing until I emailed her last week. I sent her the opening chapters and asked for her opinion. I swear, until then, I hadn't contacted her. When she emailed back, that was the first time I heard about Annaliese. Until that moment I had no idea, Scott, no idea at all she was ill. If I had, I'd have come back."

"Would you?" he asked, his gaze steady.

"Yes." I met and matched it. "Yes, I would have done."

He looked down at his hands, his face as unreadable as ever.

"So, who was he?" he asked quietly. "The man with Annaliese, who was he?"

"It was Luke," I replied, and he sat back in his chair, his face outraged.

"Luke?" he exclaimed. "But she'd only just met him. He was the son of her oldest friend. She was practically his aunt. For God's sake Eve, she was old enough to be his mother. Why on earth would Annaliese have risked her marriage, her reputation, everything she was, for the sake of a quick roll in the sack with a pretty boy like him?"

"I don't know," I said, and couldn't help smiling at the indignation in his voice. "But it was him. I remember now the first time I saw Luke, I thought how much he looks like you."

"Does he?" Scott looked affronted and placed his cup and saucer gently down on the tray.

"Why did it upset you so much, Eve? When you saw them, thought it was me, why did you leave and go so far away? Even if it had been me, why would you have cared?"

"Don't you know?" I replied, looking steadily at him.

He dropped his eyes first and looked away. I saw his hands close briefly into fists. He stood, seemingly at a loss for words, and walked to the door.

"I'll let you get some rest," he finally said. I felt a quick, hot stab of disappointment.

"Eve?" His hand on the door, he paused and glanced back.

"Yes?" I answered quickly, hope flickering.

"I understand this is probably the wrong thing to say and probably completely the wrong time to say it, but I was wondering when you've had a chance to settle back in, find your feet, as it were, whether you'd ... well, that is, if you'd consider, maybe, going out for dinner with me?"

"Dinner?"

I looked at him curiously and noticed with interest the twin spots of faint colour which burnt on each cheek.

"Do you mean on a sort of date?"

"Umm yes," he replied. "If you like ... yes ... a date. Maybe we can start again, you and I, get to know each other from scratch, as it were..."

His voice trailed away. He looked at me, and I realised it was the first time I had seen him visibly discomfited.

"No," I said carefully. "I don't think that's a very good idea, Scott..."

I paused, and took a deep breath, groping for the right words.

"Of course," he quickly replied. I heard with dismay the coldness in his tone and saw the shutters slam closed behind his eyes.

"You're quite right, I'm sorry to have bothered you, Eve."

He opened the door and was gone, leaving me frozen for a second, before I leapt across the room, threw open the door and rushed after him.

"Scott, wait!"

He stopped, his back solid and implacable. I reached him, slipped my arms around his sides, rested my forehead on his broad back, and felt his taut resistance.

"God, Scott, you really should give a girl a chance to finish her sentence," I protested. "What I meant, what I was trying to say is ... don't you think we've wasted enough time, you and I?"

He was silent. I felt his back tense. He needed more, needed me to spell it out for him.

"I don't want to start from scratch," I said slowly. "I don't want to take the time to get to know you again. I already know you and don't want to waste another second of our lives apart, not when I can be with you now, in your arms and your bed."

I stopped and held my breath. I had played every card in my hand, gambled everything I had he still cared for me, still loved me ... it was up to him now.

Slowly he turned. My arms fell to my sides, my gaze remaining fixed on the floor. I was afraid to look up, afraid to look into his eyes, afraid of what answer I would find there.

"Eve," he said, and then again, "Eve."

My name.

That was all he said.

It was enough.

I lifted my eyes; saw the answer I had hoped for and a smile, brazen and arch, slipped onto my lips.

"I once made you a promise," I purred. "A promise I now intend to keep."

"Oh?" he murmured; his eyes locked on mine. "What promise was that?"

"I promised to seduce you in front of the fire, then take you to bed and do it all over again," I replied, and saw the heat leap into his eyes.

"I like a woman who keeps her word," was all he said and allowed me to lead him, unresisting, back into my room.

He silently watched as I closed and locked the door behind us, pushed him down onto the sofa and stood before him, slowly undoing the side tie which held my wraparound dress closed, easing it off my shoulders to pool in a black heap around my feet. I stood before him, clad only in a black lace corset, thong, and stockings.

"My God, Eve!" he breathed. "Do you always wear such memorable underwear?"

"You're not still thinking about those damn socks, are you?" I laughed.

He lifted a brow at me in mock reproach. "I'll have you know I have very fond memories of those socks," he replied archly. "Have you still got them?"

"I threw them away," I said. "After..."

My voice trailed away, and his face clouded, both of us reminded of the horror of Mimi's attempted suicide.

"But..." I moved closer, lowering myself slowly onto his lap. "If it's schoolgirls that really float your boat, I know where I could buy a St. Trinian's outfit, complete with a hockey stick."

He groaned, ran his hands over the lace of the corset, cupped my waist and pulled me closer.

"Tease," he murmured, teeth nipping gently at my neck. "Does it come with the hat as well?"

I murmured an assent, and then his mouth was on mine, and I was lost to all rational thought, all reasoning, lost in the taste, feel, and smell of him.

Finally, I was where I belonged, where I had dreamed of being for so long. I was home and it felt like heaven.

He feasted hungrily, like a starving man confronted with a banquet. Where there had been tenderness was ferocity, a wildness.

I tore at his shirt, feeling buttons pop beneath impatient fingers. His hands tugged at my hair, pulling me closer, our mouths hungrily consumed.

"I'm sorry," I gasped, pulling away. "I meant to do this slowly, to seduce you, but I want you so much it hurts, I can't wait, please Scott, help me..."

He lifted me off his lap and fumbled with his zip. Clumsily I tried to help, hands shaking, pulling him free of his clothing, and moaning with greedy desire as he sprang up, aroused and ready, his thumbs pushing aside the flimsy scrap of black lace which was now the only barrier between us.

He paused for a heartbeat, then with one glorious swift thrust entered me, twin cries of need and want erupting from our throats, nearly two years of estrangement and separation being the only foreplay necessary.

His hands were everywhere, pushing down the corset to release my breasts, claiming them with his mouth, savagely pulling, suckling, taking me to a knife-edge of pleasure so keen it was borderline pain.

Gripping my waist, he moved me urgently up and down, rising to meet me at every downward plunge as I ground myself onto him, sobbing with ecstasy.

"Eve?" I heard the question and felt my body respond with a quickening of its own.

"Yes," I cried. "Now, oh, God, now..."

He paused, one still magnificent second, then thrust upwards so deeply I felt I would surely split in two, pulsating and throbbing, his hot seed exploding into my ripe and ready womb.

I trembled on the very edge of my orgasm, then free fell into the chasm, the top of my skull lifting off with the force of a climax that sent shockwaves racing through my body.

We gasped, and cried out together, voices hoarse and guttural at the magnitude and power of the tremors.

I slumped, drained, and exhausted, my face resting on his shoulder, feeling his chest heaving beneath me. His ragged breaths, loud in the still room, matched only by my gasps for air. Finally, I shifted slightly and felt the sticky disgorge between my thighs.

"I'm afraid we've ruined your trousers."

"I'll buy another pair," he shrugged in uncaring dismissal, arms tightening around me.

We sat that way for what seemed hours, before he finally slipped from me and we undressed each other properly, fingers tender and loving.

Leaving our clothes in a heap by the fire, we slid between the sheets, holding each other close, watching the firelight reflect in each other's eyes.

"Eve?"

"Hmm mmm?" I sighed drowsily, waves of contentment lapping over me.

"Are you going to go away again?"

"Not unless you come with me," I replied, and felt his body relax in relief.

"Only, I don't know what I'd do if I lost you again," he replied carefully. I pulled myself up on my elbow and looked into his face, seeing the anguish there and genuine emotion.

"I'm sorry," I whispered, "for rejecting you, but I was in shock. Every time I looked at you, I saw us covered in Mimi's blood. By the time I came out of the shock, it was too late. You'd made it quite plain you despised me."

"But I didn't," he replied. "I understood why you'd pushed me away but didn't know what to do about it. I talked to Annaliese, and she advised waiting, giving you time. I wanted to confront you, but she seemed so sure it was the wrong way to go about it ..." he paused, and I remembered the day I'd come across them talking together in urgent whispers.

"The thing is," he continued, his voice even and calm, "it's always been you, Eve, since the first moment I saw you lying under that tree, all wild child hair, and the longest sexiest legs I'd ever seen. It's always been you. When I tended the blisters on your feet, I thought I'd explode from not touching you, but you were so young, so very young, and you looked at me with those innocent trusting eyes. I'd have felt like a complete bastard if I'd tried anything on."

"You'd have been in for a surprise if you had," I murmured. "I was so churned up with lust, if you'd touched me in that way, I think I'd have thrown you to the floor and had my wicked way with you there and then."

"Really?" He looked at me with interest, and his kiss brushed across my forehead, tender and amused.

"Then you joined the group, became a friend, and it seemed impossible to change that, though God knows I wanted to. As the years went by, I began to despair you'd ever consider me as anything other than a friend."

"It was the same for me," I retorted. "I wanted you so badly, yet you treated me like a silly little sister, someone to indulge and tease, not someone you wanted to strip naked and carry off to bed. And what was the meaning of all those other women, then?"

"I was trying to make you jealous." He squirmed sheepishly.

"Well, that part of your plan worked." I sighed.

"I even smoked one cigarette a day, even though I'd given up because sometimes you'd come and sit on the steps with me ..." He paused and grinned wryly. "Isn't that pathetic?"

"Very," I agreed casually, shrieking as he rolled me over and pinned me to the bed, his mouth nipping at my neck and shoulders.

"What happened, Eve?" he asked. "That last day on the island, what happened between you and Luke? Did you have sex with him? It's all right, you can tell me. I'll understand if you did, I want there to be no more secrets between us."

"Nothing happened," I replied. "For a moment I thought I could go through with it. I was so hurt and confused by your constant rejection of me, that I decided to sleep with him as a way of getting back at you. But, when it came to the crunch, I couldn't do it. I stopped him, told him I was in love with someone else, and he was very nice about it. He asked me to go to New Zealand with him for a holiday, separate rooms, and everything, gave me a friendly hug to show there were no hard feelings, and that's when you came in."

"I thought ... I assumed ..." Scott paused and cupped my face in his hands. "I was certain I'd lost you to him, was wild with despair and frustration and didn't handle the situation very well. I couldn't bear the thought of you going away with him, of another man touching you, being with you, that's why I overreacted on the beach. When you jumped into the lake and swam away from me, I thought I'd lost you forever."

"I came to your room," I interrupted. His face stilled and he stared at me.

"You did, when?"

"When I got back to the Hall, I went to your room. I wanted to see you, talk to you; find out once and for all if there was any chance for us. But you weren't there. Your bed hadn't been slept in. I panicked and thought maybe you'd drowned in the lake and decided to go to Annaliese, tell her everything, ask for her advice, and that's when I saw her and Luke, and..."

"And thought it was me," he finished, sighing, and shaking his head. "Do you think we'll ever find out why she did it?"

"I don't know. Perhaps it was a desperate one-off fling, I mean, after all, if Robert's gay then maybe ..." my voice trailed away, and I raised an eyebrow at Scott.

"Yes, how about that?" he murmured.

"Robert and Ferdie ..." I wrinkled my nose. "That's going take some getting used to."

He nodded in agreement, then rolled onto his back taking me with him so I sprawled over his chest as his arms tightened around me.

"So, where were you?" I asked casually. "When I came to your room, and you weren't there, where were you?"

"Out looking for you," he replied. "I came back to the Hall to see if you'd come home, but your room was empty. Annaliese came to her door; I asked if she'd seen you and she said she hadn't. I remember she seemed distracted, concerned about something, and practically ordered me out to look for you, following me to the top of the stairs." He paused; brow creased in memory.

"As I came downstairs, Luke walked in and I tackled him, demanding to know if he'd seen you. He vowed he hadn't, not since the island, and I believed him. He offered to come with me, but Annaliese called to him, asked him to stay, and said she had something to talk to him about, so he went upstairs. I went out to the car, got my torch, and began to search the woods for you."

"We must have missed each other by moments," I murmured. "I went to the gatehouse, I was angry, upset, and was going to find Luke and tell him I would go on holiday with him. Not that I think I would have gone through with it, but the mood I was in that night I wanted to punish you, to show you that even if you didn't want me, there were plenty of other men who did. When I got to the gatehouse though, Luke had already left. Caro and I argued, she called me a whore, slapped me around the face, and ordered me to stay away from her precious son."

"She did what?" Scott stared at me in shock; then a smile tugged at his mouth. "And how did you respond to that?"

"Told her I was going to go and shag her son's brains out."

He gave a low laugh and shook his head.

"I wasn't going to, of course," I continued. "She'd made me so angry I wanted to hurt her. So, I came back to the Hall, found Annaliese and Luke, assumed it was you and ran away, although come to think of it, I do remember seeing a light in the woods. At the time I didn't think anything of it, but I guess that must have been you."

"Yes," he agreed wryly. "That was me."

We lay silently for a few moments, reflecting on the whim of fate and meticulous timing which had led to the events of that fateful night.

Then, as if both deciding at that exact moment it was in the past and we should waste no more time on it, turned to each other, mouths meeting, hands caressing. I felt the riptide of desire rise, running my hands over his perfect body.

"Eve," he murmured into my hair. "Is it time to seduce me yet?"

"Oh, yes," I whispered, pressing kisses onto his neck and chest.

Next moment we froze as a knock came at the door.

"Eve?"

It was Mimi's voice, low and anxious. We looked at each other in consternation.

Pressing my finger to his lips, I slithered from the bed and hurriedly pulled on the robe lying across the foot of it. Belting it tightly, I opened the door a crack and peered blearily at her as though she had woken me from a deep sleep.

"Oh Eve, darling, I'm sorry if I woke you, I was concerned about you, about how you were dealing with the shock."

"I'm fine, Mimi," I reassured her. "Thank you, but I'm fine. I want to get some sleep. I'll think about it in the morning."

"Of course," she murmured, paused, then smiled knowingly. "Good night, Eve," she raised her voice slightly. "Good night, Scott."

"Good night, Mimi." His voice was dryly amused.

I stared at her in astonishment, and she patted me on the arm.

"I'm so pleased," she said. "For both of you. I know Annaliese would have been thrilled. I believe it's what she always wanted."

She turned and hurried away down the hall, leaving me to close and lock the door, leaning on it in surprise, meeting Scott's amused expression.

"How on earth do you think she ...?" I began, then stopped when I saw our clothes lying in a pile on the hearthrug, realising they would have been in her direct line of vision.

Later, after Scott had been thoroughly and completely seduced, we lay once again in each other's arms. It was late, the fire had dwindled to glowing embers and we were sleepy.

"I find it very hard to show emotion," he said. I opened my eyes, straining to read his expression in the dark.

"There are things about me, Eve, things that happened in my past I need to tell you about, things you need to know..."

"No, there isn't," I reassured him. "I already know."

"Oh." He was silent for a moment, considering what I'd said.

"Ruth?" he finally asked, and I nodded in the darkness.

"Yes, she told me in Jamaica before the accident."

"Then, you understand?"

"Yes," I agreed. "I understand."

There was another long silence.

I wondered if he had gone to sleep. My eyelids grew heavy, and I was letting myself slide under the blanket of unconsciousness when he spoke again.

"It will always be you, Eve. I think I'm the kind of man for whom there can only ever be one woman, so if that's a problem for you, you'd better say something now."

"It's not a problem," I reassured him.

There was another long pause.

I waited, hoping, and praying he would finally be able to say the words I needed to hear.

"I suppose, maybe, we should, perhaps, get married?"

His voice was casual, almost offhand in the darkness, yet I sensed his tension, heard the racing of his heart beneath my ear and felt the trembling of his hands as they held me.

"Oh, I think so," I replied, as casually as him. "After all, someone needs to make an honest man of you."

He relaxed, his arms tightening possessively around me, and then his voice came again, the words low and sweet, like honey.

"I love you, Eve."

"I know," I whispered back. "I love you too."

The next morning, I was awoken by hot urgent hands, building me up, arousing me, forcing me into an ever-tightening spiral of desire which exploded into a hasty and passionate coupling before I even opened my eyes.

"Just thought I'd let you know," he gasped, when we could both talk again, "I intend to wake you like this every morning now for the rest of our lives."

"Oh, good," I panted. "I'll cancel my gym subscription."

We showered together, touching and caressing in wonder at the novelty of us, loving and holding beneath the hot foaming water, both reluctant to leave the sanctuary of my room, instinctively fearing the reality of the outside world.

I dressed in clothes I hadn't worn in a year, realising as I pulled my belt two notches tighter how much weight I'd lost.

I laughed at Scott's consternation when he found he had nothing to put on, his clothes from the previous evening ripped and stained from our savage reunion in front of the fire.

Finally, he pulled on my pink robe and with me acting as point man, we hastily rushed along the hallway and darted into his bedroom, shutting, and locking the door behind us, breathless with shared laughter, the sudden realisation dawning that his bed lay behind us, pristine and untouched.

By the time we eventually made it downstairs, the breakfast room was empty of all but Robert finishing his coffee and reading the paper.

We entered together, completely, and utterly a couple. He looked at us with surprise, which quickly spread into understanding and delight.

"Well!" he exclaimed, dropping the paper to the table with a thump. "It's about time. Annaliese would be so happy. She told me it was her secret wish you two would ..." He paused and blushed slightly, "get together," he finished lamely.

I laughed with delight at his mild embarrassment, wiggling out of my chair to rush over and kiss him on the cheek, before sliding back into my place beside Scott, my hand seeking his under the table.

"I have an unfinished piece of business to attend to," Robert announced cryptically, draining his cup, and rising to his feet. "So, I'll leave you two lovebirds alone and see you both later."

We tried to eat breakfast, managing coffee, a corner of toast, and fruit, our eyes, and hands constantly seeking each other, and I felt giddy with the joy of it.

"What do you want to do today?" Scott enquired as we finally pushed away our plates, both admitting we could eat no more.

"I suppose I'd better go and rescue my car from the high street where I left it," I replied reluctantly. "It's a hire car and I need to get it back today, plus it's got all my worldly goods locked in the boot."

"I'll come with you," said Scott instantly. "It's a lovely day. A walk through the woods would be very ... pleasant."

I blushed at his obvious meaning.

"I'll run and get the keys," I murmured and hurried to get my bag from my room.

When I came back downstairs, I discovered Robert and Caro in deep discussion by the front door. Her face was set and grim, and the normally mild-mannered Robert seemed to be stressing something to her.

She looked up at him, expression mutinous, then finally seemed to capitulate and nodded a sharp single nod of agreement.

I stopped on the stairs, wondering when it would end. Even now, with Annaliese dead and her bombshell dropped, it still seemed this Hall and the people within it were riddled with secrets.

Robert hurried off into the library. Caro was left alone on the step, her face impassive. She glanced up and saw me.

Did something pass over her expression – guilt – a pang of something that could have been regret?

"Eve," she said, her voice rough with the Irish brogue which became so much more pronounced under stress. "Come with me, please, I need to talk to you."

"What about?" I bridled at her imperious tone.

"What do you want to talk to Eve about, Caro?" Scott leant against the door of the breakfast room, his stance casual, his tone even, but I could see the tension in the set of his shoulders, the firmness of his jaw, and knew he was concerned for me.

"That's none of your business, Scott," she snapped and turned back to me as if dismissing him.

"Ah, but I'm afraid that's where you're wrong, Caro. As Eve and I are now engaged to be married, anything that concerns her also concerns me."

"Engaged?" Caro's voice faltered, and she glanced from him to me as though expecting us to deny it. When neither of us did, she sighed and nodded, an unexpected smile crossing her face.

"Well, congratulations, I suppose," she stated flatly. "Annaliese would have been pleased. I know it's what she always hoped for. Very well then, come, too, if you must."

She turned and stomped from the Hall, not even glancing back to see if we were following her. We exchanged startled looks.

Scott shrugged, then stepped forward and held out his hand. I ran lightly down the last few steps and took it.

She led us to a formal knot garden at the back of the house, seating herself on one of the ornate wooden benches which ringed a pool and its gently burbling fountain.

Hesitantly, we sat on the next bench. A sudden fear gripped me, along with an intense reluctance to stay, as if I knew what she was going to tell me, knew and didn't want to hear.

Sensing my disquiet, Scott's hand tightened.

"Annaliese wasn't your mother."

There was no preparing the way, no softening of the blow. Caro launched it at me like a grenade, leaving me gaping and shocked.

"But ..." I stuttered. "Last night, on the video, she admitted she was."

"No, she didn't," stressed Caro impatiently. "Think about what she said."

"She agreed it was her name on my birth certificate," I said slowly, trying to remember her exact words. "And she talked of me as a baby. Are you telling me she lied? That she didn't know me as a baby? That her name wasn't Anna Louise Kennedy?"

"No, she didn't lie, she did know you as a baby and her name was Anna Louise Kennedy, but she wasn't your mother."

"Then I don't understand ..." I began helplessly.

"She wasn't your mother," she continued. "I am."

CHAPTER XI – JUDAS

"With one word I could have stopped everything."

It was a shock, but I wasn't surprised. Before she said it, I'd known; known what she was going to say. Maybe on some subconscious level, I had been unable to accept Annaliese as my mother because I'd known it wasn't true.

So now I surveyed Caro steadily, feeling Scott stiffen beside me, his hand squeezing mine.

"I see," was all I said.

She blinked as if surprised at my lack of reaction and ran a hand through her close-cropped hair. Hair that frizzed in the rain the way mine did.

"I need to tell you," she said. "It's what she wanted, no more lies. For over forty years she has protected me and looked after me. Now it's my turn to protect her, protect her name at any rate.

We were born in the same small village in County Cork, where we lived next door to each other in a pair of farmhands' cottages at the end of a long narrow track. I'm two years younger than Annaliese, so for all my life, she's always been there. Neither of us had a mother. Mine had died delivering me, and both Annaliese's parents were killed in a car crash, but that's where any similarities between our lives ended."

She paused, her eyes unseeing, casting her mind back over the years and events between the young girl she was then, and the bitter woman she was now. Beside me Scott sat, silently watchful.

His grip never loosened, and I felt a sudden clutch of thankfulness in my heart that no matter what happened now, I would always have him.

Against almost insurmountable odds we had found each other, and I knew nothing would ever keep us apart again.

"Annaliese was raised by her grandmother, an English woman. She moved to Ireland to be close to her only family, and when her daughter and son-in-law were killed, she stayed to raise Annaliese. She was a remarkable woman, a poet, and a wonderful human being. It's from her that Annaliese inherited her talent and her strength.

"My father, on the other hand, was a hard, intolerant, and bigoted man. Deeply religious, he made my life a living hell. Were it not for Annaliese and her grandmother living next door, I'm not sure I would have survived my childhood."

She paused and took a deep breath.

"You have no idea what life was like for me, how bleak and ugly. A small Irish village in the nineties was not much more advanced than one in the previous century.

"I grew up in fear of eternal damnation, in complete ignorance of what real life could be like.

I envied Annaliese, envied her for her grandmother and her beautiful, happy life, I even envied her vocation, her absolute certainty of what her future was to be."

"Her vocation?" I interrupted, my voice husky.

"Yes, Annaliese wanted to be a bride of Christ, a nun," clarified Caro, and smiled wryly at my start of surprise.

"It's true. It's all she ever dreamt and talked about. She was saving every penny she could to have a dowry to take with her when she entered the nunnery."

"A nun?" I murmured, trying to reconcile the idea of outgoing, vivacious Annaliese locked away behind the walls of a convent. And yet, somehow, it would have suited her, a life of quiet spiritual contemplation.

"There was a boy, a young man really, Ryan O'Connor. Tall and good-looking, he could have had any girl in the village but there was only one he wanted, and she was unavailable.

"He pleaded with Annaliese to forget about being a nun, begged her to go out with him, to give him a chance, and the more she turned him down, the more determined he became.

"Then, one day, he came to her with a ring he had saved up for and pleaded with her to marry him. Refusing to take no for an answer, he told her to think about it and meet him that evening by the old oak tree."

"What happened?" I asked as Caro fell silent.

She looked at me through her thick-rimmed glasses, and I fancied I saw an echo of remembered fear.

"Annaliese hated hurting anyone, but she didn't love him and wouldn't give up her dream of becoming a nun. In the end, I offered to take the ring and a letter she had written and meet him by the oak. I would hand them to him, then it would be over, and he would leave her alone.

"So, Annaliese sent me to meet him, alone, not knowing he'd spent the day drinking in the pub with his mates and wasn't in a mood to hear any answer except yes."

"What did he do when he found you instead of Annaliese?" I asked, but again, a part of me already knew.

"He raped me," she said flatly, "I was sixteen, but not like the sixteen-year-olds of today, I was innocent and didn't understand what was happening until it was too late."

I stared at her, frozen by her words, made the more horrifying for their stark simplicity.

"When he finished with me, he roared off on his bike and left me lying under the tree. That's where Annaliese found me when she came looking, concerned because I hadn't come home. I don't think I've ever seen anyone as guilty as her when she realised what he'd done; what he'd done to me because of her.

"She took me to her grandmother who cleaned me up and tended my wounds. She wanted to call the police, but I wouldn't let her. I knew what my father was like, and I was afraid of what he'd do to me if he found out I'd been with a man before wedlock."

"But you were raped," protested Scott, his voice ringing with indignation. "Surely no man would ever blame his daughter for that?"

"Oh, my father would have done," replied Caro sadly. "In his world there existed only black and white, good girls and whores. I was now one of the whores."

"That's horrible," I murmured. "What happened? Was Ryan ever brought to justice?"

"Of a sort," replied Caro. "Two months later he came off his motorbike and went under the wheels of a car. The next week I confided my secret fear to Annaliese. She told her grandmother, who arranged to take me to a doctor in a town far enough away no one would know. He confirmed it. I was pregnant. Pregnant at sixteen by a boy now lying in a graveyard." She took her glasses off and rubbed wearily at her eyes.

"You must understand what it was like. An abortion was out of the question. It's hard enough now for girls who get caught in Ireland, but back then it was next to impossible.

"We talked endlessly about it. Finally, Annaliese's grandmother came up with a plan. Her oldest friend ran a small guesthouse in London. It was decided I would go and stay with her until the baby was born, and then it would be placed for adoption.

"Annaliese was to go with me, she was adamant about that. I don't think her guilt would've let her do anything else. So, it was all arranged and two months later, just after I turned seventeen, we came to England. I left a note for my father, telling him I had gone to look for work. I knew he'd be angry, but I couldn't tell him the truth.

"Once we were in England, Annaliese got a job at a supermarket and supported us both. I'd intended to work, too, but the pregnancy was a hard one, I suffered from sickness the entire nine months and my state of mind was fragile, to say the least."

"You were in shock from the rape," stated Scott quietly.

"Perhaps," agreed Caro. "Nothing seemed to matter, not Annaliese, not the baby. I couldn't even bring myself to care whether I survived the labour or not. I think in a lot of ways I felt it would be easier if I simply died.

"I felt numb, I knew Annaliese had brought her bride of Christ dowry with her and that was what we were living off, together with whatever wages she managed to earn, yet I didn't even feel guilty about the fact she'd given up her dream for me. She arranged everything, and when the time came, she was in the labour room with me."

She looked directly at me.

"It was a difficult labour, and it hurt terribly. I think because I was so young, I tore inside and had to have surgery. When I finally saw my baby, you, I felt nothing but resentment for this little scrap of life that had caused so many problems. Then I saw the way Annaliese was holding you, looking at you, and knew we had a problem."

She paused, and when she continued her voice was pleading, as though begging me to understand how it had been.

"The plan was to have you adopted. Annaliese agreed, we all agreed it was the only option, the best thing, but ... Annaliese changed her mind. She fell in love with you and wouldn't hear of having you adopted. She changed the rules.

"We went home, and it was like she was your mother. She did everything for you because I couldn't even bear to look at you. She even chose your name. She called you..."

"Eve ..." I interrupted softly. "She called me, Eve."

"Yes," agreed Caro. "She called you Eve, but when it came to registering your birth, I got my way and my mother's name was put down as yours, Melissa, although I put down Annaliese's name as mother."

"Why?" I asked.

"Because I was so afraid my father would find out. Annaliese readily agreed to her name being used. In a way, I think it pleased her.

"Anyway, we struggled on for a while, Annaliese worked every hour she could at the supermarket, using her staff discount to buy you nappies and formula. Her grandmother sent you clothes from Ireland and I saw the way the future would be.

"I saw that Annaliese was going to devote her life to you, knew if she did, she would never achieve anything. She was writing by then, evenings when you were asleep and any other spare moment she could, would scribble desperately in her notebooks.

"I read some of it and even I could see how good it was. I was determined Annaliese should have her chance at greatness, that her life shouldn't be ruined because of you."

"What did you do, Caro?" I asked, with a deadening sense of inevitability.

"I persuaded her to submit her manuscript to an agent, and then when a couple of months went by and she hadn't heard anything, made her telephone them.

"Annaliese still had a slight Irish accent at that point. The secretary misheard her name and that's when Anna Louise became Annaliese.

"She went to meet the agent. When she came back there were stars in her eyes. I knew she was in love. I laid my plans carefully."

Caro stopped and looked away, unable to meet my gaze.

"I pretended to bond with you, and I began to take care of you. At night, I would sing you lullabies, the words choking in my throat, telling myself it was all for Annaliese. She was so happy and kept telling me how pleased she was that I was so much better.

"I lulled her into a false sense of security, so she felt confident enough to go away on her honeymoon. She'd been reluctant to go and leave you with me, knowing I was unable to look after you."

I felt tears prick the back of my eyes; could see the events so clearly, so vividly. Annaliese, torn between her love for Robert, her shining plans for our future together, and her love for me, her concern at leaving me alone with my mother, a woman so traumatised by post-traumatic stress and post-natal depression she could barely care for herself, let alone her baby.

"She planned to tell Robert on their return, to introduce him to us and to persuade him to advance Annaliese some money on her book so she could set us up in our own home.

"But I knew her real plan was to adopt you as her own and I couldn't let her destroy her marriage before it had even begun.

"What man would want a strange child? What man wouldn't wonder if perhaps it was his new wife's little mistake? No, I couldn't take that chance."

She fell silent, lost in the echoes of the past.

"What did you do, Caro?" Scott asked, sensing I was unable to form the question.

"We had dinner together, the three of us, the night before the wedding. She was so happy; she sparkled and bubbled like the champagne she bought to celebrate. She chatted all through the meal, all those plans, hopes and dreams.

"She kept hugging you, kissing you, promising you the earth, and all the while I sat there like Judas at the last supper. I knew how he must have felt, loving Christ, the weight of betrayal dragging his soul down to hell, the lies on his lips.

"I watched her and knew it was the last time we would ever be together this way, the last time she would ever be able to trust me. So many times, that last evening, I almost said something. With one word I could have stopped everything. But I said nothing. I couldn't. I was doing it for her, so stayed silent.

"The next day, she married Robert and went away on her honeymoon. When she came back the deed had been done. It was too late. You were gone, adopted."

"What did she do," I asked, through lips numb with cold, "when she came back and found you'd given me away?"

"I thought the shock would kill her," Caro stated flatly, eyes large and mournful behind her glasses.

"Robert had to go away on business for a few days and she came rushing round, loaded down with presents, desperate to see you, bursting into the room and calling out your name, and then her face..."

Caro paused and a lone reluctant tear slid down her cheek.

"Her face, oh dear God, her face when she realised you were gone – when I told her what I'd done. I can still remember as clearly as if it were yesterday how white she went; how her lips went blue, and she swayed. I thought she was going to faint.

"It was then it truly hit me what I had done, what I had taken from her. I had given away her child. I don't think she ever truly forgave me for it."

"And yet you remained friends," Scott said dryly, and Caro glared at him.

"Annaliese was an amazing person. The most forgiving and generous soul that has ever walked God's earth. She made a promise to stick by me because she felt responsible for what had happened to me, and she kept that promise even though ... She paid for me to go to college, to learn business and secretarial studies. When her book was published and she became successful, she hired me as her assistant, and no one ever guessed we had known each other before. We were safe. We had jobs and money and were secure."

She paused and shook her head.

"But I should have known, should have realised she hadn't let you go that easily. She searched for you and in the end, five years later, she found you.

"When she told Robert, she wanted to move out of London, I didn't realise it was because she'd found out where you were. I believed her story of wanting to be out of the city and came with them because I could never leave her and because my marriage had by then failed."

Caro's expression turned regretful.

"Not that it ever had any chance of succeeding. We should never have married, Eddie and I, we were so different. I was so young, only twenty, and I thought I could still have what other women had – a normal life, a marriage, children even – but I couldn't.

"Every time he touched me; I remembered. His love wasn't enough you see. He loved me, but I couldn't love him back, not enough anyway. The marriage was on the rocks when I found out I was pregnant.

"At first, I was determined to have the baby alone. I don't know, perhaps in some way, I was trying to replace the baby I'd taken away from her. Then he was born, and I couldn't even bring myself to look at him, so when Eddie asked for custody, I let him have it, I let him take my boy away. It was for the best ..." She faltered, swallowing hard.

"It was best for the boy," she continued. "Eddie loved him. He had a large, close-knit family. It was a chance for Luke to have love and stability in his life."

"Of course," I breathed, realising something obvious. "Luke's my brother."

"Half-brother," she corrected.

"That's why you warned me off him," I cried, horror drenching me at the thought. "I assumed it was because you'd always hated me and couldn't bear the thought of him being with me, but all the time it was because he was my brother and if I'd slept with him..."

I stopped, hand flying to my mouth in repugnance at the thought. Then the world twisted on its head and at last, I understood.

"Annaliese," I breathed. "That's why she did it, that's why she slept with Luke that night! It was to make sure I didn't."

"That's right," agreed Caro. "Luke told me you were going away with him. I could hear in his voice, see in his eyes how much he wanted you. Then, when you left, I believed you were going back to the Hall, to him. I panicked. I phoned Annaliese and told her the unthinkable was about to happen. I pleaded with her to do something, anything, to stop it.

"She begged me to let her tell you the truth, but I couldn't, I just couldn't. In the end, Annaliese agreed to think of some way to stop you from having sex with him, although I didn't find out what until later."

"The plan backfired, Caro," I remarked bitterly. "You see, I thought it was Scott with Annaliese, and that's why I left."

"And she lost you again," Caro stated. "And this time she couldn't find you. Then she got sick, the tumour was diagnosed, and it was too late. She died without seeing you, knowing you believed the worst of her, and it was all my fault. I'm so sorry, Eve. She begged me to tell you the truth, but I wouldn't hear of it and held her to her promise."

Silently, I imagined Annaliese's despair upon receiving the news from Caro. The girl she loved as a daughter was in danger of unknowingly having an affair with her brother.

Unable to take the simple path of telling the truth, bound by a sacred oath made nearly thirty years earlier, I could almost feel her panic as her mind raced through her options.

Then, she encountered Scott desperately looking for me, knew how much he loved me, and realised if I went away with Luke it would be the end of any chance for us.

So, she'd got rid of Scott, sent him on a wild goose chase to look for me in the woods, knowing full well I was on my way back to the Hall, had taken Luke upstairs and ... here my imagination stalled.

"I'm so sorry, Eve," Caro said again, I heard the raw emotion in her voice. "Can you ever forgive me?"

"I don't know," I murmured. "I don't know, Caro. So many people were hurt to protect your secret. I'm not sure I can ever forget that; in fact, right now, I'm not even sure I ever want to see you again."

"But I'm your mother!" she exclaimed in shock, and I stared at her levelly.

"No, you're not," I replied. "It's true, I have been fortunate enough to have two mothers, but they were Patricia Stephens and Annaliese Macleod. They are the women who loved and raised me. They are my mothers, not you, Caro, never you."

She stared at me for a very long time, then bowed her head, and made no attempt to stop me as I stood. Scott rose beside me, and we walked away from her.

We left her sitting there. We didn't look back. We paced in silence, my hand clasped firmly in his, I could feel his concern, yet he said nothing. For almost the first time, I was thankful for Scott's silent nature.

We passed the small silver birch, quivering slightly in the gentle breeze. In unspoken agreement, we stopped to gaze at its bright youthfulness; its promise of great things to come.

"Give me the keys to the car, Eve," Scott demanded. I looked at him in surprise.

"Why?"

"I'll get the car," he offered. "Why don't you stay here for a while and visit with her?"

I blinked back my tears, realising how fortunate I was to be loved by a man who perhaps knew me better than I knew myself. I nodded, released his hand, and slid my arms around his neck, pulling him to me in a tight embrace.

"I love you," I whispered.

"I know," he replied steadily, "and I love you too."

Then he gently took the key and was gone, leaving me to settle myself on the soft grass beneath the tree, looking up through its dancing leaves to the blue, blue sky above.

With my eyes closed, I fancied I could feel her presence, could almost hear her soft breathing, smell her light fragrance, and realise the words I'd spoken to Caro had been nothing more than the truth.

In every way except biologically, Annaliese had been my mother. She had been the one who'd fed and clothed me, who'd sung me to sleep, who'd changed my nappies and bathed me, and it had been her loving arms I'd been taken away from, to be given to my other mother.

I wondered what would have happened if Annaliese had been able to keep me. Would it have turned out the way Caro feared?

Would Annaliese have thrown her life away? Or would she have still had the determination and the willpower to succeed, even with a child in tow?

I tried to imagine a life lived with Annaliese as my mother. A light breeze caressed my cheek like the touch of her hand.

I smiled and opened my eyes to find Robert standing there, a bouquet of white roses in his hand, his expression gentle and tender.

"Hello Eve," he said. "Are you all right?"

"You knew, didn't you?" I said slowly. "You knew Annaliese wasn't my mother."

"Yes, I knew," he agreed, sitting carefully on the grass beside me.

"How? How did you know?" I asked, looking at him curiously.

"When Annaliese and I were trying for children we discovered she had a medical condition which prevented her from conceiving. She was born with it, so I knew you couldn't be her child. Also," He paused and smiled. "When Annaliese came to me on our wedding night, she was a virgin."

"Did you know all along that Caro was my mother?"

"No." He shook his head adamantly. "I had no idea, not until last night, not until Annaliese led you to believe she was. Well, I knew that couldn't be true, so realised she must be covering up for someone very close to her. I tackled Caro this morning and she admitted everything, finally agreeing it was time you knew the truth."

"Thank you," I murmured.

He leant forward and gently kissed my brow, then stood and laid the roses on the ground at the foot of the tree, paused for a moment contemplating their soft creamy white perfection, then turned and lightly ran his finger across my cheek, before walking away with swift sure steps back to the Hall.

I stayed, the sun warm on my face, thinking about the last two days and how much my life had changed. Eventually, Scott returned and found me, dropping down to sit on the ground beside me, his hand running gently through my curls.

"I need to go somewhere this afternoon," I began.

He nodded.

"Okay, where are we going?"

"No, I need to go somewhere alone," I continued, and saw the old uncertainty in his eyes.

"I need to go and see my parents. They don't even know I'm back yet."

"I don't mind coming," he said.

I leaned forward and gently kissed him.

"Scott, I will give you the rest of my life, but today belongs to my parents; I owe them so much. They've done everything for me, yet for the past ten years I've done nothing but shut them out of my life." I saw in his eyes he understood.

"What are you going to tell them?" he asked, and I took a deep breath.

"The truth, I'm going to tell them the truth."

EPILOGUE

"She cannot be blamed for what she did,"

It had been a mild winter, a bright and early spring, and I thought how well the little tree had established itself in the eight months since it had been planted. It had become my favourite spot in the whole garden, and Scott had one day surprised me by arranging to have a large comfortable bench placed beneath it so I could sit in comfort and visit with Annaliese.

I always felt her spirit was somewhere close by when I listened to the wind rustling the leaves and saw sunlight gleaming on its silvery trunk.

My book had been published. I held a copy of it in my hand which I had brought to show Annaliese, and my fingers were constantly drawn to the smooth brightness of its cover, gently tracing my name picked out in gold.

In a strangely reflective mood, I found my mind turning over the events since her funeral last September.

I had visited my parents that afternoon, realising in their relief at my safe return, how selfish I'd been to simply vanish, leaving them with nothing more to cling to than the odd emailed message to remind them of my existence.

I allowed my mother to fuss, for once not being annoyed by it, waiting patiently until the small things had been settled, and we were all sitting with cups of tea and biscuits.

Then, I told them everything.

It was a long tale.

Dusk had fallen before I finished. At the end of it, my mother had tears in her eyes and my father looked dumbfounded that his daughter could have had such happenings in her life, and he be completely unaware of them.

Much to my surprise, my mother had been deeply sympathetic towards Caro.

"She was raped at sixteen, Melissa, had no counselling and no help to overcome that. She simply had to get on with life, yet all her choices had been taken away. She cannot be blamed for what she did, for being afraid, rather she's to be pitied."

I heard my mother's words, understood their meaning, and felt shame at my attitude to Caro, vowing to be kinder and to try to build bridges with her.

My mother became very excited at the news I was engaged and started twittering in that way I suppose all mothers do at the thought of their little girl becoming a bride.

Despite her protests that it was too soon, we were married six weeks later in the small church in which Annaliese's funeral had been held.

Both Scott and I had known and liked the vicar for eight years, and when we visited him, requesting he perform the ceremony, his smile had been broad and avuncular. He would be only too happy to, he stated, continuing that he knew Annaliese would have been pleased, as she had once confided to him her hopes for us.

Walking home together, afterwards, Scott had commented wryly, "Did everyone know we were supposed to be together, except us?"

The wedding was simple and stylish.

When I walked down the aisle of the church packed with all our friends and family, my hand resting lightly on the dark blue sleeve of my father's best suit, feeling the smoothness of my creamy silk gown rubbing against my skin, I felt such a moment of sublime happiness it had seemed too intense to be borne.

Scott turned to watch me approach, his face wearing its habitual mask of indifference, yet I knew the signs to look for now. The slight muscle that moved at the side of his mouth, the tension in his shoulders and the look that burnt deep behind his eyes. I knew I was much loved, and that this day was one we had both longed for, but never imagined possible.

As he took the rings from Mimi, who, much to her surprise and delight, Scott had asked to be his best woman in memory of Andrew, and slipped the band of gold onto my finger, I felt his hand tighten over mine, the power of his emotions trembling under the surface.

I had arranged the honeymoon and took him to Jamaica for a month, renting Reg's beach house which had been my refuge. I took him to the restaurant and introduced him to Reg, holding my breath when the two men silently sized each other up. Then Reg's perfect teeth flashed in a smile of welcome and I knew everything was going to be all right.

During the first week, I watched as he relaxed, allowed himself to believe this was real, that I was there with him, and would never let anything part us again.

I showed him my island, re-visiting places and people who had become part of my life during my year of exile. Gradually, the pace of the island crept into his soul, and I watched him discover the joy of trusting in another person.

By day we swam, scuba-dived, and explored the island by jeep. By night we made long passionate love, our bodies making up for so much lost time.

He and Reg shared a mutual enjoyment of chess, and I would lie in the sun, watching through sleepy eyes as never-ending games became intense, both players evenly matched.

On our first night on the island, lingering contentedly over a delicious meal of fresh local fish, he'd commented that just because he didn't drink, it was no reason for me not to, that he really wouldn't mind if I wanted some wine with dinner. But I simply smiled, shook my head, and sipped my fruit punch.

I can still remember the look on his face later that evening after we'd finished our delicious meal and wandered back along the beach to our little nest to make lazy love together when we lay sprawled on the bed, and I told him my news.

I suppose it shouldn't have surprised him, that on the very same day we bade goodbye to Annaliese, new life had been created within my womb. But it took much reassurance from me before he finally believed, his self-control cracked, and he almost cried for joy in my arms.

His surprise was nothing compared to my own, when we went for our first scan, eager to see pictures of our much-wanted baby, and saw not one, but two little shapes moving together on the screen, and listened to their twin heartbeats, throbbing quick and fierce.

I shifted uncomfortably on the bench, my hand rubbing automatically at the vastly extended bulk of my stomach. Even though Scott thought it beautiful and amazing, and cherished my swollen body, I was tired of being fat and cumbersome.

I longed for the twins to be born, growing impatient to hold them in my arms. Their names had already been chosen and the whole Hall had been turned upside down in preparation for the arrival of Sam and Anna.

A postcard had arrived only that morning from Robert and Ferdie. They were in Italy but planned to travel back next week, to ensure their presence for the all-important arrival.

I smiled, thinking about the worldwide travelling those two had embarked on, sending back postcards and gifts from every corner of the globe, their love and happiness in each other's company apparent.

I glanced up at the tree, thinking how pleased Annaliese would have been.

Before he left, Robert had placed mine and Scott's names on the deeds to the Hall and had reassured us it was our home forever. Returning from our honeymoon, tanned and happy, we had started our married life here together.

We both loved the Hall, feeling it would be almost impossible to consider living anywhere else and were delighted to have such a wonderful home in which to raise our children.

The courtship of Miles and Mimi had progressed upon much more sedate and gentle lines than that of our own, yet they seemed to find much joy in each other's company.

Although I felt Mimi would probably never love as wildly and passionately again as she had with Andrew, I knew she loved Miles very much.

Only that morning at breakfast, I had seen a secret look pass between them and Miles' hand rest gently on her stomach, so I wouldn't be surprised if there was a little announcement from them this evening.

And what of my relationship with Scott?

I knew many considered my husband to be a cold fish, completely devoid of emotion, unable to love. I heard the mutterings of those who wondered exactly why I married him.

They don't see the looks he gives me when he believes himself unobserved, the subtle touch of his hand each time I'm near to him. They cannot know the love that burns and throbs behind the closed door of our bedroom.

Sometimes I would compare Scott's love for me to a well-made-up fire, which, on the surface appears cold and dead, but move the coals slightly and see underneath the glow of a fierce, ever-burning fire, constant and sure.

It is enough for me.

It is more than enough.

I know I am the blood that courses through his veins, the reason his steadfast heart continues to beat.

I am a woman who is confident in the knowledge she is loved, wholly, completely, and passionately. In return, his heart has been given into my safekeeping.

There is a rustle in the undergrowth, and I turn my head to look, as the beautiful male peacock struts arrogantly out from amongst the bushes, followed moments later by the shy and demure little brown peahen.

Poor lonely Humphrey had died many years before, and I had missed hearing the unearthly cry of the peacock echoing around the grounds of the Hall.

After mentioning this to Scott one morning, he immediately set the wheels in motion and located a pair of peacocks to take up residence on the grounds. Their species not being on the endangered list, he had been able to arrange a private purchase and this tame pair who had been hand-reared since they were chicks soon settled into their new home.

They paused not far from me, and for a moment the male stared at me – his black eyes as still and as impenetrable as Scott's – then moved protectively in front of his mate as they stepped delicately away through the undergrowth.

I watch them go, then move uncomfortably again on the bench, feeling a sensation I'd never experienced before, but with the instinctive knowledge of a woman, recognised immediately and knew my due date of some three weeks hence was one I would be pre-empting.

In the distance I saw Scott coming from the Hall to bring me in and smiled at the ease I saw on his face, knowing with a few quiet words I would soon be changing that expression to one of tightly controlled panic.

But I knew that he would then simply do what he did best and cope, taking me quickly and without fuss to the hospital so our babies could be born.

I struggled to my feet, the strong urge bearing down through my body and gently placed a hand on my stomach, feeling it surge and ripple beneath my touch. With my other hand, I grasped the tree, bending my forehead to the smoothness of its trunk.

I closed my eyes and for a moment simply stood, feeling the silent communion, then a rogue breeze rippled through the slender branches, rustling the leaves with a joyful sigh.

I smiled, sensing Annaliese so strongly it was like she was there beside me, her hand caressing my cheek, her loving gaze embracing me in its warmth.

"Thank you," I whispered, and waited for the next chapter of the book of my life to begin

THE END

ABOUT THE AUTHOR

Julia Blake lives in the beautiful historical town of Bury St. Edmunds, deep in the heart of the county of Suffolk in the UK, with her daughter, one crazy cat, and a succession of even crazier lodgers.

Her first novel, The Book of Eve, met with worldwide critical acclaim, and since then, Julia has released many other books which have delighted her growing number of readers with their strong plots and instantly relatable characters. Details of all Julia's novels can be found on the next page.

Julia leads a busy life, juggling working and family commitments with her writing, and has a strong internet presence, loving the close-knit and supportive community of fellow authors she has found on social media and promises there are plenty more books in the pipeline.

Julia says: "I write the kind of books I like to read myself, warm and engaging novels, with strong, three-dimensional characters you can connect with."

A NOTE FROM JULIA

If you have enjoyed this book, why not take a few moments to leave a review on Amazon,

It needn't be much, just a few lines saying you liked the book and why, yet it can make a world of difference.

Reviews are the reader's way of letting the author know they enjoyed their book, and of letting other readers know the book is an enjoyable read and why. It also informs Amazon that this is a book worth promoting, and the more reviews a book receives, the more Amazon will recommend it to other readers.

I would be very grateful and would like to say thank you for reading my book and if you do spare a few minutes of your time to review it, I see, read, and appreciate every single review left for me.

BEST REGARDS
JULIA BLAKE

OTHER BOOKS BY THE AUTHOR

THE PERENNIALS TRILOGY

Becoming Lili – the beautiful, coming of age saga
Chaining Daisy – its gripping sequel
Rambling Rose – the triumphant conclusion

THE BLACKWOOD FAMILY SAGA

Fast-paced and heart-warming, this exciting series tells the story of the Blackwood Family and their search for love and happiness

BLACK ICE

An exciting steampunk retelling of the
Snow White fairy tale

THE FOREST ~ A TALE OF OLD MAGIC ~

Myth, folklore, and magic combine in this engrossing
tale of a forgotten village and an ancient curse

ERINSMORE

A wonderful tale of an enchanted land of sword and sorcery, myth and magic, dragons, and prophecy

ECLAIRS FOR TEA AND OTHER STORIES

A fun collection of short stories and quirky poems that reflect the author's multi-genre versatility

If you want to know more about the young honeymooning couple that posted Eve's letter, then read their story in

Sugar & Spice

Book Three of

The Blackwood Family Saga

Printed in Great Britain
by Amazon